I0681633

WHEN SHADOWS FALL

A Novel

By

NILDA ABERÁSTURI

ISBN: 978-0692527306

Cover photo:

Sunset At Kuting Reef
By Gerardo Aberásturi

Back cover text by Susan Astor

Available from amazon.com and other retail outlets
Available on Kindle and online stores

Printed in the United States of America

July 2015

To Buddy

Into my heart an air that kills
From yon far country blows:
What are those blue remembered hills,
What spires, what farms are those?
That is the land of lost content,
I see it shining plain,
The happy highways where I went
And cannot come again.

XL - The Shropshire Lad

Alfred Edward Housman

Also by Nilda Aberásturi

Half-Forgotten Things
Vignettes From A Life, A Memoir
With Txomin Aberásturi

Translated to Spanish
Cosas Medio Olvidadas
Viñetas de Una Vida, Memorias
By Juanita Aberásturi Wonderly

The Constant Heart
A Novel

Prologue

*I*t used to be called The Laurels, that house at the end of Amalfi Drive in the Pacific Palisades. For a long time it stood, deep in the cover of the laurel trees that Denis Richards had commissioned to be planted around the property when he first brought his bride to California, stood in majesty, as sedate and proper as the people who had it built and who lived in it for nine years. Then it was sold and the new owners had it renovated, and added to, and modernized so that now, except for the skeleton of the original, it bears little resemblance to the house that the Richards built.

The immense music room where once Denis Richards honed his magnificent voice was converted into a ballroom for the endless parties that fill the lives of the present owners. The eucalyptus and avocado and citrus trees which in days past grew in fat abundance and which were the pride of the man of the house, were mercilessly felled to give way to an indoor swimming pool, the one outdoors not being enough for the present owners' unceasing stream of guests. The orchids are nowhere in sight, needing constant nurturing as they did, which the present owners did not have the time nor the inclination to give. Only the roses that have escaped the renovation crew's machinery remain, asking for no attention and no care, and receiving none, obediently sprouting their blooms all the year through, filling the air with their rose-scents, rambling over fences, climbing over posts, their hardy roots and branches more vigorous and stalwart than the fragile girl who planted them and cared for them because they gave her husband an immense amount of pleasure.

When, the next day after he met her, Denis Richards first brought this girl, who was called Laura, to his New England hometown to meet his family, the laurels were in spectacular bloom and so was she. He wanted to keep that picture in his memory, that pink springtime when he fell with a resounding thud for that girl who later became his bride. And when he married her and brought her back with him to California, he surrounded the property with laurel trees and called the estate The Laurels.

But the name never caught on. At first his family and close friends tried to oblige him and called his house The Laurels, too. But then, when everybody else referred to it as The Richards' House, his family just gave up, until it became simply Denis'. Denis Richards was just too overwhelmingly famous for people to call the house by any other name but his.

Now the house, if it is called anything, is called Rowdy House, with its incessant stream of guests who share the new owners' pursuit of the good, boisterous life. When the noise and the laughter and the shouts drift down the valley, the people who live in the vicinity would remember the time when the Richards lived there in quiet dignity, that couple dazzling to behold, the tall, handsome husband with the golden voice and his young, exquisite wife with the elegant ways, and again they would recall their story, more poignant and haunting than any of the movies Denis Richards ever made.

For some time after the house was sold, the plank of wood bearing the words 'The Laurels' clung to a laurel tree. Then the new owners bought the adjoining lot as well and promptly razed the laurels that divided the two properties, to make the two one, and that plank of wood, that last piece of link to the past, fell by the wayside, and was trod on by muddied boots, until it sank, no longer needed, into the soft, sad earth.

It has not been called The Laurels, or even The Richards' House, not in a long time.

BOOK 1
DENIS

1

*T*he city had been stifling for days, the cloud that hung over it hovered for as long as it could, tenaciously holding on to its cache of vaporous rainwater like a miser, until it became too saturated and the lightning that knifed the gray skies sliced its bloated middle. With a thunderous rumble, it disgorged its hoard in a deluge of blinding and uncontainable rain. And it poured, pausing only at times to gather its breath, then again upending its buckets of reserve. Winds reached out, snapped leaves from stems and slapped them on windowpanes. Sewers could not hold the unusual inundation, and the rushing waters, breaking away, dislodged debris and garbage from their hiding places, clogging gutters and immersed the streets with flash flood and flotsam.

From where he sat, Denis Richards could see the rain pouring outside the dining room windows. When Los Angeles poured, he observed, it really did an excellent job of it.

The phone rang; it was his mother calling. "Denis, we just read the reviews and we are so happy for you. All such excellent notices."

He had just finished reading the papers himself. The reviews, of the movie and of his voice, were all excellent. It looked as though he had a winner again, just like his previous picture. These had been good times for him. His concerts and recitals and shows were getting impressive reviews and their recordings were selling briskly. There was nothing he could do wrong, it seemed.

His first movie, which came out a year ago, was based on a runaway bestseller about an opera singer. It was tailor-made for him, almost as if the author had him in mind when she wrote it, and Charles, his manager, went after it with all he had. He knew that the movie would give Denis the broad exposure that opera could not. Everyone expected the movie to be a success—there was a whirl of publicity even before the book came out, then it stayed in the best-seller lists for months and an Italian director snapped up the movie rights. There was an even greater whirl of publicity when the producers started the search for actors to appear in the film, but nobody expected the enormous success that it became. It was a dream of a movie---the music lush, the settings magnificent, the leads good-looking---it became the summer's surprise hit. Such a big, unanticipated hit it was, in fact, that the producers scrambled for another movie to follow in its wake.

The author was commissioned to write a sequel, and she whipped up a new book in weeks when the first one took her four years to write. It followed the same formula that made the first movie the big success it was---great and great-looking actors, stirring music, and a moving love story that lingered in the mind long after one had left the movie theater. This time, Charles did not have to sell Denis. There was no question but that he would play the lead again. After the first movie, Charles never had to sell Denis again. Offers poured in, some of stories without a single musical note in them. If there was a story with romance in it, they wanted him. Revivals of old musicals were brought up. He had always dictated his own terms, had never compromised, even in those times when he did not have the clout to do so, but it was more satisfying to do so now, knowing that what he wanted he got. When he made it clear that he was not appearing in a movie if he could not sing in it, songs were slapped, sometimes haphazardly, into the story line.

Now, with all the splendid reviews and the spate of publicity that surrounded it, this second movie could be an even bigger success than the first one.

*   *   *

His first movie labeled him an 'overnight sensation.' Sensation might be true. A giant of a man who filled the screen with his handsome, masculine looks and the theater with his magnificent voice, he was indeed a sensation. All the papers praised his 'elegant, lyric baritone' and his manly performance. But 'overnight' was hardly accurate.

He burst into the world of opera when he made his debut as *Don Giovanni* at the Metropolitan Opera in New York City and took the audience by storm. That was five years ago. Before that, there were little concerts and recitals that generated trickles of excellent reviews, first in Europe where he did the rounds of opera houses to gain experience. By the time he came back to America, amidst outstanding reviews, he had already made a name for himself. But it was the Met debut that made him a star. The audience cheered, critics went overboard in praising his rich and strong and virile voice, raved about his masculine performance and his arresting stage presence, called him the perfect Don Giovanni and perhaps the best of the crop of young baritones who had sprung up all over the world. Since then he had ridden far and high, to exultant reviews every time he performed, in almost all the important concert stages of the world. Comparisons of his voice to that of the revered baritone Dietrich Fischer-Dieskau's were rife. Long before he went to Hollywood, then, he was already a respected presence in the international world of concert and opera and was far from being 'overnight.'

Although he liked making the movies---the money was good, more than he ever imagined---it was his recitals and his concerts and the making of his records that he found more satisfying. His records, of opera and lieder, won extensive praise and critical acclaim, recordings of his interpretation of the Mahler song cycles won coveted prizes, and while crossovers---recordings of popular music by classical artists---were getting a flagging from critics, his recordings of songs of Irving Berlin, Cole Porter and Jerome Kern were called 'excellent choices of remarkable good taste' and became best sellers. Tickets to his concerts and recitals were sold out months in advance.

* * *

His mother was calling from Laurelfield, their hometown in Connecticut. A cousin was getting married and he had been planning this trip home for quite some time. He looked at the window again and at the whipping rain outside. Few things could get him down, but intermittent days of dark and gloom just fed his homesickness. He had not had a respite from his unrelenting schedule in a long time. Yes, it would be good to go home for the weekend, get away from gloomy Los Angeles, share this new triumph quietly with his family; breathe in the perfume of country air again, be fussed over by his sister and nephews again, and be smothered with spoiling and mothering by his mother again. Just for the weekend.

"So when are you coming," asked his mother.

"I shall be there Saturday, maybe by lunch time. I still have some business to attend to in New York."

His mother lived with his sister, Bess, in Laurelfield, visiting him in his Los Angeles apartment only when she ran out of excuses not to come. Even then, her visits were short. Then she complained of the weather, how she could not live in a town with only two seasons, just rainy and sunny, that she missed snow in winter, that she had to be back east when the leaves turned in the fall, that she missed her garden in spring. And don't even mention Christmas. "Christmas with no snow and it's scorching outside?" she'd say. Denis accused her that she just missed Bess' two children. "When you have your own children," she said, "I'll stay longer. And I do wish you'd hurry. I'm not getting younger and neither are you."

When the money started coming in, and so much of it, he thought seriously of buying a house. Then maybe with a garden his mother could be persuaded to stay longer.

Going to work one day, absorbed and distracted, he took a wrong turn and passed a house so startlingly like what he wanted but could not define. He stopped for some minutes to gaze at it. After that, he took that route every morning, even though it was more circuitous than the one he usually took. After some inquiry, he learned that the house belonged to Roger Williamson, the movie producer, that Rich Stevens of Stevens Architects of New York designed the house. Roger Williamson, New York born and bred, started his career in Broadway before he went to Hollywood and started producing movies, and he and Rich Stevens went a long way, before Hollywood, even before Broadway. When fame and money came, there was no question but that only Rich Stevens would design the Williamson house, and he designed for him a structure that became his signature in a list of award-winning designs.

Later, Denis learned that a piece of land along the way was up for sale. He went to look at it one day and it was immediate love. A good part of the six acres was situated on a promontory, it had a magnificent view of the Santa Monica mountains on one side and the ocean on the other, it was replete with fruit trees and it even had its own citrus grove. He even liked the name of the street – Amalfi. Thomas Mann, whom he thought was one of the greatest German writers of the century, used to live just down the road. Not that it mattered, but it was nice to know. He knew straightaway that this was where he was going to build his house. Visions of his own version of the Williamson house floated persistently in his mind, gripped his imagination and just would not let go. He bought the land and decided to have Rich Stevens design his own house for him, too.

Thus he was passing by New York, to visit Stevens Architects, before going to Laurelfield for the wedding.

2

"Good morning," said Denis, is Mr. Stevens in? Well, good afternoon really," he corrected himself, darting a glance at the clock on the wall. "It's past twelve, I see."

Laura Steiner looked up from the papers she was checking and saw him standing there, a man big and tall, light hair burnished bright, carrying manly authority in his stance, a match to the very masculine voice she just heard. "Yes," she said, "it's past twelve, and Mr. Stevens is out to lunch." She smiled up at him.

"Lunch time, and maybe not a good time to," he left the sentence hanging.

In the business that Denis Richards was in, gorgeous women came and went, and steeped as he was in his work, they went.

He must be getting old, he had thought many times lately. He would be looking at a gorgeous woman and catch himself thinking of things far removed from gorgeous women---the concert that he thought was a good move, or the appearance that he shouldn't have missed or the contract that he should have revised. There was a time when the sight of a pretty pair of legs or a well-filled blouse could always turn his head and there was no place on earth where one could find more of them than in Los Angeles. But there was a glut of these women there, littering the grounds of that industry that swallowed stunning women in hordes, that they had started to look the same, and not one had anything different to offer to get him excited about. So he remained detached, standing on the fringes of superficiality and shallowness, of loud laughter and empty stares, untouched by overtures that let him know things could progress quite pleasurably if he were so inclined. But he was not. For a long time now, designs to cultivate a feminine relationship had been relegated to the lower rungs in his inclinations. There were times, of course, when something in a walk or a glance made him take a second look, but these times were few and far between, and with no effort on his part to spur himself on, a third did not come.

The last time the sight of a face such as this cut him short in mid-sentence he could not remember. Now this girl in front of him looked up and smiled at him, a scintillating play of teeth and eyes and lighted face, and took his breath away.

"Well, past twelve," he heard himself say again, unconcealed admiration written on his face.

She belonged to a family whose two sides were famed for beauty, a family noted to have produced more beautiful people than any other, where being beautiful came with the package. Beauty was a heritage they took lightly, because it was a thing that they had not worked on and therefore was something not to be overly vain about, certainly not a feat in the league of achievement in school or in business or in the arts. At least, that was what Cecilia always impressed on her children, so that, although Laura always knew she was beautiful, she also knew that in a field full of stars, she was not even the brightest and so took no needless pride in it.

"Yes, it's past twelve and not a good time to come, everybody is out to lunch. Excuse me, please." She answered the ringing phone. "Our ad in the paper? Yes, we did advertise for an architect. Yes, yes," she answered between pauses. "You could just mail your résumé. Well, but of course you may bring it over yourself, if you so wish, some applicants do. Yes, that's right, 9 to 5. All right then, thanks, bye." The firm had advertised for an architect for a week now. The response was quite good, but Rich Stevens said the applicants were not what he had in mind. He told Laura if she wanted the job, she could have it. But she politely declined; she would work there for the summer, after which she was going to Columbia University. She arrived in New York a week before and had just completed the requirements for, and been accepted to, the graduate program of the School of Architecture at Columbia University in the fall. "Well, let's see what today's batch brings," Rich Stevens had said.

Laura looked up at Denis, still standing before her. "Oh, I'm sorry. I've been having so many of these calls. Ah, you were looking for Mr. Stevens, you said? He'll be back after lunch."

"Maybe I could wait." He did not have anything to do, anyway, and he did not mind sitting there just watching this girl. He glanced at a stack of résumés in front of her and tried to make conversation. "Many applicants for the job?"

"Well, a bit," she answered. Was he applying for this job? He did not look like a job applicant, she thought, but what did she know? This was the first job she ever had; she did not know what people did in offices. "You could come back later, or you could leave your résumé, and we'll call you. Did you bring your résumé?"

"Oh, ah...I, ah..." He was at a loss for words, a rare occurrence for him. "No, I did not bring a résumé."

"It's all right, you could just mail it in, if you wish."

Denis looked at her, amused. He was aware that there must be a number of people who did not know him. But to have an example as stunning as this one sitting in front of him now, surveying him with glancing eyes! "I guess I don't know much about résumés," he said. He glanced at a stack of papers in front of her, saw the one on top that looked like one.

"Maybe I could look at this while I wait." He picked up the paper on top of the stack.

"Oh, I'm sorry, that's mine." She tried to retrieve the paper, the copy of the one she sent the firm when she applied for the internship, a copy she was reviewing and tossed on top of the stack when Denis came in. But he had already gotten hold of one end of the paper and was not letting go.

"It's all right, I'll give it back to you," he said. "I'll just sit here and see how these things are done."

She did not know whether to insist on getting the paper back, which would entail more action on her part. She let it be.

He sat down on a corner chair while she continued with her work. There must be better ways to spend a Friday afternoon than watching girls, even one who looked like this, but he could not think of anything else he would rather do at this moment and let his eyes feast unhampered as he allowed her to step tentatively into that part of him that for a long time had stayed unvisited by female company.

She stole glances at him and each time caught him looking at her approvingly and she reveled in that approval.

"I really must go out to lunch now," she said after a while. "You could wait here. Or you could have lunch meantime."

"Where does one get lunch around here?" he asked.

"You're not from New York?"

"I came in from L.A. this morning," he replied.

"Well," she hesitated, "there's a place around the corner. Food is kind to your stomach as well as your pocketbook."

"Is that where you're going?"

"Yes, actually."

"May I just come with you then?" he said.

"Well," she hesitated, "I guess, if you wish."

She stood up and poked her head into the next room. "Mary, I'm off to lunch now. You'll take care? Thanks." She reached for her jacket, put it on, nodded at him, and headed for the door.

He shrugged into his trench coat while he followed her out of the building. She threaded her way through the crowd, with him keeping in step behind, taking notes unhindered, regarding the shapely legs, the slim frame, the wind-whipped hair.

It was a small place she led him to. Tall walls covered with creeping vines bounded two sides and on the far end, a waterfall cascaded down a center wall, like a sheet of cellophane rippling in the breeze, ponding coldly on rocks and plants and sullying cigarette butts. There were a few tables scattered around, with seats rooted to the ground, and benches under pink-flowering trees. She spied a table under a cherry tree that had just been vacated. "If you'd watch that table I'll get the food." She looked at him expectantly, not knowing what to do next.

"I'll get the food, you stay here," he said.

"No, you don't know what I want in my salad. Why don't you just guard that table. There will be a crowd here very soon. Any particular thing you want?" she asked.

"I'll have whatever you'll have. Let me come with you."

"No, no, just guard that table."

He took the seat facing the waterfall, his back towards the street, anonymity provided by his broad back and his trench coat. He pulled the coat collar forward and up, hiding a good part of his face, while he looked over her résumé.

She came back with a tray of food. She looked at him sitting there, half his head buried in his trench collar. With a hat, she thought, he'd look like Humphrey Bogart, albeit more handsome and in grander proportions, in an old black-and-white movie, seeking concealment from, or maybe looking for, a villainous Claude Rains. "I got a salad for myself but I thought," she left the sentence hanging, eyeing him. He was a big man---not a swell of fat, not a ripple of muscle, just built big and broad and very tall.

"I thought you might need more, so I got a burger for you, and a Coke," she finished the thought. "I hope that's all right with you."

"Oh, yes, thanks." He opened the food wrappers. "So how much do I owe you?" he asked.

She picked up the receipt. "Yours came up to, ah, let's see." She named a figure.

He dipped his hand into his coat pocket and came up with bills. "Let me pay for everything."

"No, of course not, just pay for your own."

"I have money, see?" he said, pulling out more bills.

"So have I."

He took big bites from his sandwich, chewing and swallowing with his entire mouth. Everything about him was big. Back home, they'd say that everything about him was 'American size.' One big hand held his food, the other her résumé. "Hm," he said. "A BArch, going for your Master's? Hm. Then why are you doing reception work? Why are you not applying for this job?"

"Oh, that is just for one week; the girl is coming back Monday. Today is my last day, actually. Next month, I work there as an architectural intern for the summer."

He took another big bite, worked on it, washed it down with a long swig from his Coca Cola. "Now, aren't you a bit too young for these accomplishments?"

Her brother Franz had always told her to keep that brain under wraps; it would surely scare the boys away. But nothing, she was sure, could easily scare this man who looked as though he could do the scaring, with that huge frame and that very male bearing. And a huge appetite to match. She could not remember when she was as fascinated just watching someone eat.

"How old are you, anyway?" he asked. He had demolished his sandwich and had gulped down the last drop of his drink.

"Old enough. Do you want me to get you another sandwich?" She was not even half through with her salad.

"Thank you, no. And how old is old enough?"

"Well, I'll be twenty next month."

"Oh, oh, oh, not even twenty yet, still a teenager," he laughed. Even his laugh was big and booming. "Isn't this Swiss school one of those institutions that teaches little rich girls which knives and forks to use, what wine goes with what, and finishes them to become perfect wives to rich husbands?"

"Don't be a snob. I studied public relations there, which according to my brother, Franz, I am in most, in dire need of," pronouncing the last words with emphasis, "and a course in Oenology, which my cousin Joe says is a must for survival," she countered, still at her salad.

It was not only her smile that dazzled him. His one regret in life was that he never completed his education. Now he was looking at this twenty-year-old who studied at a Swiss finishing school, had a degree in Architecture, was going for her Master's from an Ivy-league school, and with such a face!

"I have to go back now," she said, wiped her lips with a lacy handkerchief, tucked the handkerchief into the breast pocket of her jacket. "Why don't you stay, then you could work on your résumé. Bring it over later." She started to gather their litter but he stopped her.

"Let me take care of that."

"All right, thanks," she said and again flashed him that smile that lighted up her entire face. Then she walked, almost ran, away. She turned, saw him looking at her, nodded and left him bedazzled.

He took out the straw from her half-drunk Seven Up, took the bottle to his lips, and the drink went gurgling down his throat. He sat there, deep in thought, an amused smile flitting across his face. Then, with a laugh too exhilarated to repress, he gathered their trash and slid it in the trash bin. He looked for her phone number on her résumé, looked for a phone booth, and called her. "Is it okay if I did not bring in that résumé today?"

"Well, of course it's all right. It's late, and the boss leaves early Fridays, anyway."

"Good," he said.

"Have a nice weekend, then," she said.

"Wait, what time do you get off?"

She took a few seconds before she answered. "Five."

"Do you have any plans, are you going anywhere?"

"Well," she hesitated quite a long time, "well, I was thinking, I have never been to Central Park, I thought maybe," she hesitated again. "Maybe I'll walk over there or something."

"Never been to Central Park? You don't go to Central Park alone the first time; you need somebody to show you around."

"You? I thought you're not from New York."

"Central Park I've been to. I'll wait for you in front of the building. Oh, I'll bring coffee. How do you like yours?"

Habit prevailed. He was always master of the situation. Even at an early age he led; as a child he decreed the games his group of small boys played, as a young adult he marched to his own beat and the others followed. He stayed unswayed by others' opinions, and so his opinions swayed others. He knew his own mind, early on knew what he wanted to do with his life and when he traveled the road to get it, he did not tarry by the wayside, and arrived faster and surer than the other men in his town. He took things into his own hand, now presumed that she would not mind him going with her, presumed that she wanted coffee.

She did not mind and she wanted coffee. "Regular, one sugar, plenty of milk."

"Got it. See you then."

He could hardly wait for the hours to pass. Hey, what am I doing? he thought. True, she was beautiful, but he would see a stream of beautiful women each day and had not paid one undue attention. In fact, he had not given much thought to women for some time now and, preferring his own company, kept to himself and his music. When he had to promote his picture or his record, or had to attend a function, which was not often, his managers provided his companion for the evening. On these occasions, he was always his usual charming and engaging self, so handsome, so gallant and alas, so elusive. And such a perfect escort, his date always had a most pleasant evening and hoped for another one that never came, for although he enjoyed himself on these outings, on his own, he did not seek out a second date until the next time when his managers decided that another exposure was good for publicity and arranged another evening out. These events were few and far between that he had not been romantically linked with any girl and developed a reputation for being very private, very reclusive and very hard to land.

Now he reflected upon this afternoon with pleased surprise. He had not only actively sought to go out with this girl but was looking forward to it with a delicious sense of anticipation. Anyway, he told himself, he had no plans for the afternoon; it was perfect weather for Central Park, there was nothing to be concerned about. No need to see Rich Stevens today, another time would do. She did not even know who he was, he laughed.

Well, she was just a kid, half, or thereabouts, of his thirty-seven years. He wondered what kind of music she listened to. Girls her age did not listen to classical music, much less to opera. Still, he was excited and consulted his watch several times, only to find each time that the hand had moved forward only a few seconds.

The afternoon was nippy, still early June, and a slight wind had risen, but he slouched into his trench coat more to hide his face from the crowd than from the chill. He leaned against the building wall where he could see her when she came out.

She emerged from the building, paused, and crossed the street when she found him. There was nothing coy about her. She was not adept in the art of flirtation, not having been exposed much to the opposite sex to practice it on. But she did have the raw material every girl was born with---the instinctive sureness in the power of a smile to melt. She poured out a wide, white smile that momentarily stopped short his natural breathing processes. "What have you got there," she asked, looking up at his eyes.

And in the ability of a glance to confuse.

"Now, let me see," he said, losing his place. "Well, ah, yes, what have we got here now, hm, coffee and this thing they call danish. Hungry?"

"A bit. Let's eat in the park." They walked and did not talk much. It was after five and people were starting to stream out of office buildings unto sidewalks, gazing at shop windows, eyeing the other gazers. For most of the way, she had to walk ahead of him. He liked the elegant air she had about her, the regal way she carried herself.

A sudden wind rose, caught her hair and flung it outward, he was sure it did, as wind was wont to do to young girls' hair in movies of romance that his professed unsentimental, masculine side used to deride. Why, he thought, he had not looked at a woman with so much pleasure in a long while.

3

The park was not crowded and they walked a bit until they found a spot fronting onto the lake.

"That looks perfect. We can sit under the tree and have our coffee." He turned his back to the path to hide his face from passersby and spread out his trench coat on the grass under the tree.

"No," she protested, "you're going to stain it."

"That's all right, it needs cleaning anyway," he said of the coat that he spent much money on just this week to bring to this trip. He helped her sit on it. She took off her jacket, folded it neatly, placed it by her side and put her handbag on top of it.

Yellow dandelions spotted the ground. He gathered some, tied them into a posy with a dried blade of grass and presented the bouquet to her with a flourish.

"I wish they were orchids," he said. "I may be paraphrasing somebody's quote, but the sentiment is strictly mine."

"Like Mr. MacArthur's bag of peanuts to Miss Hayes?" she asked.

Behind the eyeglasses, he squinted one eye, a habit when he was rapt in attention. "You've heard of Helen Hayes?"

"Who hasn't?" she said.

Indeed.

She laughed. "When Charles MacArthur first saw her, he handed her the bag of peanuts he was holding and said he wished they were emeralds. Later, it's said, after he married her, he did give her a bag of emeralds and told her he wished they were peanuts. You know, I have wondered about that. A bag of emeralds? How big a bag were they talking about?"

"Don't believe everything you read in the papers." I guess old movie stars you've read about, he thought.

"I do read about movie stars," she answered his thoughts, startling him. Witches he had heard of where he came from, met one he had not, witchcraft had never been practiced on him, and if it was on this bewitching afternoon, he lay open and welcoming to it. "At least when I have time," she qualified.

"There's this anecdote I read about once, Helen Hayes, I mean," he said. "They had a maid who was so star struck she gushed, 'My folks are so classy, even the faucets in their bathrooms have their initials.'"

She was silent for a bit, figuring this one out, but comprehension dawned in a split second. "Oh," she laughed, flashing all white teeth, "I get it, hot and cold, H and C on faucets, Helen and Charles. Oh, that's good."

So are you, he thought, catching on fast.

"I like these," she said, looking at the dandelions, "simple, uncontrived. Thank you very much."

"I know something like that, but much lovelier."

She knew where this conversation was going if she allowed it. Then she might find herself in that unfamiliar field called a flirtation and might flounder into foolish indignity. She chose not to allow it and kept still.

She fumbled to stick the posy in her hair, and he came near to help her. "What's the perfume?" he asked.

"Chanel #5," she replied.

"I like it," he said as he surveyed her. She was small boned, willowy almost. Her arms, now freed from her jacket, were long and surprisingly full. Her gray eyes were fringed with thick lashes, her eyelids had a hint of shadow, compliments of Ms. Chanel again, but bewitched as he was, how was he to know that? But it was the smile, with that perfect curve of teeth, that he would always say was his undoing.

"Yes," he said again, "I like it." He was not thinking of perfume anymore. He smiled and said gently, "With an afternoon such as this and a girl with a smile on her lips and flowers in her hair, what more could anyone want?"

"Coffee, maybe?" she said.

He laughed and handed her her coffee and the pastry in a paper bag.

He seemed eager to please her, and she did not have the heart to tell him that the coffee had turned tepid and she did not care much for sweets. She took one bite and said, apologetically, "Would you mind if I just saved this for later?"

"You're not hungry?"

"Maybe later," she said.

"Oh, I'll finish it for you if you don't want it," he said, and demolished the pastry in two bites.

She laughed. "I've never seen anyone eat with such enjoyment."

He wiped his mouth with a paper napkin, wiped his hand carefully with it, put the soiled napkin in the brown paper bag that had held the pastries, and looked at her. "Perfect," he said.

"Want to work on that résumé? I brought paper and pen. Oh, I don't even know your name."

"Richards."

"Just one name?" she asked.

"Denis. Denis Richards," he said softly, wanting to prolong this anonymity, going easy on the sibilants, clearing his throat.

"Denis Richards," she said, testing how it sounded, then pronounced judgment. "An okay name."

He laughed, a hearty hahaha, and realized---he was happy. "Just an okay name? I think Laura Steiner is a lovely name."

"I think so, too," she said, "But everybody calls me Lauren, after Papa's grandmother."

"Everybody calls me Denis," he said.

"How else?" she gurgled a laugh. "Now finish your résumé, then you could give me back mine," she urged.

He stayed her hand, which was taking the pen out of her handbag. "Such a radiant afternoon. Surely a day such as this was made for something more interesting than résumés. Let's do that another time."

"Well," she hesitated, "all right."

She rested her head against the tree and looked him over. He reminded her of the man in that Gershwin song, a man big and strong, and very tall. The afternoon sun had come out full and bright, shone on his light hair which grazed his collar with waves that looked like they met the hairbrush with resistance, snapped back and settled into that stylish hairdo. His eyes, behind the becoming rimless glasses, were gray; his face looked honest and kind. His mouth curled at the corners when he smiled, which he did often. He looked clean-cut and very neat, although his clothes looked as though they were picked off the rack, without much thought or concern. His black shoes were buffed to a shine and looked conservative. In fact, except for the hair and the stylish eyeglasses, he had an air of restraint about him, of being reserved and staid.

"So what's the verdict?" he asked, holding back a grin.

"What?" she said, then laughed. "Oh. Well, the face looks honest, the figure looks, uh, healthy."

His laughter boomed. "Healthy! God, you're such a sweet girl." He was quite intoxicated. When did this begin, he thought, this awareness that things had sprung up alive around him, as in an animated movie, with trees and flowers snapping up to life and a giant brush splashing them with vivid colors, and he came alive with them, suddenly awake to the sky so blue, the trees so green, the tulips at their feet in show-off red and yellow? Dandelions poked their yellow heads through the greens and the sun streamed through the trees unto the lake, made the water glimmer, dripped golden sunshine on the dappled grass and danced on her hair, speckled the brown with glints of gold.

Ah, so much beauty! He breathed deeply of the New York air that until now he swore wreaked havoc on his sinuses.

"Tell me about yourself," she said.

"Well, let me see now. I come from a small town in Connecticut. We were poor. No, we were not poor, we just did not have money, all the time. I have a sister, Bess, she's married and has two children. My mother's name is also Elizabeth; she's called Betty.

"My mother and father were divorced when I was 15. There was no money in the house, so I had to stop school and took a job to help out. It was a hard time for my mother, with two children to support, with what little she got from teaching piano. I remember there was nothing but cheese and bread and milk for stretches of time. Once I asked why there was nothing but cheese in the house and my sister said that was the only thing they had in the line. Then I realized they must have stood in line where the social services people, I think they were, gave out food to the poor. To this day, I could not look at, much less eat, a cheese sandwich."

Too bad, she thought; she loved cheese. On her rare adventurous forays into the kingdom of food, one delight was trying out new cheeses and she had not met one she did not like. No matter.

"Back where I come from," she said, "nobody with your looks ever needs to be without money. So many rich girls there will just snap you up. Just give them your western name, and gorgeous children and you could get to be a passable vice president of their companies. My *Tito* Ray, my father's only brother, well, he's married to my *Tita* Maggie, of the really rich Gomez family, I mean, really rich. *Tita* Maggie's sister, Gilda, came home from Italy with this so magnificent Italian husband, with a name to match: Alberto Rossetti. You know, as in Dante and Christina." She paused, not quite sure if he knew these poets she was talking about.

"As in Christina Georgina?" he said.

"Yes," she chuckled, glad that he knew. "Later, they had these children who looked just as magnificent as their father, with those long, heavy lashes, we wondered if they had a hard time looking out at the world. Anyway. Alberto started working in the corporate office of the family's company and became one of its vice presidents. When their first baby came, Gilda gave Alberto this big, red car, an MG. Everybody snickered and called him Mister Gomez, you know, MG. Oh, but those children! I'm sure Gilda wouldn't have minded giving Alberto a new MG every time she had one of those just adorable babies. Oh, sorry I interrupted. Go on with your story."

"Well," he continued, "my father married again and my mother really took it hard. Of course we did, too, but it was harder for her." He paused and inhaled deeply. He looked at her for some time, biting his lips. He wondered why he was telling her this; he never liked to talk about his family, certainly never about his parents' divorce. But she had an air about her that drew out confidences, and he was comfortable with that. He wanted to tell her, and stranger still, he wanted to let her into that part of his world he did not usually invite others to visit. "Did I say I left school after graduation? There was a family to support and I was now the man of the house."

"What a sad story. I'm so sorry. Is that why you're not married?"

"How do you know I'm not married?"

She looked at his hand, "No ring."

"Oh, that," he shrugged, trying to sound unconcerned. "I hide it when there are girls around."

"Are you?"

"What?"

"Married?" she pursued.

He laughed. "No, no, never found the time. I was too poor, you see. And then, when I stopped being too poor, I was too busy. No, never found the time."

Well, that's all she needed to know, but she loved his voice and pressed him.

"Go ahead, tell me more."

"Well, I did all kinds of work, but I always knew I could sing. Not only that I could sing but that I loved singing more than anything else. There was no money for formal lessons, but there was this lady who was an excellent voice teacher. My mother offered to give her children piano lessons if she would give me voice lessons. After that I went to Philadelphia, and one lucky day, I auditioned and got a part in an opera presented by a local opera company. I must have been quite good, I got good reviews in the next day's papers and attracted the attention of Mrs. Meredith, one of the opera company's benefactors. She offered to lend me money so I could train with another reputable voice teacher. Later, this teacher said I was getting too good, and he did not have much left to teach me and recommended that I studied with another good teacher, a better one, he said. But this teacher had to go to Vienna, so that, so as not to interrupt my studies, Mrs. Meredith lent me money again so I could go. I was in Vienna, and in Europe, for seven years."

He paused, and she pressed him, "And?"

"There's not much more to tell. I have since paid every penny of that loan."

"With drawing?" she asked.

"What?" he looked at her, puzzled. He had forgotten drawing. And then remembered. "Oh, well, not really. As I said, I do whatever I can. But mostly by singing, wherever, whenever I could." He laughed, he couldn't help it.

"When did you take up Architecture?"

"Well, now, Architecture. That's a story for another day. One day I'll explain everything to you." God, how precious, he thought. He had not spent a more enjoyable afternoon in so long.

She read somewhere that opera did not pay enough, that some singers had to resort to teaching or did other work not related to opera, or not even related to music, to earn their keep. What a pity. With the dearth of opera singers who looked good enough to die for, or even just to fight over, they should have kept him. Well, architecture's gain.

"That is quite a story," she said.

"Quite a hard story, you mean. Now, enough about me. Tell me about yourself."

"After your story? I'll bore you to tears with mine."

"I'm sure there's nothing about you I'll find boring. Come now, tell."

She shivered and reached for her jacket.

"Oh, I'm sorry, it's getting chilly and I did not notice." He helped her up and into her jacket. "Are you hungry?"

"I don't know. I mean I don't think so. I'm sorry. I guess I'm still thinking of your story."

"Don't think about that anymore," he said. He bent down to retrieve his coat and dusted it of leaves. "Here, put this on, it's getting cold."

She looked at the trench coat. That enormous thing would look like a tent on her, she thought. "Oh, no, please, I'm fine, really."

"Let me take you to a good place to eat. You haven't eaten at all."

"I don't want you spending your money on me. Let's buy some things, then we can cook them in the house. Do you know how to cook?"

"Do I know how to cook?" His eyes crinkled in held-back laughter, his mouth opened in a wide smile, with a hint of an overbite, a lot of teeth. One side tooth, askew, slightly edging another out of its place for space, saved the smile from being too perfect.

"You smile like a Steiner, teeth, overbite and all."

"You don't have an overbite." At least just a faint shadow of it, which made the perfect curve of teeth more alluring.

"You should see us Steiners before our parents had our teeth fixed. So, do you know how to cook?"

"I'm sorry, I guess just eggs."

"Me, too," she said and they both laughed. He laughed often, and at everything, she noticed.

"Come, let me take you to a good restaurant, where all we have to do is eat and leave."

She shook her head. "Too expensive. Don't waste your money. Let's see what we can do with those eggs." She hesitated. "I shouldn't be bringing you home, though. My Mom always tells me not to talk to strangers, much less bring them to the house."

"You said I have an honest face. Don't you think you can trust me? Besides, I don't think I qualify as a stranger anymore," he said. "Haven't we known each other for how long now?" He consulted his watch, a Rolex, one of two expensive things she noticed he was wearing, the other, the trench coat, he was shrugging into now. "Seven hours? And haven't I poured out my life story to you already?"

"All right then. I have some bread and eggs in the house." Remembering his enormous appetite, she added, "No meat, though, I'm afraid."

"That's fine."

4

*S*he had an apartment on Riverside Drive, overlooking the Hudson River. Somehow, it did not surprise him that she lived in this elegant house. From the window, he could see the early evening lights of New Jersey flickering across the river, and the necklace of lights on the George Washington Bridge glittering like gems under the first stars of night and the muted gray cast of the fading day.

"Ah," he said, taking a deep breath, "look at that view."

She stood behind him. "Sometimes, in the evenings, I would play my records and just sit here, listening to my music, looking out this window, looking at that view."

Concerned that perhaps she had exposed a part of her she did not want to lay bare yet, she switched to another tract. "My parents bought this place a long time ago, and had it rented to some people working in the United Nations. Luckily, they were transferred to Switzerland, which was convenient for me. We bought their furniture for a song. They are such fine pieces, don't you think so? I stay here for the two years it takes to finish my master's degree."

"What records?" he asked.

"Classical records, mostly. Oh, Berlin, Cole Porter, Jerome Kern, too." She added, smiling, "And Gershwin."

Could she possibly stand opera? Was that too much to expect? "You like opera?"

"I don't know much about it, just the standbys---*The Barber of Seville, La Traviata*, and of course, the one I love best, my first opera, *La Boheme*, which I saw in Covent Garden, in London, with my brother, Franz, and my cousin, Joe. It was Joe's birthday present to me---formal dress, orchestra seats, dinner after, the whole works. He thought every girl should be initiated into opera with *La Boheme*. He was right; I cried. Hey, I was only fifteen."

He had not sung *The Barber of Seville* and *La Boheme* in a long time. Driven to perfection, he felt he had outgrown Figaro and Marcello and had nothing new to offer to the roles. But if she wanted him to, why, he would do them again, for her.

"Well, that's about all. I like some operettas, though. Is *Merry Widow* an opera, or an operetta? We saw it in London, too. That I loved," she smiled widely, all white teeth, "very much." There was that disconcerting smile again.

"Alone? This house is too big for you."

This jumping through topics was unsettling, but he did not lose her.

"Not really. My cousin Ann lives in a studio two doors away. She's not a cousin really, more like a cousin of a cousin. She works as an accountant with Stevens and helped me get the summer job. She's away though, left this morning for a weekend at the Jersey shore with her friends. She'll be back Sunday, so maybe you can meet her then."

"Why didn't you go with her?"

"She went with her friends, whom we don't share. Besides, I'm a working girl, remember?"

He followed her to the kitchen. "We're going to have *tortilla de patata*," she said. "Very Spanish. She washed some potatoes and he helped her pare and slice them.

She went to the cabinet and took out a small bottle of olive oil. "Others like their potatoes deep-fried, but I just fry them in enough oil, not too much, like so." She went to the fridge and took out four eggs. "You may beat the eggs, while the potatoes are frying." She transferred the fried potatoes into a plate, added more olive oil in the skillet, and poured in the beaten eggs. Then she tipped the potato slices on top of the eggs. "Now this is the part I am proud of." She placed a plate on top of the skillet and flipped the skillet, shifting the egg-potato mixture from the skillet to the plate.

"Impressive," Denis said.

"Yes, wasn't it, though?" She put the skillet back on the range top and slid the mixture back to the skillet. When it was done, she took out a small platter and slid the omelet into it. "Perfect," she said, "if I may say so myself. Took a lot of practice, too."

"I am impressed."

She took a small curtsy. "Now you may help set the table."

"Hope you like," she said when they were seated. "This is the only dish I know how to make."

"I thought that's what finishing schools do, teach you how to cook and things like that."

"Well, it's just that I don't really like to cook, really," she shrugged in apology.

"Then you don't cook," he said earnestly, "you don't have to do anything you don't want to do." The silver and crystal caught the lights from the chandelier above and the ridges on the decanter of sherry flashed with the borrowed lights. Looking back later, he would pinpoint to this exact moment when, gazing at her face aglow in the velvety light, her hair shining like a halo surrounding her face, he awakened to find he had fallen, unaware until it was too late, then happily was past caring. He was lost and nothing could pull him back. He was going to take care of her, hire a battery of cooks to cook for her, sit her in place while servants waited on her, make her his own.

"Drink? I only have sherry. Say when," she said, pouring sherry into his glass.

"When," he said.

She poured some for herself and took sips as she watched him enjoying her handiwork.

"For someone who doesn't cook, this is good. In fact, this is really good."

"Thank you, I'm rather pleased with it."

They talked while they ate. Mostly, he talked while he ate while she listened while she ate. She had a calm, quiet way about her. There were stretches of easy conversation, then silences, infrequent but comfortable.

She gathered their dishes and proceeded to the kitchen.

"You may help with the dishes," she said. "I'll wash and you dry."

He hummed while he dried and she stayed quiet to catch the tune. She knew the song, she heard it played often, *The Way You Look Tonight*. He put the dried dishes on the shelf, at the same time watching her watching him. Carried away, he sang in earnest, looking at her, and finished the song.

This is what great singers do, she thought, pick up a great song that had turned lackluster from too much use and sing new excitement into it. "I've heard this song sung many times, but never quite like the way you did it. Could anybody train that voice to be better than that?" She looked so serious, he wanted to make light of it.

"That's it, that's it. It was not that good. Or I'd be singing at the Met. Ah!" He laughed heartily at his own joke, a staccato hahaha which she would later find he did often. "Come, come, really, it was not that good," he said, still laughing, while she just stood there looking at him. "How about dessert?"

She opened the fridge and looked inside. "Want ice cream?"

"Love ice cream."

She laughed. "Tell me, what food don't you like?"

"Cheese sandwich," he answered readily.

They drifted into the living room, sat down on the deep comfortable sofa and ate their ice cream.

"Now tell me about yourself, what's with the Philippines?" he asked.

"Well, I am from there."

"But there's nothing Oriental about you." Her skin was very white, her hair was light brown, flecked with gold. "Even your name is not Oriental."

"Well," she began, "let's start with Papa's side. His grandmother was English, his father was from Switzerland. That's my father's side. My Mom's father came from Spain, from the Basque region of Spain. And there was an abundant showering of European blood before that. So I'm sort of a mongrel out of Europe."

Remembering some Filipinos he had met, he said, "You must stand out in your country. I mean, you look so different from the other Asians I've seen."

"A lot of people think that, but that's not so. Where I come from, there are many who look like me, many who were educated here and in Europe and married Americans or Europeans and have children who are as white. My brother, and especially my cousin Joe, they look even more European than I do.

"I guess not much have been written about my country. What you hear mostly is the negative side, the poverty, the corruption, the red light districts, which, of course, you can find in London, too, or on Forty-Second Street, or in several other large capitals of the world, for that matter. But then, I guess, it's the negative stories that sell. Nobody had ever bothered to show the many wonders one can find in my country.

"Few people know, for instance, that we are the most westernized country in the east. The official language in offices is English, the medium of instruction in schools is English. Books in libraries and in bookstores are in English. Private schools are excellent. People dress in fashionable western clothes that are featured in Vogue magazine and other up-to-the-minute western fashion bibles. National newspapers are in English. American bestsellers and records of American artists are in bookstores and record shops. (*Mine aren't*, he thought, *or you just never looked?*) American movies are shown in all movie houses. (*But mine you've never seen.*) Cultural events are in English, too. World famous pianists and ballet dancers and other artists have performed there. (*Let's see what Charles has to say about this, fine manager that he is.*) Major plays and Broadway musicals had been presented there. Once, we attended a recital by Van Cliburn that, as always, glued us to our seats, and an excellent presentation of Tom Stoppard's *The Real Thing*. Really enjoyable performances.

"I have yet to meet a Filipino who does not know a smattering of English, and that includes the people in our hacienda. On summer vacations in my grandparents' house, I remember sleeping to '*This is the Voice of America in Easy English,*'" she did a good imitation of the VOA announcer that made him smile, "which my aunts listened to every night. I started reading *Time Magazine* and *Newsweek* and other American magazines when I was still this high because a recent issue was always in the bathroom. Reading is a passion in my family and in a lot of families I know. Like everybody else I know, everything we read is in English. In our houses are bookshelves overflowing with books, in English. Letters and notes we write each other are in English, and conversations, though sometimes sprinkled with dialect words, are almost always in English.

"There are so many who, like me, look occidental. Do you know that the Spaniards colonized us for more than three hundred years, and after them came the Americans?"

"No," he said. Or anything else about that country, he thought, that produced girls such as this who, with a smile, moved his heart to precarious levels of beatings.

"They did. That's almost four hundred years of intermarrying with Europeans and Americans. So many members of my family studied or vacationed abroad and married Europeans. In my family alone, especially on my Mom's side, so many aunts and uncles and cousins studied or vacationed in Spain and came home with..."

"Prized Spaniards?"

"Yes," she laughed. "I have so many relatives who are even more fair-skinned than I."

Than I, he noted. She spoke grammatical English, like a schoolteacher. Yes, the schools must be excellent. "I guess I was surprised because I've known some people from that country and they certainly don't look like you at all."

"Maybe there are many of us who don't want to live here, we come here to study and then we go home. Home, the gentler shores of a land far away, where faces are more smiling, the stride is slower, and life is more kind." A few more of those yearning looks, he thought, and she could take him home with her.

"You have your life pretty much planned."

"Yes, come to think of it, yes, I have. But it's not an exciting life. A husband with a 9 to 5 job. Maybe we will work together in one office, which would be great. Then we'll go home together, catch an occasional movie, or have a quiet dinner in some quiet place. If we are short of money, then maybe we'll just take long drives or long walks, or just spend quiet evenings at home."

"It sounds like a great life. But if you marry somebody who has a lot of money, then you can have all the quiet dinners in all the quiet places anytime you want."

"I don't think money is all that important. Sometimes, a lack of money is a good thing, too. It keeps a marriage stronger, keeps the family closer."

"Who said that? That's an absurd assumption, spouted by people who think that no money means they can't do Europe this year." She looked up at him, his intensity caught her off guard and surprised him, too. "Oh, Laura," his voice softened considerably, "that's just a romantic notion, romanticized by people who have money."

"That's not always true. There are people who stay happily in love, despite and still."

"If you are talking of Robert Graves, my dear, he was having a romantic streak. There's no despite and still in poverty. When the roof leaks, and the table's bare and she hasn't bought a new dress in a long time, she lets herself go and he looks for romance somewhere else."

This seemed to be a sore topic for him and she let it be. "May I get you more ice cream?"

* * *

"So tell me more about your family," he said when she came back with his ice cream.

"Well, there's Papa, his name is Francis, and my Mom, her name is Cecilia. There are five of us. I have an older brother, Francis, too. We call him Franz. Then me. I was named after Papa's mother, Laura, but my family calls me Lauren. My grandfather's mother was called Lauren, and he was the one who called me that."

"Why Lauren? I think Laura is a great name."

"Filipinos have this penchant for nicknames. We just can't seem to call people by their real names, no matter how short the name might be. I have this friend, her name is Fe. She would introduce herself with 'My name is Fe, but you may call me Ping, for long.'" She laughed heartily. "Anyway. After me comes a younger brother, Ignacio, like in Loyola, you know, the founder of the Jesuits, the Society of Jesus; he was a Spanish Basque, too, like my mom. We call Ignacio Nacho. He's always wanted to be a Jesuit, so I guess he'll be one. Then I have two younger sisters, Maricris and Isa. Except for Franz, who is studying at Oxford, they will all be here Tuesday. They are passing by New York on their way to Europe. Would you come to dinner and meet them if I asked you?"

"I shall be honored."

"Then you're asked."

"You're not going with them to Europe?"

"No, not this time. I have to finish my Master's."

"But that's not until September."

"Oh, I'm working as an architectural intern at Stevens for the summer, remember? I start next month. I'm thinking of doing the other America this time, the smaller cities, you know, on weekends maybe, when I don't have classes. We have been to almost all the big cities, here in New York and in the West Coast, but I have not been to the other States. I'd like to do that this time around."

"Just the cities? Have you ever seen the countryside? Have you ever been to New England? A small town in Connecticut, that's where I come from."

"New England," she said, "located in the northeastern corner of the United States of America. There are six states that comprise New England," she recited in one breath, "Maine, Massachusetts, New Hampshire, Rhode Island, Vermont, and the best of the six, Connecticut. Right?"

He looked at her intently, not knowing what to make of her. Are you for real, he thought. Do I touch ground tomorrow and find you're just an ordinary girl with a gift to surprise? "Well," he said, "that was excellent. I couldn't have done it better. Or faster."

"Don't get carried away. That was just elementary geography. But I should know. I went to Wellesley, remember? Wellesley, M A."

"Oh, yeah, I forgot, Wellesley, M A."

"You were telling me about countryside New England," she prodded.

"Well, actually, Connecticut first," he said, once again connecting, "Laurelfield, Connecticut, my hometown. Lovely this time of year. Lovely all time of the year. Come with me tomorrow," he said earnestly. "Come and meet my family. Come and see this town I was born and grew up in. Come with me to Laurelfield. A cousin is getting married Sunday. Honor us with your presence."

"And meet your family?" she asked.

"Yes. Come and meet my mother and my sister."

"I can't do that."

"Why not? I accept your invitation to come to dinner Tuesday and meet yours."

"Because. What will my Mom say?" She laughed at the thought of her Mom. "You know, except for one occasion, which was a disaster anyway, I was never allowed to go out alone. Either my brother, or my cousin Joe, always chaperoned me."

"Not in Europe, they didn't. And certainly not in Wellesley, M A."

"Well, I guess old habits die hard. I was in Switzerland only one summer and Wellesley, M A, is not a party school. I fell in the company of these girls who did not think that life revolved around boys and parties and going out, whose idea of fun, in fact, was going to estate sales, and museums and libraries. Mostly, we spent hours just enthralled with all the astounding volumes Wellesley has in the Reserve Room, and I would stay up late reading poetry as well as Jane Austen. Once, we went to an estate sale and Gretchen, my roommate, found a rare edition of the poems of Edna St. Vincent Millay, Morocco-bound, gilt edged all around, a treasure! We congregated on Gretchen's bed that night, reading the poems." She looked at him and smiled. "Four girls who found their kicks in forays into auctions or estate sales or antique shops, looking for things older than themselves."

"How could a boyfriend thrive on that?"

She lowered her eyes, which had never left his. "No boyfriend yet. But one day soon." Her glance grazed his lips briefly, before it finally settled on his eyes. "Hey," she smiled, "give me time, the day is still young."

The smile reached out to that part of him that had stayed untenanted, and those glancing looks woke up what slumbered there too long. This is going to be harder than I thought, he thought, quite overcome by that look. "So what do you say?" he finally found his voice. "Spring in Laurelfield is something you shouldn't miss. Do come. This is the first step to New England, we'll go up north next time."

At that moment, she wanted nothing more than to go with him, wherever he would take her. She looked away, exhilarated with the thought. "Oh, I don't know, that's rather a big step to take," she hesitated.

"Look at this honest face. And what could be more honorable than to take you home to meet my family, attend the wedding of a cousin? My mother would be so pleased to have you. You shall be a guest in our house and shall be treated with the utmost respect. You'll find that I am such a gentleman. Come, please say yes."

She wavered. "Well, I have always wanted to see Hershey, where those chocolates are made, but..."

"Good," he jumped at the opening, before she could change her mind. "Great. It's settled then. Hershey first it is. I'll pick you up tomorrow, at 8. Would 8 be all right with you?"

"Isn't that too roundabout for you? Hershey is, after all, in Pennsylvania."

"Roundabout? We have the whole weekend. I'll take you to Hershey first, then we'll backtrack going up to Connecticut. In fact that's even better. Then I could show you Connecticut you haven't been to turning back. We'll stay the night in this old-fashioned mansion that had been converted into a lodge. Then Sunday, home." He was clearly excited, a contagious excitement that got to her, too.

"Only if I paid for my own room."

"Oh, come on, you're my guest," he protested.

"I really don't want you spending money on me, at least not until you have found a job."

Oh, for heaven's sake, he told himself, this is not amusing anymore. He had transcended to a different place from the one he was in this afternoon. It was a charming entertainment, then, somebody who did not know him, who thought he was out of work, who would not even let him spend money on her, thinking he had none. Now, it had become an entirely different matter. He had ceased to be amused way back. Tell her now, he urged himself.

"Would you believe me if I told you that I have money, really I have, a lot of it."

Well, a lot of money is a relative thing, she thought. "Hold on to it then. You never know when you'll really need it."

"Oh, all right," he surrendered, then continued, still in the same tract. "But you'll just love New England's countryside, Laurelfield, in spring, summer, autumn, too. And winter is just glorious. We'll do these next time around."

Then the clock chimed the hour. "I did not realize it was so late," she said. "Guess we better call it a day if you want me to make it tomorrow. I must have eight hours of sleep or I can't see the end of the day."

* * *

He called her when he reached his hotel. "Were you asleep, did I wake you up?"

"No, I just finished my bath, now I'm reading myself to sleep."

"What are you reading?"

"Just some poems. Do you like poetry?"

"Oh, I don't know," he hedged, this baritone whose favorite concert fare was Mahler's and Schumann's and Schubert's music, set to poems of Ruckert and Heine and Hugo. And the poems of Walt Whitman that he so loved. "Read me one now."

"Oh, I don't think so, these are just love poems, I don't think you'll like them."

"Try me."

"All right. This one is by Edna St. Vincent Millay. By the way, she's from New England, too. Anyway." She cleared her throat and started to read.

"When I too long have looked upon your face,
Wherein for me a brightness unobscured
Save by the mists of brightness has its place,
And terrible beauty not to be endured,
I turn away reluctant from your light,
And stand irresolute, a mind undone,
A silly, dazzled thing deprived of sight
From having looked too long upon the sun."

She couldn't hear anything from the other side and asked softly, "Are you still there?"

"Yes, I am," he replied, just as softly. "That was wonderful. Now I am your pupil and I want more. Look, I don't think I can sleep anyway. Why don't I come over again and you read me more poems."

"If I don't sleep soon, I shall not be able to make it tomorrow. We'll do the poems another time. Call me when you leave your house. I'll wait for you downstairs, no need to park."

He tossed and turned but couldn't get her off his mind. He had been feeling this keen sense of expectation all afternoon, knowing something good was going to happen. He had never known anyone quite like her before, a young, exhilarating thing who swept away his cobwebs, stood him alert and alive in a flowerful field where breezes wafted sweet, promised joys too staggering to contemplate. If this is love, then this is how love should be, a joy, an exhilaration, he wanted to shout, to laugh, but most of all, he wanted to hear her voice again.

"Forgot to say goodnight," he said when she picked up the phone. "Goodnight."

"Goodnight to you, too."

He hung up the phone reluctantly. He opened the blinds to the lights of New York. He lay down on the bed, contemplating the view before him, the skyline all ablaze. New York, like him, was sleepless, too.

How could he know when he flew in this morning that Fate, unpredictable, inscrutable Fate, had laid out plans that left him reeling, happily, helplessly. He turned over and burrowed his head deep under the pillows, then turned over again. For the first in a long time he was completely happy, breaking out in uncontrollable laughter, bursting out in silly song. Try though he might, he could not wipe the grin off his face, and thus, smiling idiotically, he finally fell asleep.

* * *

Laura looked at the clock. Eleven o'clock. With the twelve-hour daylight saving time difference, they should be almost ready for lunch in Manila. "So what time are you coming in, Mom?" she asked when Cecilia answered the phone.

"With customs check and everything, we should be out at nine in the morning, that's Tuesday, New York time, of course." Cecilia gave her the airline name and flight number. "You don't have to meet us, we'll take a car service."

How she wished she could tell her about Denis, but she did not want to alarm her. Let her spend the next hours in the plane in peace.

"Until Tuesday, then," she said.

"Until Tuesday, and take care."

"Safe trip, Mom, and I love you. Tell Papa I love him, too."

5

*L*aura was waiting for Denis when he drove up. He helped her with her bag, which he stashed neatly in the back seat.

The day was gorgeous, the drive more so, through rolling hills, then stretches of meadows, past white churches with belled steeples, a boy with his hat slouched over his face dozing under a tree, red brick farmhouses with white picket fences standing in isolated patches. White cows wearing black masks over their eyes stopped grazing to gaze at them, mooed commentaries to each other, dismissed them for the more interesting task of thinning out the grass underfoot. These were scenes she had read in books, seen in magazines, perfect as a picture.

It was still early summer, the tourists had not descended in full force, and Hershey was relatively quiet when they arrived. He showed her the gardens, where tulips and mums and especially roses were in spectacular bloom. This was his turf. She might have been to all the places in the world tourists go to, but she had not seen this. Now he was showing it to her, she liked it and he was happy.

"Have you been to a flea market?" he asked her. She shook her head. "Come, there's a big one along the way."

They arrived at an open market, where vendors had spread out their wares on tables, on grass that had turned brown from too much traffic thrust on it.

"Here," he said, taking her hand, "let's see what they have."

They found hats they liked, made of straw, and she bought one for herself and one for him. He bought sunglasses for them both, *Raybans*, $10, the sign proclaimed. "I hope they don't make us cross-eyed by the end of the day," he said. He hoped the sunglasses, with the hat, would make him far away removed from that Denis Richards. There were all sorts of jewelry, and socks and hosiery, and sweaters and various chocolates by the pound, of which he bought a bagful.

"Oh, look at this," he said, showing her a sweater, "handmade and not expensive too. Which one do you like?"

"Please," she protested, "I don't need one."

"You don't want me to buy you anything, do you?"

"It's just that I have so many sweaters already. Can we just look around without buying anything, at least not things we don't need?"

"Don't you ever buy anything you don't need, just splurge on something, just because it's spring and you're feeling happy?"

She folded the sweater carefully and put it back.

"Well, look there, perfumes, let me get you a bottle. It's such a nice day, let's do something frivolous and buy something you don't need, at least this. Come on." He was holding a good-sized bottle of *Chanel #5*.

"All right," she capitulated, "but that's such a big bottle. Just get me a smaller one I could put in my handbag."

They arrived in Valley Acres at 6 and registered at a hotel that had been renovated from an old mansion.

"Tired?" he asked solicitously, looking at her face in that sweet, searching way of his that she, and unbeknownst to her, countless other women, found so appealing. "Would you want to rest a bit before we have dinner?"

"I'm all right, though I'd like to take a quick shower. I feel so dusty from that flea market. Just give me a half hour." He carried her bag to her room.

"I'll come back for you in thirty minutes."

Her room was large, with a French door leading to the garden outside. The bathroom had an old-fashioned bathtub sitting in the middle. She was glad there was a shower. She read once that the actress Joan Crawford had the bathtubs in her house removed because she thought it was unsanitary to sit in one's own bathwater. Her feelings exactly.

She had showered and changed and was ready when Denis knocked on her door.

"Is your room as large as mine?" He surveyed the room. "Do you like it?" he inquired, eager for her approval.

"Do I like it? Just look at that bathroom, and that bathtub sitting there. And that garden outside, with all those rambling roses. Rambling roses! Last time I saw rambling roses was in my grandmother's garden. Thank you for bringing me here. Yes, I like it. It's amazing what they had done to this old house."

The owners had put in all the conveniences that their guests might require while taking pains not to lose the old-world ambiance of the old house. "If I believed in another life, then I'd say that I must have lived in a time before this, a time long ago. I just love things that are old, even my ideas and opinions tend to be old-fashioned most of the time."

"Good, then you must like me. I'm old, with ideas and opinions that are older."

She laughed. "I'm known in the family as the square. Papa says that it's because I lived with my grandmother a long time."

"I'm glad, I mean, I'm glad you're old-fashioned. I guess we're a pair then." She turned so she wouldn't have to look at him.

"Look at that garden. Have you ever seen anything more magnificent?"

He came near her. "Yes," he said. She knew he was not looking at the garden.

"Those are my parents and grandparents," she said, wanting to head off his attention from herself. She nodded her head in the direction of the bed. He turned and saw a couple of framed pictures she had arranged neatly on her bedside table. "I like to have their pictures around. Sort of keep me in line."

She went to the table. "This is Mommy and Papa."

He took up one of the frames. It was a weird feeling. He thought he was looking at an older version of Laura in both of them---that smile from the woman; the piercing eyes, the rest of the face, softened in hers, from the man; light hair from both of them, the resulting blend stunning him now.

"It was her smile that Papa says got him. He is good-looking, too, Papa, and quite dashing. They say he took one look at my Mom and never looked at another woman again. And that is remarkable, since Filipinos usually have another woman on the side. When I think of my parents, I see them holding hands. As Lerner and Lowe would say, they are still *happ'ly ever-aftering*. Do you know that we never heard them quarrel? I'm sure they must disagree sometimes, but we never heard them quarrel. I think that's rather remarkable."

"Is that where you got it, your smile?"

"No." She looked at the picture, quite discountenanced by his looks. "My face is a Steiner's, everyone says. I'm built like my

Mom, though, thank goodness. The Steiners are big men, like you."

"What color are his eyes?" he asked.

"Gray, like a lot of other Steiners." She looked up at him. "Like yours." But even just looking at those eyes, never leaving hers, shortened her breath and she had to look away.

"These are my grandparents," she said, looking at the other picture, "Papa's parents. Her name was Laura, too." It was an old picture. The woman was sitting primly on a chair, wearing a flowing dress. The man, with a mustache, hair slicked back, wearing a light suit, perhaps white, was standing a bit behind, one hand slightly on the woman's shoulder. There were those piercing eyes again, Denis noted. He looked at the woman. She bore a strong resemblance to the Laura standing next to him. She had the same light hair, had the same regal way of holding her head high, the same stately bearing, the same sureness of self that, although falling short of conceit, still seemed to say, hey, you couldn't find better.

"The other Laura," he said.

She laughed. "I like that, 'the other Laura,' my grandmother." She picked up the frame and looked at the picture. "One summer when we were on vacation in our hacienda, my brother Franz and my cousin Joe and I were looking for things in the attic. We found an old cedar trunk, you know, that wood that smells so sweet. Inside we found a packet, tied with blue ribbon, of letters my grandfather wrote her when they were acourting. Such stirring, poignant letters they were. They transported me to another time, when they were young, and so much in love."

"What was his name?"

"Francis, like his father, and like my father and like my brother. So many Francises in our family. My brother is the fourth generation Francis."

"How did he happen to go to the Philippines, your grandfather, I mean?"

"His family was originally from Switzerland. He was sent to the Philippines to manage the company's business. Their firm installed and maintained the machinery used in the sugar centrals. He was the one who called me Lauren, after his mother.

"My grandfather worked in the city and my grandmother lived in her parents' house in the hacienda, which was an hour's drive from the city. My grandfather would visit my grandmother every evening, always under the watchful eyes of one aunt or another. But sometimes, my grandfather would arrive at the hacienda rather late, when the family had already retired. Then he would climb up the vines that clambered up the balcony outside my grandmother's bedroom." She laughed. "How could she help but fall in love with him? He was so romantic.

"He wrote her every day. Every single day. I still have those letters in my room in Manila. Someday, when you can find the time, you may read them. I also found this," she said.

She picked up a book from on top of the table. It was bound in leather, in rich burgundy. "That goes wherever I go, too," she said. "He gave that to her."

She handed the book to him. It was Petrarch's *Canzoniere*. The book was old and well handled, its pages frayed from having been leafed through too many times.

"Petrarch was an Italian poet. He loved this girl Laura for twenty-one years and wrote poems of his love for her. Then she died, on the anniversary of the day he first saw her. He kept on loving her, and for ten more years, kept writing more poems about her. Three hundred sixty-six poems he wrote in the *Canzoniere*. I've kept that book all these years."

He flipped the pages until he came to a silk-marked page.

She looked at the page he opened. "One day, Petrarch met Laura in the streets of Avignon and she said, 'Petrarch, you are tired of loving me.' That incident produced that sonnet, one of the finest sonnet beginnings written."

He read the poem that she had marked:
Tired, did you say, of loving you? Oh, no!
I ne'er shall tire of the unwearying flame.
But I am weary, kind and cruel dame,
With tears that uselessly and ceaseless flow,
Scorning myself, and scorn'd by you. I long
For death: but let no gravestone hold in view
Our names conjoin'd: nor tell my passion strong
Upon the dust that glow'd through life for you.
He closed the book slowly. "That was great. It must have been a magical time. How tragic it must be to go through life not ever knowing how it feels to love like that."

"Or to be loved like that," she said. "I think I was born in the wrong time. If I had a choice, I would prefer to have lived in that time long ago."

"Maybe you did."

"No," she chuckled, "Catholics don't believe in reincarnation. We don't get recycled. We believe in an Absolute Creation. When God created me, He started from absolute scratch. So I'm me, completely and totally Laura Steiner, not somebody else's spirit, or body or soul. When I get out of here, I get out of here. My soul would go back to heaven and my body would turn to dust. Some people say that sometimes we do come back, to finish some unfinished affair, close an open book. But that's just a romantic notion. Who knows, really? But if I should come back, I come back as a ghost of me, not as a living entity recycled from somebody who was gone."

"I'm glad you are here now, exactly the way you are, instead of somebody else from some time long ago. What a loss it would have been for me had you been here at some previous time and I missed you." He held her gaze and she couldn't look away.

"If people were meant to be, they'd find each other, no matter where or when. I mean," she faltered, thoroughly confused. "I don't know what I mean." She laughed self-consciously, "I guess I have not come out of my reverie yet. I am still thinking of my grandfather and grandmother." She tried to make light of it, "or I just must be hungry, I don't know what I'm saying." She turned and started fumbling with the clasp of her bag. "I cannot seem to open this bag." He came behind her. She was conscious of his nearness, conscious of his clean, manly smell, conscious that he was looking at her.

"Here, let me," he said gently, taking hold of the bag. He stood close to her and he could smell her perfume, storming his senses. Ah, that Chanel thing should be outlawed.

They bent down at the same time to unfasten the clasp and in an inevitable surge, flowed into each other, and ribbons of light flickered in front of her before she closed her eyes, and all the starlight and moonlight of years that she stashed away as she waited for him flashed inside her head as he pressed her to him and enveloped her in his massive embrace. She drew in chunks of breaths lest she'd drown in his sweet, sunshiny smells. He leaned down and seeking, took her lips in his and in the uncharted realm of this foreign enclosure, she foundered and was lost. This was exactly how she pictured their coming together, this corny scene of bending down at the same time and finding each other. But she was a great believer, even in corny scenes, and more so in magic, and she knew it would happen just this way, and she never found her way out again, or tried to.

And he, man of the world that he thought he had become, grown resistant to smiles and glancing looks and other feminine adornments, just gave up his defenses. His fences toppled over, his barricades came apart. She stormed and occupied, neither asking permission nor seeking approval. "God, to think that I almost missed you," he said huskily. "I could have gone to Stevens next week and you would not have been there anymore, and I would have passed through this life not knowing that I could be capable of this thing that I feel for you now." All the years when he thought he would never feel a full, overflowing emotion such as this, all the voids that had stayed too long unfilled, came completed at this moment. She opened herself up to him and he found himself drowning in a deluge of emotions.

There was a knock on the door. He hesitated, loathed to leave the bewitched state she had led him to. But the knock was insistent and he had to let go.

She opened the door and a lad stood there, his arms laden with towels. "You called for towels, miss?" he asked.

"Yes, I did." She relieved him of his burden, dipped into her pocket and gave him some bills. "Thank you so much."

She went to the bathroom and arranged the towels neatly on a small table. She had to keep on talking, more to herself than to him, otherwise she would have to look at him, and she was not ready for that. "I used up all the towels when I showered, and called for more. What thick towels they have, one would think that in a hotel like this...."

He did not let her finish. He knew she was not thinking of towels. He spun her around but she refused to look at him. She was so slight, a perfect match to his immense frame. He must have crushed her, did he frighten her, she looked flustered still.

He held her face in both his hands. "It's all right," he said gently, trying to reassure her. "It's all right. Are you hungry, would you like to have dinner now?"

"If you wish," she answered inaudibly.

"Then let's." He smoothed her hair, then held her chin until she had to look up at him. He smiled and every confusing thing snapped back into their previous lucid arrangements. "They serve dinner on the terrace here. Would you like that?"

"Whatever you want. You're my guide, remember?"

"All right then, we go."

The terrace was dimly lit. It was still early, and most of the tables were empty. He chose a secluded one and she let him order for both of them. Somebody was tinkling on the piano and a girl was crooning Duke Ellington's *In A Sentimental Mood*, languidly moving and shaking shoulders and hips in obvious delight to the music.

"Let me show you the rest of the town," he said when they were done with dinner.

He drove around a bit but it was a small town and a ten-minute drive covered whatever there was to see of it. He drove to the edge of the town, up a small hill, and in silence they watched the lights of the houses below. The moon was out, big and yellow, bathing the countryside with a pale light. She looked at his hands gripping the wheel, big, strong hands with big, strong fingers, and was soundly stirred. Steady now, these are just hands, she told herself. Then why am I asphyxiating just looking at them? He reached for hers and she wound up in his arms, being held tightly. She was suffocating again and had to come up for air, but he was not through and well, she thought, I'm young, it's not going to kill me.

"Come," he said huskily, "things are getting out of hand, let's go dancing."

He brought her to this small, intimate place with soft music and softer lights. The dining room opened to a terrace outside, lit by a moon that had since gone hazy, where a three piece band was playing and couples were dancing. From their small table in one corner they could see a young girl, hear her singing Antonio Carlos Jobim's *Once I Loved*, with gusto, scaling with ease and evident enjoyment the high notes she herself shaped, adlibbing shamelessly.

He was not much for dancing; they hardly moved, they hardly returned to their table. He was much for the little, gentle things though, kissing the palm of her hand, touching her face, caressing her hair.

"Ah, so much hair, smells so good, too."

"Thanks to you. You paid for the bottle. You smell good yourself. I did not know you smoked."

"My father used to smoke a pipe and when he went, he left a collection. When he was not there anymore and I felt at odds with myself, when there were things I could not seem to get a grip on and I needed to connect, I picked up his pipe. A disastrous luxury I can't afford, I know, but which I indulge in once in a great, big while, when things come up in my life I desperately want to share with him. Yes, I do, smoke a pipe, but very seldom, when yon moon turns blue. You don't like it?"

"I love it." She loved everything about him, his low laugh, his clean masculine smell of newly laundered shirt, aftershave lotion and pipe tobacco and the way she fit in his arms. He was like that man in that Gershwin song, big and strong, not just coming along into her life but bursting into it, the man she loved. "I still can't believe that so much excitement happened to me these past few hours than happened to me in my whole life. I did not know yesterday how good it is to be dancing here with you, being held this way by you, as though I'm yours, as though I belong to you."

"You do. I've staked my claim. You're mine now and I shall never let you go and I shall take care of you all my life." He held her face between his hands. "Marry me tonight."

"Tonight? I guess all the priests have retired for the night."

"Priests?" He had not thought of priests.

"Priest. Singular. Who did you think would marry us?"

"Oh, a priest, singular, definitely."

"You're not Catholic?"

"I'm afraid not."

"Are you what they call a WASP?"

"No," he laughed, "not even a bee. Don't hop around, don't sting, not interested much in flowers. Until yesterday."

"You don't take me seriously at all," she accused.

"I'm sorry. I'm just too happy, I can't help myself." He touched her face and said seriously, "My family is Methodist. But we are not a religious family. I have not been to church in a long time. Does it matter?"

"To my family, I'm afraid it will. Papa will be disappointed if he can't walk down that aisle with me, in that church filled with flowers and three hundred of his friends. As for me, to be honest, I'm past caring, about anything."

"We're going to a cousin's wedding tomorrow, will you marry me Monday?"

"I have to ask my parents' permission. They're coming Tuesday. You're meeting them, remember?"

"Tuesday, then." he pursued.

"But why the hurry?"

"I've waited so long. Now that you're here, what's there to wait for? Besides, I have to be back in L.A. in two weeks, that has been arranged a while back, I cannot disarrange that now, and there's no way I am going back without you. And I do want to take you away after the wedding, even for just a few days, so it has to be next week."

"Are you absolutely sure? After all, you've known me but a day."

"That's long enough. With some people, it takes less than that, a moment, that's all it takes. You looked up at me and smiled, and that was it for me."

She looked at him, "Catholics cannot be divorced, I'm sure you know that. If you marry me, it's a no-return-no-exchange deal."

"No satisfaction guaranteed or my money back?" he asked.

She shook her head. "Once you take me out of the store, I'm yours for life. So you see, you have to be very sure."

"And if I don't satisfy, you don't return me?" She shook her head again. "Great," he said, "that's how I want it. We're stuck with each other. Hey, I think I'm going to like this religion."

They held each other in silence for a bit, then he resumed. "So how about Wednesday?"

She laughed. "You do have a one-track mind, haven't you?"

"I do. So how about Wednesday?"

"It's just that everything is so new to me. Don't let's hurry things. You're the first boyfriend I ever had. I want to know what it's like being courted, going steady. Let's go acourting first. You could ask me for a date, bring me flowers when you come for me. Let's hold hands in the movies, we could steam up the back seat of your car. That's what the girls in college did. And for a change, I'd like to have some really earthy, lusty sins to confess.

Let's take small steps and not hurry things too much. There's so much I haven't done."

"But of course we shall do all this, I promise we'll catch up. Tell me what you want and we'll do all of them. We can do all these things, all the things you missed, I bring you flowers, hold hands in the movies, fog up the backseat of that car, after we are married. I'm sure those things are permitted married people, too. I can still court you even after we're married. You'll find I am a most romantic fellow. Come on, say yes."

She touched his hair. "How about Saturday. That's the Blessed Virgin Mary's day. It's a good enough day to get married on."

"It's settled then. Saturday it is. You've made me the happiest man tonight. You won't regret this, ever. I'll take care of you. No one could love anyone as much as I'll love you. Let's get a ring as soon as we get back. And let's not tell my Mom yet, I shall make it a surprise."

He noticed that there was just a sprinkling of couples left on the dance floor. "I guess they want us to leave," he whispered. He walked her to her bedroom door.

"Had I known kissing was this good, I wouldn't have waited this long," she said.

"I'm glad you did."

"I'm glad, too. I don't think I would have liked being kissed by somebody else."

"No, it wouldn't have been this good with anybody else; nobody kisses like I do."

"You're a modest big fellow, aren't you?"

He laughed. "It's late and you have a long day tomorrow. I'm taking a cold shower, and you, young lady, are supposed to be in bed, it's past your bedtime. I'll arrange for the desk to give us a wake-up call. Goodnight, sweet." He kissed her lightly, placed his hands on her shoulders and steered her firmly inside her room.

He went to his room and called his mother.

* * *

Sunday dawned bright and clear. Laura woke up early and couldn't go back to sleep. She opened the window and inhaled deeply of the crisp June air. A breeze brought in the fragrance of all the flowers blooming in the garden.

She showered and took her time dressing. She was drying her hair when Denis called.

"Did I wake you?"

"No, I had been awake for some time. In fact I'm almost through dressing," she answered.

"Meet you in the dining room in thirty minutes," he said.

He ordered coffee while he waited for her. He saw her first, lingering by the door, searching for him. He sprang from his chair and watched her walk towards him. How many men would burst their vests to have one such as this to bring home to their mothers? She must have cornered the market on elegance, exuding class even in casualness. He pulled out her chair and waited for her to sit down before returning to his own. "Hungry?" he asked.

"Not really. I'll just have coffee. I really can't eat so early in the morning. Maybe just toast with my coffee." She placed her hand on top of his. "Can you take me to church?"

"We can go this afternoon. Is that okay? I'll come with you."

"Yes, of course."

"We'll be there in an hour." He took both her hands and put them to his lips. "Did you sleep well?"

"Yes, thanks. Did you?"

They were causing a lot of excitement among the guests, but he, who before had been so fiercely protective of his private life, did not even seem to notice, or care.

6

This was the New England he was proud of, the hometown he wanted her to see, all blue skies and yellow sun, and the wall of spectacular pink and white blossoms.

"What are those?" she asked in wonder.

"You share the same name. Those are laurels, our state flower."

It was a spectacular show. Clouds of pink and white clusters covered the landscape. "Actually, this is one of the best years. They were not this magnificent the last time I was here. I think they're showing off for you.

"Oh, wonderful. I'm so happy they are."

They passed a quaint bridge spanning a brook, rustling and gurgling past them through paths strewn with pebbles and algae.

"Wildflowers abound in Connecticut. Come, let's walk a bit." He stopped the car and they wandered by the side of the brook. He came back with a sprig of white flowers. "Look at these. These are wild mints, native to Connecticut, here, take a smell. They came out early for you." She took the spray from his hand, bent towards the while petals and breathed in deeply the sharp smell of mint. "And those are hemlocks, you've read of them, of course, highly poisonous."

A frog surveyed them indifferently, then dismissed them, finding them less interesting than the lily leaf riding the rushing water.

"Tired?" he asked when they were back in the car. "We'll be there soon."

"I'm not tired." She surveyed him while he drove. One hand gripped the wheel strongly, the other idled on his thigh when it was not needed, or when it was not groping for hers. Hair peeked from the cuffs of his shirt sleeves under the sweater, scattered down the back of his hands, dispersed into fingers almost as big as cigars, before fingernails cut short and clean. She wondered how hands, so ordinary and taken for granted before, fingers that used to be just appendages, could take on such voluptuous proportions now that they belonged to him.

She reached out and touched his face. "You must have been the best-looking boy in your neighborhood. Were you?" She ran her fingers on the hairs on his wrist. "Tell me about yourself, about your folks, about this town where you were born and grew up in. Tell me about when you were a small boy. Your mother must have loved you very much. Did you ever get smacked? Bet she never disciplined you. Did she or did your Dad?"

"Whoa," he laughed, "may I take my time?" He removed her hand from his arm, laced his fingers with hers. "Now, did I get smacked by my mother? No, I was my mother's boy, you see, but I was also a good boy, was most well behaved. I was born a gentleman; everybody says so. No, I can't remember being smacked by my mother. By my father, no, not either, but then, I was also my father's boy. Anyway, he was seldom home, so I had the run of the house."

"I knew she didn't. Even when you misbehaved, I'm sure she just looked the other way."

"Well, we did not give our mother much trouble. Early on, we were aware that she had enough problems with our father gone, so we did not misbehave, did well in school, were very good children. Then Bess got married to James, had two boys, Jody and Jamie, whom my mother dotes on, and I went away. Even now I'm no trouble at all. You don't know how lucky you are. You get the boy who never misbehaved, the man who does not play around." She laughed but he looked at her seriously. "That's true, ask anyone."

She wished the drive were longer, but they arrived sooner than she wanted.

"So here we are," he announced.

A tall, big woman hurried over to Denis and gave him a big hug. He turned to Laura. "This is Laura."

"We are pleased to meet you. You must be tired from the long drive. Come in, come in." She was a towering woman, broad, big-boned, with a face that was long and horsy, almost mannish. She could not be that old, but her face had the expression of one who was resigned to carrying a heavy load, a face grown old before its time. Behind her the entire family had come out from the house and was surveying them. That must be

Bess and her husband and the two kids. Bess was a younger version of her mother. With a thick middle, her broad figure beginning to go, Laura could see where she was going. It was difficult to imagine that they were Denis' mother and sister. He must have gotten his handsome looks from his father, then. Laura shifted her eyes to the man standing beside Bess. A drought of beauty on one side, a surfeit of it on the other. Here were good looks too much for one man. Yellow hair, startling blue eyes, Paul Newman in the flesh, with a mischievous smile lurking on his lips, James, Bess' husband. Laura wondered how he ever got together with Bess. She looked at the two children. Jody, and this must be Jamie, both carbon copies of their father, thank goodness for that.

"Did you grow up in this house?" she later asked him. They had just come back from church, and were drinking tea in the porch.

"Well, this is rather a young house and I'm not. No, we grew up in a small house, in the other side of town. Actually, I bought this house for my mother." They were seated on a swingy sofa; she leaned and kissed him on the check. "What's that for?"

"You bought your mother a house."

*   *   *

Too many things were happening too fast. Time fled, things blurred. She did not remember much. But what she did was filed neatly in folders and laid away in a cache inside her head. She remembered the church, old, with ivy clinging to its walls, too many people, the evening wedding ceremony, the church filled with candles, the unfamiliar non-Catholic wedding rite, the reception at the back of the groom's massive house. And the dance after.

Denis was holding her close and her nose, buried in his chest, took in his smells, of things masculine, of sharp-smelling soap and shaving lotion and a shirt that a breeze from some sweet place must have blown dry while it danced on some line under the sun.

"Change partners?" They turned and Laura saw a good-looking couple, he rather young, with blue eyes and yellow hair, she, blonde and much, much older, well, at least older, with a low-cut dress that revealed overflowing proportions. Laura found herself relinquished into another's arms.

He held her lightly, away from him, frankly looking her over. After some while he said, "So how come a pretty girl like you is going out with a handsome man like that?"

"Just lucky, I guess."

"Aren't you a bit young to be dating an older man?"

"Aren't you a bit young to be dating an older woman?" she shot back.

"Sorry, not guilty. I was just commandeered so she could cut in on you."

"And why is that?"

"Oh, well. They were an item once, you know, but that was years ago, did not last long, over in due time." He stepped back to survey her and looked at her quizzically. "He had always been partial to blondes." Then he smiled at her brightly. "I do know, though, someone who isn't."

"I'm sure you do."

"Yes, I do. Why don't we leave the older generation to their older, boring ways and go somewhere and get to know each other?"

"Thanks but I think that older generation is coming over to claim me now."

They watched as Denis hurried towards them, the intruding woman cast off to wherever she came from.

"Thanks, Craig," said Denis. He took hold of Laura's hand and steered her away and she allowed herself to be led. "Let me show you the rest of the house," he said "This is the trellis," he announced with a flourish, "and this is the door to the kitchen," he opened the door, "and this is the kitchen." Then he pinned her against the wall. "And this is the fellow who missed you." His body pressed against hers blocked all lights and troubling thoughts of bothersome blondes and when he chewed on her lips, Craig went away into the blue night, forgotten, as he should be, and with him, the yellow-haired woman with breasts too big for her too-small dress.

*   *   *

"Now it's your turn. Tell me about yourself," he said. They were driving back to New York. "How did you get to look the way you do?"

"Well, I told you about my parents and my relatives scattered all over Europe. Actually, there are so many others in our place who look like me. Did I tell you that the Spaniards colonized us? They were in the Philippines for more than three hundred years. Then came the Spanish American War. You forgot to Remember The Maine? Anyway, the U. S won the war and annexed former Spanish colonies, the Philippines included. The Americans came and stayed for another fifty years. That accounted for a lot of intermarrying, and many children who are white. The Americans," she said, warming up on the subject, "they wanted to liberate us from the Spaniards, from what they called the yoke of Spanish imperialism.

"But then of course, after they defeated the Spaniards, they stayed and wanted to impose on the Filipinos their own brand of imperialism, you know, American style. You did not know that?"

"No," he said, taking her hand and putting it to his lips, not quite interested in what the Americans did a hundred years ago, in a land on the other side of the world, whose only feature that interested him was that it produced this girl. "Somebody was remiss with my education. Steeped and soaked me in culture and neglected history."

"You want a short refresher?" Actually, no, he did not. But she did not wait for his reply. "Well, the Americans routed out the Spaniards, but instead of granting the Philippines independence, as the Filipinos expected, they stayed and ruled, too, just like the Spaniards. Even Mark Twain said he became an anti-imperialist when he saw what the Americans did to the Philippines, that instead of liberating the country, America wanted to suppress it, that instead of America being the protector, it was now grounding its heels on the people it was supposed to be protecting. That's verbatim Mr. Twain.

"The Filipinos, of course, did not like it one bit. There followed one of the bloodiest wars in the annals of American, and Filipino, history. Like all wars, it was most savage, too, almost a quarter of a million people dead, the bulk of whom were, of course, Filipinos. One historian even calculated that more than one million Filipinos died during that war, which made it an act of genocide on the part of the Americans. A staggering, brutal war it was. Whenever an American soldier was found dead, every Filipino in the village, man, woman and child, were lined up and a Filipino was shot until a confession was extracted. In a village where some American soldiers were massacred, the American authorities ordered all the Filipino males shot unless the perpetrators surrendered. These males included boys in their teens or even younger. Villages were burned. Those who surrendered were concentrated in camps without food. In the course of days, more than a thousand Filipinos died, and were pushed into graves they were ordered to dig out themselves. Sounds familiar?

"But they were a hardy people, those Filipinos. There sprung up the Bolo Battalion. Bolos are something like machetes. Well, bolo-brandishing Filipinos went up in bolo-arms against what, just recently, they called their liberators, who were wielding guns, of course. Undaunted, the little brown people swathed their little brown bodies in thick fabric, and sometimes in interior tubes of tires, which constricted their blood vessels, and deterred profuse, fatal bleeding when they were hit by American bullets. This gave them a few seconds of reprieve to still charge and fell the enemy with their bolos, before they, themselves, fell on the ground, dead. This staggering around after they were hit wouldn't do, the Americans said, so they asked Mr. Colt to come up with what is now called the forty-five, with heavier bullets with impact so strong it knocked down the little enemy, pronto, bolo and all. This was why the Colt forty-five came about in the first place, really, you did not know that? That's true, the Filipino's kinship with the forty-five. Don't laugh, that's true, look it up." Her fingers played with his hair. "A bloody, long-drawn-out, expensive war that cost the American people more than half a billion dollars, a staggering amount at that time. Well, the Americans won the war, of course. After that, they had to get back that money they lost. Of course. For fifty years they stayed and made the Philippines an American outpost. Almost all the goods sold there were Made in America. There were products, too, that were Made By Americans, judging from the white children who cropped up after that, and their white descendants who are still there. There," giving his hair a final twist, "the American-Filipino conflict in a nutshell."

"Wow," he said, feigning wonder, "a whole history of a savage war, logistics included, and all I wanted to know was how you got to look this way." He looked at her seriously, shaking his head, and she laughed. He had this way with him, she would find out later, of taking her out of her serious moods and into irresistible laughter. "Drawn into international conflict and given a historical dose of man's inhumanity to man, just because I wanted to know where you got that face."

She was laughing now. "Man's inhumanity to man! You should hear what I have to say about the Second World War and the Japanese' inhuman occupation of the Philippines. That," she said emphatically, "was an inhuman man's inhumanity to a small, defenseless man whose war it was not even, in the first place. One day, when nights are long and you have the ears, I'm going to tell you horror stories to curl your toes."

"Oh, please," he said, "no more wars. Let's make that piece of history a love story. We once lived in those times, you and I, we fell in love, and were the Romeo and Juliet of that time, your country at war with my country, with both our countries vehemently against our falling in love, but we prevailed. No asinine schemes, no stupid misunderstanding, and definitely no poison kept us apart. We prevailed and populated that country with children who looked like you. Now, that's the kind of history I want to listen to. No more wars now," he said. "Tell me about when you were growing up, tell me about the other Laura."

"What else is there I haven't told you? She had three children, my *Tito* Ray, Papa, and there was a girl, also named Laura, who died when she was little. I was my grandmother's special girl, maybe because I was named after her.

"I used to spend a lot of time with her in the hacienda. Sadly, she died before I finished high school.

"Anyway, I went to the graduation ball with the two handsomest men there that evening, my brother Franz and my cousin Joe. Joe, the best-looking Steiner, I always say, because he is. Better looking than Papa or my *Tito* Ray, or RJ, his brother, or even Franz.

"Then it was time for college. I wanted to become an architect. Franz and Joe were already in England, Papa thought at first I should go there also. Papa and *Tito* Ray went there, you know. But I wanted to come to the States. Mom's sisters went to Wellesley, so they decided I could go there, as well.

"After Switzerland, I went to Wellesley and from Wellesley to you. That's all there is to know about me. A short, uninteresting story. I hope you find me pleasing, sir. My family shelled out a lot of money to make me acceptable to you. "

7

They reached New York about seven. "Are you hungry?" he asked.

"A little," she answered. "Look, there's a small place there. Maybe we could get a burger there or something."

The place was dimly lit. "Let me order for you," Denis offered.

"All right," she replied.

He took both her hands in his. "Did I tell you how much I love you? There is nothing truer than that."

She looked at him, at how serious he was. "You were never divorced, were you?" she asked cautiously.

He laughed, shaking his head. "No, not that."

When they were done, he paid and left a hefty tip. She would notice this of him, that he would always leave a substantial amount for the waiters. "Now, I would like to take you to the movies," he said.

"Now?" she inquired.

"The movie starts at nine. We can still make it."

The parking garage was in front of the movie house. He let her out of the car. "I'll just park there. Don't move, okay?"

He sought her hand and held it tight when they were finally seated. She found it strange that he did not even ask her whether she wanted to see this particular movie.

She slid back into her seat and wanted to adjust her skirt, but he was holding her hand tight and would not let go. The lights went out and the movie started. She was reading the credits and saw the name Denis Richards but that did not register. Then there Denis was, big as life, starting to sing to this woman. The color was very flattering, he looked very handsome, she looked stunning.

"What's happening here," she said under her breath. She watched the movie, hardly breathing. Then with his face and the woman's face occupying the entire screen, that Denis Richards kissed that woman. It was just a slight kiss and Laura could feel

Denis looking at her. She tried to disengage her hand that he was clasping tight but he refused to let go. Then he sang solo, a stirring performance, she thought in spite of herself, then they sang together, he and this blonde movie star, after which he kissed her again, this time, longer and with more passion than the last.

"I think it's time to go home," she said and walked out of the movie house. He scrambled out of his seat to catch up with her.

"Oh, please, listen," he started but did not finish. She had stopped so abruptly that he almost fell over her.

"I'm listening," she said coldly.

"I'm really sorry."

"You are in the movies." Her brows furrowed, "you are in the movies. How was I so stupid as to think you were looking for a job. Look at you." She snorted a laugh. "You sell that expensive trench coat and you don't have to look for a job for, how long, months?" He tried to hold her hand but she pulled it back. "Let me think first." She was not even looking at him. She was talking more to herself than to him. "I got myself engaged to somebody in the movies. All right, first let me do this, let me disengage myself first. Then let me go home and sort things out."

"There's nothing to sort out. And what do you mean disengage?"

"I," she pointed a thumb at herself, "consider myself disengaged. You don't have to follow." She looked at him, shaking her head. "Now you may take me home."

She was very calm, it unnerved him.

"No, no, no, we have to talk this out first. I'm sorry, all right?"

She looked at him, contrition written on his face.

"All right. Now just take me home. My brain is not functioning right now. Please."

He heaved a deep sigh and proceeded to get the car.

She straggled to the farthest end of the car. He reached out to touch her, "Please just let me be for a while."

Then they were in front of her apartment. He jumped out and hurried to the other side to open the door for her. She stepped out of the car, got her bag from the backseat and looked at him, her head held high.

"Goodnight," she said.

"Can't we talk about this, please?"

"I'd rather we didn't," she said, fumbling for her keys. "I'm tired. I'm taking a shower and I'm off straight to bed."

Somewhere in that pampered, catered-to, fawned-over childhood, he thought, she must have been told that she was as perfect as a girl could be and she believed she was and acted like she was, holding herself straight and tall and as imperious as any royal could be. But where yesterday this regal air delighted him, now it exasperated him.

* * *

The room was lit by the streetlights when she entered. She went through all the rooms, switching on all the lights. She then called Ann and was relieved to find her in.

"Stop it right there, I'm coming over," Ann said. She was running through her story so fast, Ann did not grasp everything she was telling her.

"Are you telling me that you spent the weekend with Denis Richards? The Denis Richards? And he asked you to marry him? And you did not know who he was?" She knew some people who were in this world but were quite out of it but in this department Laura was without peer.

"Oh, Ann, have you heard of him, have you seen his movies?"

"Yes, I have and yes, I have, at least one movie."

"What I can't understand is why I've never heard of him."

"Well, you don't watch movies that often. And you don't go to the opera. Since you haven't seen a Denis Richards movie, or heard a Denis Richards record, you did not recognize him. He has not been around that long, in fact, what you saw last night was only his second movie, but surely even you must have heard of Denis Richards. He had made quite a name for himself in the musical world before he went to Hollywood."

"The name sounds familiar, but then every Tom, Dick and Harry is named Denis and Richard, my apologies to Mr. Goldwyn." They both laughed at the absurdity of it all.

"What are you going to do? You have to pick up that phone sometime," said Ann.

"I'm not marrying a movie actor! God, I need that like I need a toothache. I couldn't possibly know how I could handle marriage to this so public a person. And how long could marriage to these people last?"

"Maybe it's not so bad, Lauren. I seem to recall reading somewhere that he is a private person too, that he keeps pretty much to himself. And no rumored girlfriend. Maybe that is possible, even in his kind of work. I just have not read much about him."

"I can't be married to a public person. All I want to do is just stay in my own quiet corner and be left alone. I can't have that, married to him.

"Let's not be too hasty. Calm down and think things over. Why don't you go to the library tomorrow and check him out."

"The library? He is in the library?"

"He's an artist," said Ann patiently. "Yes, in the library. There's one for the performing arts at the Lincoln Center. Read up on him. What you find out might not be so bad."

* * *

Denis called several times the next morning but she did not answer. He called Stevens but was told she was not in. But of course. Friday was her last day. On the chance that she could help him, he asked for Ann.

"Denis Richards? Yes, I'm Ann."

"I have been trying to get in touch with Laura but nobody is picking up her phone. I have to talk to her."

"I think she'd rather not talk to you at the moment."

"I'm sure I could explain if you'll just tell me where she is."

Why not, she thought, he was not like the other movie stars. If the tabloids were to be believed, he kept pretty much to himself and had not been linked romantically to any girl. Besides, what harm could he do her in the library, with so many people there.

"She went to the library. At the Lincoln Center."

"Thank you, Ann, thank you so much."

8

*T*he Lincoln Center. It had been the center of his life for many years. He remembered his New York debut at the Metropolitan Opera singing Mozart's Don Giovanni to a resounding, standing ovation. The critics the next day were all praise for his performance, gushing over the way he sang the Serenade, the Champagne aria, calling him the definitive Don. He remembered, too, recitals at the Avery Fisher Hall across the square; the elation, the exhilaration, the downright humbleness he felt the first time he worked with Leonard Bernstein conducting the New York Philharmonic. Heady days for a young man who had worked long and hard to achieve his dreams and did, to acclaim more favorable than he ever imagined. Immersed as he was in the making of his two movies, however, they only filled a void in his finances and he did not find in them the soul-satisfaction that he got from opera and song recitals and recordings. And so he was coming back next season, to do a recital at the Avery Fisher Hall and another Don Giovanni at the Met.

The Library for the Performing Arts was located at the back of the Metropolitan Opera House and he had to walk a bit to reach it.

He went to the information desk and was told that there was a reading room on the main floor and another one on the third floor. She wasn't on the first floor. He did not bother with the elevator and took the stairs two steps at a time to the third floor.

There she was. He could see her reading from one of a pile of materials in front of her. He went inside to where she was seated. He saw pictures and articles of himself spread out in front of her. She looked up and saw him there, looking at the papers spread out before her, looking at her. She returned his look without any expression on her face.

"Please," he said, "I have to talk to you."

"I'd rather not talk now, I am in the middle of something here."

"I must talk to you. So will you please come outside with me?"

"I can't. I am doing something here." She was trying to keep her voice down, so as not to be heard by the other people around them. But Denis, all six-foot-four-inches, a-hundred-something pounds of him, even if he were not Denis Richards, was just not the kind of person who would go unnoticed. By now, they both had caught the attention of people in the room and eyes and ears were on them. People had recognized him and they were causing a flurry of excitement.

He tried to take her hand, but she pulled it back.

"What do you think you're doing," she sputtered. "Have you lost your mind? Everybody is looking at us."

"Of course I've lost my mind. Now, will you please come outside with me or shall I continue, right here."

"You won't dare."

"Oh, but I would," he said. He would too, she thought.

She looked up. There was a hum of excitement in the room, everybody was watching them now. She stood up and gathered her reading materials. He tried to help her, but she turned her back to him, blocking the way, so he couldn't reach the magazines. She scooped them up, returned them to the counter and proceeded to go out.

He turned to the faces looking at them, shrugged, spread out his hands in an apologetic gesture and, in that voice familiar now to every woman in that room, said, "I am sorry for the disturbance."

He was reassured, "Oh, we did not mind at all." "Hope things turn out all right." Accompanied by titters, "If she doesn't want you, we're here."

She went to the elevator, pressed the button and the elevator opened for them.

"See, that's just what I mean. You can't keep anything about you private. Everybody wants to know what's happening in your life. And I, I would be drawn into so much display; I don't think I can take it. God, just the thought of it unnerves me."

They left the elevator and she took long strides to get out of the building, with him behind her, trying to catch up. They reached the part of the square that was lined with benches. He tried to hold her arm, then her elbow and she kept on shaking his hand away. Finally, with as much authority as he could muster, he said, "Just give me ten minutes, okay, just listen to me for ten minutes."

He steered her towards one of the benches at the far side of the square, where they could have a semblance of privacy, and sat her with her back towards the path where people were passing by.

He took both her hands in his. She tried to pull them away but he wouldn't let go. "Will you sit still? You're not even giving me a chance here."

"*It was not that good or I'd be singing at the Met,*" she mimicked him. "You really thought that was funny, didn't you?" He laughed, he could not help himself. That really was funny. "*I don't know much about poetry,*" she intoned. "Why, those Mahler recordings and those crossovers that sold all those copies and made you so much money could keep you away from the drawing board for as long as you live. And let's not even talk about the movies, for crissakes. And *architecture, that's a story for another day?*"

He tried to look serious but failed and she glared at him. "I'm sorry," he said, frankly laughing now, "it's just that you look so, so, I'm sorry, really. But I really don't know much about Edna St. Vincent Millay, that was all I was saying. I am really sorry. Please forgive me and don't be angry anymore."

"It's just so unfair. Had I known you were an actor, I would never have gone out with you. Why the lie, I cannot understand." She looked very upset.

"There was no lie. I never told you anything that was not true. The rest you just presumed. My only fault was that I did not correct you. At first it was amusing, meeting maybe one of a dozen people in New York who did not know me. But that did not last long. I did want to tell you, before the day was over, but I had gotten myself in too deep, and then I did not know how to tell you."

She was not angry, really, just sad. "It's not going to work. I am a very private person. I don't like going out, I don't like crowds, I don't like any kind of attention focused on me. You, whatever you do, the press will just lap up. And above all, when I get married, that will be it for me, no more second chance. It's just that one time. I shall be stuck to that one man for life. So you see why I can't take a chance on you?"

"Haven't we covered that ground? Haven't I told you I want to be stuck with you too, for the rest of my life. What do you think I have been trying to tell you?"

"How could you possibly kiss that woman the way you did last night and not feel anything? And how many more women will you kiss that way, and say it's just part of your job? And how many more movies do I have to endure and each time wonder if this is it, the movie that ended me and started her. I just want a simple life. And let's not even speak of that dreaded D word, for crissakes!"

"And you sincerely think that only an unemployed person could give you that? Look at me. I'm still the same person I was yesterday. How could things change so fast just because I happen to be doing this kind of work? And how can you be so sure that I could not be faithful to you? You're so afraid of divorce you can't even mention the word. What do you know of it? You who have seen nothing in your family but holding hands and sweetness and affection. You have not even heard your parents quarrel.

"I am a child of that dreaded D word and I will tell you how it is. You're awakened in the middle of the night by bitter arguments and harsh words and afterwards, the heart-rending weeping, always the weeping, and your eight-year-old, ten-year-old, twelve-year-old heart goes out to her but you can't hate him. He is your father, after all, and a good father, too, he had been. Then, tired, worn out, and resigned that there is nothing to salvage from years of contention, he walks out, and your fifteen-year-old head tells you what your fifteen-year-old heart refuses to acknowledge, that that's the end for them. Then you must stop going to school, something you have loved doing, you are the man of the house now and must help bring in the money. Then one heartbreaking day he gets married again and you know that there's no need to hope anymore, he is not coming through that door ever again and your heart breaks with hers. That is the reality of divorce that you have only read about, if that. How could I subject myself, or someone I love, to that again? I was there and I'm damned if I'm going through that all over again."

"I'm sorry. I did not mean to bring that up."

He touched her face and after that impassioned outpouring that she brought about, she let him.

"If you are a hundred and one percent sure the first time around that this is it and you work hard to make it work, whether you are a singer or movie star or whatever, I believe you can make it work.

"What I do is sing and if I'm paid better singing in the movies, fine, but I don't have to be there exclusively. I am not an actor. I am a singer, and I sing wherever it takes me, in recording studios, in concert halls, in opera houses, there." He nodded his head towards the Met. "I sang there for three years. I am singing Don Giovanni there again and doing a recital in the Avery Fisher Hall next season. There are other things I can do besides acting, but I must have you there with me. Whatever you want, we can always work out, as long as you're there. What I'm saying is, whatever you want goes. You shall direct the traffic in this family."

She could just imagine her directing him, this immensity who exuded maleness in his every move, who had mapped, clear-eyed, the course his life was going to take and never wavered, who knew from the start what he wanted and went straight ahead despite all odds, and got it, who had an opinion on everything and welcomed the chance to defend it.

"I can't ask you to give up anything for me. You worked so hard to be where you are now."

"I'm not giving up anything. I only did two movies. That does not qualify me as an actor. I don't really relish acting, anyway. In fact, I'd enjoy being an actor if it were not for acting." His voice softened. "It's too late for me, can't you see? I can't go it alone now. You have to be there."

Why must she give him up just because he happened to be famous. He was right, he was still the same person he was last Friday when he burst into her uneventful world like a fabled knight. Could she turn back now and get on with her safe, sheltered life and still be happy? Why, she did not even know how happy happy was until he showed her. Would she really prefer twenty secure, solid, ho-hum years if they were without him?

She looked at him and relented. "You could have any woman you want. I don't know why you want me. We are so different. I just want to sit and observe; I am surrounded by my books and my music and I am happy. You are sought out by people and they scare me. I don't know how it can all work out. We don't have anything in common."

She was relenting. He wanted to hold her, but he didn't dare. This was still a fragile peace in here, he dared not do anything to break it.

He took her hand. "Except that I love you and you love me, and that's more than enough to start with." She rose. He caught her by the waist and when she did not resist, he did not let go. "If we are together, there's nothing we can't work out. Just give it a chance."

She seemed composed, though, he noticed with relief. "Are you hungry?" he inquired, "I haven't eaten all day. Do you still have eggs in your house?"

9

enis was in Laura's apartment when her family arrived. Francis entered the room first, then Nacho and the two girls. And Cecilia came in. Laura might claim that she was a Steiner through and through, but Denis could see her clearly in Cecilia, in the trademark smile, in the regal lift of the head, in the elegant bearing.

Francis Steiner looked at his daughter and said, "So, Maria Laura, what have you got to say for yourself?"

Laura looked at Denis and he took the gauntlet from her. "With your permission, sir, I would like to marry your daughter."

"You would, huh. From what I heard, plans were made even without that permission. You have even set the date, so I'm told." He sighed. He was tired. "What's the rush? I don't understand. You only met him Friday."

Denis said, "Well, Sir, I am sure, and since she is also sure, I don't see why we have to wait."

"Sure?" Francis addressed Laura; he was too exhausted to tackle Denis. "How can you be sure? You're just a child. You have never even had a boyfriend before, as far as I know."

"Mom was not much older when you married her, and you were the first one for her too. I don't think she has ever regretted one moment of it. You said that all you did was take one look at her and you knew. How could that be different from this?"

"She was not a teenager, Lauren." Actually Cecilia just turned twenty when Francis married her, after a whirlwind courtship. Whirlwind my foot, thought Francis. This is whirlwind, and in stories of dizzying-pace courtships, this will surely take the prize hands down. Compared to this, his courtship of Cecilia was one that dragged its feet and took a good two months. The wedding was trumpeted by the media as the wedding of the year or the decade, depending on which newspaper covered it. Never mind that his brother Ray's wedding the year before to a daughter of Jose Gomez was more lavish, was more widely covered by the press, and was also called the wedding of the decade, thanks to the Gomez millions, and the penchant of the Gomez girls, mother and three daughters, for everything social. Birthdays, charity affairs, fund-raisers, or just plain parties were graced by one Gomez girl or the other and assiduously reported in the society columns.

Poor dear, Francis thought, looking at his daughter, not only will you not have a wedding of the year, you are not even marrying inside the Church. Mixed marriages were performed in the rectory. This made him most sad.

Cecilia was wiser than Francis where their daughter was concerned. They had always been close; she had always been privy to her daughter's thoughts and feelings; to her uncompromising values, which were so like her own, to her friendships, which were few, to her dreams, which would never shake the world. She just wanted a marriage to that man her father promised her would come along some day. Cecilia would smile at her childish dreams, until she laid eyes on Denis, and recognized him, no stranger to the scene, in fact quite familiar and most expected. One look was all she took and she knew there was no way Laura could be persuaded to pause, catch her breath, think things over. Cecilia recognized in him the ideal Laura kept in some secret, scented drawer where treasures were hoarded, brought out as reminder when temptations threatened, the decided winner in a field with no encouraged or welcomed contender.

Francis looked at Denis, grimaced, turned his face the other way, as if the sight of that so-good-looking face was too much for him. "She just doesn't have a clue what kind of life you people live."

"If you want guarantees, I can't give you that. Nobody can. Even that someone from your own world can't. My parents' divorce affected me in ways I don't want to go into now. But I vowed I would never go through that harrowing experience ever again. I understand how you feel, Sir, this industry has a tainted name, and rightly so. But I guess you don't read the trade papers. If you did, you would have read that I have kept a clean name. I steer clear of the social scene; I keep pretty much to myself. Why, I have not gone out with a girl on my own for so long I can't remember. When I do go out, it is always for publicity and arranged by my managers."

Francis interjected, "But why this week? At least give it some time. This, this is so sudden."

"I have a week free, then I have to be in L.A," said Denis. "This is an engagement that had been planned a long time ago; I cannot back out now. And I am not going back without her."

Francis Steiner looked at Denis, standing there in front of him, unbending and resolute, and at his daughter, who looked just as determined and just as hard to budge. "Well, it looks as though everything has been planned already." Francis sighed and at last really looked at Denis.

Nacho, sensing the break in his father's reserve, extended his hand to Denis. "Welcome to the family."

* * *

Laura and Denis were talking, when a commotion drew their attention. Two young men had entered the room and were kissing and embracing everybody. They strode across the room with a poise and self-confidence of those who were born to generations of great wealth. It was apparent they were related. They both wore glasses and both of them wore light-colored sport coats and casual slacks, with ties peeking from under vests in shades of mist and rain and blue skies and slivers of sun, the picture of casual elegance.

"Franz," whispered Laura. Denis saw him walking towards Laura, arms outstretched, with a happy grin on his face. She dropped Denis's hand holding hers and went to him.

"What have you been up to now, Maria Laura?" said Franz, embracing his sister.

"Come and meet him," she answered.

He kissed her and went over to Denis. "Welcome to the family, I suppose."

"Thanks," said Denis. The other one then, the taller and fairer one, was Joe. Denis saw him enfold Laura in his arms, this extremely handsome boy, embraced her, then held her face with both his hands, and looked at her searchingly. "Are you happy?"

"Oh, Buddy, yes, yes."

She pressed her face into his chest.

"Then that's all there is to it. If you should find it's not what you thought you wanted, if you should ever be troubled, you know all you have to do is whistle and I'll come flying."

"I know."

She took his hand and with a broad smile on her face, pulled him to where Denis and Franz were standing.

"My cousin, Joe."

Behind the eyeglasses, gray eyes surveyed Denis intently. Then unsmiling, he extended his hand. "Joe Steiner," he said.

10

*A*nd so they were married, with Denis' family, Peter, his best friend, and Charles, his business manager, and their wives in attendance, and Ann and Laura's family.

He brought her to a land awash with sun and was entranced by her delight at discovering every new thing he showed her. If she was full of awe and wonder, more so was he, amazed at how one girl could change his life completely. He was a person asleep who woke to a world of riches and beauty far beyond his expectations. She basked in his devotion, thrived in so much care and blossomed with his passion. They were a perfect complement to each other; he was all confident, sheltering male, she was all delicate, vulnerable female. He was a magnet that drew intoxicated, languorous gazes from her that his answering looks encouraged and that she did not think to contain. And if she was radiant, more so was he, all controlled excitement in his stride, looking younger than he ever did, with a face that was lighted by a hundred-kilowatt bulb she must have switched on inside him. "That must have been one hell of a honeymoon," Charles observed.

             *   *   *

They started building their house, this time with her ideas woven into the original design while she supervised the building of it.

They settled into a routine that, by other people's standards, seemed downright boring. He was true to his promise. They led exceedingly private lives, stayed clear of the social scene, and became famously reclusive.

He was a kind man, patient in his ways, a caring friend, an indulgent husband, a fervent lover. And she, most pleasant of surprises, turned out to be the wife he had only heard or read of, from some far away part of the world too removed from the careless, unmindful one he was used to. She lavished on him care and attention and love that were all new to him. Everything he needed was always there, all he had to do was utter the wish and it was done. Work days, he would wake up to find her bathed and dressed and ready for the world. He would drop her off to church before going to work and Mario, Milly's brother, would pick her up after Mass. Laura had started growing roses and Cecilia arranged for Laura's old nanny Milly and Milly's brother, to come. He became her gardener, driver and Man-Monday-to-Friday.

Denis would call her in the middle of the day and they talked while he had his lunch. Or he would call her and they would meet somewhere for lunch. Sundays were special days. He called it Laura's day, one day a week that he was exclusively hers and that he devoted solely to her. Just the two of them, no work, no business, no phone calls. Just a day to enjoy each other. He attended Mass with her, then they took long drives, went on picnics, or just stayed home, but it was her day. His friends did not even bother to phone, he never answered their calls, anyway.

They loved the days when he did not have to go to work. They would wake up late, linger in bed, shower together, make long, lazy love, then have brunch in the dining room, or on the terrace, and savor the day as it stretched, long, indolent, theirs alone.

When the weather permitted, Milly would pack a hamper and they would take long drives and have small picnics. Laura would bring a blanket for them to lie down on and Denis would study his notes while Laura would read her book, once Christina Georgina Rossetti's.

"Rossetti," he said. "Do you remember that Rossetti fellow you were telling me about? You know, Mr. Gomez, MG, remember? Are they still together, do you know?"

"Yes, they are, with their roses and their orchids, and their lovely children."

She couldn't get over the fact that he was so even tempered, so easy to live with, so normal for someone as celebrated as he was. He was not given to temper fits and people he worked with had nothing but praise for him. She was proud of reviews that praised, which were often, and questioned those that criticized, which were seldom.

"Critics must criticize," he shrugged, unconcerned. "Besides, it's not the critics that bring in the money." And judging from the way his fans filled concerts halls for his concerts and bought up his records as fast as they came out, they did not care much what critics thought, either. His records were money makers, his concerts sold out months in advance and his name guaranteed a full house, always.

By July, Denis finished his engagement. They prepared for a long vacation in Manila, and invited Peter and Charles and their wives, Marta and Ellen, to go with them. And off to Manila they went.

11

The plane landed early in the morning but the Manila International Airport was already bustling with people. "Travel business must be booming," observed Denis.

"You'd be surprised at how many of these people are just meeters," said Laura. "When someone comes home from abroad, usually a busload of friends and family comes, too, to meet them, thus filling these spaces." She looked at her husband, a good fair head taller than all, hat and dark glasses offering vain concealment.

Cars were waiting to whisk them off to Forbes. They passed an iron gate where guards, seeing the two familiar cars, pressed buttons that lifted the barrier and cheerily waved them through. They passed through cool streets banked by massive leafy trees that looked as though they had been there for centuries, past houses of disparate architectural styles, all impressive, all luxurious.

Cecilia was waiting for them when they arrived. She turned to Denis and flashed a smile that he would find was a trademark of the women of this house. This is my mother-in-law, he thought as he kissed her on both checks. In twenty, twenty-five years, I shall be old and doddering, and my wife will still look like this--- slim, with hardly a wrinkle on her face and no matter what her age was, still a stunner.

Would his father have strayed too far and too often, Denis thought, from one affair to another, had he someone like Cecilia to come home to, instead of the dowdy, nagging woman that his mother had become over the harsh, hard years? Never a raving beauty to begin with and overwhelmed by a merciless fate that dealt her a philandering husband and disadvantaged circumstances, his mother just stopped caring and let herself go and in the process, Denis always thought, let his father go, too.

Thus it came about that all the women Denis had been attracted to had always been beautiful first and foremost. No matter for him a bright, or a sexy, or an interesting woman if she was not beautiful to start with. The charm, the intellect and what other attributes attracted a man to a woman came later. And when, in that later, that beautiful woman did not show qualities stimulating enough to hold his interest, he just dropped the matter and buried himself deeper in his music. Maybe, like everything else he did, he was testing his limits and thus, holding firm and not giving in, he did not settle for less, and became one of the industry's most hard-to-land bachelors. But then of course she came. With that face that took his breath away the first time she broke into a smile for him and everything that followed after that that left him reeling, he never had a chance. She caught him when he fell, ripe and ready and hers for life.

* * *

In the nineteen fifties, Manila overflowed. All sources of commerce were isolated in this city and the people from the provinces flocked to the capital: students went there to attend the better colleges and universities, others to earn a living. It was already apparent that the city could not handle the sea of humanity and must extend itself to the suburbs. Before this happened, the Steiners and their other cousins and friends who had the money knew where to put it and invested heavily in real estate.

The Steiner house was enormous, nestled on a luxuriant property of foliage, flowers and opulence. Francis commissioned one of the country's foremost architects to build the house for him and what Francis got was a structure so splendid The Steiner House was always mentioned when accolades were heaped on the architect's full and honored career. There were six enormous bedroom suites and from various points of the house, through glass windows encircling whole widths of walls, one could see the gardens outside, lush with greenery, splattered with colors. The living room opened unto the lanai where small parties and dancing with close friends were held. From their bedroom window Denis could see Cecilia's roses blooming in profusion, strutting their stuff on this brilliant, summer morning.

Everything about the house Denis loved. And everything about his wife and her family dazzled him---the world of privilege that created them, the gilt-edged upbringing that produced the quiet elegance about them, the breeding that endowed them with a finesse that filled him with awe, all the things in fact that he dared not even dream of in his deprived youth he found in them now.

Laura found Denis standing on the terrace outside their bedroom, looking at the moon that had risen yellow against an opal sky, ruler of the night tonight, when stars and clouds, seeing no contest, went into early retirement. She went behind him, groped inside his shirt, circled her arms around his waist, and felt his skin warm under her arms.

He pulled her closer to him, "Why is the moon bigger here than in L.A.?"

"It's not even full yet. It will be in a couple of days, and I know a place where it rises fuller and bigger and brighter than anywhere in the world."

He turned around and faced her. "And where might that be?"

"Above the sea. Behind palm trees. On a white beach in Santo Niño, Mom's hometown. Want to come with me?"

* * *

They took a plane to Santo Niño. Ships plying passenger routes were the most popular mode of transportation from island to island. These ships could be comfortable, too, but for those who could afford the much more expensive airline fares, the faster planes were, of course, more convenient.

A jeep was waiting for them at the airport to take them to Santo Niño, which took another hour, through roads traversing a mountain, passing scattered communities of nipa houses, carefully tended, with flowers bright against bamboo fences and frangipani trees in full yellow and pink blooms, some of which winds scattered on yards ridged by coconut-midrib brooms. Women sat on bamboo stairs, braiding their daughters' hair. Men squatted by the roadside, grooming brilliant-colored fighting cocks.

"What are they doing?" Denis inquired.

"Exercising those fighting cocks, comparing notes," Laura explained. "They are in no hurry. They don't have anywhere to go until breakfast, which is still a good two hours away."

"It's so peaceful here," Denis said, taking deep breaths. "Even the air smells different."

"Be careful with the rag weeds there. They could invade your sinuses and give you a full-blown allergy." She looked at him. He always seemed to be showing her things, teaching her, guiding her into worlds foreign to her. She felt that, in her confined life, she had nothing much to contribute. Now she showed him a part of her that was foreign to him, too. He was pleased and she was delighted.

"It's a good life the people have here, time does not fly as fast, life could be tasted more fully.

"Of course all this is also conducive to lazy living. The coconuts are harvested four times a year, rice twice a year. In between, for their everyday needs, they grow their veggies and fruits in garden patches, raise their own poultry and pigs, and how much time could that take? They are left with plenty of time to take it easy, strum their guitars, fondle their fighting cocks, listen to soap operas from their radios, hold dances in the village square for the feast day of whatever saints they set their hearts on. Once a week, on market day, they go down to town to sell a few chickens or fruits and vegetables. With the money, they buy a few cans of sardines or fish. Schools are free up to high school. Good schools, too. It's summertime all year round, and, yes, the living is easy. "

"How often did you spend summers here?"

"In Santo Niño? Every year. If we had to go abroad, we stayed a few days. If not, we stayed longer."

* * *

Santo Niño, at last. Budding trees lined the long driveway that led to the house. Their first impression was an abundance of flowers. Clumps of orchids with bouquets of white blossoms clung to tree trunks and on the whole length of the long driveway, bougainvillea and begonias dripped with blooms. Gardenias, headily fragrant, and the ubiquitous frangipani, bloomed everywhere, pink and yellow and the new lavender. A riot of colors flamed everywhere.

At the end of the driveway, the house stood in majesty, a massive structure of white, with wooden verandahs stained brown, like a strip of girdle encircling its girth, looking like the Mediterranean houses Denis had seen. They passed a black iron gate and entered a room light and airy and high-ceilinged, with sunshine pouring through tall glass windows. The two-story living room was separated from the formal dining room by two steps going up. On one side of the house forming an l, a library separated two bedroom suites of Celina and Carmela, Cecilia's sisters who lived in the house. In the living room were white chairs and sofas and wide chaises inviting rest and even sleep. A black iron partition with curlicues partly hid the informal dining room. This one was also large, with a big round table in the middle. Everywhere, the house was white and brown---white walls, white furniture, white cushions, brown wood, brown folding doors that led to verandahs, brown overhead fans lazily cooling the house. Flowers filled vases scattered around the rooms.

Celina and Carmela ushered them inside while maids brought their bags up a staircase that led to bedrooms upstairs, large and breezy with tall windows and lace curtains fluttering in the sea breezes. An enormous four-poster bed with white embroidered bed covers and lacey pillowcases sat in the middle of the room. Balconies overlooked the grounds teeming with flowers.

"I'm sure, if there is a paradise, it would look like this," observed Charles.

After they had freshened up, they came down to brunch, served by two maids on the loggia that spanned one entire side of the house.

Breakfast, Denis would soon find, usually at 7 after Mass, consisted of rice, sausages, homemade ham and fried eggs, brewed coffee and toast and homemade jam, mango today. A killing feast, the first of five meals they had for the day. At around 10, coffee was served, with cookies and fruit. A heavy lunch was the main meal of the day, a table laden with various meat and vegetable dishes. Then everybody repaired to bedrooms for the midday nap. So that was why the siesta was necessary, Denis observed, so the body could rest while the digestive process was going about its business. The siesta was a ritual nobody tampered with. Even the maids retired to their bedrooms and a quiet pervaded the house. At 4, the house hummed with activity again, and the family had *merienda*, the afternoon snack taken after the siesta, although snack was hardly the word to describe the spread of cakes, cookies, and whatever native delicacies the cook had cooked up that went with the manly coffee, brewed and fragrant and strong. At 8, the church bells rang the hour and dinner was served, over conversation and reminiscences that lingered until it was time to retire. From their bed, Denis would hear the faraway sound of the washing waves, while the moon, topping the trees, spilled white moonlight into the room, past the quivering curtains, through the long windows, washing his wife's body with an iridescent glow.

They spent the next days in lazy abandon. They slept late if the mood struck them, had brunch and spent the rest of the day on the white, fine-sand beach, swimming, exploring caves, or just lying on the blanket they spread on the sand, under the leafy shelter of the *talisay* tree that overhang unto the water and shaded a part of the beach. Sometimes, Denis, Charles and Ellen and Peter and Marta would go hunting for seashells, while Laura would stay behind and sleep, and breezes blew strands of curls across her face. She couldn't seem to get enough sleep here, Denis noted.

Some days, they came home for lunch, after which everyone repaired to their bedrooms. Denis would read in bed, while his wife would listen to the whirring of the fan overhead, and, again, sleep.

Nights were balmy here, often still. Most times, after everyone had retreated to their bedrooms, they would steal away and come to the beach. These were the hours they both loved, lying on the blanket on the warm sand, concealed by the canopy of leaves, after everyone had retired for the night, on these white nights when moonlight streamed into the sea, silhouettes of coconut trees swayed on the horizon, and the waves, breaking the silence with their unending strain, lulled people in their houses well unto dreamland.

* * *

"Race you to that dinghy out there," Laura pointed at a dinghy resting at the far side of the water. The moon was high and she and Denis had escaped quietly from the house after dinner. But Denis could never catch up with her. She was just a better swimmer.

"Later, sweet, let's just look at the moon first." They were on their blanket on the sand, under the shadows of the overhanging branches, watching the moon rise, big and round and yellow as she promised, flooding the beach with a ghostly glow. In the hush they stayed wordless as the coconut trees reached high to touch the sky, while the moon played hide and seek with some scattered clouds, and the waves tumbled into the shore and lapped at their toes.

"Ah, this is a place one could only dream of," he said.

She leaned over to face him. "We could stay here longer, you know," she touched his face and he playfully bit her finger. "Would the world miss us too much if we stayed away longer?"

But his life was planned for him for long stretches at a time, running a course charted by Charles and a host of other managers. A protracted, unscheduled vacation was just one luxury he could not afford. If he idled, he would cause a reaction of people, like domino chips, tumbling towards inactivity they could not afford either. There was nothing he could say to her. They just had to make the most of the few days left to them. He put his arm under her, flipped her on top of him and flipped the blanket over them both. He then pressed her head down to his. They never went moonlight swimming.

They stole away every night and came back to this strip of sand, until the round moon waned to a crescent, then disappeared completely, and not even a sky full of stars betrayed their presence on the beach and they did not need the blanket to cover them anymore.

* * *

A steady drizzle drove them indoors the next day. After lunch, everybody retreated to bedrooms to rest. Denis brought up some magazines to read and in a little while he could hear Laura's even breathing and knew she was asleep. She was so relaxed here, so at peace, and so sleep-hungry. After a while, he gathered his magazines and wandered downstairs to the library to return them. Shelves overflowed with books: a complete set of F. Scott Fitzgerald's works, everything about Hemingway, all his books and books about him, Mann, Hardy, Paine, Conrad's Heart of Darkness. Books old and worn took up a separate, glass-fronted bookshelf. Volumes on Thomas Aquinas, books on saints. Had she read all these, that girl upstairs barely out of her teens? He continued his search. There were volumes of poetry: Walt Whitman, A. E. Housman, Shelley, ah, Edna St. Vincent Millay. He took the book out, opened it and saw his wife's neat handwriting, Maria Laura Steiner, and a date on the bottom. She was fifteen then. He opened the next page and on it was written in a man's lean script, in small letters: girl cannot live on aquinas alone, must have poetry, too. It was signed j.

She was awake when he came up, stretching like a cat, looking at him through eyes heavy-lidded from too many nocturnal hours on that beach. She stifled a yawn with the back of her hand.

"Who's j?" he asked, although he was sure he knew.

She looked at the book in his hand. "Oh, my book of poems! I searched everywhere for it but I couldn't find it, so Joe bought me another one. Where did you find it?"

"In the library."

"So that's where it was." She held out her hand for the book and Denis handed it to her. "Joe wanted me to read Thomas Aquinas, but that was too much for me, so he gave me poetry, too. Easy poetry I wanted, lest he plied me with Shakespeare." She looked up at Denis and smiled. "Hey, I was just a kid." She leafed through the book. "Recess reading, he called this."

"Did you read all these books downstairs?"

"Most of them, yes. Several of those are Joe's and Franz'. Even on vacations they brought armloads of books. They assigned me reading material every night and I had to give a report the next day."

"And you did?"

"I had to. They said they did not want a mentally indolent mascot. Those two were awfully hard teachers."

"Well, look at you now."

"But they never taught me what I learned from you." She held out both arms, smiling at him invitingly. "Come," she said, "I miss you."

The day cleared in the afternoon, and the family had just finished their *merienda*. "Come to church with me, let's make a quick visit," Laura invited Denis, "then let's walk over to my cousins'."

"If you're going to visit Ernestina, could you bring her some of these guavas," said Celina, putting some fruits into a small basket. Ernestina was the wife of one of Cecilia's cousins. "She has been hankering for guavas these past weeks."

"Hankering for guavas?" asked Laura. In this part of the world, hankering for guavas usually meant a celebration some nine months later.

Celina laughed. "It's really unbelievable. Their youngest is already fifteen. She couldn't believe she still could have another

child. She is so embarrassed she has been hiding in the house."
Denis took the basket from Celina.

The street going to church was lined with giant acacia trees
that must have been planted a hundred years ago. People sat on
their immense roots protruding from the earth as though they
were chairs.

The townspeople left Denis pretty much alone. Children
gawked, followed him around and giggled when he looked at
them and favored them with a smile. The grown-ups, though,
were more bashful, would smile slightly or shyly nod at him in
greeting. Laura took Denis's free hand in hers. "Do you
remember I told you about my Mom's family, about how my
Mom's cousins intermarried, and about those children who
resulted from those marriages?"

"Yes," said Denis.

Laura had told him about these cousins of Cecilia's. Theirs
had always been an isolated family. There were too many cousins
and they had always been sufficient unto themselves. Although
they grew up in schools in the city---the girls in the Catholic
boarding school for girls and the boys in the Jesuit boarding
school---when they came home they spent their vacation among
themselves, holding their own parties in their own houses. When
they went to dances they danced with each other. They went
swimming and boating and partied and dined, among themselves.
Consequently, cousins fell in love with cousins, cousins married
cousins, and married cousins produced an alarming number of
children with genetic flaws.

Lest he be burdened by such a catastrophe, Cecilia's father
watched over his daughters like a hawk. At a young age, he sent
them to school in Spain, where nuns supervised a rigid, religious
discipline. When they came back, they were sent for further
studies to an exclusive Catholic boarding school in the city, as far
away from Santo Niño as was possible. When they came home to
Santo Niño for vacations, he limited their social activities, totally
forbade night swimming and with relief, surrendered Cecilia to
Francis, Jo to Doctor Enzo and the other two girls to the arts and
sciences and whatever studies the universities offered, away from
home and disaster.

"Who can explain what chemistry surges in our veins that we
fall in love with that one person, even though we know we are in

for disaster, but there is just nothing we can do about it?" Laura looked at Denis. "Ernestina is one of those who have one of these children."

"Should she be having another one then?" Denis could not understand how they could be bringing children into this world, with this frightening risk.

"The Church does not allow artificial birth control. Though some priests leave this issue to one's conscience, some consciences are more inflexible than others. And so they have to resort to the rhythm method, which is exceedingly unreliable. Hence, those children."

12

ome," Denis said to his wife, pulling her to him, "story-telling time." They were back in Forbes, but he was still steeped in stories of the past that had shaped and molded his wife.

"What else is there that I haven't told you?

"Tell me about the other Laura and her Francis. That story I love."

"Well, he was an engineer, his family was originally from Switzerland. His company sold the equipment used in the sugar centrals. His company sent him to San Sebastian to manage the business, you know, sales and installation and maintenance and such. My grandma's family did not approve of him. For one thing, he was not Catholic. Interfaith marriages were either unheard of or extremely frowned upon in those days. But the family capitulated when he converted. With those looks, at least he could *'mejorar la raza,'* improve the race, my grandma's folks said.

"Do you remember that I told you my grandmother kept a diary? Would you like to read it now?"

"Do you think it's all right?"

"Of course it is. I'm sure if she were here now, she would approve of you most wholeheartedly."

She went to the chest of drawers and took out a box. Inside were packets of letters tied with blue ribbons and a small book with a cushiony cover of multi-colored paisley designs.

"Why don't you ask the maid to bring me a glass of milk and a plate of those cookies Cook just baked."

"The *lenguas*?" she asked. Cook had just baked a batch of *lenguas del gato*, cookies as delicate as a cat's tongue that Denis loved.

"The *lenguas*, yes. A heaping plate, please. Then I'll just put my feet up here, like so. There, now I'm ready for an afternoon of *lenguas* and love letters and this diary."

13

*M*y name is Laura Marquez. Today, I turned 13 years old and my Tita Rita, my father's sister, gave me this diary. She said I am always writing and since I write well, I might as well write about my life. I do like to write. After I have put down my thoughts in writing, I don't feel so sad anymore. I am glad my Tita Rita gave me this gift. I used to just scribble on pieces of paper that I threw away afterwards. Now I have this diary to talk to when Teddy, my brother, is busy and does not have time for me, which, I am sad to say, is often. Teddy, whose name is Teodoro, is 16 and my only brother. Although I think he is my best friend, I don't think I am his. He has many friends and is always going out with them, but he is a boy and can do things I cannot. Still, he is good to me, bringing me candies when he comes home. But lots of times I get lonely and I wish I had a sister.

Papa's name is also Teodoro, and everybody calls him Ted. After he graduated from the Ateneo de Manila with high grades, his family sent him to Oxford, in England. When he graduated, he came home, with my mother. He said he did not want to leave her behind and married her before he came back. Of course Papa's family was dismayed that he got married abroad and to an Englishwoman. They were married in London in a civil ceremony, a marriage performed by a justice of the peace, which, in our intensely Catholic family, was not considered a marriage at all and they were married again in church, in a lavish wedding, attended by family and a few hundred friends and maybe the entire town.

My father is an unico hijo, an only son. He has three sisters, my Tita Rita, the eldest, who is married to my Tito Tomas, and they, also, have two children; then there are my aunts Elena and Emilia, both unmarried.

Mama is the most marvelous-looking woman I have seen. She has a full head of light brown hair, eyes they call sapphire blue, and very white skin. She is almost as tall as my father, who is himself quite tall. Everybody says that I look like my mother, but I don't think so. I think she is much prettier.

We live in a big house with several servants. My bedroom is white, also big, and my maid Rosa sleeps on the floor, on a mat at the foot of my bed. Rosa has been with our family for a long time and has taken care of me since I was born. She is good at sewing and taught me how. After lunch when I take my siesta, she embroiders our initials on towels, and on pillow cases. She sews laces on my pillow cases and bed covers and curtains. Every night she tells me stories to make me sleep. They are boring stories and really make me sleep. Mama does not tell me bedtime stories at all. She goes out often and comes home when I am already asleep.

~ ~ ~

Last night Papa and Mama had a fight again. They are always fighting. Mama likes going to parties or to Tita Carmen's house to play monte or mahjong. My Tita Carmen's house is even bigger than ours. Way off the living room on the first floor is an enormous room where her cousins gamble. Papa says Mama should stay home more and take care of us children and be there when he comes home. Mama says she doesn't want to stay home and just take care of the children and grow old before her time.

Before, when they quarreled, Mama would start crying and then I would hear Papa's voice comforting her. Now, she cries longer and her voice gets angrier but I don't hear Papa consoling her much. When I tell Teddy this he says I should be asleep instead of listening to our parents fight. I really don't want to listen. But my room is next to theirs and I cannot help but hear them, especially Mama. When she is angry, she does not care if she wakes up the entire hacienda.

I wish Mama would stay home more often, too. Before, my father used to accompany her when she went out.

Later, he said he was worn out from too much partying. Now, except for family celebrations when everybody in the family is expected to attend, Papa stays home and my mother goes out without him.

~ ~ ~

My grandmother Emilia, Papa's mother, lives in a big house not far from ours. She lives there with her unmarried daughters Emilia and Elena, Papa's older sisters. Everybody loves their house, but I don't like it; it's too big and dark with heavy and dark furniture. I like our house better, with all these windows where the sun comes in early in the morning and wakes me up.

My grandmother has a Japanese gardener and their garden is big and formal. I don't like the garden either. I cannot run around it. I am afraid of stepping on some forbidden plant and I am afraid of the Japanese gardener, with his slits for eyes. Most of the time I cannot understand what he says, with his sentences without any L and full of Rs. But he seems kind and would dig into his pocket and come up with candies for me.

~ ~ ~

My grandmother came to visit us today and she and my father went to the formal living room. I knew it was an important visit. For less important business, they have coffee in the family room, served by the maids. When they want to be alone, they use the formal living room. When you are a little girl, the older people tend to forget you are there or they think you cannot understand what they talk about, so that, even though I was sitting on the floor at my grandmother's feet, they talked as though I was not there.

"Teodoro," said my grandmother. She calls her children by their proper names, not by their nicknames as everybody else does. "Surely when you married her you should have known that you could not keep her in the house, just taking care of your household, just waiting for you to come home. If you wanted somebody like that, you should have married our kind, one of us."

"I'm so tired being husband and wife, father and mother," said my father. "Sure there are servants, but they don't function when there's nobody there to manage them.

And you cannot believe the rows she has with them. It seems that every time I come down to breakfast, there's a new servant there. Nobody wants to stay, the way she treats them. Rosa stays because of Laura. And I don't want the child to have a new maid every week, so I pay the tuition of Rosa's children and she borrows money from me almost every month which I conveniently forget. But Jane (that's my mother's name) just does not understand that that's why these people work as servants. If they knew better, they would be out there doing something else.

"Household work is just over her head. Yesterday, she wanted to make a blanket for Laura's doll. How hard is it to make a doll's blanket? You just have to cut four sides of a piece of cloth. But she had the maids running all over the place, get this, get that, do this, don't do that, you are doing that wrong. The new maid was almost in tears."

I saw this picture in a magazine and fell in love with the lacy doll's blanket. I showed the picture to my mother and asked her if she could do that for me. I wish I had not. Now, my father is upset with her. It is really my fault.

Papa was so agitated he had to take a drink. "And the worst thing is, she never finished it. It was just too much for her, a tiny blanket, for crissakes." (That is one of my father's favorite expressions, for crissakes.) "It would be funny if it were not so pathetic."

My grandmother laughed, too. I don't think it was funny, though. I think it was sad. "But why didn't she just ask Rosa? That's why we have all these servants."

My grandmother does not let anything trouble her. Born to great wealth, she grew up with this truth: there is no trouble too big that money cannot fix. Experience had taught her that if you have the money, there is always somebody who will do the work for you.

"Because Laura asked her to, and she has not done anything for the child in a long time."

"At least she wanted to do something for the child. Basta con la intencion."

"No, Mama," my father said, "intentions are not enough. Once in a while, one must come up with something more concrete than just intentions. And what about, the road to hell is paved with good intentions?"

My grandmother laughed again. "Well, as I said, you should have married your own kind."

~   ~   ~

I have been feeling sad all day. And afraid. Last night, I went to the bathroom and when I came out I saw Papa going back to their bedroom. He had just come out of Gloria's room. Gloria is one of our maids and, except for Rosa who sleeps in my room, she and the other servants have rooms way off the kitchen. I went back to my bed but I couldn't sleep. After a while, I heard Mama come home. Then the grandfather clock that stands in the hall boomed dong, dong. It was two o'clock.

~   ~   ~

I wanted to talk to Teddy yesterday but he went to the city and did not come home until quite late. I am feeling sad. And afraid.

~   ~   ~

I talked to Teddy today and he said maybe Papa just wanted to ask Gloria something. I pray he is right. But at 2 in the morning?

~   ~   ~

Last night they had a fight again. This time was the worst that I have ever heard. Mama screamed that she was leaving. Papa said no, he was leaving.

~   ~   ~

Today, we are at Tita Rita's house in the city. This morning, Tita Rita came to the hacienda to fetch Teddy and me. She said we are going to spend a few days with her in the city. Since this is a school week, I find this rather strange. Also, Mama's eyes were red from crying, so I know all is not well at home. Mama said that Papa was out so I could not say goodbye to him, but he would come to the city later. She then hugged me for a long time and gave me a long kiss.

~   ~   ~

We have been with Tita Rita for almost a week now. Mama came the other day and we went shopping. I asked where Papa was and she said he will be coming later. She asked me if I wanted to transfer to the school where my cousin Margo, Tita Rita's daughter, is studying. They had already planned for Teddy to stay with Tita Rita and study at the boy's school with Tita Rita's son, Tommy, so would I like to stay with Tita Rita, too? Of course I would. Except that I would miss Papa and Mama so. But Mama said it was all right, they will come to visit often.

~   ~   ~

Mama came to visit us today. She said that, since Teddy and I are going to school in the city, they have decided to buy a house here so that she could be with us all the time. She said that Papa will just come to visit as he couldn't leave his work in the hacienda.

~   ~   ~

I had a lot to do, transferring to a new school, moving to a new house that we bought, that I had not written in this diary for quite some time.

~   ~   ~

We bought this big house in front of the town plaza. I have been busy decorating my bedroom. My maid, Rosa, helped me put up the curtains and the pictures. It would have been an exciting time, except that I have not seen Papa for a long time. When I asked Rosa about this, she put a finger to her lips and said, "Sshh, you ask too many questions."

~   ~   ~

Today I asked Mama when Papa was coming to visit us and she cried. I had to console her and said it's all right Mama, I shall not ask again.

~   ~   ~

My grandmother came for us today and brought us back to our house in the hacienda. How I missed that house. I like the house in the city, but I love the house in the hacienda. How I missed my bedroom, too. When I was there, Papa came in. I was so happy to see him that I cried. He held me tight and kept on kissing me, and then I noticed that he was crying, too. He said he was going away and will not see me for some time. I did not want him to cry some more, so I said, it was all right, Teddy was there to take care of me while he was away.

~   ~   ~

Today I came home from the city and while I was putting my wardrobe in order, I found this, my diary. I had written on a few pages, what do I expect. I was only 13 then. Maybe this vacation, I shall fill up the other pages, take up where I left off, a long time ago.

~   ~   ~

I am 19 years old now. So much happened in six years. The last time I wrote here, my father had just come to visit me. What I did not know then was that he had just left my mother. Later, he went to live on another island across the bay, and brought Gloria, our maid, with him. (Remember her? I saw him come out of her room at 2 in the morning and felt so sad and afraid then.)

The first time I knew that my father left my mother I cried bitterly and was inconsolable for days after that. It was Teddy who inadvertently told me. He did not mean to at the time. I was only 13 and in his eyes, too young to understand these things. What was there to understand, my young heart told me, he left our mother and us and went away to live with our maid.

"Why her?" I asked Teddy, through my tears. "She is not even pretty at all." In fact, she was less than not pretty and my mother was one of the best-looking women in the province. Now that I am older, I am trying to understand. Did he maybe think that one attractive and flighty woman was enough for a man in one lifetime? It was as if, by leaving my mother for Gloria, he made a statement about women who bring to a marriage beauty of face and not much else. She is my mother and I love her so much but I have to say to you, dear diary, what I have never said to anybody else. Although I never countenanced what my father did, when I try to understand why he did what he did, I come up with the same answers. My mother was not a good wife to my father. She was not there when he needed her and nagged him constantly when she was there. This is not a judgment against my mother but just an observation of a daughter who did not see much of her mother, who saw her father try to be all father and mother, wife and husband, provider and manager, fed-up listener to a strident, discontented woman, and got tired and worn out in the process.

Nobody could understand why my father did what he did, why he cut off all ties to his family and went away to another province. It is a common enough practice for the master of the house to sleep with the maid. Although this is conduct not exactly condoned, it is one of those common-enough practices from which society turns its collective head the other way. So there are needs of the master that the mistress of the house cannot completely satisfy. So satisfy them in some bedrooms way off the kitchen. That is often done. Never right, but often done. But one does not leave wife and children and family, and most of all, so much family money, to go off with one's maid and live a life of scarcity and want, especially if the wife looks like my mother, and the maid is as homely as Gloria. Once again, it provided grist for the scandal mill.

My grandmother disinherited my father, not so much because of the scandal that ensued, not so much that, intensely Catholic as the family was, he was blatantly living in sin, but, being the woman that she was who had money all her life and who always got what she wanted because of it, she thought that without money, my father would come back. When my father spurned her money and chose to live with what little he had, it was a great disappointment and heartache for her to find out that what her money could not buy was the most important thing in her life, her only son.

My father never came back to us or to our town. He bought a small parcel of land with what little money he had, planted it to coconut, and lived, to him, a different, simple and hard, hard life. He was a proud man. Hurt that my grandmother took my mother's side, he never asked for money from her or from any of his sisters and lived on what he got from his small property. Later, he and Gloria had two children, two girls, and he, who grew up amidst so much comfort and luxury, just could not bear the hard life he had set for himself. He contracted tuberculosis.

Maybe my mother saw how heartless my grandmother could be. If she was capable of cutting off her only son, she could always do the same to her. My grandmother inherited her money from parents of enormous wealth; it was her own money over which she exercised complete and absolute control. She had her own definition of The Golden Rule: the one who had the gold, ruled. I don't really know whether, when my father left my mother, my grandmother threatened to disinherit my mother, too, if she did not clean up her act. I had grown into a young woman, and could not sit around unnoticed as I did when I was a child, but not exactly an adult yet to be privy to adult talk and decisions.

Little by little, my mother retreated into her own world. Now she does not go out anymore, just stays in her room most of the time. It's ironic that now, when my father is not there anymore to plead that she stay home, she stays home.

We always believe my grandmother had a hand in my mother's transformation. Or maybe it just shattered her that my father could leave her for Gloria, plain, commonplace, nobody Gloria.

Would the hurt have been less had he ran away with a younger, better-looking woman? Could she have then faced her friends with a less defiant look and say, and believe it when she said it, that hey, he was the one at fault, it was his, it was not hers? As it was, it was hers. When a husband turns his back on a wife as stunning as she, turn his back even on family and money, for a maid that he could have anyway without benefit of marriage or anything resembling commitment, it leaves the wife without even a face-saving line of defense.

She never forgave him. And he, unyielding, never gave her her revenge. He never made a move to reconcile, with her or with his family, and not doing so, made everyone know that he would rather live the hard life he had chosen for himself than come back.

When my father left our house but not our lives yet, before he left for another island with that other woman, there was still time for her, my mother, to have put things to right, and give themselves another chance. But she was too proud for that and never tried. He always did things for her, he was always the one who gave in when they argued, he was always the one to try to make peace when they quarreled. He waited on her, was always at her beck and call. She would say, Ted, do this or Ted, I want this and her wishes were as good as done. And so she waited for him, for that man who had always loved beauty, who had spent a fortune surrounding himself with things of beauty, and wasn't she the most magnificent adornment in his life? Maybe she thought he would come to his senses and back to her, in time. But that time never came.

What was it about those parties and those friends that made her turn her back on a good marriage and a good man? Were there indiscretions on her part? Was this why my father was so unyielding? I heard rumors but as I said, I was too young to be privy to answers and too old to be unnoticed when the adults were in discussions, so I was never sure if there was. Looking back now, maybe I did not really want to know.

Did it hurt him to raise his two new children in territory exactly opposite of that in which his own mother had raised him? Did he justify it to himself that it was not the circumstance but the values that mattered? Or was it that there was only one choice left to him, to come back, and that choice was unacceptable?

~   ~   ~

Once, we had a one-day break from school. Since it was only a one-hour drive from the city to the hacienda, whenever there was no school the next day, my grandmother would send the car to the city to bring us to the hacienda. My grandmother now took a direct hand in our upbringing, giving my mother this final slap---if she could not manage her husband, she could not manage her children as well. These were her grandchildren, my grandmother liked to say, heirs to an immense fortune (my grandmother liked to point this out). Surely their upbringing belonged to hands more capable than my mother's, which, my grandmother made clear, meant hers. I always hated it when my grandmother called us 'the Marquez heirs,' as if we were prized horses in procession for public inspection.

That night, I was surprised that the car did not come for us. I spoke to Teddy about it but he told me not to worry, it was all right. Teddy is always hush-hushing me, but he is the only brother I have, so I don't get upset, given that I don't have a choice.

The next day, Teddy woke me up early. "Come, Laura, get ready, we're leaving in fifteen minutes."

"Aren't we having breakfast first?"

"We'll have breakfast in the ship."

"Ship?" I was taken aback. Did I mention that our family owns one of the biggest shipping lines in the country? That's where our money comes from, from ships and lands so vast you could go up the highest peak of that tall hill yonder and look around you at the sea of sugarcane but your eyes couldn't see one end of the land to the other. Money begets money, and from the wealth that they derived from those lands, the ships followed.

"Hurry, Laura," Teddy urged, "and don't take too long in that bathroom or you stay behind."

I had seldom been in one of these ships, never having gone far. It was a marvelous day. Teddy and I went to the ship's bridge, where the captain showed us how to work the wheel. The nice man even allowed me to turn the wheel myself, which made me rather pleased with myself. The water was smooth and we passed several islands, some small, some not so, most of them uninhabited, all of them impressive. What a pleasant time we had on that ship.

Soon enough we arrived at our destination. The boat docked at a long wooden pier.

"Where are we going?" I asked.

"Stop asking questions, Laura. You'll see when we get there," reprimanded Teddy. But I could see that he was excited.

There were calesas, horse-drawn carriages, waiting by the pier. We boarded one that did not look as decrepit as the others, the gaudy paint on its roof and its body not yet peeling off, although the horse attached to it looked just like the others, old and tired-looking, blinking its eyes in a futile effort to drive away the flies that have settled there. I was excited, never having ridden in one before. Whenever we went anywhere, we always took the car, which I liked, as long as they were just short trips. Long trips I hated, which were always a chore and a production, with the driver preparing the car, another maid helping me dress, Rosa preparing my things---baby powder, hand towels, a bottle of water, a glass, small sandwiches. Why Rosa bothered, I never knew. I'm sure my grandmother made her. I don't eat the sandwiches so I don't have to drink the water so I don't have to go to the bathroom. One time I really had to go and we stopped by this eating-place along the way. There was only one bathroom, with a sign outside, "His and Hers, but not together." It was a clever sign, it was not a clean bathroom; I never had liquid on the road again.

Teddy gave the cochero, the calesa driver, the address and down the street the horse trotted, every once in a while prodded by the driver's whip, unnecessarily, I thought, since the horse's gait never altered. The horse took its own sweet time, clip clop, clip clop, the whip regardless. But I guessed a driver had to drive, and a horse driver had to use a horsewhip.

We had arrived. Teddy paid the driver and we alighted. I could never think of this moment without crying buckets of tears. There he was, sitting on the porch that ran the entire front of the house, his shirt hanging on his thin frame, his feet shod in wooden shoes. He had always been a handsome man, but his appeal lay more in the confident, masculine way he carried himself, in the intelligence and strength of character that showed in his face, in his being such a gentleman. But I thought this strength never manifested itself more than it did this day. Frayed, determined, looking older. My father.

He looked at us when we reached the gate of the bamboo fence, then shook his head and closed his eyes, as if to dispel an apparition that had constantly haunted him, then looked at us again, from one to the other. When we did not disappear and he was sure that we were not some specter from his past, he shot out of his seat and ran to us. I don't remember what words were spoken. We were laughing and crying, kissing and talking at the same time.

The commotion drew from inside the house two scraggly-looking children, bare of feet, clean of dress. And

Gloria. She looked exactly as I remembered her, tall, thin, plain Gloria.

It was an exciting day, being with Papa again, getting acquainted with two sisters we had never met. Gloria, still the maid, kept out of sight. At lunch, of boiled chicken with potatoes and cabbage, and white rice, she shyly declined to sit down at table with us, saying she had things to do in the kitchen. For the first time in our lives, we ate at a table without a tablecloth, on thick plates, with not silver silverware, drank tap water from thick glasses meant to withstand battle, without servants hovering to serve us. From my father, there was neither self-consciousness nor apology. Nowhere in his house was there a vestige of his former life.

The house was not as small as I first thought it was, at least it was bigger than the other houses in the neighborhood. It was a typical barrio house, made of nipa and bamboo. But what struck me about the house was its cleanness---everything was shining. There were two bedrooms. The children's beds had mats on top of them, and a blanket folded neatly on top of a pillow, just one pillow, no mattresses, no sheets, no bedcovers. There were a couple of books on the bedside table, a crucifix on the wall over each bed, a rosary hanging from the iron bedstead. It was a tidy, very clean house; everything seemed to be in its place. Since we were not expected, I assumed this was how it looked every day. If his life was not in order, at least his house was, and I was happy for little crumbs for him.

The yard, too, was especially clean, with a bed of begonias lining the walk that ran from the gate to the porch of the house. Outside the windows were flower boxes and more flowers.

But all good things must end. The ship hooted, giving notice of its departure, and we had to go. We left with mixed feelings, happy at seeing Papa again, sad to see how poor he was. Teddy scolded me. "Poor," he snorted, "is poor in spirit, poor of character, poor in fortitude. Papa has no money but poor he is not." Sorry about that, Teddy.

"By the way, Laura, this trip is our little secret. If Mama doesn't ask, don't tell," cautioned my brother.

No need to worry. Mama never asked. Not that time, not at all the other times when we went again. She never visited the hacienda after we moved to the city but I was sure she must have known. Our absence from the hacienda on those days must have been commented upon, since my grandmother arranged our lives like a martinet, giving Rosa a written schedule from which rigidity we, or at least I, may never stray---wake up at 6:30, shower, then breakfast at 7, school at 8, lunch at 12, home by 4, homework and books and music or ballet lessons, then dinner at 8, bath at 9, then bed. The car was at the door Friday afternoons to whisk us to the hacienda for weekends, back to the city Sunday evenings.

My mother never met anything head on. My father did everything for her, took our temperatures when we were sick, tucked us to bed with a hug and a kiss after our prayers, conferred with teachers when parents were called, answered our little questions--from Teddy, about girls, from me, why being a "proper" young lady was so important. On top of these, he provided all the luxuries a woman in my mother's position must have: splendid clothes, fabulous jewels, an expensive car, a more expensive house, unlimited money. All he asked of her was just to be there for him and for us. Spoiled as she was by my father, when he was no longer there, her way of coping was to turn her attention the other way, as though, if she did not think about her problems, they would just go away.

My mother had a limited command of the local dialect and would take on a vacant look when the local dialect was spoken, the dialect which, when garbled by her, was even harder to understand than her British English, anyway. In this land where English is spoken, however imperfectly, even by the servants, she never bothered to extend her vocabulary. My father, gentleman that he was, spoke only English when my mother was around, so much so that we became more comfortable in English, and so spoke it exclusively in our house, even when later, my mother was more absent than present in our lives.

I was sure that she must have heard the servants talk about our absences from the hacienda, and must have gathered, at least, a gist of what she heard. If she did, she knew that there was nothing she could do; so she never asked, and I, forewarned, never volunteered.

We visited my father a few times after that, when we had one-day school breaks in the middle of the week. I wanted to go more often, on weekends, but Teddy explained that my grandmother wanted us in the hacienda on weekends and the only time we could go was when we had one-day breaks on weekdays, which I protested was not often enough. I started sending the two girls little packages---clothes, shoes, books, little things for little girls, necessities for me, luxuries for them. And money. Teddy and I saved part of our allowances, which we sent the girls through the ship's captain every week. But our allowances were awfully small. I had all the clothes and shoes that I needed, exquisite dresses and expensive shoes, and everything else I wanted. When I needed or wanted anything, all I had to do was ask and one of my aunts would take me shopping. We went to exclusive schools, lived in an enormous house, were driven around in an imported car. In short, we had all the trappings of luxury but, alas, little money. My grandmother held a tight rein on her purse strings, believing that little money was good discipline for children.

Once, in one of our visits to my father's house, we were sitting on the porch after our usual lunch of chicken with potatoes and cabbage. Sometimes, when my stomach was full, my brain became dull, or so Teddy had the habit of telling me. But fools rush in where angels fear to tread, I often hear it said, and I was the former and not the latter. Without thinking, I asked my father, "Are you happy here?"

Teddy darted me a look that could have felled me right then and there. But I guess my father knew that one day, I'd ask him that. He shrugged a shoulder and said, "I am at peace here. Gloria is not given to small talk. Sometimes, we don't talk for hours. She takes care of the children and they don't fuss and intrude too much. I have all the time to read." He had always been a passionate reader, stacking up shelves in our house with books, boxes of which he brought back with him from London, more he bought through the years. All this he brought with him when he left.

"My needs are anticipated and met," he continued. A far cry then from his life with us, where we all went to him for everything, for concerns big or small, and nobody was solicitous of his needs.

The dagger of my thoughtlessness and inconsideration smote my heart. Yes I was guilty, too. But I was only a child then. "I'm older now, almost 14. If you come back, I'll take care of you." I tried to hide the tears in my voice.

"You have taken care of me, more than you'll ever know." He touched my hair, full and thick and fair, just like my mother's, he used to tell me. Everyone says I look just like my mother, especially now that I'm older. Sometimes I look at myself in the mirror and see her in my glances, in the way I hold my head, in my face that is hers all over, the fabulous face of the Englishwoman my father loved so at one time. Did I remind him of her, of things that were for him past, maybe regretted, but surely not forgotten?

"The only things I miss are you two," he said. "But I tell myself that you just went away to school and will be back soon. It's easier to bear when I know that you are well."

One night, in one of our weekly dinners at my grandmother's house, she asked me about our trip. Except that he had lost some weight, I thought my father looked all right, I told my grandmother. How was I to know that he had contracted tuberculosis? By the time we first visited him, the disease was already slowly ravaging his body and that was the reason my grandmother arranged our visits.

Consumption should be visited only on the rich. Although there is no cure, a consumptive's life could be prolonged, and in comparable comfort. However, like a hungry monster, it is a disease that demands good food, plenty of rest, a lot of care, which spells money, which my father, son of one of the richest families in the land, did not have. With him, five years was all it took.

When we learned about it, it was too late. One day, my grandmother heard that my father was coming home from Manila after one last futile attempt at a cure. He was coming home in one of our ships. He had to, there was no other means of transportation from Manila to San Miguel, the town on the island where he now lived, or I was sure he would not have set foot on ground that he had set firmly in the past. He never forgave my grandmother for taking my mother's side and disinheriting him; she thought that without money, in time my father would relent and come home. My grandmother boarded the ship when it docked in our town. My grandmother had one last meeting with her only son. What transpired on that meeting I never knew; I only pray they made peace with each other.

We steel our hearts to compassion and sympathy and understanding, all in the name of principle---I say on my grandmother's part, it was more pride; nobody had ever thwarted her before---hoping that time will heal all rifts and bring a loved one back into our lives. And the days turn to years. And still we wait. He'll come back, maybe tomorrow, surely in time.

Did it break her heart when she saw her son, saw that emaciated body that he had become with her help, or rather, that he had become without her help? And then again, would grandmother let on if it did?

What heartache transpired in that ship I never knew. Probably she told my aunts Elena and Emilia. They made one last trip to San Miguel for one last reunion, with an only brother who, if they had but made an effort, might, just might, have enfolded them back to him. And then again, maybe not. But they did not try and so they never knew. Now they'll never know.

Even in death he did not have the peace he was denied in life. My grandmother insisted that he be buried in the family mausoleum. Gloria insisted that it was my father's wish to be buried in San Miguel and would our family defy a dying man's wish? Maybe he did wish that, maybe Gloria just wanted it that way, knowing that it would be hard for her to visit him if he were buried in the family mausoleum in our town. Me, I believe her. She had always been meek and quiet. I do not think she had it in her to invent the story of a dying man's wish and stand up to it in front of my father's family. My grandmother had perfected this withering look, a countenance unnerving even to one with a constitution stronger than Gloria's. I was sure she could not tell a lie and weather that look.

While they were engaged in acrimonious battle, my father's body waited.

In the end, Gloria relented. After all, she did not have any legal right to his remains. Once again my grandmother prevailed. When had she not, ever?

Tito Tomas, Tita Rita's husband, was sent to San Miguel to arrange for a Mass with Gloria and the two children in attendance. My grandmother ordered one of our ships to make this special trip to San Miguel to bring my father's body back to our town. Another Mass was said, with the family, and the whole town, in attendance.

Another Marquez event. This family had given so much to this town: jobs, scholarships, endowments, outright money, and, lately, as if it felt a responsibility towards its entertainment as well, more than its share of excitement, some sordid, some not, all giving the town days of feigned concern and secret enjoyment. The production was the same---big money, big scandal---only the players change.

My mother was not there when we buried my father. Again she pleaded sickness. I was sure my grandmother had her hand in that, too.

Early in life, I was taught that a lady should never show emotions in public. Pillows are there, to comfort the head as well as to hold the tears. My grandmother, whose edict---do what I say and do what I do---nobody dared ever defy, stood in stoic silence while her only son's coffin was interred into one of the niches in the family mausoleum, supported on the arms of her equally stoic daughters. Whatever they, and the other members of the family, felt was buried inside their stoic selves. A few tears and a few discreet sobs were allowed, otherwise the only one who wept openly was myself. So what if I was not a lady today. Once with much sorrow, I lost my father, then with joy I found him again. This day, I lost him one last time, finally, irrevocably, forever. I felt that, with so much sorrow heaped on my 18-year-old heart, I had a right for once to put down my armor. With a deluge of tears and heartrending sobs, and not for the last time, I grieved my father's passing.

When my father left my mother, my grandmother made it known that she was leaving my mother a lot of money, as much as what she was leaving her own daughters. She revised her will, leaving her vast properties in Manila to my mother. She hoped that this strategy would entice my father to come back to my mother, and hence to the family.

My grandmother died two months after my father did, without changing her will and, since it no longer served the purpose, without putting the Manila properties back to her daughters' names. Again, for the second time in a few months, there was something my grandmother did not foresee and could not control: time running out, that thief stealing again in the night when she least expected it.

Without meaning to, and most certainly not wanting to, she left my mother an exceedingly rich woman.

By this time, however, my mother did not much care. Somehow, when her husband left her for homely Gloria, the blow to her ego left her with no desire for living, at least for living high. Crushed, humiliated, she never recovered from the blow of her husband's perfidy. When my father left, my grandmother took over the management of our household and the care of Teddy and me. Every decision was made by my grandmother, informing, if the whim takes her, but not consulting, my mother, leaving her, my mother, with nothing else but time on her hands. What enjoyment she derived from the parties and the games vanished when she realized, or so she thought, that she had become the object of gleeful gossip, of spurious pity, a curiosity.

I remember asking her once about her family. She told me that her father and mother died when she was still a young girl. She did not have any brothers and sisters and the aunt who took care of her had died long ago. I remember thinking how sad life must be without any family at all.

Now, even with my grandmother gone, she keeps to herself and never went back to her former self.

14

$\mathcal{T}$ he sun had set and the room had darkened, but Denis did not notice, until Laura came into the room. "Can you still see? It's dark already." She slipped out to go to Cecilia's room when Denis started reading the diary but obviously he did not notice. She switched on the lamp on the table by his side. "Where are you now?"

He showed here the page he was reading. "This is a sad story," said Denis. "What happened to these people?"

"Toward the end of her life," Laura said, "my grandmother Jane never went out of the house. When she died, she left Teddy and my grandmother Laura so much valuable property in Manila, and made them enormously wealthy. Much later, when my grandmothers Elena and Emilia passed away and the passions kindled by this tragedy cooled off, Teddy took care of his father's new family. He sent the two girls to the best schools in Manila. They married well and their children, Papa's cousins, are doing very well. They are now living abroad."

"What happened to Teddy?"

"Oh, he became a Jesuit. He worked in the missions that were run by his Order. He died at a very old age."

"Oh, my goodness, Jesuit missions!"

She settled herself next to him and he put his arm around her, the better for her to read the pages with him.

"Go on, there's more," she said.

15

*T*he death of a loved one dampened my taste for writing. But as one love went out of my life, another came in. And so I'm picking up this diary and my pen again.

His name is Francis Steiner. Laura Steiner. I fell in love with his name and took it for my own even before I laid eyes on him. He is Swiss, an engineer, sent over by the company to manage the business that sells and maintains the machines that run the sugar centrals, and from all the excitement he is generating, remarkably handsome.

Parties at Tio Benigno's villa are affairs we always look forward to, parties for cousins mostly, and parents, a pleasant way to catch up on time spent away from home while at school. The conversation is stimulating and the food always excellent, whipped up by their cook, whom they sent to a Senora Tina to learn the intricacies of Spanish cooking. What the cook comes up with is a delicious gastronomic marriage of Senora Tina's recipes and the cook's own inventive discoveries.

Tio Benigno's villa is enormous, filled with all the appurtenances of wealth, and seems to have jumped out of the pages of some home magazines. After dinner, there is always dancing on the terrace under the moon, if there is one, or under the stars, of which it seems there are more in that part of the world than anywhere else.

~ ~ ~

I had just graduated with a degree in Literature, major in English, and tonight, Tio Benigno, always proud of me, was giving a party in his villa in my honor.

Have you ever felt somebody's eyes boring into you and you look up, involuntarily, and sure enough somebody is indeed staring at you? I turned and saw him, a gold-haired head taller than the rest, gray eyes watching me, with that steadfast gaze that held mine. Him, the subject of the excited girlish chatter I had heard so much these past weeks. No wonder he had whipped up such tumult---his was the handsomest face I had ever seen.

He walked towards me, this tall, light-haired joy, drink in hand, sure of purpose, gray eyes unwavering. He stood looking at me without speaking.

"Did I pass inspection?" I asked.

He laughed. "Yes, a long time ago," he said, "nine minutes to be exact. One minute after I saw you. Oh, would you care for a drink?"

I smiled at the thought of a 19-year-old girl drinking at a party. Unheard of. But he is a foreigner in our shores and does not know better. "No, thank you," I said.

"Something to eat?" he asked.

My smiled broadened. This was the villa of my uncle, where summer parties were almost always held, and he was inviting me to eat. "No, thank you," I said.

"Marriage? No, no, no," he said, "not yet," holding up his hands. "Don't answer that. If you said no thank you again I could just drop dead from despair, right here at your feet."

I laughed. "I have not seen you around."

"Oh, I'm sorry. My name is Francis. Steiner. And I know yours is Laura. And I'll tell you the strangest thing. My mother's name is also Laura, though she is called Lauren, but still, if that isn't fate I don't know what is." He held out his hand and held mine in a firm grip. And he never let go after that. I won him without even entering the contest. And was the talk of the town the next day, and many days after that.

Oh, to be loved by a man as he loves me. All these years I had been a plant asleep. Then all at once I burst out. I bud. And I bloom. We take long walks, hand in hand, even in the rain. I'm sure the gumamelas were never this red, the gardenias never gave out such a heady perfume. Even the sugar canes never looked this fat (he has never seen anyone eat sugar cane before). I can almost taste the sugar on my tongue, the sweet juice that drips down my hand when I bite into the stalk, sweeter now, I swear, than at any time before.

He brings me books and chocolates and flowers. He writes me letters every single day, Sweet Notes, he calls them. Yesterday, he wrote, 'The night is so quiet, everybody must be asleep and I am here looking at that full moon outside my window and missing you. I hope you miss me, too. There is no minute in the day that I do not think of you. Would that I were a witch, then I would ride my broomstick and be with you this minute and we could watch that moon together.' He closes his letters with Terribly in Love.

He brings me books of poems. Yesterday, he gave me a treasure of a book, Petrarch's Canzoniere. I read the poems many times and still cannot get enough. I feel as though I am the Laura Petrarch was singing about, that I am the Laura who inspired him for many years. I wonder what experiences in life poets go through, suffer through, laugh through, love through, to come up with these words that stir the senses so. Petrarch saw Laura in church and immediately fell in love with her. Sadly, she was already married. But she remained his muse even after she died, inspired him, inspired those love poems out of him. She appeared to him in sleep one night and when he awoke, he knew that she had died.

Now I shall put this down, this diary of mine. This was started by a young girl a long time ago, a sad girl often left alone, not outgoing at all, who found solace and comfort in writing. That lonely girl had become me, no longer lonely, in fact completely happy.

Tomorrow I shall become Laura Steiner. I have found someone to share my hours with, and who delights in sharing them with me. Maybe once in a while I shall pick up my pen again, but only to leave a record for posterity. But not out of loneliness, never again out of loneliness.

16

"What a sadly moving story," Denis said. "What happened next? Tell me more."

"Well, they married and lived happily ever after and produced *Tito* Ray and Papa and a girl named Laura who died. And you finished the cookies."

He laughed. "Be a good girl and call for more milk and more cookies. Then tell me more stories."

She called the kitchen and then snuggled back into his arms. "What else is there I haven't told you? After that Francis Steiner married my grandmother Laura, he parlayed her inheritance into a respectable fortune. He bolstered the shipping business, went into international shipping, and when Papa and *Tito* Ray took over, they made it the largest shipping line in the country. I guess that about plumbs that story dry. Would you like to hear about what your wife did when she was growing up?"

"Very much."

"The summer after my grandmother Laura died, Franz and a girl named Regina whom Franz was in love with at that time, and Joe and I spent two whole weeks in the hacienda. We decided to renovate the attic and that's where we found this trunk full of my grandmother's things, old dresses of lace, books with flowers pressed in their pages, these bundles of their love letters, and this diary. Did you finish the love letters, too?"

"Uh huh," he nodded.

"From the hacienda we went to Santo Niño and stayed for another two weeks, taking long hikes in the country, moonlight swimming, going to the barrios and dancing in the streets. It was one of the happiest summers I had."

"Joe seemed to be always with you," Denis said.

"Yes. He and Franz were inseparable. Joined in the hips, Mom would say. More like joined in the heart, I say. And I was honored to be their mascot. I went wherever they went, even though they made me their gofer. Gofer cigarettes and lighter, gofer more wine, gofer more tapas. Joe brought armloads of books that I was assigned to read, too. He had a big hand in my education, literary and otherwise, which really shaped me.

"One summer Joe went with us to Spain, which upset *Tita* Maggie, that's Joe's mom, since they went to Madrid the year before and Joe did not want go with them. But he had never been to Guernica, Joe reasoned, and would not want to go there without Franz. You know Mom's father came from there. We had a great time there.

"Franz and Joe would disappear into a *taverna* in the afternoon and come out late in the evening, garrulous and contentious and, of course, drunk. They would come home and argue at the kitchen table until the wee hours. Joe. He could drink anyone under the table. But for all the drink that he consumed, I've never heard him slur his words, or seen him stagger when he walked, or do any of those stupid things we typically associate with being drunk.

"From there we toured Spain, saw a bullfight, those two crazy boys ran with the bulls, well, just a couple of blocks or so, anyway. We saw Picasso's *Guernica* in the Museo in Madrid, that awesome painting of the horrors of the Spanish Civil War. That summer was one of the happiest. They say that youth is wasted on the young. Well, not really, not on us, youth wasn't.

"I guess I was a disappointment to my father. While *Tito* Ray will have Joe and RJ to help him out, Papa has only Franz. Nacho is the Lord's share and they never begrudge Him that. But I could be a great help, doing so well in school. But I never had the Steiner's head for business. And so the burden of helping Papa will be placed squarely on Franz' shoulders when he is done with school. Poor Franz."

"How about Joe?" Denis wanted to know.

"He'll be there, and will take over when he's done with school, too. But *Tito* Ray will also have RJ, so Joe will not have to carry as much responsibilities. Besides, he will sit on the board of the companies of his grandfather, his mother's Dad, Gomez Enterprises, Limited that enterprises almost all aspect of business in the country and is anything but limited, which will fill his hours and of course his pockets. *Tito* Ray has always disapproved of the way *Tita* Maggie's family spoils Joe, but Joe just charms. Don Jose, that's *Tita* Maggie's father, starved for a male heir after so many years of producing girls, just dotes on him, spoils him terribly, floods him with money. There was great jubilation when Joe was born. Gomez Enterprises declared a holiday and gave its employees the day off and they say that no baptism in memory rivals his in grandeur. Don Jose asked *Tita* Maggie if Joe could carry his name, Jose Gomez the Second. That upset *Tito* Ray, that he could even suggest it and even *Tita* Maggie did not dare prevail upon *Tito* Ray to indulge Don Jose on that. Don Jose gave Joe an MG when he turned sixteen. An MG! Even if we had as much money, which we don't, Mom would never spoil her children the way Joe is spoiled.

"Anyway, it is stipulated in Don Jose's will that when he dies, Joe will have an equal share in his estate, I mean, his estate is divided equally among his three daughters, and Joe. He is the son Don Jose never had. And so, with so much money, Joe does not have to lift a finger to maintain his lifestyle.

"When they come back from Oxford, he and Franz will manage the provincial part of Steiner. Joe will work there because Franz will work there, he has nothing else to do, and he knows he is expected to carry on when *Tito* Ray steps down, but his heart is not really there."

Did all roads in her life lead to Joe? Denis wondered. Somehow, no matter how far they wandered, they ended up to him. "So where is it?" he asked.

"Huh?"

"His heart, where is it?"

"Not very much in girls, I'm afraid. If girls are there, and they usually are, he takes them, but he is not good at starting and following through. There were a few in college, one or two in England, too, according to Franz, but nothing came out of those. Where is his heart? In his books and his music and his bottle most of the time, I guess."

You guess. Oh, my dearest, when your father said you did not know anything about life, he had no idea just how much you did not know. In fact, he had no idea how much he did not know, either. "I'm so glad you were at Stevens' that day," he said and took her in his arms. And she had no idea what brought on these little acts of tenderness that never failed to move her and she added another star to his already-studded approval card.

Soon, September was on its way, summer was gone and vacation time was over. There was work to do and a living to be done. They went back to California and Denis prepared for a scheduled concert at the Avery Fisher Hall at the Lincoln Center in New York and immediately after that, he was singing the role that he was fast making his own, that of Mozart's *Don Giovanni*, at the New York Metropolitan Opera.

17

*L*aura marveled at how much work went into the preparation for an opera or a concert or a recording. Denis did everything with characteristic thoroughness. He read the score first, after which came the meticulous research. He assembled books on the theme of the program and read those. The language teacher saw to it that each foreign word was pronounced and phrased perfectly; the voice teacher taught him how to make his body handle each note and made sure that he did not falter and crack up in the higher ones. And there was Peter, who was always there in all these, the one person he trusted, his outside ears, who listened and made sure that no note come out flat or strident or, heavens forbid, out of pitch.

After every pointer was carefully noted, he isolated himself in his study and with that awesome brainpower that saw and photographed every period and every comma of every sentence, he went into the process of committing everything to memory.

He had the utmost respect for his audience. He would go through a two-hour concert without glancing at notes. Once, he sang three sets of songs, four to five songs in each set, more than a dozen songs in all, and he never once had to look at notes. In that vast repository inside his head, whatever he learned, stayed learned.

He set at the outset a high standard for each performance and was exacting in its execution. It was unthinkable, and unheard of, that he would come on stage and glance at the notes on the music stand during a performance, an anathema to him and a needless annoyance he spared his audience. "These people came from far and near to hear me sing. I could at least do my share and memorize my lines." By the time he came out on stage, the complete performer, every line and every note of every song was firmly etched and embedded in his head.

This compulsion for perfection produced powerful performances that earned him a following that stayed loyal even after an abundance of newer and younger baritones started to crowd the international operatic rolls.

Mahler was his composer of choice in recordings and recitals, each carefully chosen piece a delight to him in giving and to his audience in receiving. The *Kindertotenlieder*, one in Mahler's song cycles, was, to Laura, the most haunting in his repertoire. When he would sing it, she would prepare herself for the last song, her favorite in the cycle, the one she had listened to a dozen times in records, but which never failed to move her. He would start *In diesem Wetter, in diesem Braus*, feet planted apart, closed fists hammering in the air the pain and anguish of the Ruckert poem, with that voice that would have thrilled even Mahler himself. But then, from the very first, she found in him a clear case of the singer more than the song, and he moved her in all the songs he did, from the tuneful crossovers, to the exhilarating operas, to the difficult lieders.

He encouraged her feedback and liked to insert her preferences in his programs, the show-off songs she loved, Don Giovanni's tongue-twisting *Champagne* aria, *Chansons Madecasses* that Ravel wrote for a mezzo, and *Wintersturme* that Wagner intended for a tenor, striding about the stage with arms outstretched or buried in his pockets, passionate but always dignified. His voice filled the halls with its incredible range and richness and climbed to the rafters seemingly without effort. Surely, no boundaries confined his voice, surely he could have soared higher had the song not given up.

* * *

Tonight, at the Lincoln Center's Avery Fisher Hall, Denis' first concert after they got married, his program consisted of, for the first part, songs by Rachmaninoff and Ravel. Cole Porter, Irving Berlin and Jerome Kern songs made up the second part. These were the programs that he enjoyed, where he could shed off his formal self and include these love songs that he marked with his own inimitable, intimate touch and that always swept his audience away.

* * *

He came out, looked up to where he knew Laura was seated and found her in an instant, and started to sing, and she knew that he was singing to her, knew that he was brilliant this night because she was there, knew that the songs flowed like velvet and flashed like gems because she gave added meaning to them. He made love to her that night, in a hall packed with two thousand seven hundred people, and he could not have done it with more fire and intensity had they been alone. She sat still through the thunderous applause, the curtain calls and standing ovations, too moved to move, as exhausted as though she went through an actual convergence with him.

That was how he introduced her to his second love.

18

hey celebrated Laura's twenty-fifth birthday with a quiet day at Forbes, though quiet was not exactly the word. Everyone was there, sisters and brothers, with spouses and children.

Franz and Hazel gave her a fertility tree, a small tree of bronze with a jade at the tip of each branch, believed to curry favors from the god of fertility.

Manuel and Isa gave her a subscription to Playboy magazine, "To show Denis. After six years, maybe you need to look at pictures."

With Maricris pregnant, Isa with twin girls and Hazel having a baby every year, it was inevitable that Denis and Laura would get the ribbing.

"So now it's fertility we're into," said Denis.

"It's more like infertility," said Hazel.

"I don't need a baby," said Denis, unperturbed, pulling his wife to him, "I have my baby right here."

"You do need a baby," said Hazel, "You cannot imagine how these guys enrich your life." She started to poke little Chris' neck and the baby made cooing sounds. There seemed to be children around her always, a boy clutching her skirt when she walked, another boy at her feet when she sat, and the new baby in her arms wherever she went.

"Haven't you heard of birth control?" Maricris asked her.

"Oh," answered Hazel, "we did try that contraceptive jelly once, what was its name, but that was a mess. I mean literally a mess," she said, rolling her eyes upward. "You had to wait 15 loooong minutes for it to work. Franz asked, 'Is it time now?' and I said, no, not yet. Five minutes later, he asked again, 'Is it time now?' and I said again, no dear, not yet. After another interminable five minutes, he asked again, this time, he was really getting aggravated. No, dear, I replied, not yet. And then when it was time, I said, it's time now, Franz. But he's had it.

"Thanks,' he said, 'but I don't want to anymore.' And we never tried that stuff again."

Everyone burst out in laughter. "Poor Franz."

That night in bed, Laura asked Denis, "Do you mind it when they tease you that way?"

"No," said Denis. He was comfortable with his own self and with Laura's family and never minded their ribbing. "Do you?" he asked her. She did not answer, so he said, "You do."

"Why don't we have a baby, Denis."

"Why don't we. Let's, right now." He started pawing her.

"Denis, I'm serious."

"So am I."

"Denis, please," she chided, then looked wistful. "Oh, wouldn't it be just wonderful, to have a little boy and he'll look exactly like you."

"What if he turns out to be a big girl and looks like my mother?" They both laughed.

"You are such a bad boy."

He took her face between his hands. "Do you want a baby because you want a baby or is it because everybody else is having one?"

"Don't you want one?"

"Sweet, you're all I want. But if you really want a baby, then we'll try for a baby."

"You mean that, dear, you'll go to the doctor with me?"

"Doctor? What doctor? There's nothing wrong with you and definitely not with me. I just have to apply myself some more, that's all, although at the rate we're going, I don't know what more is possible without giving me a heart attack."

"And a ribald bad boy at that," she said, trying to hold a straight face. "But you'll go to the doctor with me?" she persevered.

He sighed in resignation. "Sweet, I'll go to the ends of the world with you, but why a doctor? Believe me, let's just try some more, and more often, and you'll get your baby boy."

After that, he promised to go, but with his crazy schedule, they never got around to it. And in the end, she stopped asking him and he was glad she seemed to have forgotten.

How could he explain to her that a baby was the last thing he wanted? Everything in his life was perfect now. She went with him everywhere he went. When she wanted to finish her master's degree, he scheduled their time so that when she had classes, he had no shows. His concerts were scheduled only when she could go with him. He knew too many husbands who strayed because their wives were too engrossed in the children and the husbands were left to their own devices. He knew of too many husbands and wives who drifted apart because he had a career to pursue and she was anchored to home and children. He had seen too many marriages fail because priorities were not set clearly from the start. His was this marriage, and in his work, where gorgeous women abounded and with the kind of physical person that, quite simply, he knew he was, he could not chance her absence. A baby would surely upset that snug world he had made for them both. To explain that to her now would seem cruel and heartless, and her opinion of him mattered a great deal to him to allow her a glimpse of how selfish he could become where she was concerned. All he knew was that she was the most important thing in his life and he would do everything to keep her there, happy and content and in love with him. And so, for her only wish that he could not give her, he hedged and hemmed and hewed and promised without any intention of doing anything about it, and was unashamed, sure that he was doing this for them both. He showered her with more care and attention and when she thought that what was wrong with him was a given that couldn't be helped, he did not set her straight. So be it.

"It is really hard, trying to have a baby," Laura confided to Franz. But she talked to the wrong person.

"Oh, I don't know," he said. "I don't seem to have any problem with it. And neither has Hazel."

19

*D*enis took great pleasure in being with his wife's family. He was the only husband he knew who loved his mother-in-law.

But it was Isa's irreverence that clearly gave him a lot of amusement. Once in Manila, they were in the terrace after having *merienda*. Denis was comfortably stretched out on a sofa, his arm around Laura, who was curled up against him. They family had guests, two oversized former classmates of Maricris. They were members of the opera guild and were selling tickets to an upcoming operatic event. "Thanks for the support," said one of them. "We have to go now, feed our souls, you know."

"I think too much soul-feeding have gone into the hips of those two," observed Isa, "or do you think opera just makes for wider hips. I mean, it ain't over till the fat lady sings and all that. I think opera really does something to one's weight," eyeing Denis who, despite Laura's care, or maybe because of it, was starting to take on prosperous proportions.

"Don't start with me, Isa," Denis warned. "I am too comfortable here. I am not taking you on today," which sent everyone laughing. Denis had an air about him that discouraged uninvited familiarity, but all that was lost on Isa.

One sweltering day, too hot even for Manila, the family was at poolside, holding sweating glasses of cold drinks. Although wives were taking care of husbands, getting them iced tea and whatever went with it, Manuel was fending for himself.

"Quarrel?" Denis asked Isa.

"He said I have small breasts."

Manuel looked at his wife testily. "I did not say that. I just said compared to your sisters."

"Well, compared to whoever or not, I don't have small breasts," Isa retorted angrily. "You just have big hands."

* * *

The family had grown since Denis first joined it six years ago and he had been witness to almost all the important milestones in its members' lives.

He and Laura went to New York when Franz and Hazel got married (and caused a minor traffic jam when his fans espied him coming out of the church with Laura). Now Franz and Hazel had three boys, three children in just as many years of marriage.

They came to Manila when Nacho was ordained a priest and he remembered shivers down his spine at the solemnity of the occasion.

They stayed for a short vacation when Maricris married a Swiss named Stefan, a concert pianist like herself whom she met in Europe, and they had a big church wedding.

They missed Isa's big day, though, although big it wasn't.

When she started going out with Manuel, one of the *pelotaris* playing in the *Jai-Alai*, the family was against it. You're much too young, and he is much too handsome, was Francis' objection; sounding much like the time Laura met Denis. Isa had grown into a willful young woman, headstrong and resistant to discipline. No pliant, obedient Laura nor level headed Maricris was she. She was her own woman, and would brook no comparison to her two older sisters. She had become very sensual, "sexy" was the term the boys used and Francis so abhorred. Francis liked to point out that the white hair on one side of his head he got from a rapacious government that throttled private business, and gave Isa credit for the other side.

Francis was reminded of that other Steiner daughter who, on her own and without any help from a stifling government, gave Ray his own head of silver hair. His daughter Madeleine had by this time shed two husbands and was well unto her third.

* * *

The game of *Jai-Alai* might have been played in ancient times by the Greeks, but the Spanish Basques refined it into what had become the exciting game it was today. The game started out as handball, a ball or *pelota*, hit by the hand to a solid wall. Later, the Basques developed the *cesta*, an elongated basket that caught the ball before it was bounced back to the wall. Like most things Spanish, *Jai-Alai* had a special beguilement to Filipinos. Aside from being an exciting game, it gave them a chance to gamble, to bet a peso with dreams of going home with a hundred. Since the game started in Spain, *Jai Alai* was played mostly, and mostly better, by the Basques, with strange Basque names like Larrazabal and Aberásturi.

Mostly good-looking and highly paid, *pelotaris* were much in demand by the girls, and Manuel was good-looking and highly paid indeed. When he first saw Isa, he was riveted by her looks. When later he started going out with her, he was riveted by the world of wealth and opulence that she opened to him. From then on, he was relentless in his pursuit of her. When he was not with his *cesta,* he was with her. Isa declared that they were getting married. Francis was furious and adamantly refused to hear about it. Isa was just as adamant. "We are getting married, that's all there is to it."

"They will, you know, with or without your consent," Cecilia said later. "We should know her by now. And without our support, he could take her away. Do we really want that? I don't. I don't think I could stand that, and neither could you."

Francis knew that with Cecilia feeling that way, he would not be able to stand it, either.

In the end, Francis relented.

Isa declared she did not care for a lavish wedding. Impatient, she just did not want to wait. They were married in a quiet evening ceremony, attended by just a handful of Steiners. Manuel did not have anybody from his family. Spain was much too far away.

So was California. Laura and Denis missed that one.

* * *

"A penny for your thoughts," said Denis. He went to the terrace to look at the moon and the radiant night and found Maricris standing there. He did not have as close or as comfortable a relationship with her as he had with Isa. When he and Laura were just newly married, and she, Maricris, was younger, she was more playful, trying to match Isa's outgoing nature, but as she grew older, she became more like Laura, more quiet, more reserved, more an observer than a participant, and Denis respected and did not try to breach that distance. Later she became a concert pianist and when she married Stefan, they lived in Switzerland and their visits home did not always coincide.

She looked at Denis, deliberated a moment whether to take him into her confidence. "What do you say to a sister when you think her husband is having an affair?"

"I'm not," he said.

Maricris laughed. "No, you aren't. You know what, when you married Lauren, the family had a lot of misgivings. We were sure that she was going to have a difficult marriage. Of course Papa thawed fast when he read quite often that Denis Richards did not play around. You turned out better than any of us expected."

"Thanks. Now, what is this about an affair? Since I am not having one, and you only have one other sister, what has Manuel been up to?"

"There has been talk, a lot of it. Maybe it's true, maybe not. But I think if there's smoke, something is burning somewhere and Isa should start sniffing to find out what is."

"Does Laura know about this?"

Maricris shrugged her shoulders. "I told her, but she is just hopeless. With her, there aren't two ways about things. It has to be undying love, or none at all. I'd leave him, she says. Easy for her to say, she does not have children to think of."

"That doesn't make it any less painful," said Denis.

"Well, she'd leave you, if you were having the affair, you know that." He did not answer, and she continued. "Sometimes a husband can be attracted to other women, but that doesn't mean that he doesn't love his wife. You should know that, in the business you are in; you must have been attracted to a few other women a few times."

He let that pass without comment.

"Maybe there are just some areas in a husband's life that a wife is not satisfying, but that does not mean he's ready to call it quits. Also, I believe that it takes two to whatever. Isa could sometimes be thoughtless, as you well know. She just opens her mouth, and what comes out, though not really intended to hurt, hurts just the same. 'English is broken here.'" She sounded exactly like Isa, Spanish accent and all, taunting Manuel, that Denis had to laugh.

"Have you talked to her about this?" he asked.

"No, I don't know how to go about it."

"Does your Mom know?"

"I don't think so."

"Maybe you should talk to her."

She thought about this for a while and heaved a sigh. "Yes, I think I will." She looked at him and smiled sadly. "Thanks, Denis."

He had not really given her a good look and now was surprised to note that she was lovely in her own way, if you did not compare her to her other two sisters. Hers was a quiet loveliness, falling short of Laura's breathtaking beauty and certainly not in the league with Isa's stunning, sensual attractiveness. But lovely she still was, and the smile, which seemed a family trait, taken from Cecilia, never failed to dazzle.

* * *

"Where's Manuel?" Denis asked. They were having *merienda* on the terrace. Everybody was there and Manuel was conspicuously absent.

"Playing tennis," answered Isa.

Laura, reclining on the sofa, head on Denis's lap, one arm dangling lazily by her side, bare feet and long legs stretched out from white shorts, cool as the frosty glass of soda she was holding in her other hand, belied the entire cool picture and said, "His name is being mentioned with that Vargas woman."

Isa shot her an angry look. "They just play tennis. Nothing to that," she replied, defensively.

"Tell him not to play constantly with just one woman. Aren't there any men he could play with? He's causing a scandal. A philandering husband, that's all the scandal the family needs now."

"Oh, philandering, for crissakes. You make it sound like he's having an affair with every woman he meets!"

"Does it have to be," Laura mimicked her, "'every woman'? How many does it take for you to put your foot down? Maybe he has too much time on his hands." Manuel had stopped playing *pelota*. There was a scandal about rigged games, an inquiry followed, and although his name was cleared, he stopped playing, anyway. Isa said he had plenty of money put aside to put up a business, but after that, she asked Franz if she could work in the company, and the family believed that Manuel's money might not have been that plenty, after all. "Maybe he should be helping out Franz and Joe. Then maybe you don't have to go to work, with small children like those."

"Oh, shut up, for crissakes," Isa fairly screamed. "Don't you think he has heard enough of that? It's already coming out of his ears. You just look down on him because he does not come with pedigree. You're just a snob, Laura."

"I most certainly am not! And I don't look down on him because he comes from a poor family and you know that. How can you say that? It's not even money we're talking about here. I just want you to open your eyes."

"Mine are. Yours aren't. Not everybody can have a husband like yours. Some of us have to contend with less. Just once in a while, why don't you get down from your pedestal, read some of those trashy magazines that you so look down on, mingle with hoi polloi. You'll find that imperfect humans populate this world. Then maybe you'll develop a bit of compassion. Try it. It should do your soul some good." She passed Denis, glared at him, "Get yourself a real woman once in a while, you don't know what you're missing." She gathered her children and, with the white-uniformed maid trailing behind, stormed out of the house.

An embarrassed hush filled the room. Stormy scenes were never displayed. She and Manuel seemed to trade insults often that it was surprising how much she was defending him from her family's criticism. Laura stood up and left the room. Cecilia heaved a sigh and went back to her thoughts. Nobody made a move to dispel the quiet.

Denis rose. "Excuse me," he said and followed his wife to their room.

She was looking out the window when he came in. He stood behind her, and as was his wont, moved her hair to the side and kissed the back of her neck. "You all right?" he asked gently.

"I'm sorry but I just felt I had to say something since nobody else seemed inclined to do so. I just cannot understand how she can have him back to her bed knowing where he came from. And you, if you ever did that to me, I just want you to know, you can start looking around again, because I'm out of there."

Book 2
Joe

1

*W*hen they were not rehearsing his parts, Denis liked to spend his time inside his dressing room reading or doing crossword puzzles. He could wait for his wife for hours while she did whatever she had to do, and not mind it, as long as he had his crosswords with him. Lately, however, the crosswords were getting much too easy for him. He could breeze through two or three without much effort. Today, he finished one and was too tired to start another. He had zipped out of the house this morning and forgotten to bring a book, too.

It had been a hectic day for him. He had left the house early and had told Laura he might come home late. He had a very full morning and now he was exhausted.

He looked outside at a cluster of men in jovial discussion. On slack days, he liked to swap jokes or chat with the crew or the other cast members. Maybe he should do that, he thought, the air should do him good. He flexed his shoulders. He was exhausted! He wondered what his wife was doing. Well, doing what she did mornings---puttering in the garden with her roses, swimming or planning menus with Milly. He wished he were home.

He was about to call her when his phone rang. He let it ring a couple of times before he picked it up.

"Denis, Susana here."

"Susana? Susana? Well, well, this is a pleasant surprise. I haven't heard from you in a while. Are you in town?"

He had not seen her since that day in Laurelfield before he got married six years ago, that day he brought Laura home to meet his family. She had written him a few times---when she got her first big break in the opera in Philadelphia, before she went abroad to study, when she came back and had her first U.S. opera. Each time, Denis sent a card, in encouragement, in wishing her success, in congratulations, but was too busy with his own life and never caught her performances.

"Yes, I'm in town and I leave for New York tomorrow. Can we have lunch? Oh, Denis, it's been such a long time, there is so much to talk about."

He knew he couldn't spare the time. But he knew he couldn't quite refuse her either. They had been cordial even after their relationship broke up. Well, not exactly broke up so much as petered out. They were childhood friends, lived in the same block, went to the same school. They had the same ambition---to make it in the world of opera. She was the first girl he went out with and, a few years older than he was, she initiated him in the art of the boy-girl merging that served him well later in his life. They took up where they left off when, years later, they both found themselves in Philadelphia, perfecting their voices, learning new languages, trying out for operatic parts. She was the kind of woman who did not appeal much to him, the hard, emasculating, traffic-control kind of woman, characteristics that became more prominent when acceptance, success and fame were too long in coming. Even in their younger days, she had that fierce, determined, hard-edged look about her that he thought unbecoming, an abrasiveness that he found quite unattractive. What he wanted was a softer, more caring kind of woman, one who was there to support him and love him and hold his hand and she was definitely not that. But they were lonely in a lonely town and they turned to each other. Then his breaks came and he got too engrossed in his career. The affair had cooled off long before he left Philadelphia. Then he was swallowed up by a success even bigger than he ever hoped for or imagined and he never looked back. But they remained friendly and now he knew he just could not beg off.

"I guess I could skip over for lunch," he said.

She named a hotel not far from the studio. She was waiting for him at a corner table in the dining room when he arrived.

"Denis Richards, more handsome than I remembered, if that is at all possible," greeted Susana. "Marriage agrees with you."

"You look great yourself," he said, "and that without the benefit of marriage." He kissed checks and continued, "unless you went and got hitched and did not write me."

"You'll be the first to know. So, how's Laura? I saw your picture in the papers when you were in New York. She looked just fabulous."

"Marriage agrees with her, too. A great institution, marriage. You should try it some time."

"Ask me anytime you're ready. You know I'm always ready for you," she said seriously, surveying him with darkly made-up eyes. Denis laughed this off. Flirtation was child's play to her and he did not want to be pulled into a territory that had long been laid to rest in the past. He had left Susana long before their affair ended, long before he left Philadelphia.

"Look, can we order first? I'm sorry, Susana, but I can't stay very long." They made their orders, hers a salad, his, the usual roast beef sandwich.

They caught up with the six years and then he had to leave. "I'm sorry I have to rush. Take a rain check, will you? I'll do better next time. Don't be a stranger, write again, and keep me posted." They exchanged goodbyes and he left. She looked at him as he rushed out, an imposing figure to behold. There had been other men when Denis went out of her life---a few when she was struggling with her career, more when success came, but after Denis, the rest had a hard time measuring up.

In his haste, Denis did not notice that he left his handkerchief on the table. Susana picked it up, called out to him but he was gone. She sat deep in thought, then pressed the handkerchief carefully to her lips and went to the desk to ask for information.

* * *

Laura was in the den when Mario came up. He was holding a silver letter tray with a white, embroidered linen cover. An envelope sat on it. "This came for Sir Denis," he said.

Laura looked at the envelope with a hotel's emblem and name on top and a woman's scrawl "Denis" on the center. Just "Denis."

"Who brought it?" she inquired.

"There was a limo and the driver brought it up."

"Thank you, Mario."

The fat content had bulged through the envelope's seal and popped the flap open.

She picked up the tray and perfume assailed her nose. Careful now, she told herself, you had never opened other people's mail, and you are not about to start now. She brought the tray inside their bedroom and placed it on Denis's bedside table. She looked at her watch. Two o'clock. He should have called long before now. Well, he said he would be rushing today. She looked out the window, at the sky too blinding-blue for January, at the leaves shivering in the light breeze, but her eyes were riveted to the tray. She did not have to open Denis's mail, she told herself, this one was already open. She fingered the envelope and saw a piece of cloth inside. She pulled it out and held up Denis's handkerchief. There, on one corner, were his initials, the small, gray letters dsr. Denis Sebastian Richards. She had the initials embroidered on towels and pillow cases and pockets of his shirts. And handkerchiefs. This one was soiled with lipstick, redolent of perfume. Then a note, folded in half, swirled languidly to the floor. She picked it up daintily with thumb and forefinger. Again she let her gaze travel out the window, at the radiant day outside. She looked up, as though looking for succor from somebody up there, but found none.

She knew even before she flicked the note open that curiosity would kill her and that satisfaction would not bring her back. There was that feminine scrawl again. "Denis, as always, a pleasure. Thank you so much. P.S. You left this in the hotel." It was signed Susana. Then she remembered. A dance floor in Laurelfield, a woman with hair too yellow and breasts too large for her too-small dress, cutting in on her and Denis. ("They were an item once; he had always been partial to blondes," that young man had said.) "Denis's three Bs," Charles said when they read an item in the papers about a concert Susana gave, "blonde, big breasts." "And what?" she had asked innocently. "Darling," said Charles, "that's three already." "Don't be crude in front of my wife," said Denis, and swatted Charles with the folded newspaper, more annoyed, she thought, than was necessary.

She stood there, heart pounding, eyes smarting, feet stamped to the floor.

Then the phone rang. "Hi, dear," said Denis. "I'm sorry I wasn't able to call earlier. God, this place is a madhouse. Have you had lunch?"

"Yes," whispering the word.

"What did you have?"

"Milly's *laswa*, as usual." Boiled vegetables with shrimps. Then almost inaudibly, "Have you?"

"Yes. Roast beef sandwich, as usual." He talked for a few more minutes, then said, "Oh, I'm afraid I will be late again tonight. I'm sorry, sweet. I was hoping we could finish my part first, but I don't know, I don't think so. I'm really sorry. You know what, I was thinking. Why don't we do New York when I'm through here, would you like that? Yes, New York would be good, you'd like that, wouldn't you? We'll talk about it tonight, all right? I love you, dear," he said as he put the phone down.

"Methinks thou dost protest too much," she said grimly. She always tried not to mind his long hours. He had work to do and knowing that in whatever he did he always strove for perfection, she never cramped his style. If long hours were what it took, then long hours were what she let him take, in peace. She never questioned, never fussed, never doubted. Trust, not vigilance, was the rule she went by in her marriage. But trust was not easy in the face of confirmation marked by lipstick, reeking with perfume.

She sat still for a long time, taking deep breaths. Then she put the handkerchief and the note carefully back inside the hotel envelope, went to the bathroom and angrily scrubbed the perfume off her hands. She phoned the airport, filled a small bag, and called Mario.

"I have to go home. Take me to the airport, please."

"Home?" asked Mario. He was used to her, this kind girl whom he had served faithfully for so long, and home to her had always been this house and that equally kind man. The Philippines, her family, was always referred to as Manila.

"You can tell Sir Denis when he comes home that Papa is sick." When she made her weekly call to Manila yesterday, Cecilia told her that Francis had the flu, but it was flu season there, and he was feeling better, nothing to worry about.

"I hope he's better soon," said Mario.

"Thank you, Mario."

She was a chance passenger and barely made it. The plane was leaving almost at once. But she had only a small hand-carried bag that she did not have to check in, and first class was not often full.

* * *

Mario met Denis at the door when he arrived and took his briefcase. "Where is she?" Denis asked, the same question he asked of Mario or Milly, whoever one of them opened the door to him when he came home, all these years, the first words he uttered every time he came home, where is she?

"She left for Manila, sir, I thought you knew."

Denis stopped in his track. "Left?" he asked, eyes narrowed, perplexed. "Left?"

"She said the Señor is sick. I drove her to the airport. I thought you knew," Mario repeated.

"Did anyone call from Manila?" Denis thought that maybe she called him at the studio but he couldn't be reached.

"I don't know, sir."

He scaled the stairs two steps at a time. He stripped off his jacket, flung it on a chair and sat down on the bed to call Cecilia. Then he saw the envelope, propped up against the lampshade on his bedside table, the silver tray with the embroidered cloth sitting empty next to it. Even before he touched the envelope he knew it was bad news. He saw the hotel logo, saw the familiar feminine scrawl "Denis" on the center, could smell the perfume, and it was unsealed. He picked up the envelope with fearful fingers, pulled out his handkerchief, read the note on the hotel stationery and was chilled to the bone. He tried to recall his telephone conversation with Laura. He was in such a rush, he thought he would tell her about Susana's visit when he came home. Too late.

He called Cecilia, hoping that Francis was really sick, that someone did indeed call, that Laura was asked to come home. But even before Cecilia answered the phone, he knew that was not so.

The talk with Cecilia did not bring relief.

This was the first time she went back to Manila without him. This was the first time she left their house without him. In fact, this was the first time she went anywhere without him. God, they did not even quarrel. What was there to quarrel about? He had loved her passionately from the first day he met her and every day in their lives, in everything he did, he showed it. He was a besotted lover, unabashed and unashamed of it amid the ribbing of his friends and the teasing of her family that he was "under," under her thumb. There was nothing about her, or his life with her, that he cared to change.

He could do nothing for the next hours while she was in the plane. He went to his study and pored over his lines but it was a futile effort and he gave it up. He paced the floor to tire himself but couldn't sleep when he went to bed. He had never stayed in this house without her. For six years, he would hurry home to her when his day was done and she was always here, waiting for him. He had never been angry with her, and he wasn't now, putting all the blame on himself.

Sleepless, he went to work the next day, and for the first time in his career, bungled his lines. He sleepwalked the hours until it was time to call Manila.

Cecilia answered the phone. "May I speak with her, Cecilia."

"Denis, she did not want to come home. She wanted to be alone and went to a hotel. But she's registered under another name, what, she did not want to say, so there is no way you can talk to her. She promised to be here tomorrow morning. You can call then. I don't even want to ask what this is all about, Denis."

"And I don't think I can tell you. Just believe me when I say that all this is a stupid mistake and if she wants me to suffer for it, she has succeeded immensely, but to deny me the chance to explain is very unfair and unjust."

But there was nothing Cecilia could do for him.

2

*J*oe was waiting for Laura when she entered the Manila airport terminal building. She went straight to his arms and stayed there without moving. She was safe there, nothing had ever hurt her when he was around. After a while, he looked at her and said, "Checked-in bags?" She shook her head. "Very well, come then."

He took her hand in one of his, carried her bag with the other, and they threaded their way through the throng milling around the terminal.

"Yours?" she asked, when he opened the door of the spanking new Citroën for her.

"Papa's," he answered. He swung her bag to the back seat, waited for her to enter, closed the door after her, went to the other side and entered the car. She felt the big car rise a few notches from the ground.

"How did you do that?" she asked.

"Pushed a few buttons," he replied. He searched her face. "How are you?"

"I'm glad you came for me. I don't think I could face anybody else right now. How come you're here? Thought you were in San Sebastian."

"Monthly meeting. I was at your house when Mario called that you were coming home. As usual, I volunteered my services."

"How's everybody?"

"Your Papa was sick, but he's better now. I'm invited to dinner tonight. Everyone will be there."

"Oh, no," she said, chagrined. She did not want to talk about Denis, she did not want to talk about her marriage, she did not want to talk at all. All she wanted was to be left alone. "I don't think I can face anybody now. I don't want to go home, Bud. Can you take me to a hotel?"

He looked at her, but if he was surprised, or did not think much of the idea, he did not say. He nodded slightly and steered the big car out of the airport and into the highway. Typical Joe, asking no questions, expecting no explanations.

From a distance Manila Hotel loomed, its white facade shining bright in the glaring, morning sun. She had always loved this hotel. A long time ago, they would drop by for *merienda* in the dining room overlooking Manila Bay, and they would linger over sandwiches and coffee until the banks of clouds turned purple against the red sunset sky and that spectacular ball of fiery orange that was the setting Manila sun dipped into the waters and the sailboats with their triangulated sails scattered on the horizon composed themselves for the night. Sunset Over Manila Bay, celebrated in books, paintings and song! Before going home, they would roam the corridors, pretending they were guests and Joe would pluck a flower from one of the vases along the corridors and stick it in her hair. The lobby was filled with ornate furniture all carved and wooden. Paintings of Philippine scenes by Filipino artists covered walls, an outsized one in the middle stood larger than life. The dark figures clad in traditional Filipino dress looked down on them like stern sentinels in frozen captivity, looking quite scary. They reminded her of the giant statues of the World War II Memorial to the Landing of Leyte that they saw when they went to that province when they were little. That was a frightening group they presented, that Memorial, determined-looking marble men wading through marble water to marble shore: General Douglas MacArthur towering taller than his six-foot-something frame and his already tall reputation, returning as he promised, dwarfing General Carlos P. Romulo who reached just a breath above his waist. "Is he really that short?" Nacho had asked. "He just looks short," defended Francis, "but here," he tapped his forehead, "he is every inch as tall." At least he did every countryman proud when, belying a nondescript stature, he shone brilliantly as the first Secretary General to the United Nations. The figures looked so real they sent tingles down Laura's spine and, afraid they were going to scoop her up, she scampered back to Francis' arms in panic.

Laura was not surprised that Joe would bring her to this hotel now. They entered the lobby that had stood still in time. The carved furniture was still there, so were the Filipino paintings, the vases of flowers, too.

"Register in another name," Laura told Joe. She smiled when he wrote on the hotel register 'George and Ira Gershwin' and they both laughed when the girl at the desk asked, deadpan, "Any relation to the brothers Gershwin?"

"Here, Ira," Joe said to Laura, "let me take your bag."

Eccentric behavior from visitors did not elicit comments or curious looks. Manila teemed with tourists, and with their looks, they both could pass for European tourists anytime. Tourists spilled unto these expensive hotels, and strange, foreign deportment was looked on with indulgence and tolerance as another one of those idiosyncrasies, familiar and expected of foreigners. Later, when the fateful events unfolded and both their pictures occupied headlines and magazine covers for weeks, nobody in the hotel remembered that they came together to this hotel this day.

Her room was light green and very lavish. The bed in the middle had a satin cover that matched the covers of the sofa and the cushions on the two green chairs grouped in the sitting area. A radio sat on a console against the wall. Joe fiddled with the dial until he found the classical music station and Rachmaninoff's *Second Piano Concerto* filled the room.

"Rach's Second," she sighed, "ah, how I love that piece. Have not listened to it in quite some time, though." She sat on the bed and looked at him. "Selfish me. I did not even ask you how you are. How are you?"

"How else? The question is, how are you?"

She smiled wanly. "I'm just tired. I think I'll just sleep. You may go back to the office, I shall be okay."

"I don't have to go to work today, I'll go tomorrow."

"Is that company still solvent?" she said. "Maybe I should be selling my shares?"

He laughed. "Go ahead and sleep. I'll just sit here and read." He pulled out a paperback from the pocket of his jacket. "Brought my book, see?"

"And he shall have a book wherever he goes," she said. She looked at the book on his lap. "*Brideshead Revisited*? How many times have you read that?"

"Still reads like new."

She arranged her head on the pillow and stifled a yawn with two correct fingers. "When I wake up and you're not here, I'll know you were a good boy and went back to work." Her voice was sleepy and muffled under her hand as she composed herself for sleep. "And Bud, thanks for being here," she said and closed her eyes. In a little while, he knew that she was asleep. He took off her shoes and put them neatly under the bed. He stood there looking at her, at the frown on her brow. He touched her face gently with flitting fingers. After a while, he called Cecilia. He settled himself on the sofa and watched Laura for a long time. Then he opened his book where he left off at the airport.

She slept for hours. She would open her eyes, see Joe reading and, reassured, drift back to sleep. Denis floated in and out of her dreams, kissing away her ache, smiling at her sweetly, somehow not the evil face unfaithful husbands were so often depicted to be, so real she woke up feeling more depressed. Crystal mornings, crisp air smelling of pine, clear brooks rushing over smooth, white stones, she thought, trying to lift herself out of her depression, an abundance of laurels in bloom. No, not laurels. Laurels meant Denis.

She turned her head and saw Joe fast asleep on the sofa, the book clasped to his chest. His long legs, clad in jeans, were stretched out before him, his feet in white socks and loafers, one of several he owned. He owned the most pair of shoes of anybody she knew, and that included Denis.

Sleep had wiped away the perpetual look of concern on his face, making him look like a little boy. She smiled looking at his pink shirt. A long time ago, when pink was still entrenched in the province of women's fashion and other men were balking at wearing such a female-associated color, his confidence in his sense of style and in his masculinity was overwhelming that he would wear pink, and not think twice about it, knowing that nothing could detract from his very male look, and that he looked good in it.

She remembered that summer in the hacienda when he got his first pink shirt. Franz gave it to him in jest for his feast day, the feast of St. Joseph, running out of ideas on what to give a cousin who had everything.

"Pink? Why pink?" he asked, looking pained.

"Why not pink? I would not mind wearing pink," said Franz, who would not be caught dead in it.

"I would not mind wearing pink, either," Laura echoed.

Joe put the shirt on and yes, it looked good on him.

He turned to Laura. "You like it?"

"I love it. Looks very good on you. Yes," she said, nodding her head in approval. The best looking Steiner, she always thought him, in a family with an exorbitance of good looks.

How their lives were intertwined. She could not remember a time when he was not there when she needed him, in the sad and happy times, in the familiar and newly discovered places, in the mornings and evenings of a youth that she always thought was perfect, a long time ago.

Thank God for good things that never change, this cousin who was always there for her.

She rose, went over to him and kissed him on the check.

He opened his eyes but stayed still, watching her leaning over him. He knew if he stirred, she would go away, as she always did in his countless dreams, invading his nights, then leaving him empty and heart sore when he awoke.

She gave him a slight smile. "Hi, sleepyhead," said. "No, no," she held down his shoulder when he started to get up, "go back to sleep. I'll just take a shower."

He found his bearings, wiped the sleep off his eyes with the back of his hand. "I fell asleep," he said thickly. He held her arm, there leaning over him. "Are you hungry?" he asked.

"If you are."

"Want anything special?"

"Anything you want."

"All right. I'll make reservations while you bathe." He called Cecilia again. "She just woke up. I'll take her to dinner. No, we haven't talked yet. She seems okay."

She came out of the bathroom, her damp hair combed back, carrying a towel, dressed and ready but without her shoes, which Joe had left under her bed. She sat down on the bed and started to wipe her feet with the towel.

"Here, let me," he said and knelt in front of her. With the towel he dried her feet. She had the small feet of Spanish women, Cecilia's feet, deep-instepped, rose-heeled, the nail polish stark red against the white skin. Ah, he thought, perfect.

"There," he said. "Powder?" he asked and looked up at her.

"Forgot to bring," she said and smiled sadly at him.

He saw the anguish on her face. He paused, hesitating to enter that area that he allowed himself only in his imaginings, but he could not help himself now. "Damn him. How long has this been going on? And how often has he been doing this to you?" He raised himself up and sat on the bed beside her. She tried to avoid his eyes and averted hers, looked at the window but there was none, tried to blink the tears back into where they came from. He smoothed a tendril of hair that, now dry, had sprung away from the rest, slicked back, still damp. "Oh, Bud, I can't bear to see you like this. Can you tell me about it?"

Here he was, her champion all her life, the one person who had never hurt her. And breaking down, she did, through muffled voice and heartrending sobs, breaking out of her in torrents that his tender concern fed.

He looked at her, at how miserable she was, and all the years of holding back seemed wasted, squandered in vain. He had stepped back, because he was told he would not be good for her. That was what he had been made to believe, and for what? Just to let someone else be exactly that. No, be worse than that. How often had that husband cheated on her and how often had she suffered like this?

He held her while she wept, and through the deafening drumbeat that was his heart, he could feel hers pressed closely to his own.

And so it happened, at the moment when she was most vulnerable, hurt and angry at what she thought was her husband's infidelity, unprotected by the perfect marriage that had always shielded her. And he, seeing how much she was hurting, this wondrous being whom he had loved for so long, had loved for as long as he could remember, was too overcome to stop the onrushing emotions that he had worked so hard to subdue. He had not had a drink since she arrived, but not even this cold, singular sobriety could help him now. He fell, headlong, helpless, past caring, into such sweet deeds, deeds that, before this, happened only in his dreams, his long smoldering storms at thought of her bursting forth unrestrained, fires that he had banked exploding inside him until he feared his heart would burst open. And she, who grew up believing that things were so because Joe said so, was caught up with him, caught off guard when it started and then quite powerless to stop him, not knowing how.

* * *

He came down from that height to where he had been transported and passed her, looking at him with eyes fringed with those impossibly thick lashes. He held her close and shuddered at the fact of her nearness. He wanted to weep in gratitude, get down on his knees in supplication: Oh, God, let this day last just a little bit longer, leave that sun alone in that sky, hold back those stars from coming out, stop those clocks from telling time. Please God, just a little bit more, just a little bit longer, and You can do with me what You will. But later.

He felt her stir. He touched her face gently. "How are you?"

She looked at him with mournful eyes. "Twenty-six years of nothing sins that bored those priests to tears, then, faster than I could say mea culpa, adultery and ince...."

"Don't," he said with such force it stopped the awful word from pouring out. He covered her lips with his hand. "Don't," he repeated, quietly this time. "I wish I could say I'm sorry, but I'm not. We did not plan this to happen. I have not seen two people who have tried more to do what's right. But we are not divine and could fall. And God forgive me, but I'm not sorry it happened."

He ran his fingers through her still-damp hair, slid his hand behind her head and brought her face up close to his. "Marry me," he said passionately. "Divorce him and come with me. We shall get an annulment."

"What are you saying?" He was swamping her with surprises.

"I love you. Ever since I can remember, I've loved you. I cannot remember a time when I did not love you. Before I knew what love was, I'm sure I already loved you. All these lonely years I could not let you go."

If she had led the life of a normal teenager, hang out with friends, gossiped with them, went to movies with them, read what teenagers read, and had a more energetic social life than the zero she actually had, she would have known that these things could happen, would have seen it coming and would have steered clear. But she was reticent and retiring, her involvements private and familial, her interests less worldly, more cerebral. She was pliant and not at all headstrong, and was easy for Cecilia to discipline, and did not rebel at an upbringing more strict and more protective than was the trend at the time or was good for her. From Cecilia's protection she graduated to Denis', more sheltering and exclusive than Cecilia's even; Denis, who filled her days, who hurried home to her at the end of his, who couldn't stand a night without her and carted her wherever he went. And so at twenty-six, married for six years, she was still as naive and as guileless as when she got married, and was laid exposed and vulnerable to Joe's passion, uncontrolled now that he had laid it bare and open, at last, before her.

"But why had you never told me?"

"How could I? There was nothing I could have done against the family's objections. Oh, the furor we would have caused."

"Still, since this had something to do with my life, I wish that you had told me, had let me make my own decision."

"You were so young, our parents, *Tita* Ceil, would have been so against it, and I did not think I could take her on at that time. You had always been such a compliant daughter, I could not risk antagonizing her and in the process, maybe you, too. I would have been so alone, you see. But I had no intentions of giving you up. In time I knew I had to tell you. I was just biding my time. You were such a child, I could not believe you could be swept off your feet so fast. What was it about him, anyway? Less than a week, that was all it took him! God, I can't even begin to tell you how I felt when *Tita* Ceil called to say you were getting married. I did not want to come to New York with Franz, and yet how could I let you go without seeing you? You read about heavens falling about you and hearts breaking to pieces and you say to yourself, surely books exaggerate, writers embellish. And then it happens to you and yes, the heavens do fall about you and hearts do break to pieces. You broke my heart, Laura Steiner."

"Oh, Bud," she said and touched his face gently.

Bud. He and Franz went to Europe with his parents and when they came back, she said she missed him, she did not have a buddy to play with when he was away. Play with! But she was only twelve and that name established for a lifetime how she regarded him, more than hero, more than teacher, more than giver of attention---a buddy she missed when he was away.

* * *

He lay on his back, looked up at the ceiling.

"Do you remember that time when you came home from Wellesley for Christmas vacation and there was a party Christmas Eve at your house? Even now, I can still see you clearly. You came in while everyone was already there and you looked just ravishing, I knew my breath caught in my throat. I had always been careful with the way I looked at you when people were around, but I hadn't seen you in months and you looked different. You had filled out somehow and you showed it in that very sophisticated dress. I tried not to think of you in a physical way, or I knew I would be undone, but that night you just ravished me, I knew I could not hold myself much longer. I knew it was time; I had to tell you before you went back. And then fate, or rather, my grandfather, stepped in.

"That old man. We were always so attuned; he always seemed to know how I felt about everything. He must have seen how I looked at you that night, must have known that I could not keep things to myself much longer.

"Anyway, that night. I was already in bed, listening to my music when he came into my room. 'Mahler's Fifth,' he said. 'How haunting that Adagietto is. Mahler wrote that movement when he was courting Alma, before he married her, you know?' I knew. You read that in the accompanying notes of records, but I did not say anything. I knew he was making small talk before he launched into something bigger.

"He sat on my bed and said, 'Do you know that I love you very much, even more than I love my own children, have I told you that?' 'No, you haven't,' I said, 'but I know.' 'You have made me very proud of you,' he said. 'You are everything I would have wanted my own son to be. Well, maybe too overly fond of the bottle, but to each his own way of facing the world, I say,' he smiled. 'But, on the whole, I'm very happy with how you've turned out, with all the spoiling that everybody did of you. Going for your master's degree from that school, no less.' I was always glad I worked on that, if only because that was the one thing he had always been most proud of about me. Sort of his armor when people say I drink too much, like saying, that may be so but look, he's at Oxford, going for his master's.

"Then the clincher. 'Laura, she looked lovelier tonight than I ever saw her.' I knew then that that was why he came, to talk about you. There was nothing I could say, and he continued,

'Cecilia did a very good job with her children, but especially with that one.'

"Again I let that pass without comment. 'You know,' he went on, "if circumstances were different, and for your sake you don't know how many times I've wished they were, I would be the first to tell you that you couldn't make a better choice and that you have my blessings.' I was about to protest, but he held up a hand. 'I've known how you feel, for a very long time.' He smiled a small, wan smile. 'Sad to say, circumstances are not different and for that, my heart aches for you, too. But you are responsible for the children that you bring into this world and your children's children after that. I know it's an awesome responsibility to know that your choices now will have repercussions for generations to come but that's how it is. And knowing Cecilia's unfortunate family history, I don't think you could take a chance. Think of Laura, and the heartache, and the devastation, when children like those pitiful cousins of hers start coming. The guilt would be more yours than hers, since that girl looks up to you and would do anything you say. And in the end, the decision would really be all yours. Have you seen those unfortunate children?' I nodded. 'And you allowed yourself to go farther?'"

3

hose Unfortunate Children. The Cousins. Whispered words in childhood that he and his brother and sisters often heard in undertones. The grown-ups used to shush them when they asked questions and for a long time The Cousins inhabited their infantile imaginations as the white-gowned something lurking in a mysterious room down a long spectral corridor, the ghost who could leap at them if they got too familiar, the ashen-faced child furtively peeking out a doorway they glimpsed in their peripheral vision who disappeared once they turned their heads, the secret that everybody knew was there but nobody talked about.

Close as they were, it took a long time, they were quite adults, in fact, when, without any prodding, quite without emotion, Franz opened up and told him about these cousins, the disastrous results of inbreeding in Cecilia's family, those heartbreaking, tragic, genetic aftermath of cousins marrying cousins, the shadows that darkened a corner of Cecilia's otherwise pristine perfection.

He had been to Santo Niño numerous times before he saw one of them. She was propped up in a wheelchair, this girl of indeterminate age (fifteen? twenty?), long white legs stretched out in front of her, head lolling to one side. At first he thought she was asleep, sitting there so still. Then, at the sound of their voices, she turned and looked up at them, a face so hauntingly tragic, with the blankest eyes he had ever seen that sent shivers down his spine, and those feared figments of long-ago imaginings came back to haunt him.

Laura cooed at her. "Hi, Cari, we came to visit you." With one finger she tickled her neck. Cari smiled and cooed back at her, non-words, unintelligible, unbearable. She grasped Laura's finger and wouldn't let go. Joe could not take it and, sick of heart, walked away.

"She's so lovely," he said later.

"She's a mongrel, too, like me, with ancestors all over Europe," Laura said.

Later he asked Franz. "Did you say there are others?"

"Yes, but I don't think you will see them. They're not exactly hidden, but visits are not encouraged either."

But he did see others, in other visits, some not quite as touchingly tragic as this one, but still wringing his heart, filling it with dread. These could be your children, he warned himself, if you don't wrest yourself away from this obsession with Laura. But of course he was never able to be free of her, no matter how much he applied himself.

How long ago that time was and how frightening the specters it conjured, but the long years and the dark shadows could not touch a love that knew no dimming.

Now he looked around him, at this room in Manila Hotel, the height of luxury at any other time, now looking tired and jaded and uninspired against the white rooms, the petal-strewn bed with gossamer curtains, the ceilings of stars and deep blue skies where, in his compulsive imaginings, he would have brought her to, the first time they would have come together, for what meaning would his wealth hold if he could not use it to get the opulence beyond imagination that he would lay at her feet. But although there were no limits to the luxury with which he longed to cover her in his fantasies, in his reality, he would scrounge for crumbs if they came from her and be thankful for them.

He turned towards her. "What I did not say to my grandfather was that I did not have a choice where you were concerned. Despite the bad genes, through all the other women, I just could not get you out of my system. Reason and judgment and choices, or even a strong will, had nothing to do with it. I simply just loved you, that was all there was to it. But if I was willing to risk hell for myself, I could not pull you down with me. I loved you too much for that. And so, what else could I do but carry this burden all to myself?

"Six months later, you were falling in love, although alas, not with me, and a few months after that my grandfather was dead and I had not told you both how much I loved you, besides Franz, the two people I love most in the world. So many things left unspoken, so many regrets."

"I cried so when I received your letter telling me of his death, so full of sorrow, and I wanted to comfort you but I was a world away," she said. "I loved that man, too, you know that. Such a cultured person. I've always found it amazing how different he was from his own children and how so much alike you two were."

"It's like insanity. It skips a generation," he said.

"That's not so." They both laughed. He twirled a curl of her hair around his finger. So many times in the past he had wanted to do that, and as many times had to rein himself in.

He became serious and took her hands in his, small things in his big ones. "You do love me, too, don't you?"

"Oh, I do, you know I do." She held his face and said earnestly, "but not this way."

"But not this way," he repeated, breathing deeply. "Well, no matter. I have enough love for both of us. I shall love you like you could not imagine a man is capable of loving a woman that you could not help but love me in return. I'll wait. I've already waited a lifetime, what else can I do. In time you'll learn. I shall be a patient teacher, as I have always been."

"You were not. You were a hard teacher. Thomas Aquinas when I was just a kid! I did not tell you lest you'd think less of me. But he was difficult to read and he bored me, you know."

He laughed. "I knew, that was why I did not press you too hard, went easy on you. But you did learn to love him, didn't you? And you could learn to love me too? This way?"

She looked at him sadly. "Oh, Bud, can't you see how impossible this is?"

"How impossible can it be? You're not going back to him after this. Then let's get an annulment. Can't you see? This is a second chance for us and I'm damned if I'm giving you up again. Not again. I need you, God, do you even have an idea how much I need you? I just can't let you go ever again."

He had always been there when she needed him, he was always doing things for her and for their other cousins, he knew before she did when she needed anything, always anticipating her needs, but she never knew him to need her or anybody, except perhaps Franz. He always seemed sufficient unto himself; she had often marveled at how complete he seemed, if he just had his books and his bottle, and a liberal sprinkling of Franz.

"I need you. Without you I might as well be dead. Do you know how terrible it is to be dead before you die? Really dead. But I was, dead all these years, not seeing you, not being able to talk to you, knowing I could never have you. I was a walking zombie days and dead drunk nights."

"I still think you should have told me."

"Would it have made a difference? Would you have loved me, too, had you known?"

Maybe not, she thought. She was taught early on that she shouldn't, she mustn't, think of him as anything but a cousin.

"Anyway," Joe said. "I almost did tell you, that summer we were in the hacienda before you went to Switzerland, remember? We were in the attic and we found those love letters tied with ribbons and the *Canzoniere*. And you cried reading those letters."

"Yes, I did," she remembered. "Franz kept on saying, 'Will you stop that sniffling. I can't understand what you're reading.' Then he went into a tirade about how women cry when they're happy and when they're sad, and when they're angry, and when they're etcetera, etcetera. He was such a scold."

"And I felt an ache in my heart, looking at you sitting on that floor, in that lacy dress." He had stayed immobile looking at her, the afternoon sunlight suffusing her and her hair with a muted glow, making sure that that moment stayed in his memory forever for, no matter what fate dealt him after that day, he knew he would never again see a picture more perfect than she was at that moment. He still carried the memory of that summertime deep inside him where special riches were kept, even after all the fruits had fallen on the ground, and the flowers had shaken off their heavy petals, and the summer fragrance had turned heady with the earthy smells of ripeness. And sometimes, when missing her seemed beyond enduring, like a miser he would open the floorboards and take out that memory, hold it tenderly in his mind, savor it with all his senses. Then he would put it back just as tenderly, snap shut the floorboards of his memory and hit the bottle until reprieved by drunken oblivion. "Looking back now, I don't think I have ever been as happy as I was that summer in that old house. It seems to me that all the times in my life that I recall as happy were because you were there. And you were happy that summer too, weren't you?"

Yes, she was.

4

*T*hat lazy, golden summer that could blind with so much beauty. The oleander and frangipani trees wore a riot of blossoms, the gardenias were too waxy white against their too-green leaves, and the cosmos, white and yellow and the new lavender, waved in the breezes, clamoring for space, lightweights trying to edge out Cecilia's roses---the old, fragrant ramblers and climbers that she liked better than the tea roses---their stems thick with blooms, leaning lazily against white picket fences. The air was heavy with all the earthy smells and bees droned everywhere. Wisteria clung to terrace columns that reached the second-story balcony of that big house. They did not even know that wisteria grew in the tropics, but there they were, had been there ever since they could remember, maybe brought over by their grandparents from abroad, the blue-violet petals clustered among the leaves in profusion. Once in a while, a breeze coaxed the petals gently from the stems and they came whirling, twirling down in slow motion, rested languidly on the ground below and on the terrace floor, and the red bricks were strewn with the blue and violet blossoms. The big house blazed white in the sun, blue and white antique ceramic pots scattered on the wide porch choked with begonias and hydrangea that they called million flowers. Gladioli and crepe myrtle lined pathways, like so many sentinels in colorful uniforms.

What a glorious time it was. Franz was in love. Her name was Regina and she, too, went to Laura's school. She was a class ahead of Laura, although Laura could not call her a friend. They would smile and nod in greeting when they met in the school corridors and that was about the extent of their friendship. It was not until Franz met her in one of Laura's school dances, and they went out a few times, that she went out of her way to be nice to Laura. Laura neither liked nor disliked her. Regina was just one of those people who did not leave much of an impression on her. Then home on vacation from Oxford, Franz met her again at a party, some forgotten embers sparked anew and they started going out in earnest.

He invited Regina to visit San Sebastian and they spent two whole weeks in the hacienda, the two of them and Joe and Laura for chaperones.

That summer! The trees were heavy with fruit and Franz showed off, climbing to tops of guava trees, dropping the fruits to the girls waiting below, and they would catch the fruits with their skirts. Milly made guava jelly and guava jam and all sorts of guava recipes until Franz protested, "Enough! We smell of guavas already."

They found avocados that had dropped from the trees, concealed like chameleons nestled among the grass, some ready for eating. "Do you know that this is one fruit that cannot ripen on the tree? You have to pick them and put them away to ripen," Franz told Regina. "Go, Lauren, take these to Milly, tell her to make salad for lunch."

"Why me?" Laura protested.

"The youngest gets to gofer, or get scolded, isn't that the rule? Or you don't want to be mascot anymore?"

"The mascot is also the gofer?"

"Do be a good girl and obey your elders," said Joe indulgently.

"Aw, all right," said Laura, resigned.

They spent hours in the attic, going through their grandmother's trunk, where they found the letters, the books of poems with flowers pressed on their pages, Petrarch's *Canzoniere*, and the diary.

They found long, lacy, embroidered dresses from the trunk. Milly aired and sunned them and Laura tried them on. "You look good in that," approved Franz.

"Have Milly put your hair up," said Joe. All summer long she wore the old dresses, had her hair rolled up and looked like a picture from the past.

They decided to renovate the attic and Franz and Joe came up with pink paint and some frilly materials they had dug up from somewhere. But Laura thought of their grandmother as a no-nonsense woman, more Marlene Dietrich than Jean Harlow, and would surely disapprove of pink and frilly and, being the artist in the group, they made her manager of renovations. They drove to the city and bought white paint, instead, and some light blue, striped material for bedcovers and curtains, tons of food, cartons of cigarettes, and of course, the ubiquitous, requisite Spanish brandy---Fundador, and the more favored Carlos I. "Know what?" said Franz, "maybe we should buy shares of Pedro Domecq, the way we just guzzle this stuff."

Franz let Laura take sips from his drink but she had one too many one night and had a miserable hangover the next day, and never tried the stuff again. Joe let her take puffs from his cigarettes but one time she inhaled too deeply and went into a paroxysm of coughing and hurt her nostrils. But she liked the smell of cigarettes, and just swirled the smoke in her mouth before blowing it out, the original did-not-inhale kid.

"I don't know how your Mom could choose Wellesley over Oxford," said Joe. She had just graduated from high school and hoped she would go to England, too, since Franz and Joe were already at Oxford. Cecilia's two younger sisters went to Wellesley, however, thought very highly of it, and talked Cecilia into sending Laura there.

'Wellesley should be good. If I get to be like my Mom's sisters, that would be quite an accomplishment. You yourself said they are two of the classiest people you've met."

Joe did, but he never imagined that they could be instrumental in sending Laura to another continent far removed from the ones he knew.

"I don't know how Mom could think three months in Switzerland could finish you. I should think you'd need three years. At the very least," said Franz, stressing the last four words. She was going to the finishing school in Switzerland in June, after which she was proceeding to Wellesley in September.

When they had had enough of work, they picnicked on a grassy knoll under flowering trees, where Franz and Regina spent the afternoon talking, Joe reading and Laura sleeping.

"She has to sleep after she eats," observed Franz, looking at Laura composing herself for sleep.

"She sleeps after everything," Joe observed. "I have never seen anyone for sleeping. How tall are you now? Five five, five six? And you're just sixteen. Better put a lid on it. You'd be taller than all the boys and you'd never get a date."

"How tall are you now? Six, six one?" Laura mumbled sleepily, "and you're just nineteen. Anyway, I'll never be taller than you, and you'll always be there."

"She can't even get a date now," said Franz.

"Girls don't grow after sixteen," she said.

"Not so," said Franz, "remember Sister Marian? When she was sent to Ireland by the Sisters of Mercy, she guzzled down the good sisters' supply of milk and they sent her back two inches taller, remember?"

One night it stormed. Lightning pierced the sky outside, thunder rattled the windows and the wind shook doors and rafters. It was a night just perfect for telling ghost stories and playing Spirit of the Glass. They wrote numbers and letters on a big, square piece of brown pattern paper. Then they each placed a finger lightly on a drinking glass and, to their horror, watched the glass move. They accused Franz of pushing the glass, Franz, looking innocent, accused Joe of doing it and in delicious fright, they watched the glass glide over the paper even after the four of them together had lifted their fingers off the glass. But pushed or not, the glass did move and gave them preposterous answers to their equally preposterous questions. After that, Regina and Laura refused to sleep in their bedrooms and they all decided to sleep in the living room, the four of them, Regina and Laura on the white, wide, deep-cushioned sofas, Franz and Joe on the floor, on mattresses the maids had pulled from some beds somewhere, and they slept there for the remainder of the vacation. They walked to town and Franz and Joe, having exhausted their bottles of brandy, bought Tanduay Rum, the only respectable drink they could find in the country stores, and the two spent the nights drinking.

"Here," said Franz to Regina, handing her a drink, "try this." She handled her drink too well they suspected that that was not her first.

The girls did not want to give up the day and, sleepy-eyed on the sofa, listened while Franz and Joe, on mattresses on the floor, the drinks on the floor between them, begrudging the hours wasted in sleep, talked until dawn.

"Why didn't you ask Emily to come?" Franz wanted to know. Joe had been going out with Emily, an American who was studying at the university in Manila, and Franz had hoped something serious would come out of that.

"He broke off with her," Laura volunteered.

"That's not so," corrected Joe, "she broke off with me."

"Broke off?" Franz sat up in his surprise.

"'My dearest Joe,'" Laura held out her hands, pretending to read from an imaginary letter, "'I can feel that you need some time off from me and so I decided to spend a month with my parents in the States. I do hope, Joe dearest, that things will be different when I come back.' Sure," she chortled, all mischievous merriment, "things will be different when she comes back. She won't see him again. Hahaha," she threw her head back and laughed heartily.

"You're such a bad girl, you know. Next time, I won't let you read my mail," said Joe, but her laugher was infectious and he could not help but laugh, too.

"Why didn't I know of this?" asked Franz.

"I was going to tell you, in due time," replied Joe.

"But I thought," Franz did not finish, then was exasperated. "But why? Beauty like that you don't find every day, bright, too. I thought she was the only girl you went out with who could discuss Aquinas between kisses. What happened to that?"

Joe laughed. "Well, she also went the way of those who kissed in silence."

"But why?" persisted Franz.

Joe shrugged his shoulders. "Guess, like my drink, I like my kisses straight, too, sometimes. She just did not know when to spout Aquinas and when to shut up." He shrugged, "Sorry." He poured more rum into his glass. He looked at Franz frowning at him. "I don't know, Franz. Things just got boring, that's all."

"Bored with that face? You know, with the kind of brains you're looking for, the face most often is boring, and with the kind of face you're looking for, the brain usually is boring. It's very seldom the twain meet. What more do you want?"

"I don't know. Maybe she was trying too hard it was not fun anymore, who knows. I'm not like you. You have to hold everything in your hands and quantify it and qualify it and analyze it to death. I can't explain why I feel this way about one thing and not that way about another. I just feel. All I know is that I feel strongly about some things and not about others and I don't even know why."

"That's bull and you know it," Franz said. "Don't give me the I-don't-knows. You're just too lazy and too selfish. The truth is that you just don't want to share that precious space in there that you treasure so. That was it, wasn't it? You just don't want anybody in there."

"You're there."

"I'm there, too," piped Laura earnestly. Joe and Franz looked at her, looking so serious, forgotten until she spoke, and they both laughed.

"We should not be enough for you," Franz relented. "Rouse yourself up a little bit."

Joe took a drink from his glass and grimaced. "Ah, the day will come, no hurry."

"Famous last words of a lazy person. I don't know what will happen to your social life when I shan't be there any longer."

"Ah, but you will always be there. You know, whither thou goest," he started laughing.

"Me too, me too, whither thou goest I go, too," said Laura.

* * *

They rose with the sun, awakened long before by the incessant chirp-chirp, chirp-chirp of birds nesting on the trees outside the windows, then they walked the kilometer to church to attend Mass. After Mass, they went to the marketplace and, seated on long bamboo-slat benches in front of a bare wooden table, ordered *chocolaté* and *puto*, that delicious confection made of sticky rice, the perfect mate for the *chocolaté e*, they called it, *chocolaté espeso*, so thick it refused to drip fast enough from their spoons. Then they walked briskly home, to take care of the calorie-laden breakfast, but when a *bagon* stacked with sugarcane passed them, they hitched a ride, their legs over the side dangling in time to the chug chug chug of the slow-moving open train. They taught Regina how to eat sugarcane---choose the fattest cane and with your teeth, tear away the bark and suck the pulp to extract the sweet juice.

A tenant who was charged with gathering tuba from the coconut trees gathered young coconuts for them, and they drank the milk and scraped and ate the still-translucent meat straight out of the shell, with the milk oftentimes dribbling down their cheeks unto their clothes. Sometimes they found, among the bunch of coconuts, a macapuno, that aberrant coconut offspring filled entirely with meat without the usual milk, and Milly made macapuno pastillas and macapuno ice cream for them, with fresh milk, extracted just that morning.

Franz and Joe would come up with silly anecdotes they read somewhere. From Franz: "Know what the cow said when she was milked by one of those machines?" "What?" "'Somehow I miss the personal touch.'"

They were in their element when they had had too much to drink. "There was this drunk, see. He staggered out of a bar with a bottle of whiskey in his back pocket. Well, he slipped and fell flat on his back. He scrambled to his feet, fearfully checked his back pocket and felt something wet there. 'By god,' he cried out, 'I hope it's blood.'"

"Your sentiments exactly," said Laura.

Milly boiled fresh milk and after it had cooled, Franz and Joe fought over who would skim the thick skin that had formed on top of the milk. Then Franz would drink from a glass and come up with a cream mustache, which he would wipe away with the back of his hand, spreading the cream over his checks, and which Regina would wipe with her handkerchief or kiss away.

Milly, who adored the boys, whipped up her special Spanish dishes that were their favorites---*callos* and *paella* and endless plates of her incomparable *tapas,* a must when they were drinking, just pure eating pleasure when they were not. "What are you chewing there?" Joe asked Laura. She dipped her hand in her pocket and came up with a chunk of *tapa.* "Ay, girl, that's why the dog was following you, you smell of dried meat," he chided but tossed the meat into his mouth.

Joe was a giving, caring person and although his quietness gave the impression of indifference, he had a sincere interest in the lives of the battery of servants and tenants who attended to their needs, who supplied the services that made their lives easier and more comfortable, inquiring after them and their children in a caring fashion, paying tuition fees or hospital bills with his own money, and these servants and tenants returned his kindness with adoration. "You spend so much money on these people," Laura observed once when Joe wrote out a check for a hospital bill of one of their tenants.

"Remember this," Joe said seriously, holding her chin so she had to look at him, "you are a big tree. I hope it shall never be said that people cannot take refuge in your shade."

That lazy summer! They spread out blankets on the grass under the trees, amongst the flowers, and the wind shook the branches of the frangipani trees and their fragrant, satiny flowers rained down on them. Franz and Regina would converse in mellow tones while Laura, who could not take so many sleepless nights, would doze wherever her head found anything to lean on. Joe beside her would read a book from one of the bundles with which he had armed himself, dipping his hand into squat jars of peanut brittle while he read, or *lenguas del gato* that Milly baked, and from inside the house, they could hear Maria Callas singing Mimi from *La Boheme*, or the sweet strains of the music of Brahms and Schumann, and Laura's great love then, Rachmaninoff, drifting through the open windows.

"I wonder how Grieg came up with these haunting names for his pieces---*Elegiac Melody, The Wounded Heart, The Last Spring*," Laura commented.

"Yup," said Franz without missing a beat, "*'March of the Dwarfs.'*"

"And *'Morning Mood',*" said Joe. "Come, let's see what Milly is whipping up for breakfast."

And Grieg's *I Love Thee*. To this day, Laura could not hear this piece and not recall those afternoons, of Regina playing the record over and over again, lest they put on another classical piece that she found interminable and unrecognizable. Franz had played that piece and told her, "There, that should not be too hard for you," and indeed it wasn't. But just that one piece, again and again, determined to have a foot inside their door, but deaf to the strains of the classical music that they so loved. It was the only classical piece that appealed to her ears, ears that preferred the crash, boom and rumble of rock music, records of which, of course, she could not find in the house.

Joe would sing his favorite song those days, *You go to my head*, in a low, muted voice, accompanying himself on the piano, *and you linger like a haunting refrain, and I find you spinning round in my brain, like the bubbles in a glass of champagne*.

"Oh, I love that song." Laura, catching up, would sit next to him, hum snatches of the tune, and sing a few lines with him.

You go to my head, with a smile that makes my temperature rise, like a summer with a thousand Julys, you intoxicate my soul with your eyes. Franz would join, standing behind Joe, his hands on Joe's shoulders, singing with much ardor. *Though I'm certain that this heart of mine, hasn't a ghost of a chance in this crazy romance, you go to my head.*

* * *

"He likes her a lot, doesn't he?" Regina observed to Franz one afternoon. She had always found Joe rather chilly and forbidding, talking little, laughing less. With his money, she thought, he could do what he darned well pleased. Still, it was strange how different he was when he was with Franz and Laura, how much he and Franz enjoyed each other's company, how tenderly he treated Laura, giving her all his attention and his indulgent smiles, breaking out in approving laughter at her comments, listening carefully to whatever things she talked about.

"Likes?" said Franz, "He loves her. We all do. Every brother should have a sister like her."

Serves you right, Regina scolded herself. Her sisters always said that she bore malice towards all. If that was so, so be it. She did not care.

Regina was one for gossiping, and could never understand how anybody could not be interested in who went out with whom, what they did where, who had more money than whom, but every attempt she made to talk about people was met with icy quiet from Joe and Laura. Franz, not wanting to discomfit her, would venture a few comments that would send them off laughing.

Regina remembered the time when her family did not have money. Then her father won some contract with the government, through ways that were quite suspect, she suspected. So what, her father said, everybody bribed the government. Spread the wealth, he used to say. And then they had more money than they had ever imagined. They were yanked from the inferior public schools; her brothers were sent to the prestigious and very expensive Jesuit boys' school (which the Steiner boys attended,) and she and her sisters to the exclusive, and equally expensive, Catholic girls' school.

Where she saw Laura and her sisters. Even in that school where class seemed to be every girl's middle name, the Steiner girls were in a class by themselves. And so were the Steiner boys, in that Jesuit school along the way---Nacho, that boy who always wore a smile, and RJ, cast in an entirely different mold, more tall-dark-and-handsome Gomez than fair Steiner, and Joe and Franz, tow-headed, terribly good-looking, rushing forth in Joe's MG. She remembered thinking how splendidly they carried their splendid selves, in their splendid clothes and their splendid cars.

In one of their school's social breakfasts, she saw Cecilia. She did not think she had seen a more youthful mother, or one lovelier. Most mothers of the girls were also alumnae of this school. Joe's mother, one of the fabulous Gomez girls, went there, and so did his sisters. All of a sudden, nouveau riche sounded pitiably inferior to Regina's snobbish ears. All the snobbish prejudices in her came up to the surface. She wished her own mother could buy some class, with all the money they now had. She looked at her mother, fat (pleasingly plump, she would insist), with chunks of diamonds on rings and pendants and earrings, so early in the morning, too, and suddenly, she was ashamed of her, and of course was instantly ashamed of herself for thinking so. Then Joe and Franz went to Oxford, and she did not see them again until they came home one vacation. They met again at a party, and Franz invited her to spend a couple of weeks in their hacienda.

She did not know what Franz saw in her, why he chose her from among so many, but whatever it was, she was not going to jeopardize it with her brand of snide insinuations.

Now, she looked at Laura sleeping peacefully on a blanket spread under a leafy tree, a breeze lightly blowing tendrils of hair off her forehead, at Joe and his inevitable book lounging beside her, reading while munching peanut brittle from a fat, wide-mouthed jar after he had demolished the *lenguas del gato*. Why should she insist on opening Franz' eyes, if he and his family wanted theirs looking the other way from, or better still, closed to Joe's, touching looks. It was enough that they were beginning to thaw towards her, those icebergs. She knew that Joe's opinions mattered a great deal to Franz. And so, looking at Joe and Laura, she kept her peace and looked the other way, too.

"I wish we had some records to dance to, then Regina could teach us the tango, maybe," Laura said one afternoon.

"Come, then, let's get some," said Joe.

"Where?"

"Let's drive to the city, that's where. Come on, lazy bones, get up, let's go shopping," he said. Well, good, Regina thought, all this isolation and all that music by composers long dead were getting much too heavy for her, Franz notwithstanding.

They drove to the city, with Regina and Franz smooching in the back seat. Laura stole glances at the rearview mirror. "Do they bother you?" Joe asked.

"Not unless I look, and I don't, not much, anyway," Laura replied. "All that pawing, for crissakes, I'm glad I'm not in love."

Joe chuckled. "Your time will come, and then you'll like it, too. Just don't hurry it, okay?"

"Did you like it as much with Emily?"

"I liked it as much with Emily, yes."

"With Ana too, and who else went before her?"

"I liked it as much with Ana, too, and who else went before her, yes. Who else went before her, anyway?"

"Ah, yes, Sherry, her name was. With her, too?"

"All right, all right, let's not confuse the two here. I like it very much with my sherry, in a glass, poured straight from the bottle."

"Heh, heh, heh, funny man." She paused, "did you and Emily really discuss Aquinas between kisses?"

"She discussed, yes. I rather did not like to discuss, no. But I guess Emily did like it very much, too."

"If she had to pepper her kisses with Aquinas, then they were not exciting enough," she pronounced.

"Alas," he sighed, "I'm afraid they were not."

With the tango records, Regina picked up some Frank Sinatra records, with the song *'Drinking Again,'* teasing Joe that he should make that his own personal song. Joe replenished his supply of books and, of course, their indispensable bottles of brandy.

They laughed watching Joe dance, with a cigarette dangling from his lips, all long limbs and left feet. "Joe Steiner, never been much of a dancer," Laura said.

That perfect summer! Everyone was so happy, Franz was so happy.

At first, after Franz and Joe went back to Oxford, Franz and Regina burned the telephone lines and burdened the postal service. But the calls and the letters were not enough to stoke Franz' fast-fading fervor. And then Hazel came along and after a while, he let her nail him down.

And Joe. Laura had very seldom seen him as happy as he was that time, and certainly never after that. But then, she did not see much of him after that. She went to Switzerland, and to Wellesley, and to Denis. And then Joe kept away.

5

*B*ut that was long ago. Tonight, so many summers later, she committed the most grievous sin of her entire, blameless life with him.

"So how about it?" He touched her check gently. "If you're not going back to him, and you don't have any plans for the next ten years or so of your life, how about spending them with me?"

"Just ten?"

"I don't think we have more than that. Do you remember that woman who told our fortunes? She said we both have short life lines."

"Oh, Buddy, that was just a game. You don't believe that, surely."

"Let me tell you something. There was another game, and there was another woman, and she read the same thing. But ten is all right, I couldn't ask for more, if they are with you." He ran his hand through her hair. "So how about it?"

"Oh, Bud, I'm still a married woman, you know."

"We'll make it right. We'll get an annulment."

"Which would take years."

"I'll wait, as long as you're there."

"Years, Bud, years."

"I'll wait. Do I have a choice?"

"Oh, dearest, yes, you have. A lot of choices. Look at yourself. What girl wouldn't jump at the chance of having you?"

"Don't tell me what my choices are, Laura Steiner. Do you think, all these years, I just sat here waiting for your husband to cheat on you, so you would leave him and come to me? Did you not think that I did give myself a lot of chances and explored every single one of those choices and found all of them unacceptable?"

"Oh, Bud."

"I'll go to my lawyer tomorrow. All right?"

Her eyes started to fill. "After Susana, I won't have him back and when he'll learn about you, he won't have me back, so I guess I don't have choices, either."

"Ouch, thank you very much."

She smiled. "I did not mean it to sound that way."

"Not in my wildest thoughts would I ever take any girl on those terms, but then I could never let you go again. So you see, we both really don't have any choice but to stick to each other, as it should have been from the very start."

She heaved a long sigh. "Can you take me home now?"

"Home? Oh, please let's not go yet. Let's stay the night. You did not want to go home, remember?"

"What we did, we did not plan, so maybe in a merciful time, we might be absolved of this, but what could save us if we stayed the night, with our eyes wide open?"

Well, he thought, she's very well-schooled, this is how you want her, for despite what they just did, he could not see her as anything but straight and upright and true, for he knew he alone was to blame in all this.

"At least have dinner first. I made reservations."

"All right. But let's check out."

She took another quick shower, after which she packed her things in her small suitcase: She snapped the case close and stood in front of him, expectantly. "I'm ready," she said.

* * *

The place was lit in mellow lights, the music sweet and dinner was delicious, but all these were lost on her. She was distracted and ate silently.

From the orchestra, the singer started to sing 'Speak Low.'

"You always liked that song," Joe said brightly, trying to get her out of herself. "What was that other Kurt Weill song that used to be big with you? I remember you almost bore a hole through that record, what was that song?"

"September Song? Surabaya-Johnny?" she answered with a laugh.

"No, the other one, the French one."

"*Je ne t'aime pas*," she answered, sadly.

Wrong move, he thought. "Where is Surabaya, anyway, and what was Johnny doing in such a strange-sounding place?" he asked, angling for a shift in mood and a smile, and got a sparkle of it.

"Burma, Indonesia, I don't know, you should know."

"Come, we haven't done this in a long time," he said, taking her hand and leading her to the dance floor. He placed both his arms around her; she was so slight in his arms. "Husband not feeding you?" he said. She did not answer, and placed her arms lightly around him, her nose buried on his chest, breathing in his clean smell. "God, how I miss doing this," he murmured.

He never learned how to dance. As he used to do ages ago, he just stood there, with both his arms around her and took a side step every now and then.

"Joe Steiner, never been much of a dancer," she said.

"Hm," he snorted, "but good enough when nobody was asking you."

"Yes, my lean and dry years."

He pirouetted her, wrapped one arm around her waist and bent her over backwards, pulled her up again, took her hand and twirled her around, traipsed her through some fancy tango steps.

"What, what, what are you doing," she sputtered, surprised.

"I just want you to see that with you by my side there's nothing we can't do, not even the dreaded tango." He looked at her in all earnestness and said, "A girl can't have a leaner and drier season than when her husband is cheating on her, and I am asking you now. Leave him. We'll get an annulment. I know the family's objections will be formidable at first, but in time, they'll realize that there's just no way they can separate us. We were meant to be together." He pulled her close to him and whispered urgently. "We don't have to live here. We could live in Europe. Let me take you back to all those places you loved long ago. Don't you want to go back to Spain, look up your relatives, those relatives that for a change we don't share? You've always loved it there.

"Let's do it. Let's go abroad. We'll have the entire thing annulled." The idea took hold of him firmly. "I shall go to Vargas tomorrow and ask his advice on how to proceed. I know you would not be comfortable living here, at least not at first. If you want we can live in Spain until you have decided where. Would you like Spain? Please say yes. We could live anywhere you want, do whatever you want to do. Or until you have decided where you want to live, we could travel the world, revisit places we have been to, see new ones together. Anywhere you want to go, anything your heart desires. Come, let's look up Johnny in Surabaya."

"Surabaya," she laughed, that gurgling laughter that had always filled his heart with contentment. Then she looked at him sadly. "Oh, Bud." How could she categorize how she felt for this man? There were times growing up when she was sure she loved him more than she loved Franz or Nacho.

She remembered a time clearly, a picture that was etched vividly in her mind. She must have been thirteen; there was a party at their house. Ray and Maggie arrived with their children, Madeleine and Marybeth dressed to the nines as usual, RJ, even then strongly displaying the dashing qualities that he would be known for in later years, every inch a Gomez and not at all like a brother of Joe's but looking just as good. And Joe, her hero even then, wearing eyeglasses for the first time, and looking so handsome with them. "Daddy, may I marry Joe when I grow up?" she had asked her father. "No, dear, you may not." "Why not?" she pursued. "Because he is your cousin. Cousins don't marry. Besides, Joe is more your brother than your cousin. It would be like marrying Franz." Heavens forbid, she remembered thinking, who would want to marry Franz, stern, scolding, no-nonsense Franz? "But don't worry, you'll find someone else," her father said. "Will he be as handsome as Joe?" she asked. "Yes, just as handsome as Joe."

"How about Georgie there," somebody had teased. George Hernandez Junior, whose father was the governor of the province, and whose family had been friends of the Steiners for years. Laura looked over at Georgie, so unlike the fair-skinned, light-haired men in her family---her father and brothers and uncles. And not by a long, long shot like Joe, tall, gray-eyed Joe, the best-looking boy she knew, better looking than Franz even, Franz, whom everyone said was an improvement of their father. And what was there about Francis that could stand improving? Then smug, swarthy, swaggering Georgie appeared ungainly in her eyes.

"But he is ugly," she pronounced.

"And you're a stuck-up brat," Georgie countered, and stuck out his tongue at her, forcing it to come out long and snakelike, violet from the grape lollipop he was sucking, forcing it out so hard his eyes bulged out of his face.

"What a revolting boy," Laura declared, holding her head high, in her most haughty, imperious manner, to the amusement of everyone, and started the teasing on the part of the adults to get her and Georgie together, an idea that filled her with a revulsion, and him with a distaste, that lasted until they were adults themselves. She looked away from ugly Georgie, and turned to Joe, who was looking at her, trying to hold back imminent laughter. He rose from where he was sitting, passed by her chair, and touched her face gently with the palm of his hand. Then he left the room, and clouds dimmed the sun.

But he never ventured into the sensual realm of her life, never stepped inside the bordering lines that he himself drew. He just stood outside looking in and, loved as much as he was, she let him be. Perhaps in the end they would have ended up together, like those uncles and aunts and cousins of hers who created a cocoon world of their own that shut out anyone who did not carry their blood and their looks and their names, because, after all, what strange strains flawed their system could flow in hers, too. Perhaps. If Denis had not saved her. But he did, charging into her life, the fairy-tale prince on a white steed who seized her by the waist and carried her off triumphant into his less constricted, more open world and showed her that one could celebrate love not just with the heart, but joyously, passionately, with all the senses as well.

* * *

"Let's have one lifetime of a honeymoon," Joe said, caressing her hair, "just be with each other, catch up, we've lost so much time already."

"You said you'd wait for me. Then wait for me. Give me time to think this through. I want to be alone for a bit."

"Alone? Like, you don't want me there?"

"Just for a little while."

"How much time are we talking of here?"

"Go to your meetings. Don't come to see me. Leave me with my thoughts for a couple of days."

"Two days without seeing you." But he could never refuse her anything. He always divined her wishes and gave her everything she wanted. She never even had to ask. He sighed, "at

least let me call you. Just let me talk to you. In the evenings."
Her hesitation worried him. "Please."

"He will never give me a divorce, you know that."

"Then we'll go without. We'll just work on the annulment.
He's not going to hold on to you if you don't want him."

"He will," she said. Don't I want him? How can one just
annul six years of marriage? Annul? Erase? Dissolve? As if it
never happened, six very good years, too. Oh, Denis, was Susana
worth all this? And how many other accomplices to afternoon
trysts were there before Susana, accomplices who stayed
nameless and faceless because they were not as bold as to make
sure I knew about them? Well, how about you, she scolded
herself, not only adultery, incest, too. Suddenly, the enormity of
what they did and what they planned to do swamped her, Joe's
intensity frightened her. "I'm scared."

He pressed her to himself. "Don't be. There's nothing to be
afraid of. I'm here and I shall take care of you. Haven't I,
always?"

Yes, he would. He had not wanted much, but when he did, he
just went after it with a quiet resolve, as she knew he would do
now---put his vast resources to work, cast aside whatever dared
bar his path, and as he always did, get what he wanted.

6

*S*he locked herself in her room. Cecilia, sleepless, too, would pass her room in the small hours of the morning and hear her pacing the floor. The food that the maids left on the console by her door remained untouched until Cook got worried and voiced her concern to Cecilia.

Denis called that evening, but Cecilia said Laura refused to take his call. He called again an hour later, but still she did not want to talk to him.

"Cecilia, I'm not putting this phone down until she talks to me."

"Come on, Lauren, you cannot keep on like this. Talk to him, straighten this thing out," pleaded Cecilia.

Laura took the phone and plunked it down.

"Can you tell me what this is all about?" asked Cecilia.

"Later, Mommy. Right now I don't want to talk about it. And Mommy, I'd like to be left alone, so please don't have me disturbed. Tell Cook I don't want her knocking at my door. I shall call the kitchen when I get hungry."

Denis called again. This time, Laura took the call. "Yes, Denis Richards." Her sibilants hissed in the air.

"Denis Richards," he repeated and laughed. She called him by that name, and in that tone of voice, when she wanted him to know that she was deeply bothered. His exasperation vanished at the sound of her voice. "Oh, sweet, it's so good to hear your voice. I miss you so much."

And she missed him, missed the snug, secure, sinless world he had created for her, missed the way he shielded her from temptations, solved her problems, spoiled her. Now she had this overwhelming weight that was pressing her down and she could not go to him for relief. "Roast beef sandwich indeed," she said.

"What?" It took a while before the words registered. "But that was what I had." Now he was getting angry, she knew. "God, do you know what I had been through these past days and that's all you can say to me?" he sputtered.

"Roast beef sandwich and what, Denis Richards?"

"Don't be crude, Laura, it doesn't become you. If I wanted another woman, why would I get someone older than myself? Oh, sweet, you know nothing happened, you know that. When have I ever lied to you? And I swear, if I see another roast beef sandwich again, I swear I'll throw up. Oh, dearest." He knew getting angry with her wouldn't get him anywhere. "I must see you. I'm off to the airport now."

"No, you're not."

"Yes, I am. I'm useless here. I can't memorize my lines, I'm in no mood to sing, I definitely cannot bring myself to act. So everybody is taking the week off. Meet me at the airport? Please."

"You call Mom and arrange it yourself."

"I shall be there Saturday evening. Meet me yourself, please."

"I don't think so, Denis."

Denis. Good, that was an improvement, he thought. "Oh, Lauren, I have been crazy these past days from wanting you. Don't punish me more for something I did not do. Why, I might as well have done what it is you're accusing me of, the way you've been tormenting me. You've condemned me before giving me a chance to explain and I protest. You know nothing happened with Susana. We just had lunch. She was not even staying in that hotel. Maybe with a nineteen-year-old. You know older women never appealed to me."

"What time are you coming in?"

* * *

"Next time," said Ray to his son, "if you feel you're not up to these meetings, maybe Franz could come in your place." Ray had called Joe's attention twice but Joe did not hear him. Ray looked at Francis and shook his head with impatience.

Francis raised inquiring eyebrows at his brother.

"New girl in the horizon, who knows." Ray answered Francis' unspoken question with a shrug, looking at Joe.

It had been like this for two days. Joe was in the meetings, but he definitely was not there, looking up at the ceiling, staring in space, examining a pencil, which all seemed to hold his interest more than what was going on around him.

He became aware that they were looking at him. "I'm sorry, Pops," he said and rose from his seat. "If you'll excuse me." He was out of the conference room, no explanation given. But then everyone in the room knew him and none was expected. The people in the meeting had been with Steiners' for a long time, and were considered "family." They saw the company grow, and the Steiner children with it, were witnesses to milestones in their lives---progress in school, turnover of girl/boyfriends, acceptance to universities, engagements, marriages, births. They watched Ray and Francis groom their boys to take over one day, saw the bond that joined the brothers join Franz and Joe, too.

When Joe and Franz finished their master's degree from Oxford, they were placed in charge of the provincial operations of the corporation and would come to Manila twice a month for meetings. The employees of the company met Joe's presence in the office with mixed reaction. The older people who had been with the company for a long time were used to his quiet air of detachment, and respected and never intruded. The younger employees, however, he intimidated even when he was his gracious self, the model of good manners, always saying please and thank you for everything done for him, even bringing the girls small presents when he came back from trips abroad. Still they were daunted by him, stood apart in awe of him, fazed by just the fact of him, just being Joe Steiner, a tiptoeing respect bordering on reverence, and, yet, for being younger and more handsome, and, most importantly, unattached, he generated an excitement among the female staff not accorded even Franz, whom everyone knew was very entrenched in his marriage. The girls took special care with themselves when Joe was in town, wearing their best dresses, taking special care with their toilette. A veritable fashion show would take place, high heels looked higher, suits looked newer, scarves sprouted from necklines. Sometimes he noticed and complimented. "Black and white always looks elegant," and the girl who was blessed this way was in euphoria all day. This was especially true with Mae, the assistant assigned to him and Franz when they were in town. After all, how many bosses could a girl have who looked like a young, albeit fair-haired and taller, Montgomery Clift? Even if he did not own the company, he still would be a great, big catch.

Joe went back to his office. He knew he couldn't function until he had talked to Laura, heard her voice again. He picked up the phone, then put it down. He did promise her he'd call only in the evenings. As he did countless times a day, he looked up at the giant picture on the wall, of the three of them, taken when they were young ages ago, at Franz grinning from ear to ear, at himself squinting, with a big, toothy smile, and at Laura, in pigtails and bobby socks but already with a face that could break your heart. Ah, he had to hear her voice.

"My two days are up. Now, can I come and take you to dinner tonight?" he said when she picked up the phone.

"In fact," she said, "you may come and pick me up anytime you're ready."

"And that is now. I'll be there before you could call my name," he said.

He shot out of his office. With tires squealing, he pointed his car towards Forbes, dared anyone to cross his path and was at the house faster than a bullet.

He kissed Cecilia who met him at the door. "Have we heard from the great lover?" he asked.

"Now, Joe, there's no need for that. After all, they have been married six years and this is the only time this happened, whatever this might be."

"The only time it happened that she knew about. We forget that these things happen to these people, it's in the nature of what they do. How many more of this does she have to suffer through before you say she's had enough? Well, I say this is enough. I do not cotton to this martyrdom bit, that she made her bed, now she must lie on it." Cecilia was taken aback by his intensity. "We shall have the marriage annulled, it has been done before. I don't care what it takes, if that's what is needed to get her out, I'll get her out. I want her to know that in this house she's loved, without question, without judgment, and if she wants out, out she gets, and damned what people say."

"And you think that leaving behind six years of marriage will make her happy?"

"And you think that staying on in a marriage with a husband who cheats on her will make her happy? I cannot believe you're saying this, *Tita* Ceil. You sound as though you were on his side."

"Sometimes these things happen, Joe. That does not mean he does not love her."

"It did not happen to you. It did not happen to my mom. It did not happen to Hazel. It did not happen to a lot of women in our family. If it happened to Isa, she had always been made of sterner stuff and could stand what could just break Laura. She deserves better and that certainly is not him."

"Why do I have the feeling that you think it's you?"

"If love, given without question, asking for nothing in return, there for her alone, could make her happy, then it certainly is me. I stood by, silent, all these years, because I was told I would not be good for her. Now it seems I could have done a very much better job, and I'm damned if I'm letting her go, ever again."

The look of consternation on Cecilia's face was a reproach. He went to her, kissed her and said gently, "I love you, *Tita* Ceil, but this is how it should have been from the very start, if I were not such a good boy and always did the 'right thing.'"

Cecilia was stunned speechless, stamped where she stood.

Laura came out and saw the dark look on her mother's face. She looked at Joe, but he flashed her a bright smile, and when he looked that way, how could anything be wrong?

"Hi, what time is it? Aren't you supposed to be at work?" She returned his smile.

"I am at work. Aren't you the most important stockholder of that company? Then I'm taking care of you today. Care to go for a drive and a lobster lunch afterwards?"

"Sounds good."

"Come then," he said. He kissed Cecilia goodbye. The proprietary way he took Laura's hand chilled Cecilia. Oh, God, God, don't, oh, please, don't, not her, not them, oh, please, she wept inside her. But she knew it was too late.

"Bye, Mom." She pushed the door and ran down the steps.

He pulled her to one side of the portico, behind sheltering plants and kissed her eagerly.

She extricated herself from his grasp. "Please, Bud, not here."

"So say, where?"

"Please."

"All right," he said. Nothing could dampen his good spirits. "I'll wait."

The drive to the country was long but pleasant. "And what had the thinking process brought about?" he asked.

"Can we talk about it later? It's such a scenic drive. I haven't passed this way in a long time."

"All right, as long as I'm not going to be exiled again."

* * *

He drove with one hand while the other held hers all the way. "Oh, Bud, I haven't stopped smiling. I cannot help myself. I jump over hedges, I burst out in uncontrollable laughter, I never imagined it possible to be this happy. I plucked a flower near where I park my car and handed it to Mae. She almost fainted from shock. 'Oh, Mr. Steiner,' she gushed, eyes wide and pleased, 'how sweet.' It's amazing how little it takes to make some people happy."

"This is where I'm supposed to say, 'like you, for instance.'"

"And it's amazing how you could always divine my thoughts. Yes, like me, for instance, all I need to be happy is you, in this life where happiness is so beyond my grasp, because happiness means only one thing, you." His voice changed and he dropped her hand. "But you, you promised yourself to another. That's all."

* * *

The restaurant was fairly crowded but he had a table reserved in one private corner.

The lobster was excellent. Her appetite surprised them both, used as he was to her picking at her food, eating small portions, satisfied with little. Now, it pleased him to see her eating with relish, and he was happy. He hardly touched his food, content with just looking at her, happy with her big appetite. He watched her spear the remaining pieces of lobster on his plate with her fork and finish them for him. "I can order more," he offered.

"Thanks, now I'm full. I must have eaten enough for two. Actually I did; I finished yours, too. Sorry. But you, you haven't eaten. Want to order more?"

"I'm fine," he smiled.

She wiped her lips with her napkin, folded it carefully, and placed it near her plate.

Then she came up with her little news. Denis was coming in. She was picking him up. "Dearest, is that your idea of dessert for me?" He asked in dismay.

"He called. There was nothing I could do. If he wants to come, he'll come. I could not stop him."

"Why does he have to come? Isn't he working on some hotshot project? Could they get along without him, big star that he is? You could do this on the phone." He knew he was being unreasonable, but he just couldn't stand the thought of him near her again, touching her again, doing to her what he had been aching to do all these years.

"I have to talk to him," she said gently. She took his hand and gave it a reassuring squeeze. "You just don't end this thing over the phone. I know how he is going to take what I have to tell him. It's not going to be easy."

"He's not going to talk you into going back to him?" His voice was full of dread.

"No." She saw the stricken look on his face. "Everything is going to be all right. Now, will you take me home?"

"Come spend an hour with me before you go. One hour with me and your husband could shoot me, for all I care. Really." He looked so touching, looking at her with those pained eyes. God, she thought, how did we arrive at this point? She could not bear his hurt.

"Why, Mr. Steiner," she strove for lightness, "I believe you are trying to seduce me."

"I am. Come," he coaxed, "be seduced and come with me."

She looked at her watch. "I really have to go, really, what can I do?" She brought up his hand to her lips. "It's all right. I'll be back before you miss me."

"I miss you already." He touched her face. "I don't care what it takes. I'm not giving you up again."

7

*S*he was at the airport; the first person Denis saw when he entered the arrivals area. He did not recognize the dress. It was new, maybe Cecilia's. She seldom brought a lot of clothes when she came home, and would raid Cecilia's closets. They looked at each other while he made his way through the crowd.

He steered her to the side where there was a semblance of privacy and pulled her close to him. "God, I miss you," he said. She tried to extricate herself from his arms. This was not lost on him; he dropped his arms and let her go.

"You have checked-in luggage?" she asked.

"No."

"All right."

She did not say a word, not in the car, not even when they reached her room. She closed the door and stood there, looking at him silently. But he was not having any of it. With a couple of huge steps, he reached her, and enfolded her in his arms. She tried to wriggle out but he was not letting her go. He pressed her head back, his mouth hungrily engulfing hers, his arms crushing her to himself. He felt her yielding; she stood there limply, her arms hanging at her side, while he drowned in her nearness, shut out from the world, conscious only of her and her sweet smell, and her body pressed tightly to his.

He was a very physical man with tremendous passions and their lovemaking had always been a source of complete pleasure and satisfaction to him. Every idea he had of everything desirable in a woman he found in her and he knew that making love could never be more fervent and impassioned and voluptuous as when he made love to her. And through the years she had been that to him, a woman who satisfied him completely, a lover who fulfilled him in every way. And so he never strayed.

* * *

He looked at her, at her eyes fringed by those thick lashes, passed his finger lightly over her lips, lips that looked very red; it couldn't be lipstick, he had eaten all that already.

"I have the week off. We could stay here a few more days if you wish," he said.

"I'm not going back with you."

He refused to understand her. "Lauren, I cannot be out too long. We're already behind schedule as it is."

"I shall give you your divorce. Ask Charles to prepare the papers and I'll not contest," she said. "I shall not get a cent from you, you know that. You can keep the house. I want nothing from you. All I ask is that you keep things as civilized, as quiet and as private as possible and you keep away from Susana until after the divorce becomes final."

His hand, caressing her face, rested frozen on her cheek. He remained very still, not moving. She watched the expression on his face changing from fervently adoring to controlled anger.

"Damn you, Denis Richards. In everything I do, I would ask myself, is this all right with him, would he approve of this, would this make his life easier? My sun rises and sets with you. I never knew that there could be such pain as I went through when I thought of you cavorting in some hotel with that tart. I know now how much pain you are capable of causing me. You told me once that there are no guarantees. Well, you're wrong. There are. I'm staying here with my family, where I have never been hurt. I want safe, I want secure, I want out. I am not going back with you."

He said in a low voice, slow, deliberate, "No, no, no. Never. There shall never be talk of getting out in this house. You vowed to take me till death, and I am holding you to that. Don't think you'll ever be free of me. I would rather die than let you go. No, I'll shoot you first, then I'll shoot myself." Tears flowed freely down her cheeks, but he was not letting her off. "You want safe. What have I been striving for all these years, if not to make you safe. No wife had ever been more safe and secure." His voice rose as he spat the words. "And spoiled. That's what your trouble is, you're spoiled. Spoiled by your grandmother, spoiled by your parents, and most of all, spoiled by me. There had never been any affair, with Susana or anybody else, you should know that. If you had trusted me, just a little bit, if you had not gone rushing to the other side of the world before giving me a chance to explain, none of this would have happened. I earned that trust, damn it, and I demand it."

She very seldom saw him angry and never with her. She turned her head to avoid looking at his incensed face, but with one hand he forced her face to face his own. "I have been a good husband to you, haven't I? Haven't I? Don't you think I deserved the courtesy of an explanation before you went rushing away? Answer me. Don't you think I deserved just that one, small consideration? Answer me, Laura, don't withdraw from me now."

He saw her cringe at the onslaught of his vehemence. Did she think he was going to hit her? She was sniffling and breathing through her mouth and watching him through tear-filled eyes. God, what am I doing here, he thought. "Oh, Lauren, you went exactly where Susana wanted you to go. Is that what you want?" He held her close to him. "I know I have hurt you and I would give anything just to take this week back. Why are we letting this nobody come between us?

"There's no question of divorce, ever. I have never called it quits in my life, and I'm not about to start now. There's no getting out, that's all there is to it. It was, it is a good marriage, is it not, and worth saving? Then let's work this thing out, all right?" His voice had softened considerably, urging her, as he brushed her hair from her face with his fingers. "Okay? But I cannot carry it alone. You have to help me."

His eyes held hers and she couldn't look away. "Will you help me, will you? Answer me, Laura." He was getting angry again. "This is not one of those things you think will go away if you close your eyes to it." He might have spoiled her and given in to everything she wanted, but she also knew that when he wanted anything, he always went after it with everything he had, and got it. Now he wanted his marriage, and she knew she was not getting an inch from him if that inch threatened it.

She was not used to crying; her eyes were hurting and he loomed before her, too large and invincible and full of authority. She let out a deep sigh and let go, and gave in to the engulfing restfulness of his arms enfolding her. Yes, she missed that, missed his strong arms around her, deciding for her, taking care of her, sheltering her. And most of all, she missed the open, joyful, uncomplicated way he loved her.

He felt her deflating, but he was not letting her off. "Will you help me? Will you?" She nodded her head almost imperceptibly, but that was enough for him. He knew he shouldn't push it. "Good. Now, listen to me. I want you to know, if you still don't know it. You are the most important thing in my life, you come first with me and I would never ever do anything to hurt you knowingly. Will you remember that?"

She lifted her shoulder to make a small shrug.

"Promise me we shall never let the day end angry or hurt or upset at anything or at each other. When you left I don't think I had ever been more miserable. But we could have spared ourselves that, if you had talked to me first. I have always been there for you, haven't I? And I'm the great problem solver, remember? Then talk to me first. Is that fair enough?"

Another hint of a shrug.

"I don't want any separation again. All right? All right?" She kept still. "Don't I even get an answer?" His voice was booming again.

"I do want a divorce."

"Which you are not getting, so what else?"

"I'm having an affair."

"Then I'll just blow his head off first so you can see to what lengths you could drive me, then I'll shoot you, and then I'll shoot myself. Uh, huh," he said, nodding his head. "Haven't I told you that before?" He squinted one eye. "You did not think I was serious? Well, that you can bank on, Laura. Now, can we put an end to this divorce business?"

There was nothing else she could do. Most probably he did not believe her. But one thing she was sure of, he was not letting her go. Oh, she would think of something later. Right now, she was much too tired, all she wanted was to close her aching eyes and never open them again. She would deal with this later.

8

*W*hen she came into the dining room from church, Francis, Cecilia and Maricris, and Denis were seated at table, her parents and sister having breakfast, Denis having coffee. He sprang up from his seat when he saw her, looked at her tentatively, not quite sure what her mood was at this time. She left him to go to church this morning, adamant that he did not go with her.

"Come have breakfast, Lauren," said Francis, warmly, "I have not seen you in a long time."

Laura parked her prayer book on the buffet and went over to kiss Francis and Cecilia. "You're early, Cris," she greeted her sister.

"Brought the baby over. Have some shopping to do," Maricris replied.

"I'm happy to have you back with us, Lauren," said Francis.

"I'm glad you're feeling better, Papa."

She looked at Denis as he pulled her chair out for her. He waited until she was seated before he went back to his own.

"Coffee?" Denis asked, wanting to do something for her.

"No, thank you."

"Denis tells me you're going back tomorrow. I was hoping you could stay longer. Such a short visit. Maybe you could go see Ray today, he was sick, too," said Francis.

"I am not going back," she said.

"Not going back?" asked Francis in surprise.

Denis took a deep sigh. "Are we going through this again? Enough already, Lauren, snap out of this and let's go home."

"Why don't you go ahead, I'll just stay here for a little while and think things through."

His face clouded, she could see he was getting dangerously angry again. He took off his glasses, wiped them with a table napkin, and put them back on again, trying to conceal what emotions were beginning to surface on his face. Although his voice remained low and steady, it had taken an ominous shade.

"No, there's nothing to think through. I'm not going anywhere without you and you're not going anywhere without me. That's just all there is to it." She stood up, but the sudden effort made her feel faint. She held her hand to her forehead, while the room turned round and round about her and she collapsed in a heap.

"Now what," Denis began, springing from his chair. "Oh dear, oh dear," he said as everybody rose in alarm. He gathered his wife in his arms and placed her on the sofa, frantically rubbing her hand, not knowing what else to do.

"I'll call Dr. Rudi," said Cecilia and hurried to the phone.

Laura was wide-awake when the doctor arrived. "It must be exhaustion," the doctor said, examining her, "and then again, maybe not." He asked her a few questions, then stood up. "Wipe that stricken look off your face, Mr. Richards," he said, looking at Denis's anxious face. "You're going to have a lot of this on your hands before the baby comes."

The baby.

Oh, she had wanted this baby so much. For years she had prayed for this, longed for this, rejoiced when she was late for just a few days, and heaved a deep sigh, at first of disappointment, and later, of resignation, when once again a profuse flow would prove her wrong. Until, tired and resigned, she just stepped down from her tiptoeing watch, did not think about it again, spared herself another lashing disappointment and gave herself up to her God. He will take care of her, in due time. But please, please, don't let that time be today, she prayed now, she could not bear this complication today, oh, would that He would take care of her a month from now, a year even, but not yet, oh, please, God, not yet, not today.

But who could fathom the mysterious ways in which He went about His business? He would give her her baby today, when she least wanted it.

"Come to my clinic tomorrow, I'll give you a more thorough examination," the doctor said.

Surprisingly, Denis, who did not care much for children, but would have embraced this one for his wife's sake, now was elated. He looked at the doctor, started to say something, then closed his mouth and went straight to Laura. He knelt by the sofa, looked at her face searchingly, took her hand to his lips, kissed it fervently and looked at her face again. Now she had her wish and he was happy for her and the strange and unexpected thing was that he was happy for himself, too. "Oh, my dearest," was all he could say.

"This is great," said Francis. "This calls for a celebration. Okay, Ceil, call everyone, let's have dinner here tonight." He beamed happily at his daughter. "You're okay?" She gave him a small smile. "All right, let me call Ray. Oh, hey, good work," he said to Denis, patted him on the shoulder and went to the phone to call his brother.

Denis laughed and smoothed the hair from his wife's forehead. "Oh, sweet, how do you feel?"

She started to get up, but he stopped her.

"Stay, stay. What do you want? Let me get it for you. Is she all right now, Doctor?"

"She's young. She'll live."

* * *

"Lauren, telephone for you." Maricris called Laura.

"Thanks, Cris." She took the phone from Maricris.

"Heard the news," said Joe. "I have to see you. Come to my office. I'll wait for you." He put the phone down, not waiting for her to answer, not giving her a chance to decline.

She closed her eyes and stayed that way, unmoving, until she thought it was time to go. If she did not get a lot of traffic, she could be at the Steiner Building in twenty minutes.

"I'm going out," she announced.

"Where are you going? It's not safe. What do you want?" said Denis.

"Please," she said. "I just need some breathing space." She picked up her handbag and left before her husband could gather his wits and insist that it was not safe.

"Space," Denis repeated, crestfallen, "space."

All of a sudden Francis sympathized with this son-in-law, and was angry with his daughter. What more did she want? A better husband she could not find. "I'm afraid," he said to Denis, "you're in for a difficult time. They get this way the first few months, but in time they settle down."

"It's all right, I guess," replied Denis, looking at Francis uncertainly, looking at the door where his wife's back just disappeared, "now that I know where we're going."

* * *

She parked the Mercedes in the space marked 'Reserved.'
"Sorry, Mr. Reserved, you'll just have to park somewhere else."
The hall was empty, so was the elevator. People were busy
making money for the company.

Mae looked up when Laura came in.

"Good morning. Joe Steiner, please," said Laura.

"Is he expecting you, Ma'am?"

"Yes, he is," said Joe at the door of his office.

"Thanks," said Laura to Mae.

This must be Mrs. Richards then, thought Mae. She had read
and heard a lot about her but had never met her before. Why, she
was even more exquisite than her pictures, which could not show
that luminous skin and that elegant bearing.

"Please see we're not disturbed," Joe told Mae and ushered
Laura into his office.

He pulled her to him even before she had kicked the door
shut. "I've been going crazy from missing you," he said gruffly.

His eyeglasses intruded. He peeled them off and flung them
on the sofa. She moved her face away from his lips. His face
clouded and he released her.

From the radio, which was always tuned on to the classical
music station, Jascha Heifetz was fiddling a haunting *Chopin's
Nocturne*. "Ah, that *C Sharp Minor*, it tugs at the heart," she said.
"You've always liked that."

"It soothes this breast that you savage," he said, his face dark
and grim.

"Soothes this breast that you savage," she repeated. "Father
Clemente should hear that. It is this way with words that had
those priests wrapped around your fingers." She took his hand
and put it to her face. With her finger, she smoothed the sides of
his nose that his eyeglasses had dented.

"You bear bad news?" he asked.

She held his hands close to her breasts, breathed a sigh, and
said, "You've always told me what to do. Tell me what to do
now."

"Suppose," he said, taking his hands away from hers, "you
tell me."

"We never really believed we could do it, did we?" She
looked at him earnestly, taking back his hands. "We may not
have said it, but it was in the back of our minds. It's just so

impossible, divorce is out of the question, Denis will hound us. Marriage between us is not allowed by law, here and in a lot of other places. And how about the Church? Without an annulment, how long can we stand being excommunicated, not being able to receive Communion? Not very long, I know."

"Why don't you just speak for yourself."

"We feel the same way about everything, that's our gift and our tragedy."

"There is nothing about you, and what I feel for you, that I'd consider a tragedy."

She touched his face gently, that face, those gray eyes, that had always given her pleasure to look at, now looking at her with anguish she could not bear to watch. "We could never have made it, living outside the Church. If we could for a short spell, we'd be devastated by guilt in a little while. Excommunication and absence from the sacrament would surely shatter us."

"We'll get an annulment."

"Which would take years. Meanwhile, we would be living in sin. And that would only take care of the Church part. Taking care of Denis would be Herculean. He'll never divorce me." She sighed. "But I guess, in the condition I'm in, that's more than hopeless now."

He turned, sat down on the sofa and buried his face in his hands. She sat beside him and gently removed his hands from his face. He turned and looked at her and before he could stop himself, he enveloped her in his arms, crushed his lips on hers in urgent desperation, searched for her tongue, ate her lips, devoured her with a yearning he could not appease. He moved her head back, burrowed his face on her throat, then went back and covered her lips with his again, as though drowning in those lips could somehow lessen his hopelessness. At last his mouth left hers; he took great gasps that shook his body.

"Oh, God, God, God."

"Hush, don't anymore," her voice quivered with grief, "please, dearest, don't anymore."

He looked at her face, upturned to his, eyes misty, reflecting his misery. "I don't know how I could go back to that lonely life again."

She rested her face in his chest, on his shirt that smelled of soap and sun and a manly lotion. "For all it's worth," she said, "I still wish you had told me long ago."

"How was it that I could just pour out to you with so much ease what I could never open up to other people and yet I was able to keep that to myself for so long. Franz and you were the only ones I could talk to freely, about everything, except about the way I feel for you. And then you went away and there was only Franz, and there are things I can't talk about, even to him. The next time I saw you, you were in love and wanted to get married, so there was nothing more to be said or done, was there? You broke my heart, with a sound so deafening, surely you must have heard it, so in love though you were. Besides, I am not supposed to fall in love with you, remember? We're not supposed to tamper with nature's plans, or she deals us a cruel blow, gives us defective children, you know. We're not supposed to copulate, that would be incestuous, you know."

"Oh, Bud, don't."

"Copulate? Your husband doesn't say that word to you? Exciting word, copulate."

"Can't you see I'm hurting too?" She held him to her until she felt him calming somewhat, running her hand through his hair, holding his face. "I can't stand seeing you like this."

"Sorry. A moment of weakness."

The intercom beeped and he let it until he could not ignore its insistence. "Yes," he said curtly.

"Mr. Steiner," Mae said at the other end, "Mr. Steiner, oh, I mean your father, said he would like to see Mrs. Richards before she leaves."

"You can tell my father yes, Mrs. Richards will see him before she leaves. Now, unless there's a fire, I don't want to be disturbed. All right? Thanks."

"Not at all, Mr. Steiner, but your father is already coming this way."

He shook his head in exasperation. "Papa is on his way," he said. He looked at her, face flushed, hair tousled, lipstick kissed away, and marveled how, despite this disheveled state, or because of it, he wanted her more than ever, wanted to bury his face in that disarrayed hair, burrow his nose on that neck, drown in those lips. Oh, God!

But a lifetime of practice had made him master the art of keeping out of sight what emotions for her raged inside him. "The bathroom's there if you want to freshen up," he said, now quite calm. He picked up his eyeglasses and put them on.

She came out of the bathroom, combed, collected and composed. Through the open door she saw Joe and Ray outside, talking, Ray, earnestly, Joe listlessly. Ray turned to her when he heard her rustling about and opened his arms to her.

"I heard the news. I'm so happy for you," said Ray, kissing her on the forehead. He stood her at arm's length. "But you don't look like something has changed so radically within you. Pregnancy becomes you. How many months is it?"

"Two, I think."

"And how is that husband of yours taking it?" Everybody knew how Denis felt about children.

"He was quite happy about it, strange as it may seem."

"And well he should be. But you, how are you?"

"The doctor said I'll live," she smiled. "Papa said you were sick. I'm happy to see you're all right now." They talked while Joe at the door stood looking at her with lovesick eyes, dangerously beyond caring who saw it.

"When are you going back to San Sebastian?" Ray asked his son.

"Tomorrow morning," Joe replied, still looking at Laura.

"Francis is inviting us to dinner tonight. You're coming, of course?" said Ray. It was more a statement than a question.

"I don't think so," Joe replied, tearing his eyes away from Laura to look briefly at his father. "I have things to do," he said and shifted his gaze back to her.

"Do come. We haven't finished," she said in a whisper.

"I am. And I'm all talked out." She looked at him, hurt. He relented. "What you have to say will have to be now." He turned to his father, "I'll see you before I leave," he said, firmly dismissing him, and opened his office door to Laura.

"I'll see you tonight, *Tito* Ray." Laura said before Joe shut the door firmly behind him.

Ray looked at the closed door, aghast. What do those two think they're doing, he thought, shocked at the naked look of longing on his son's face. And his secretary drinking in everything. ("You should see the look on his face. So that's why he's never been interested in other girls, he's in love with her. You should have seen the look on his father's face. His father saw it too." "They have always been very close, since they were kids, but that doesn't mean they are in love." "If that wasn't love then it was lust. He looked at her as if he wanted to devour her.")

Actually, they did not say much when the door closed behind them. He just held her close, and they stayed that way, not moving. Then she stirred and sighed. "You'll call me sometimes?" she asked.

"No."

"Just to let me know how you are, just once in a while?"

"No."

"No?"

"It would be a little death each time I put that phone down. Do you want that?"

"No." She stayed there in his arms until it was time. "I have to leave you now," she said.

His shoulders drooped as he released her and opened his hands as though to let her go.

She held his face and said goodbye without a word. She left him, without seeing, without hearing Mae's bungled "Goodbye, Mrs. Steiner."

9

*D*enis always found visits to Manila a delight. He loved
this elegant house, he loved his wife's family, he was the only
man he knew who loved his mother-in-law. He loved it when the
other members of the family dropped by with their children. He
loved the conversation, the laughter, the easy banter. Even the
children delighted him, he who never found children charming,
but rather a necessity to be tolerated but were best avoided.

He and Laura flew in from Los Angeles this morning for
Francis' 60th birthday, which the family was celebrating with a
big bash tomorrow, Easter Sunday. Tonight there was a hush
when he and Laura came down to dinner.

"Did I miss anything?" he asked as he pulled out a chair for
his wife. He was always sure of their regard for him, never had
speculative assumptions that perhaps they might be talking about
him.

"Of course you remember Ruth, the wife of Georgie?" asked
Maricris when they had taken their place at table.

"Of course I remember Ruth, yes, Ruth and good old
Georgie, my wife's first beau." He expected some protestations
from his wife, a semblance of which she always put up whenever
he would tease her about Georgie, but she just sat there,
desultorily pushing strips of meat around her plate.

Denis certainly remembered Ruth and Georgie; he first met
them one summer vacation. They had just come out from church
when Georgie and Ruth came over to where they were standing
to greet Francis and Cecilia.

Wearing a navy blue dress that fit her slim body perfectly,
Ruth looked smart and elegant and very stylish. But after all the
stories Denis had heard about him, it was Georgie who claimed
his attention, as he approached them with the swift, sure stride of
one who thought highly of himself, the lord of the manor, master
of all he surveyed. His could have been a handsome face, had it
not a petulant look stamped to it, like a spoiled child's when
denied a demand, or if he tempered it with a smile. He had taken

off his sunglasses and was squinting at the bright sunlit morning, impatient with the ritual kissing and how-do-you-dos, anxiously wanting to get a move on. He pecked Cecilia on the check, shook Francis' hand, then Denis' when Cecilia introduced them, exchanged a few, detached so-what's-new with Laura and the other Steiners. His duty done, he walked to his car, (a Mercedes, another status symbol, Laura once said when Denis commented on the slew of Mercedes Benzes on the roads) and waited, scowling, for Ruth, who was still talking to another girl. "Well, come on," he mouthed, exasperated, when he caught Ruth's eye, and started the engine even before Ruth had entered the car. Looking at them both, Denis thought of his wife, quiet, calm, serene. No, she did not do too badly with me. Spoiled, petulant, impatient Georgie would have given her a trying time. Then again, surely not. He looked at his wife, her head held high, in one of her imperial stances, and he laughed. She could never be prodded to scurry about and dash and rush to where she was not inclined to be. She would be the one to give the likes of Georgie a very vexing life.

Yes, he remembered Ruth, very well.

Maricris continued. "Well, brace yourself now. Would you believe this? Joe had an affair with Ruth."

"An affair?" Denis put down his fork and looked up in surprise. "Our Joe? Not our Joe. You mean he put down his bottle and his books for a while and took up with, of all people, Georgie's wife? Well, well, fancy that. Isn't that the most amazing thing?" He turned to Laura but this exchange did not elicit any response from her. He looked at her in his searching way, at her face devoid of expression. "You knew about this, didn't you?" She shrugged her shoulders. "Why didn't you tell me?"

"I only learned of it today." And wept inside her when she heard. Which cruel, which perverse, which Fate of derision was this who set her sight on this most upright, most straight of men, this man who all his life lived strictly by the rules, and mocked the virtues that governed his life? Which Fate of envy was this who cast a green-eyed look at this virtuous man who always patterned what he did on what he believed was moral and just, who held sacred and never compromised what he knew was right, and in the narrow time that left no space for deliberation, lured him to forage into the forbidden territory of other men's wives, knowing he was only human and as such would surely succumb?

"Yes, isn't that just too incredible?" Maricris was saying.

"When did this happen?" Denis asked.

"Just after you left, two months ago, January, was it, the last time you were here? Remember Papa held a dinner here to celebrate the news of Lauren's pregnancy and Joe did not attend, he went back to San Sebastian that afternoon? Well, it was then, when he was there, and Franz and Hazel went abroad. It went on for almost a month and we did not have a clue, until the big scandal erupted and Joe had to leave San Sebastian. So we thought that was the end of that but the woman followed him here. Well, Franz came back from vacation and put all wrong to right, thank God for that."

"Where is he now?" asked Denis.

"Joe? He's exiled himself in the penthouse. Franz says it's over. I think so, too. I saw him receiving Communion last Sunday, Joe I mean," Maricris continued. "So I think it's over. They say Ruth is going abroad with her sister."

Now, they sat and listened and with the colorful interjections from the other family members, they pieced together what, and how this incredible thing, happened.

he Seaside Country Club was the most exclusive country club in the province and had the best facilities for meetings, conferences and parties. When Francis was in town, it was his favorite dining place to where he would take his family or invite his friends. To him, it served the best Spanish food and its *paella* and *callos* were the best in the country, although Cecilia always maintained that her cook's cooking was infinitely superior. But Francis liked the ambiance of the place and the decor, which was very old-world Spanish. In all the years that they had been going there, the food had remained the perfect same, authentic Spanish dishes, thanks to Concha, who ruled the kitchen, and to her recipes, which were handed down from generations of relatives in Spain.

The terrace was the centerpiece of the club. Fronting unto the sea, it was thought very romantic, with the garden on one side choking with fragrant roses, and the splash of the frothing and foaming waves whipping the craggy rocks, and was a favorite dancing place with the younger generation. Mostly though, the club catered to its members, the island's wealthy crowd who, after playing golf and tennis, stayed around for drinks and, very often, a game of cards.

Here, Georgie and several other landowners usually repaired to after their work in the hacienda. Their wives, those who were not somewhere else playing *mahjong* or *monte*, usually came with their husbands, and whiled away the time in the dining room or on the terrace, gossiping with the other wives, while their husbands occupied themselves in the card room. Ruth had never taken to both pursuits, the gossip and the gambling, and when she came with Georgie, would hover around the men looking in on their card game, which never interested her, and she always ended up bored.

Tonight was another one of those nights filled with ennui for her, the room heavy with smoke, the men looking grim and determined. She swore if she yawned one more time, she would dislocate her jaw. Standing at the back of Georgie's chair, she stroked his hair lightly and said, "Georgie, can we go home now?"

"In a little while," replied her husband absently, "why don't you go ahead, take the car, I'll hitch a ride with whoever. I don't know why you don't just bring your car, then you could go home anytime you wish," he complained.

He still did not get it, she thought. If she brought her car, he would stay on and on long after she was gone. Then by the time he came home he would be too tired, and he would turn his back to her and go straight to sleep.

"Never mind," she said, "I'll wait". And waiting became the order of these nights for her, in that silent, smoke-hazed room of grim-looking men intent in their game. Every once in a while, the silence was punctuated by cards being shuffled or thumped on the table or a sudden whoop of triumph when one of them hit a winner. This was not a game anymore, Ruth thought. This was addiction she neither understood nor cared to understand.

Why she even bothered to come she did not know. Here or at home, it was just the same. Boredom kept her constant company these days. She wanted to go to work, but Georgie would not hear of it. "I just don't understand this hankering for self-fulfillment. Don't you have enough work with the children? I'd think a husband and three kids should be fulfillment enough for a wife."

She had been very good in school and after graduating from high school, she and another sister were sent by their parents to Marymount College in New York. After graduation, she came home for a brief visit, dated Georgie a few times, and was about to go back to New York when she found out she was pregnant. She couldn't believe that a few minutes in the backseat of Georgie's car could get her in trouble when more experiments in New York did not produce anything. "I could be chased by a mad dog or be gored by a crazed bull and I couldn't be more flabbergasted," she told her sister. But Georgie was excited about it and so was the entire Hernandez clan when it had to be told.

They had a lavish wedding, a honeymoon in Australia, and a whooping present towards the purchase of a house when they came back, compliments of Georgie's four sisters, who doted on their only brother.

Georgie, whose head was always buzzing with business deals, had convinced his family that ranching was the next best thing to sugarcane. He acquired a vast track of grassland in the south where he planned to put in a few hundred heads of cattle. Even a honeymoon could not make him stay put. ("I am not staying in a hotel room for one week doing nothing!") So he decided on Australia for his honeymoon, where he could look at his bride and at some cattle at the same time. Off to Australia he went, pulling along the morning-retching Ruth, who managed in every possible way to give them both a miserable time. "I'll make it up to you," he mollified her, and his slightly guilty conscience. "Next year, we'll have a proper honeymoon in New York."

But there was never a New York. She had another baby less than a year later, and another one immediately after that, and by this time, even she did not care for a honeymoon, proper or not.

Meanwhile, Ruth's sister applied with an airline company where her proficiency in English and Spanish and a smattering of high school French got her a job as a flight stewardess. Her letters, and her stories when she came home on leaves---travel to those places in Europe that they had always loved, and getting paid for it, too---did nothing to lessen Ruth's discontent with her life.

She had never been a homebody. That big house that Georgie had had built for her now took on the proportions of a prison for her, its care and management a trap that thwarted attempts at seeking other occupations she was sure she would be happier at instead. Nobody in her crowd had any sympathy for her when she complained about being bored. With a house like that, with all that money, with that very good catch of a husband, it was a crime to complain, she was told. Even her best friend, Linda, to whom she complained of chains pulling her down and that if she never saw the house again, she was sure she wouldn't mind it at all, wagged a red-tipped finger at her and warned, "Be careful, you might just get what you wish for."

"My parents spent a lot of money sending me to school abroad so I could find a good job," she said, aggrieved, to her husband.

"All right," said Georgie, who, like other affluent Filipino husbands, felt that wives should stay home while husbands were out earning a living. "Work for me then. Take care of the children, run the house, go shopping, play *mahjong* afternoons and I shall pay you twice as much as anybody out there could pay you." He saw the angry look on her face and immediately looked contrite. "Why can we not be enough for you? Think of the other wives out there who would be just too happy to be in your shoes." Seeing how serious his wife looked, he added, "And what expensive shoes they are, too. Come on, I'll buy you more; be a good girl and give me a smile now." Georgie was lord and master of his house, was even lord and master of his father's house, with those women there spoiling him rotten, and whatever he wanted always went, by whatever fashion, whether charmingly, as he was doing now, or impatiently, which was rather the rule, as Ruth all too soon found out. And Ruth, knowing that this was another one of the things in their lives on which she did not have any say, did not bring up the matter again.

11

*W*hen Joe and Franz came home from Oxford, Ray and Francis decided to revamp the company. Francis felt that now that the two boys had finished their master's degree, he and Ray could relegate some of the responsibilities that had lain squarely on both their older shoulders. The provincial part of the business then was given to Franz and Joe---the running of the hacienda, the sugar central and the shipping business, while Francis and Ray took care of the Manila part.

Every year or so, Hazel brought her children home to New York to visit her folks, then two weeks later, Franz, who never took off more than two weeks a year, would follow, and they would stay for two more weeks. Most often, Denis and Laura would join them for a weekend in New York. If Denis could not make it, Franz would pack his family for Los Angeles and stay for a couple of days with Laura before heading for home. This year, however, they decided to visit Europe as well, Franz, Hazel and little Francis, and they stayed away for three weeks, leaving the two younger ones with Cecilia.

Bored, bereft, sore of heart, with Laura back into Denis' life and gone from his, Joe started to drift into the country club and there sought respite from the humdrum days without Franz. At first he stayed for a couple of drinks, then left to take in a movie and headed for home. With time hanging heavily on his hands, he stayed at the club later and later until finally he joined Georgie and his crowd. Cards were never his thing, but cards in one hand and a drink in the other were more tolerable than another long, empty night, without Franz, without Laura, alone in his room with his books and his bottle that could no longer calm him, with his thoughts from which he could not escape.

But he could not keep up with the card-playing crowd. Never unto gambling, the long hours just sitting there looking at cards brought him little relief, made him restless and when he felt he had had enough, called it quits before the others did.

Tonight, he announced, "This is it for me, goodnight."

"Hey, Joe, maybe you could take Ruth home, if it's not too much bother." Thus with these words, Georgie set their tragic fates careening into the disaster not one of them in that room, even in his worst nightmare, could have foreseen or imagined.

So it started that way, Ruth wanting to go home, Georgie unwilling to part company with his cards, and Joe ending up taking her. In all fairness, Joe cornered Georgie one evening. "You really should take your wife home yourself, Georgie, after all, it's very late."

"Just say if you don't want to do it, and I'll have somebody else take her," replied Georgie.

"You know that's not it," said Joe, annoyed. "I just think you should take your own wife home yourself."

"Look," Georgie snapped, exasperated, "when you are married and are in a position to lecture about wives, we'll talk."

And so Joe, sick of heart, longing for Laura, lost and desolate and more inebriated than usual, was easy pickings for Ruth. Everyone agreed the affair started with Franz' absence and that, had Franz not been abroad on vacation, the fateful events that followed would never have happened. But Franz was not around, and when Joe started hurtling towards that doomed affair, Franz' steadying hand was not there to pull him back.

Although they were both the same age, Franz had always acted like an older brother to Joe, had been the more decisive of the two, his the hand that set the tone of the events in both their lives. Joe had always been the dreamer; he always had a book with him wherever he went, and if the company he found himself in was not stimulating enough, which was quite often, he would sit in one corner and read until rescued by Franz. If Joe was not sleeping over at Franz', Franz would be over at Joe's. However, Cecilia frowned on her children sleeping in other people's houses, even if that house happened to be a Steiners' too, and just a few blocks away, and Joe often ended up staying with Franz. Later, when Joe developed a predilection for the bottle, ("I only had a couple," he would say. "After which you lost count," Franz would counter.) Maggie, imagining all sorts of tragic stories about driving while under the influence, would rather, too, her son stayed over at Franz' than drove home.

Joe became a constant fixture at Francis' house, first in San Sebastian when they were younger, later in Manila when they went to high school. The family would come down to breakfast and Joe would be at table, where, as the maids did for the other members of the family, a place was always set for him, having coffee, reading. Francis' family was so used to having him around that when his place at table was empty, someone, forgetting that he did not really live there, would inquire, "Where's Joe?"

After high school, they prevailed upon their parents to let them go to Oxford. After they earned their bachelor's degrees, Franz decided to stay on to take up his master's degree. Joe's parents, and most of all his grandfather, were delighted. They knew Joe would stay on, too. And when, with Franz, he graduated in the prescribed time with high marks, their hearts were bursting with pride, and thanks to Franz, without whose influence Joe certainly would never have made it.

Then Franz got married to Hazel, an American he met in London, and Ray and his family held their breath. After a patient while, they had to let it out with a sigh. Unruffled, Joe sat through the family's affectionate teasing with good humor. "This is not a race. I'll go, in due time." That was one territory Franz ventured into that Joe did not deign to follow.

He had a couple of feminine involvements after that but, as with his other female interests before that, somehow he never followed through. "Takes a lot of work," he complained.

"You're just lazy," said Franz.

"True," Joe concurred calmly.

Aside from the fact that he really did not have the inclination to go dating, he found his present life as acceptable as he could make it, under the circumstances. If Laura was out of his life, at least Franz was there, as constant as he had always been. When he wanted company, he went to Franz', when he wanted a taste of married life, he pestered Hazel. He delighted in Franz' kids, little Francis and Joey, his namesake and special favorite, and he enjoyed playing with Chris, the baby. He would regale his family with stories about them. ("Little Francis asked Hazel, 'Mommy, who is your best friend?' 'Daddy,' Hazel replied. Turning to Franz, he asked, 'Daddy, who is your best friend?' 'Uncle Joe,' Franz replied.") Then when he wanted to be alone, he hied to the seclusion of his rooms, in the company of his books, his music, his thoughts and, needless to say, his bottle.

12

*A*fter his talk with Georgie, Joe decided he had had enough playing driver. He avoided going to the club and spent his nights alone in his rooms. The few times when he did go, he did not join the men in the card room but spent time at the bar instead; then he would bring home whatever was left in his bottle and finish it off while watching old movies.

And then that fateful night, a night just made for flirting, with a pale moon sailing across the light, bright sky on a fluffy-cotton cloud, the night breeze fragrant with roses, a tropic night that women, with romance in their hearts but not much of it in their lives, only dreamed about. Such a night it was, even the waves, it seemed, flirted more insistently with the rocks. On nights like these, wives, bored with humdrum marriages and disillusioned with inattentive husbands, should lock themselves inside their houses.

But Ruth was very much in attendance tonight. She saw Joe alone at the bar, watched him pick up the bottle he had almost finished off, watched him head for his car. She sauntered over and caught up with him while he was opening the door of his car.

"Hi," she said.

Joe stopped and paused, then turned slowly and looked at her without a word.

"Leaving already?" she said, smoke in her voice, eyes black as stormy nights. "Take me home?"

He stood there for a minute, not moving, regarding her with heavy-lidded eyes. For a moment she was afraid he would say no. Then he put the half-empty bottle he was holding on the car floor and said huskily, "Come in."

Taking advantage of the closeness of Joe's car and the moonlight that gave the night a glow made for romance, and Joe's defenses downed by drink, Ruth did not look into the recesses of her mind, at lessons there learned from a strict upbringing, lessons already put to a test and failed, miserably, there in the more permissive atmosphere of New York and in the backseat of Georgie's car. What moral lapses she had now lay open and out of control. She met Joe's arms with abandon and sank deep into ecstasy, drowning in the rapture of his lips on hers and his hands clamoring for her body, the bitter taste of tobacco on his tongue, the smell of brandy heavy on his breath, that expensive men's cologne and all his other manly smells intoxicating her to a point of collapse. And then a rush of triumphant exultation, Joe Steiner, whose reserve no girl in their tight little circle had ever been able to break down, now hers, hungrily relieving his own loneliness, and his self-restraint, on her most inviting, most welcoming, and certainly most accepting self. Although she knew that she was not really the cause of this urgent groping (for Ruth never had any illusions, Joe had never looked at her with interest, very much less with desire), this silent, purposeful search that was not meant for her to gratify, or that, unwined, he would never have invited her into his well-guarded, sensual world, or afforded her a glimpse of this intimate, oh-so-lustful self, she was beyond caring, enticing him with lips and arms and eager body, to come and visit, even if not to stay.

Thus they embarked on an affair that would soon become like a drug to her, driving her to distraction with an obsession that consumed her.

Although he never set the pace of the affair---he never called her, all their meetings she had to arrange herself; he just stood outside, an observer, allowing himself to be led, to the place, to the hour, to the frequency of execution---she did not care. All she knew was that she must have him.

They graduated from the confines of his car to the big house, where he lived alone, empty now that Ray had moved the entire family to Manila.

His apartment was a large addition that Maggie had had built on the main floor of their house when he came home from England, to give him the privacy she thought he might need, but mostly to discourage him from looking for a place of his own, and at the same time to be able to look in on him when she felt the need.

Joe completely stopped going to the country club. Duplicity was never his suit; he knew he could not look Georgie in the eye while he was sleeping with his wife. Thus, on evenings when

Georgie went to the club, Ruth drove over to this trysting place, where, amongst the shrubbery and the shadows, the night cloaked her car and her adultery.

But all too soon, fate decided that their time was up. Ray and Maggie and the entire family arrived from Manila for a visit and Joe decided it was too risky for Ruth to come to his rooms where R.J. and worse, his mother, who kept saying she missed this son so, could just pop in at any time of day or night.

"You can't come here, Ruth. We have to wait until they leave."

"And when is that?" Ruth asked impatiently.

"It won't be long. They're leaving in a week," he soothed her.

But she had gotten greedy. He had become a habit that she could not do without for a day, much more a week. Like an addict on withdrawal, she became bitchy, impatient and bad tempered, and endured Georgie's nearness with gritted teeth, until she could not take it much longer.

"I have to see you, Joe," she phoned him. "I'm going crazy here."

"You cannot come here, Ruth. My parents are home."

"Meet me at the Tradewinds, then. Please, Joe, I must see you."

"Don't you think that's too dangerous?"

"How dangerous can it be? Georgie is in the hacienda. Oh, Joe, you must come. I cannot stand it anymore. Another day without you and I surely will go mad. I'll go ahead. I'll call you and give you the room number."

Against his better judgment, he went. He and Ruth had not been in the hotel room an hour when Georgie's sisters came banging on the door, almost knocking it down. The harsh words and the accusations and the tears were too much for Joe to handle. He had never been exposed to this kind of emotional upheaval before and the language that went with it. Was this the family that Laura, but for the grace of God, would have been married into? Somewhere in his life, his mother, in one of her lighter matchmaking moods, and in another one of her distorted perceptions of amusement, knowing his disdain of everything Hernandez, tried to get him together with one of these sisters, Marina, her name was, but before his mother became serious, he put a screeching stop to that. "Don't even think of it, Marguerite," he warned, using his mother's real name, as he did when he was displeased with her. "Maybe she might be tolerable, at best, if her mouth were not always open," Joe said of Marina.

Now from that scorned mouth spewed forth garbage so obscene he felt his uninitiated ears ring. Noting his red face, Marina added insult to his injury.

"You're such a hypocrite, Joe Steiner. You don't want to hear the word, but you obviously enjoyed doing it."

Although Ruth was in this as much as he was, he accepted all culpability for not putting his foot down firmly when she suggested coming to this hotel. His concern was for Ruth to survive the scandal with as little damage as was possible. Mercifully, Georgie was in the hacienda and a physical confrontation was averted, at least for the moment.

* * *

San Sebastian was the capital city of the province, a province that aspired to being richer than most in the country, abounding in rice and coconut, and the island's lifeblood, sugar cane. The Steiners owned a farm there, just outside the city. 'Farm' was really a misnomer. The land sprawled into a few thousand hectares with kilometric boundaries. Isa thus described it to Denis once. "Can you see all that land, as far as your eyes can see?" she said, pointing to a vast stretch of land, a sea of sugar cane the end of which he could not see. "Well, that's not even the entire hacienda. Farther down there, the land is planted in rice and another in coconut."

The landowners who owned lands here usually spent their time in their palatial houses in Manila. Their children went to exclusive schools there, then to finishing schools abroad, and for master's degrees, to universities in Europe and the United States. These children came back to San Sebastian for vacations with a sophistication and sheen so enviable, which the rest of the young people left behind, who were not so luckily pedigreed, imitated and followed. They allowed this refinement to rub on them, and San Sebastian and polished affluence were mentioned in the same breath.

But for all its claims to culture and cosmopolitan finesse, San Sebastian was at heart just a small town, and like many a small town, with its share of people with small minds, inclined to small-minded people-watching and tale-telling and gossip-mongering. The Steiners, the Gomezes, the Hernandezes and the other members of their class were the city's elite, their comings and goings well chronicled in the local papers' society pages, events in their lives held up with fascination for public consumption, their indiscretions grist for gossip mills, in cafes, in mahjong places, in beauty parlors.

This new Steiner scandal fed the town its share of excitement as had not been heard since *Tita* Susie was caught by her husband "in the act" with a new, young, upstart golfer at the back of the clubhouse.

It was a most incredible affair, the aftermath of which sent the families reeling. These two had known each other since childhood, but Joe had never shown any interest in Ruth, had not even looked at her. That he had never shown any interest in or looked at any girl in this town was conveniently not brought up.

Georgie, three children in tow, went back to his parents' house and Ruth, empty handed, went home to hers. R.J., who by this time had also finished his master's degree from Oxford, took over the management of the provincial Steiner and Joe went to Manila, nevermore to return.

The scandal did not stop the affair. Now, without husband and children, Ruth was free to follow Joe to Manila.

And then Franz and Hazel came back, and with them, Joe's sanity.

13

*S*o how are the globetrotters?" Joe asked when Hazel answered the phone.

"One cannot seem to get enough of Europe. Spain is just so magnificent, as usual. Little Francis just loved it there. But we missed the other children. Franz is in the bath. You are coming to dinner tonight, of course," Hazel stated.

"Aren't you people too tired for other people?"

"Hey, hey, what is this? When have we ever been too tired for you, and when did you start thinking of yourself as other people in this house?"

"See you at 8 then," said Joe.

* * *

He kissed Hazel who met him at the door. "Ah, you look delightful, delicious, delovely. The vacation did you good."

"Yes, it surely did. Come in, come in. Mama and Papa are out to dinner with friends. It's just us. Let me call Franz."

Joe took off his coat and dropped it on a chair. He looked around. He had not been here since that afternoon he picked up Laura, before Denis came to claim her back, that week he found rapture he never imagined possible, that week he met sorrow that never waned, heartbreak that never went away.

All through dinner, they talked of the trip and the amusing things that little Francis did and how much he, too, missed his little brothers. And how Spain was just blooming at this time. "I had been to many countries in the world," said Franz, "but I still say, I haven't seen as many gorgeous women as I see in Spain."

"How's Laura?" Joe asked.

"She has a very hard time with that pregnancy," said Franz, "throwing up, getting nauseous at the smell of everything. Denis said he had a hard time, too. She was quick to tears, quick to take offense; she couldn't even stand the smell of him. He couldn't understand the depression, he said. She had always wanted this baby. He thought she would be elated. He started calling Mom, for sympathy, he said. Mom said she was like that when she had me, but surprisingly, had an easier time with all the others. She'd lost a lot of weight." He paused, thinking of his sister. "But she's coming 'round now."

"I have never seen her look more radiant. Pregnancy becomes her," said Hazel. "And that skin! I read somewhere that not eating cleanses the body and makes the skin glow. Oh, what I would give to have skin like that."

"How about what you would give up, like that flan, for instance," said Franz, throwing a glance at the dessert in front of his wife. Hazel winked at Joe and they both laughed. They knew what Franz was going to say before he said it. Her yearly pregnancies had started to take their toll on her hips and Franz had been urging her to work out. "That gym is still waiting for you," he said.

"Oh well, Jim," she quipped, "he could wait," and laughed heartily at her own joke.

Franz shook his head. "Seriously now."

"Yes, dear, I'll start tomorrow," she said good-naturedly.

Franz looked at Joe but Joe was laughing, too. That was her stock answer, tomorrow. They knew she had no intentions of doing anything.

"Having little Francis there was good for her," said Franz, still thinking of his sister. "She had always loved children. I'm happy for her. Denis, too, was delighted to have us there, we lightened Lauren's mood a bit. And you know, so was I, delighted to be there. You go through periods not seeing her, and then you do, and you realize how much you miss her."

"He said he was too tired and wanted to skip L.A., but I insisted," said Hazel. "I knew Laura would never forgive us if we came home without visiting her. How about you," she asked Joe. "It's vacation time, you have not been out in two years."

"Yes," seconded Franz. "You should go. You should visit Spain again."

"Oh, I don't know." He looked absently in space, feeling the stubbles on his face with the back of his hand.

"Yes, Spain. It's magnificent now. You can't go wrong with Spain," said Franz.

Joe saw the concern on his face. "Well, maybe. But I was thinking. I was thinking of Indonesia."

Franz looked at him in surprise. "Indonesia? Why Indonesia?"

"There are some people there I'd like to look up. And then maybe I'll do Burma, too."

"Oh, Joe, really," laughed Hazel.

They laughed, as though at a good joke, but Franz, looking at Joe, thought, was he seriously considering the trip? If he was then Franz was with him, as always. "That sounds like a good idea," said Franz, nodding his head. "Let's. Maybe we can find something productive there. Let's plan it out and we'll go together."

Joe filled out Franz with things that happened with the business while he was away. "I don't know how R.J. likes it there." No mention was made why R.J. had to take over.

"Are the old folks always at your back?" inquired Franz.

"Not really. I'm still sort of on vacation. When are you going back to San Sebastian?" Joe asked.

"Hazel wants to catch her breath. Mom's going, too. She has not been there in a long while. So in two weeks, probably, after Papa's birthday."

But Joe knew that he and Ruth were very much on their minds. They carefully skirted any topic that might verge on the affair, hiding behind small talk, thankful for the chatter of the children.

"Uncle Joe," said Little Francis, "we went to so many churches there, does that mean I don't have to go to church all this year?" This made everybody laugh.

"He's such a heathen, I don't know whom he took after," said Franz. "That first Francis, maybe, what do you think? They say he was not Catholic, but I say he was not anything at all, look how fast he converted. We must stop naming our children after him. He might just reincarnate in one of them, if he isn't already in this one." He tried to hold the squirming reincarnation but Little Francis was too slippery for him.

After dinner, Hazel all too eagerly bundled the children off to bath and bed, almost with an audible sigh of relief, leaving the two cousins alone.

"Coffee?" offered Franz.

"No, thanks," said Joe.

"Well, then, maybe this Carlos I that I got from the duty-free shop. I wrapped up a bottle for you, by the way. It's among my things somewhere. I'll give it to you tomorrow." He proceeded to the bar, took out two glasses and put some ice in his. Joe preferred his drink straight. He poured a good half-glass for Joe and gave him the drink.

Joe took the glass from him with a vague nod of thanks, the ice clinking against Franz' glass the only sound in the room, the air heavy with concerns left unsaid. "All right," he said at last, "go ahead, I'm ready. Come out with it."

Franz took off his eyeglasses, ran them under the running water and wiped them carefully with his handkerchief. "I'm thinking, really, why don't you go take that vacation now, go to L.A. Denis does not have a tour coming. He has been paring down his commitments so he could spend more time with Lauren and that leaves her, for a welcome change, with time on her hands. You know they would just love to have you there. You have always been good for her, take her out of her depression, take her mind off herself. Besides, they're coming in two weeks for Papa's birthday. Two weeks away would be perfect. You could come back with them then."

Joe sighed but did not say anything.

"You need a breather, that's what you need," Franz continued. "Two weeks out will do you good. We'll do Indonesia together next time. I really think that's a good idea."

Just like that, no reproof, no recriminations, no judgmental criticism. Joe thought, he was always a class act, Franz was, a male version of Cecilia. He wondered what turns he would have taken in his life had Franz not been there all the time for him. Just look where he took himself to in the short time that Franz was not around.

Joe looked at him sadly. "It's all right, Franz. It's over. Don't worry about it anymore."

"You know I do worry."

"I know," said Joe, giving him a slight smile, "and you know I do appreciate it."

Thus, without even verging on the subject, and with his considerable influence on Joe, Franz sternly and firmly took a hand in the affair and the flame that started in his absence fizzled and burned out in his presence.

Joe had put off thinking about it, but now it hit him in full force. He would not even be working with Franz anymore. Franz would be going back to San Sebastian and he would remain here in Manila. He would no more appear at their door on lonely evenings or pester Hazel or play with the children. The long, empty days and nights yawned and engulfed him. They had never been separated for long since they were children. No Laura, and now, no Franz. How could he endure? Oh, God, how much punishment could a heart take?

"There's no way R.J. could manage San Sebastian on his own, is there?" he asked.

Franz, as always, understood. Joe did not want him to go back to San Sebastian. "Maybe not alone, just yet," he said, looking at Joe seriously. "There must be a way. We could make a study of it. You want me to take this up in the meeting?" he asked.

"Oh, I don't know, Franz. I'll think about it." He gritted his teeth, the muscles working up and down his cheeks.

"Yes, I think it's time for me to come here, too," said Franz. "The children are growing fast. Yes, that would please Hazel very much. RJ could do it alone there, with a little help. I'm sure Mike Sanz would relocate, if the price is right. He's good, you said so yourself. Once a month, I'll go over and see how things are going. Know what? I really think it's s a good idea. Let's do that. I'll talk to Papa tomorrow. "

Joe looked at him and nodded slightly. He gulped down his drink, grimaced, and put the glass down on the counter. He put his hand on top of the glass when Franz was about to refill it. For once, he did not feel like drinking. "Wow, wonder of wonders," he said and laughed, "I don't feel like more. And Carlos 1, too." He gathered his jacket from the chair where he had carelessly flung it when he arrived. "You must be tired from that long trip and it's been a long day. Say goodnight to Hazel and kiss the kids for me. And Franz, thanks."

Franz looked at him, saw the misery in his eyes, and as he did all their lives, felt that misery, too. He nodded slightly and walked him to the door. Joe's car stood in the covered driveway, spanking bright, the metal on its body gleaming under the overhead lights.

"I'll see you tomorrow?" asked Franz.

Joe nodded, looked down at his hand without really seeing it, put it up in a gesture of goodbye, went into his car and drove off into the night, leaving Franz with a terrible melancholy, for this cousin who always seemed to have everything---money that could buy him anything he desired, looks that could get him anywhere he wanted, brains that had gotten him honors without half trying---everything, in fact, that spelled happiness, but for him did not.

*   *   *

The family had converted the top floor of the Steiner Building into penthouses for family members who needed private spaces for private uses. Joe had exiled himself in one of these penthouses after he came back from that affair in San Sebastian. Although Maggie and the other members of his family felt that he would heal slower alone, without his family around him to deflect part of the hurt, for once they did not question his decision. With that frightening look on his face that fairly shouted *Leave me alone*, nobody dared.

The room was pitch dark when he entered his apartment but he did not notice. He groped his way in the dark into his bedroom. The lights outside threw a sliver of yellow through an opening in the drapes. He drew them wide open and undressed in the pale light. He dropped on his bed, shirtless, unbathed, bone tired, and immediately fell asleep, his insomniac nights catching up with him. He slept through dreams that left him gripped with longing and desire, and again, as in other countless dreams, awake or asleep, he allowed himself to indulge in them, always the same scene, always the same girl, not her on whom he had given vent to this hunger these past weeks. And then, a difference. In the dim lit horizon Georgie loomed, eyes wide with anger, pointing an accusing finger at him that made him want to hide his head in his hands in shame. He woke up covered with sweat, even his bed sheet was damp, his uncovered state notwithstanding.

He zigzagged to the bathroom, eyes half closed, groggy and still full of sleep. He put on his pajamas, then straggled to the dry side of the bed and slept for ten more hours. The afternoon sun streamed through the window when he awoke. He looked at the clock on his bedside table. Four o'clock. God, he thought, I almost slept the day through. He showered, letting the hot water steam away the sleep and the sluggishness, unfamiliar for not having been induced by drink. He dressed, noticed that his eyes were puffy from too much sleep. Then he went to keep his date with Ruth.

*   *   *

Angelo's was a small restaurant on an out-of-the-way country road. With a few large bills discreetly changing hands, Joe always had reserved for him a table for two in a far corner of the dining room, almost hidden from view of other tables by sizable fronds of palms. Lamps glimmered on walls, giving the dining room a pale glow. They always had the same table near a side door, which relieved them from the painful process of traversing through seemingly endless tables while imagined eyes bore curiously through their backs when they left.

Dinner was quiet as usual. Joe, frequently uncommunicative and not sharing much in common with Ruth, would observe and listen, while Ruth rambled on a variety of topics. Tonight, he was more quiet than usual, his thoughts still on dinner at Franz' last night. How he longed to see how she looked, four months into her pregnancy. Hazel said she was not showing yet. She would look funny with a big stomach, he thought. Why, she might even get fat, he smiled at the thought. He ached to take care of her, pamper her, spoil her until the baby came, then help her take care of the baby, for it did not matter that it was Denis' baby, if it was hers, then it was his, too. But now all he wanted was to take her in his arms, hold her, comfort her. It's all right, Bud, it was not your fault, don't suffer for it, I'm suffering enough for both of us. He sat there, distracted, toying with his food while Ruth feasted her eyes on him.

"What?" he asked when at last he became conscious of Ruth's frank stare.

"Do you have any idea how much pleasure it gives me, just looking at you, at the breadth and the height and the," she groped for words, "the handsomeness of you, at the elegant way you carry yourself, wear your clothes. Why, you look even better than those models in magazines," she said.

"It's all right, Ruth, dinner's on me."

"But you do. I think I must have loved the way you look since we were this high. At least, I've always thought you the best-looking boy in the neighborhood. In the city." She laughed, "in the world, even."

And he had never even looked at her. But then, he had never looked at any other girl. How could he, blinded by just that one face as he was, for as long as he could remember. It had taken an incredibly attractive girl as Emily to make him blink and shift his gaze, and after Emily, some others as stunning, but after a while, even startling beauty just was not enough, if it was not hers. And back to her he shifted his gaze. She was his, his creation, his hunger's only food, his quests' only destination. She was his, or better to say, he was hers, inextricably, hopelessly, without recourse, and there was nothing he could do about it.

What traits they did not share at birth, she copied, some purposefully, some unwittingly, for being with him too often, too long, until she became his echo, with his mannerisms that she made her own, too---an expressionless gaze that discouraged familiarity, a detached look that put an end to unwelcome attempts at getting close. They both had a love for reading that bordered on mania, exchanging books, exhausting the library's supply; on his part, spending a fortune until he had piles of them that required shelves that reached the ceiling, bringing her books he was through with if he thought them good and good for her. She did not recognize his censorship, her trust in him absolute. While other girls her age were searching surreptitiously for sex scenes through pages of trashy novels, she was being fed and, because Joe said so, devoured the writings of The Thomases, as she called them---Hardy, Paine, though not quite as enthusiastically, the difficult Aquinas---and the other great minds of the Catholic Church. He had a definite hand in shaping her tastes---in literature, in music, in the arts---which reflected his own. He opened her world to poetry and literature when she was barely ten, to classical music before the blare of rock music could claim her. She loved Brahms, Schubert, and her staple, Rachmaninoff, the first time she heard their music, and he searched for, and bought, different recordings he could find, even writing to music stores abroad, and would be very pleased when her preference for one artist over another coincided with his own. Later, in London, he became involved with a girl, an antique nut, who hauled him in search of ancient things, scouring out-of-the-way sources and estate sales. From these he found old and out-of-print and rare editions of books that he could not find in regular bookstores. One day, he found a rare copy of Petrarch's *Canzoniere*, a different edition from the one their grandfather Franz gave their grandmother Laura. Another *Canzoniere* for another Laura! Excited at such a priceless find, he was prepared to pay a ransom for the book, and was surprised and delighted when the owner gave it to him for what he thought was a pittance for such a find.

He would give the records and books to her in a carefully careless way, wrapped in brown paper, indifferent, casual, nonchalant. "Here, see if you like that," tossing the package at her, not letting on that he had spent too many hours and too much effort looking for them.

They swallowed solitude, covered themselves with quiet, shared an inordinate preference to be left alone. They shunned parties and superficial talk. They could listen, absorbed, to hours of music or just stay still in silence, he with his books, she with her thoughts. He would give her his complete attention, listened to her childish patter with care, to her more serious opinions mindfully, corrected and counseled when needed. She absorbed his ideas and his opinions and accepted things as so because Joe said so. He arose before 6 in time for morning Mass, which they both assiduously attended every day, a habit that stayed with them all their lives.

He deflected intimation of how he felt for her by going out with two or three of those women his mother foisted on him. Home in Manila on vacations, he must have been matched with every eligible daughter of his mother's friends. His mother would be on the lookout for girls whom she considered "nice" enough for her son and would go into her matchmaking routine. When the object of these exercises seemed interesting enough, he humored his mother. He would go out on a couple of dates, but a couple was all he managed. Ana, a daughter of a Spanish diplomat in Manila whose family became friendly with the Steiners, lasted the longest, the last month of one summer when he and Franz were on vacation; then they went back to Oxford, and she and her family later went back to Spain, and that was the last anybody heard of her. As with the others, Joe lost interest soon enough and went back to his endeavors of choice--Franz, his books, and inevitably, his bottles.

He was the first male born to the Gomez family after many years and everybody doted on him. He was the favorite of his aunts and cousins. His sisters and RJ did not mind that he was clearly their mother's favorite and they did not mind being always at his beck and call. His grandfather just adored him. He was used to people waiting on him, and they did. Franz took him under his wing, decided for him, acted for him.

There was no way he could have made open his feelings for Laura; if the family knew, the ensuing upheaval would have been more than he could cope with. Although Franz had always been in his corner, he knew that in this instance, Franz most certainly would have disapproved. Not to mention Francis, and his own father, too. And what fury his mother would have vented on Laura. Maybe that was one reason she had always been so vocal in her criticisms of her. Maybe, deep down, she saw where this devotion he conferred on her could lead to and was afraid for his sake, and this devotion was a source of constant vexation for her.

Everything about Laura aggravated his mother. Even vacations that he spent with Laura and Franz were met with disapproval and resistance and bribery. She would pay his fare, she said, if he would go abroad with them, instead, and even throw in spending money, she would add, forgetting, when it was convenient, that money never ranked high in his priorities, having more than anybody in their family. Visits to Santo Niño, especially, were a constant bone of contention between them.

"I can't understand how you could prefer to spend your vacation there than come with us abroad," she complained.

"How many times have I been abroad with you," he answered patiently, and been bored to death, he thought, with all those shopping sprees. What was the point in going with her; he ventured out alone, on his own, anyway, to the opera and museums and art galleries, because, aside from a couple of evenings at the theater and a couple at the ballet, which were musts when telling stories about their trips, she and his sisters cared more for shopping than for the things he fed his soul with.

"Well, how many times have you been there with them?"

"If you had bothered, just once, to go there, you'd see what an enchanting place it is, really, and maybe you'd even ask to come with me."

"Enchanting? That god-forsaken place? Have you heard of the word boondocks? Do you know where that word came from? It's from the Tagalog word for mountain, *bundok*, that the Americans coined after the war. Look it up. It's in the dictionary. It was in those boondocks there that the Americans hid from the Japanese during the war. That is enchanting?"

"Hid from the Japanese, indeed," he repeated, laughing. "I hope you remember that those Americans won the war."

"Oh, but of course they did. Those mountains were so dense, those Japanese never had a chance of finding them."

"I've never heard a more self-serving rewrite of history and only you, dear mother, can do that without blinking an eye." He was laughing now. His mother would twist anything she wanted, to pound down her point. "I wonder how you know, you've never been there. But we are not going to the mountains, for heaven's sake, Santo Niño is by the sea and I would rather spend my vacation there than anywhere else."

"Darling, that word means sticks, and that is exactly what that place is."

"Sticks that produced *Tita* Ceil. Let's not derogate those very elegant people. That town has more cultured people than any town I know," he said. His eyes had taken that forbidding look. Everybody knew he would never brook any criticism heaped on Cecilia or her family. When he looked this way, Maggie knew she was treading on touchy waters.

"Darling, it's just that I never get to be with you. Every spare time you have you spend with them."

"Come," he said, "let's not quarrel over something both of us can't do anything about. You know my bags are packed. Here, give me a hug." He hugged her tightly, kissed her fervently on both checks. "There, that should tide you over till I come back." It always worked. She was putty in his hands.

About the only thing Laura ever did that Maggie approved of, and most wholeheartedly, was marrying Denis and living in faraway Los Angeles.

So much conflict over just a few days with Laura! Imagine the uproar if he had announced that he wanted to spend his entire life with her!

No, he would have been completely alone. But he would have overcome anything if he were sure that Laura felt the same way. She worshipped him, that he knew, but being in love with him in the physical sense, well, she was too young for that. He couldn't have stood it if she thought him weird, or strange, and rejected him. She had always blamed her aunts and uncles for those unfortunate cousins, for looking at each other, instead of looking outward, when they were falling in love. But he couldn't give her up. He would wait, he knew he would, when she got a bit older and got out from under Cecilia's wings.

And then Denis arrived on the scene, without warning, and doused his dreams with bitter rue.

14

fter dinner, after he settled up and left the waiter a hefty tip and Angelo a heftier one, he and Ruth slipped out, unobserved, through the side door. Sometimes, if the mood struck him, they would drive around for a while, after which they would go back to Ruth's apartment. The incident in that hotel had left him with a terror-stricken aversion to hotel rooms. Tonight, they went straight to Ruth's place. He had business to take care of and now that he had decided, he did not want to tarry.

Without being able to put her finger to it, Ruth knew that the days of the affair were numbered. He was still there when she wanted him, although his lovemaking was getting angrier, more tormented, once, in anguish, wrenching out from deep within him another's name. But she had transcended to a place beyond shame, beyond pride, for when he swept her up with him in his frenzied, tumultuous lovemaking, he made it all worthwhile.

"Who's Rosebud?" she had asked him.

"What?" he turned to her, his eyes spears that took her aback. His need for *her* was getting out of hand now, refusing to be held down in some hidden part of him that had not been allowed a voice before. Very often now, he would waken and catch his voice reverberating from some dreamlike recesses of his room, Bud, Bud, Bud. Did he cry out this name and Ruth took it for another?

"Rosebud," repeated Ruth. "You were dreaming; you called out her name."

She winced as his face darkened and she saw the look that had withered so many others before her who had tried to intrude into his private world, that part of his life that was forbidden territory, even to her.

"Let's not play doctor and patient here. That had nothing to do with this. Don't mention it again." Then he wiped the stern look off his face, relented and gave her a smile. "It was nothing, really, Orson Well's Rosebud, who knows. Don't think about it. It was just a dream. Just forget it. Okay?"

Well, yes, when he smiled like that, she would do anything he wanted.

Tonight, she watched him drape his coat on a chair as they came in. "Drink?" she asked.

He shook his head and walked to the window, his hands buried deep in his pockets. He stood there looking out, his thoughts only he knew where, a picture that was becoming more familiar to her lately, filling her with dread.

She was clinging at straws, hoping that if he wanted out, he was gentleman enough not to be the one to call off the affair. She was willing to accept him on any term, halfhearted, half enthusiastic, not even (no, not ever) the initiator. And then he turned around and looked at her wordlessly, his face a stranger's, grim, forbidding, yet full of infinite sadness, and she knew that it was over, that he was just waiting for her to say the words and she had to say them.

"Do I end this or do you?" she returned his look.

He came toward her, took her hand, put it to his lips, looked at her with that sweet look that squeezed her heart and said, "Maybe we should. I do miss going to Communion."

Of all the reasons for breaking off an affair, she would never have thought of this one.

Yet, it should not have come as such a surprise. He had always been devoutly Catholic. A long time ago, when they were still young in San Sebastian, she would attend Mass every morning, in that small, sun-flooded, flower-filled church that served their community, and every morning when he was in town, he was always there, too, sometimes alone, more often with Laura and Cecilia. She remembered the times he would come in late, just in time for Communion. He would leave his prayer book on the last pew and hurry straight to the Communion rail. When he came alone, he would nod at her in acknowledgment, a half smile on his lips, but would leave without a word. When he came with Laura, Laura would exchange brief pleasantries with her outside the church after Mass while he stood by in silence. Once, they came out while she was waiting for her car. Laura came over to where she was waiting and asked, "Do you have a ride?"

"I'm waiting for our driver," she replied.

"We could take you home," Laura offered, while Joe stood behind her, his look intent behind his steel-rimmed spectacles, that intent look that made a girl, with an intake of breath, think it was for her, a part of his charm of which he did not even seem aware. The steel-rimmed spectacles were a very becoming new addition, which, with his hair swept back, made him look more handsome than she ever remembered. His eyes, too, behind his glasses looked more gray that morning than they always were, made grayer, she supposed, by the gray shirt he was wearing, those grays the Steiners were noted for.

"Thanks, but he's on his way," she said of her driver.

"Sure?" Laura asked. She nodded in answer. "All right then," Laura said. Joe smiled and he and Laura turned away as Ruth watched his tall, broad frame walk to his car. Laura waved, Joe nodded slightly before he drove away, a gorgeous expensive car, a gorgeous expensive driver. There were varying degrees of wealth among the landowners. All were wealthy, some more so than others. The Steiners were way up there. But Joe, with the Steiner money on one side and the Gomez money his grandfather left him on the other, must be up there on top of the list.

Later, when he and Franz came back from England and started to manage the provincial Steiner, every single morning he was there in church, hearing Mass, receiving the Eucharist. Although he was friendly and polite, he was never close to anybody, except to the other Steiners, Franz and Laura, and when Laura went away, there was just Franz.

She heard that he went out with a girl or two in Manila, but he had never been interested in any girl in their town. In social affairs where he absolutely must attend and bring a date, he would haul Laura from where she was engrossed in at the moment. When she was not available, and later, after she got married and was not around anymore, he went without a date and spent most of the evening at the bar with Franz, or exchanging pleasantries with some of their friends, or, when he could muster enough energy, even dance once with a few of their friends, after which back to the bar he would retreat, a waste of God's glorious creation. Later, when marriage put Franz out of commission, he, too, gave up partying, which he never seemed to have much enthusiasm for in the first place. On socials that they had to attend, the family would set him up with a date, but by the end of the evening it was apparent that his preference was more towards the bar than the girl they had dug up for him for the evening.

Of the Steiners, it was Nacho who was the most outgoing. R.J. was more Gomez than Steiner, spending most of his days in Manila, visiting San Sebastian only when his mother and sisters came. But Nacho was always the friendly one, always had a smile and a word of greeting for everyone. Then, just when the girls were starting to spring him, he entered the seminary. It was just too weird. The taciturn, introspective, reclusive ones still out there, while the one so full of charm, so outgoing, so interested in people, now inside the seminary, where he could be seen rounding the corners of the school's corridors, his white habit ballooning behind him, whistling a happy, tuneless tune, lost to the womanhood so eager to have captured him.

* * *

Now Joe was ending their affair because he missed the Eucharist. The sad thing was, on top of what other reasons he might have, Ruth knew that this one was true.

"What will I do without you," she said.

"Why don't you go abroad for a while, take a vacation. Before you know it, this unhappy time will be behind you and it will be easier to start anew."

She had to give it one last shot. "Why don't we go together, live there and not come back."

He felt a twinge in his heart. Oh, would that those words were uttered two months ago, by another's lips, lips that he mustn't think of, or he would be undone. He touched Ruth's face gently. "Start fresh, Ruthie, for the children's sake, yes, but also for yourself. You've lost weight, haven't you?" His warm concern brought tears to her eyes.

But she did not want this affair that started with a bang to end in a literal whimper. "Don't you like your women thin?"

He smiled, glad that she could be flippant. "I like you any way you are." He touched her hair gently. "It has not been easy for you, these had been sad times, I know."

She ignored it that he never said I love, it was always I like. "I would never be sad, if we could just be together."

He sighed deeply. "Yes, you would. One day, when your fire is spent, you will look back to this time in regret and you will never forgive yourself for not being there when the children were growing up and needing you."

When your fire is spent, the gentleman said. Aching for him as she did now, she could not imagine a time when this fire for him would finally be consumed. But obviously, his was. "Georgie will never give them to me."

"Maybe not yet. But time will take care of things, doesn't it always? But you have to try. They need you, Ruth."

And you don't, she thought, but you need your Eucharist. What could one do when one's rival was so formidable?

She sighed and with a heavy heart dragged herself to the door to let him out. He picked up his coat, slung it over his shoulder, and followed her. With his other hand, he held her chin up and she had to look at him. He bent his head and touched her lips with his in a whisper of a kiss, sweet, sad, one last time.

Thus it ended. He was tearing her heart out, and as with their first kiss, the finality of this last drained her to a point of collapse.

15

*T*he church that served the community was often referred to as The Church That Castro Built. Long ago, when relations between Cuba and the United States foundered, the U.S. government considerably raised the sugar quota of the Philippines. The Philippine sugar industry flourished and San Sebastian prospered with it. To thank the Lord for this bounty, the parishioners gave unstintingly came collection time and the priests found themselves with more money than they ever had. This largesse extended to Forbes where several landowners bought land and built opulent houses with money that came from lands planted in sugarcane. When the priests decided that a bigger church was needed to serve the growing community, the parishioners gave freely and generously, money poured into the church's coffers, and extensive renovations were made, courtesy, as they said, of *Señor* Castro.

* * *

This Easter Sunday morning was not different from other Easter Sundays before it. The sky was cloudless, the sun beat down mercilessly on the asphalt road, and a haze rose from the ground. Outside the church, the flame trees, harbinger of leaden Lenten days, were in full bloom, as they always were in Lent, their red flowers ablaze in the early heat. The morning, breezeless, stifled, and the ladies, seated at their pews, armed with Spanish fans, were stirring up a bit of comfort while waiting listlessly for Mass to begin.

Laura felt someone tugging at her hair, turned around and saw Joe kneeling behind her. "Hey," she breathed out, too surprised to conceal her delight at seeing him, her pleasure making her face shine. Was it because of his hapless affair? He looked thinner, she thought, older, too, but still infinitely handsome, and, with the sad look in his eyes, more so now than she ever remembered. Unbidden, she reached out to touch his lean face. He caught and held her hand and shifted his gaze to

Denis, who had also turned around and was looking at him. "Hi, when did you guys pop into town?" As if he did not know.

"We came in yesterday," said Denis.

"Come sit here beside me," Laura invited and moved closer to Denis to make room for Joe. He stood up obediently and slipped into the space beside her, at the end of the pew nearest the aisle. "You've lost weight. How are you?" whispered Laura behind her fan.

"Oh, I'm fine."

She searched his face. "So I heard," she said in an undertone.

"*Et tu, Brúté?*" he said, not smiling.

She smiled. "Come, have breakfast at the house."

"I'll be there tonight for the party," he said, "no need to overextend myself." The family was celebrating Francis' 60th birthday tonight. It was going to be a big affair, there would be too many people, too much noise, and looking at Denis and Laura, too many hurting things of which he wanted to be spared. He planned to develop an allergy at the last minute and beg off.

"Tonight is tonight," she said. "Come for breakfast."

"What have you got?"

"What do you want?"

"You should know."

"We're not going into that."

"No."

"Come then, Cook will make you Spanish chorizos and eggs and fried rice. And we have these sweet strawberries, just came from Bagiuo." His second favorite fruit, he always said, the first of course being grapes, fine fresh, better fermented, best distilled.

He looked at her with that long, searching look. How glorious she made the morning and how he missed her, and after the squalid dalliance with Ruth, never more so than today. The dark world of adultery, of stealing time with somebody's wife, the momentary gratification that turned to shame in the light of day, the guilt, and worst of all, the humiliation with the sisters Hernandez, the anger and the hurt making them spout those ugly, ugly words that made him recoil with shame and disgust whenever he thought of them, all seemed unreal and far away in the brightness of her presence.

She had gained a few becoming pounds. Her face had filled out, lessening the sharp Steiner features that on her seemed to stand out when she lost weight. He looked down. Four months unto her pregnancy, and though her arms and her breasts were fuller, she was not showing yet.

"You look great," he breathed. But then, in all the years he had known her, he had never seen her look less than great--- elegant, formal, disheveled, casual; a young girl, a teenager, a married woman, eyes raised in communion with God, eyes closed in adultery with him, eyes clouded with worry now looking at him---and always, always, taking his breath away.

Then Mass was almost over and people filed on the aisle to receive Holy Communion. Joe rose, stepped out unto the aisle, stepped back a pace to let Laura go ahead.

She leaned her head back a bit and whispered, "so you're coming to breakfast?"

"If you promise not to lecture."

She turned her head and looked at his face. She could not imagine him with Ruth. "If you promise it's all over."

"A momentary aberration, but over and done with," he said. He smiled at her sweetly and reached her innermost heart. "I'm receiving Communion, am I not?"

Then she saw his body tense, "God," she heard him say. His eyes shut close as he grimaced and fell towards her.

"Bud?" Blood spurted all over her. "Bud." Her voice held all the horror that a word could contain. "Bud!" With his weight on her, they both started to topple over.

Denis was looking at them both whispering to each other, feeling that familiar disquietude whenever he saw them together. Then, like a silent movie in slow motion, he saw blood spurt from Joe's chest, saw him topple towards Laura, saw her open her arms to enfold him, saw her mouth open in a horrible whisper of a scream, Bud, Bud, Bud. Terrified for her safety, his first impulse to protect her, he shot out from his seat and hurled himself at her, pulling her, with Joe enfolded in her arms, down with him to the floor, and covered her body with his own.

He looked at her, at her dress that was white this morning, now with Joe's blood splattered all over it. "Oh, Lauren, are you all right? Stay down, stay down, are you hurt? Oh, dearest, answer me." That voice, and the urgency in it, woke people from their stupor. All at once people scrambled for safety, fled from the scene of danger, rushed as far away from Joe, prone on the tiled floor, and Denis, sheltering his wife with his body.

Francis and Cecilia, a few pews behind, were looking at Laura and Joe whispering to each other, saw them rise to receive Communion, saw Joe fall towards Laura, saw Denis cover his wife with his own body. They both rushed towards the three huddled on the floor. Stefan and Maricris, who were seated next to Cecilia, joined Francis and Cecilia at almost the same time.

"Oh, God," sobbed Cecilia, looking at her bloodied daughter.

Francis bent down to look at Laura. "She's not hurt," said Denis, holding Laura in his arms.

"Joe?" asked Cecilia looking at Joe.

Francis knelt on the floor and turned his attention to Joe, lying there chillingly motionless, his eyes closed. He looked with dread at Joe' chest and knew that there was nothing more anyone could do for him. He looked at Denis, then at Cecilia, the horror and grief on his face telling them what his voice could not.

"Oh, God," said Cecilia again.

Francis held out his arms to her and, with both of them kneeling on the tiled floor, he held her while she wept. Then taking control, Francis turned to Stefan. "Go to the rectory and call Franz, Stefan. Then call Ray and Dr. Rudi. Tell Dr. Rudi to go straight to the house. I'm sending Lauren home now. Will you be all right?" Stefan nodded. "Then go," he urged Stefan. Again, he looked at his daughter. "How are you?" She remained silent and Denis answered for her. "She's not hurt," he said again.

Francis looked at Denis. "Better get out of here, Denis, and take Lauren home. You don't want to be here when the press comes. I'll take care of things here until Franz and Ray come. Franz or Stefan can take us home." He dug into his pocket and handed Denis his car keys. "Hurry now."

"Come, sweet, let's go home." Denis whispered to Laura.

"I cannot just leave him here. That floor is dirty and he needs care. Where's the doctor. Why is nobody taking care of him? Call the doctor, Papa."

"Go with Denis, Lauren," said Francis, "we'll take care of Joe. Franz will be here soon, and Ray, too."

"No, no, no, I can't. Oh, please, Denis, don't make me leave him. Oh, please, Papa, please." She flung herself on Joe's body and the blood on his chest clotted her hair and mingled with the tears on her face. They realized she was on the verge of hysteria.

"Listen to me, Laura," said Francis, holding her firmly by the shoulders, forcing her to look at him, mustering all the authority that had served him in good stead all these years. "Listen to me. You must get away from here. The people from the press will be here very soon. You don't want to be here when they come. Besides, you need attention yourself. Dr. Rudi will be at the house soon. You must go home. I'll take care of Joe. I promise. There is nothing we can do for him now but whatever needs to be done, I am here to see to it. Franz and Ray will be here soon. But there's something you have to do for yourself and the baby. Now go, Lauren."

"Come, sweet," said Denis, but she clutched at Joe's shirt, and bloodied her hands. She was very still, staring at her hands, her eyes wide with horror. Her face would have shocked her into an outright breakdown had she seen it, all blood-smeared, her eyes staring widely, wildly beneath her blood-caked hair. "Oh, Lauren," Denis said in consternation. He scooped her up in his arms. "Come," he said. He carried her out of the church, deposited her in the car and sped away.

When they reached the house, he helped her out of her blood-splattered clothes, and under a steaming shower, soaped away the blood and the tears and the shock. He then toweled her dry, slipped her nightdress over her head, ran a comb through her damp hair, gave her brandy which she swallowed docilely (and went into a paroxysm of coughing when the brandy hit her throat) and put her to bed. The doctor came with Cecilia and he gave her a pill that made her sleep for hours.

* * *

In retrospect, safe in the knowledge that Joe was the sole target, everyone had something to say---the bullet caught him straight in the heart, he never knew what hit him, death was merciful and swift.

Nobody heard the shot, nobody saw who did it. With people milling towards the Communion rail, and with the ensuing commotion when Joe and Laura fell, everybody was too shocked to look back at who did it, granted they knew there was somebody to look for.

* * *

Francis came to their room later to look in on his daughter, but she was fast asleep. "How's everything?" Denis asked.

"They're preparing him. Maggie is beside herself, as you can expect. I do not even want to think what Ray is going through now." He was silent for a long time, shaking his head, his eyes very red, and Denis could not bring himself to say anything. What was there to say? Francis lost a son, too, for that was what Joe had always been to him. "I have to go, you'll take care?" said Francis at last, looking lost.

Denis nodded. Even he could not describe the desolation he himself felt as he watched Francis plod heavily down the corridor to his room.

                              * * *

Denis was propped up in bed, looking at the frown on his wife's face, a book unread on his lap, his thoughts reviewing the events of the morning. Then she turned the other way and he felt her sobbing quietly beside him. He turned her over to face him and the light illuminated her tear-stained face. She put her arm across her face to cover her eyes.

"Oh, sweet, how are you feeling?" She shook her head and tried to turn away from him. "Go ahead, sweet, cry, it's all right, I'm here, it's all right." The concern in his voice opened the floodgates of her tears. She let herself go and her wails broke the silence of the huge house. He brought his body on top of hers, held down her flailing arms and held her heaving body close to his. "It's all right, I'm here, it's all right." He held her close until she was spent and tear-dried and her sobs had subsided. Soon, with vestiges of the pill still remaining in her system, he heard her breathing evenly and he knew she was asleep at last.

He looked at her, this wife of his, so innocent, so pure of heart. In her innocence did she never recognize her feelings for this cousin for what it was? Did she never sit down for a while to think over how Joe felt for her and give it a name, had simply accepted his attention as purely innocent and her due because she bestowed upon him the same kind of innocent adulation? On Joe's part, at a time when falling in love with a cousin was strictly forbidden, an immutable taboo, and given Cecilia's family history of disastrous inbreeding, with such frightening genetic results, did he look for her in other women, and not finding her, did not settle for less, and so elected the company of the bottle instead?

He touched her face, wearing that frown even in sleep. It never failed to amaze him how, after all these years, he still found so much pleasure just looking at her, delighting in touching her, hurrying home to her when his day was done. No, he thought, he could not be right about Joe. No man, once finding her, would ever give her up for anyone, for anything, for whatever reason, to appease which family, to conform to whatever rules society imposed.

Slowly, he removed himself from her, pulled the sheet up over her shoulders and quietly left the bed. Through the French window, moonlight spilled onto the room. He stepped out to the terrace.

It was one of those perfect Manila nights, perfect as only a tropic night could be. A breeze blew cool on his face; a wispy cloud drifted across a sailing moon that topped the trees. He inhaled deeply. The air carried the perfume of Cecilia's flowers. He looked up at the bright sky. "Wherever you are, I hope you are at peace, at last," he said, bidding Joe goodbye.

* * *

Laura awoke in the dead of night and felt herself wet. She touched the sheet underneath her and felt something sticky on her fingers. Then the realization knocked her cold. She tried to remove Denis's arm, which was flung across her chest. As he always did when she tried to get out of bed in the night, he mumbled, "Where you going?" half awake, his voice still thick with sleep. She wanted to get up but she was too cold to move.

She was shivering and could not stop the trembling in her voice. "Denis," she whispered.

"Yes?" he answered, his voice still muffled with sleep. "Yes," he repeated when she did not answer. She held tightly onto his arm, but still the shivering would not go away. Now he was awake. "What's wrong?" he asked as he reached across her to turn on the lamp on her bedside table. The light caught her eyes and blinded her. "What is it, Lauren?" he asked, alarmed. She held up her hand, trembling, her fingers glistening.

"I'm bleeding," she whispered, her voice quivering.

"Oh God, oh God," he exclaimed. He looked down at where her hand came from, at the sheet beneath her where this red thing had crept.

"Oh God, oh God," he called out again. He who was always master of any situation was now at a loss and quite useless. "Don't move, sweet," he said, "just stay put, okay? Don't move, dearest, let me get Cecilia, okay, just don't move!"

* * *

She lost the baby, standing there in the bathroom while waiting for the doctor to arrive, flowing out of her in a flood of red spreading on the marble floor, surprisingly, and contrary to what she had always heard, without any pain.

He was smaller than Denis's enormous fingers against which he lay in his palm, but a complete human being nevertheless, with his chalk-hued miniature face and hands and feet and his very definite sex, like a tiny, broken-off fragment of a matchstick stuck to his middle, most indisputably male, just four months inside her but already an unmistakable human being, God's remarkable creation, Denis's claim to immortality, canceled for now, perhaps canceled forever.

* * *

Maids had changed the bloodied mattress with a clean one and had changed the sheets. Denis had helped her shower and dress and had put her back to bed while they waited for the doctor.

Now, from where she lay, she could see him and Cecilia in the bathroom, working on the baby, while a maid cleaned the blood on the marble floor.

Cecilia baptized him, lying there on Denis's palm: In the Name of the Father and of the Son and of the Holy Ghost. "What do you want to name him?" she asked.

"Sebastian," Denis said readily, "after my father. Sebastian Denis Richards."

Laura was surprised at how quickly the answer came. He must have thought then of giving his son his middle name, and his father's name. Sebastian. Generations of Richards men had used Sebastian as their middle name, but his father had used it as his first name. Then she saw him brushing his hand across his eyes, saw how red his face was. Why, she thought, he's crying, and felt her heart being wrenched out. The only time she saw him cry was when his mother died of a stroke two years ago. But from her there were no more tears to shed. She had cried herself dry for Joe. Now there was nothing left for the baby. Poor thing, she thought, at least your father is crying for you. Poor baby. Poor Denis, too. And poor, poor Joe.

After a while, Denis left Cecilia to finish up and went to his wife. "I'm so sorry, sweet," he said, smoothing her hair, tears falling unchecked down his face. He held her close and she could feel his body shaking. "I'm so very sorry."

16

A juicier story had not hit the land in a long time. The press played up the tragedy to the hilt. Joe's handsome face made the front pages of magazines and newspapers for days, hugging the headlines, relegating political, economic, and financial news to a distant second in readers' interest. Once again, the family was laid open to public scrutiny. Joe's pictures, and in lesser import, Franz' and Denis' and Laura's, too, were splashed on the covers and front pages of magazines and newspapers.

The press relentlessly fettered out what it could about Joe. Stories about him filled the papers and were devoured by a scandal-hungry public.

Classmates recalled a bright, handsome lad zipping around in his white MG. They recounted the time Father Clemente told the class to study Christopher Marlowe and how Joe came to class the next day and recited the entire poem, Marlowe's *The Passionate Shepherd to His Love,* with much passion, to the applause of classmates and the amusement of Father Clemente.

Friends remembered a well-dressed, well-mannered, albeit reclusive, young man, and of course his closeness to his cousin, Franz Steiner. They pronounced views on his daily Masses even when he was having that affair with Ruth, as if to imply that once again, faith could not hold its own when tested against a woman.

He must have looked down in horror at all the press coverage he was getting, that intensely private person, at having his personal life splattered on magazines and newspapers for all to read.

* * *

They never caught the person who did it. Georgie was not in Manila at the time, in fact he was provinces away, in their hacienda outside San Sebastian, but everyone believed he had a hand in the tragic affair. You don't insult an Hernandez in such a blatant way and get away with it.

Again, the Hernandez scandal that happened a few years back was rehashed in news items. Again, it was told how, when

George, Senior ran for governor of the province, a brother-in-law, his sister's husband, ran against him. In the midst of a heated campaign, the brother-in-law disappeared and a massive search was organized. A week later, his body was found in the woods at the back of his hacienda, his throat slit, his eyes gouged out. It was a gory, frightening lesson to anyone who, in future, might have thoughts of crossing an Hernandez. The police pinned the time of death on that Saturday, coinciding with the birthday of George, Senior, when a two-day celebration was held in the Hernandez' hacienda, and the whereabouts of every Hernandez were accounted for. Now, as then, the hacienda wrapped its owners in a protective, unshakable alibi.

* * *

The Steiners expressed their wish to Ruth's family that they hoped they would be spared Ruth's presence at the funeral (as if she could summon the nerve to go). The Gomezes, not ones to have their opinions shaped by proof, or lack of it, sent word to the Hernandezes not to make the long trip to Manila to attend the funeral and immediately thereafter severed all threads of association, fragile and flimsy to start with, that existed between their families.

"Is there nothing we can do to bring them to justice?" said Franz in his futile, hand-wringing grief.

"What can we do?" said Francis. "There is just no evidence. You cannot convict on the strength of mere feelings alone, even though those feelings are shared by everybody. In all probability, the wretch who pulled that trigger already met a fatal accident."

* * *

What hair Ray had that had not turned to gray turned white almost overnight and he appeared at the funeral with a full head of startlingly silver hair. The line of cars that traveled in somber procession from the church to the burial park extended a good mile. Manila's rich came in full force to bury its dead.

Laura was still in the hospital when they buried Joe, the doctor having performed a D and C to clean her womb, while in the cemetery, the family grieved as pallbearers laid to rest Joe's body in the Steiner mausoleum.

Denis stayed with his wife all the time in the hospital, just sitting there watching her. "Would you want me to read to you?" he offered.

"If you wish," she replied dispiritedly.

He took out a book of poems that he brought with him from their library, but even that beloved voice could not soothe her troubled spirit.

Ray and Maggie and their other children came to the hospital to visit, but they were bad visits, with the crying and the sniffling and Laura just lying there, pale and haggard and silent. Denis took things into his hands and banned all visits until they could control themselves.

* * *

Even after a year of mourning passed, the weight of sorrow that had settled on the family's shoulders never lightened. Maggie never went back to San Sebastian again, refused to be even in the same planet with the Hernandezes and avoided them like a contagion. Ray lost all appetite for social intercourse and took refuge in home and work. Later, he and Maggie started the sojourns to Spain and Italy to spend time with their other children and grandchildren, visits that every year kept getting longer and longer, while Francis, sharing his brother's suffering but powerless to alleviate it, stood by helplessly. What was perceived before as a passion for privacy, at least on the part of the Steiners, now took on the proportions of intense, monastic hermitage, and for a long time, the Steiner and Gomez names stayed prominently absent from the society pages.

But it was Franz who suffered the most, missing Joe with a pain so acute he could pinpoint where he was hurting. He brought his family back to Manila, leaving the business in the province to RJ. He took over Joe's work and buried himself in a punishing, rigorous workload. He never allowed Joe's position to be filled, and forbade anyone from using Joe's office, took another room for his own, leaving everything in Joe's office as he had left it---the radio turned on to the classical music station, the giant picture on the wall of the three of them in Santo Niño when they were young, a long, happy time ago, the bar stocked with bottles of his favorite drinks, with a jumbo bottle of Carlos I, the Spanish brandy that he loved, right in the middle.

17

he Steiner Building was an imposing structure of thirty floors. The first five floors were occupied by stores and banks, the next seven floors were offices and the rest were apartments and condominiums. The offices of Vargas, Vargas and Vargas occupied the entire 10th floor, one floor below Steiner Corp, which used the 11th and 12th floors. Vargas was an old and respected law firm, older than Steiner Corp even. In fact, when the first Francis Steiner started the company, he had used Vargas (the company started with just one name) for all its legal needs until Steiner grew too big and put up its own legal department.

On this dreary, drizzly morning, Franz and Laura and Denis found themselves in the law offices of Vargas. The senior Mr. Vargas had requested their presence in his office regarding Joe's will. The other family members who benefited had been informed at a previous meeting while Laura was still in hospital.

"I don't know why he came to you," said Franz.

"I wondered that too, when he called that he was coming," Mr. Vargas said. "I thought he would be better served by your own legal department. I guess he wanted to make the will very private then. You see, except for smaller bequests, he left his entire estate to you two."

"To me and Franz?" Laura asked, surprised.

"Yes," the lawyer nodded. "All his estate he left equally to Franz Steiner and Laura Steiner. Of course you know he left a vast estate."

"When did he do this?" asked Laura.

The lawyer looked at the date. "January 30th," he said.

When he was planning to have the marriage annulled, Laura thought. He mentioned that he was going to Vargas the next day but she did not think that he would really go.

"January 30th of this year?" asked Franz. "But why make a will this year? Did he say why?"

"He came to me about an entirely different matter and afterwards, he said he might as well make a will, since he was already here."

"What matter?" asked Franz.

"He just wanted my opinion. It was not really a legal matter he wanted us to handle, he just asked my opinion," replied Vargas.

"There was nothing important to him that he did not share with me and my sister. Opinion on what?" Franz was nothing if not persistent. Mr. One Track Mind, they used to call him, barnacle-tenacious when he put his mind to anything, and Joe, who did not want to be bothered by anything, bothered Franz when he wanted anything done.

"As I said, he just wanted my opinion on some matters, that's all, just an opinion, nothing official, nothing legal." Vargas said, glancing at Denis.

"It's all right," said Laura. She reached out and clutched Denis's arm as he rose from his chair to leave the room. "You can talk to us."

"He asked about annulments; he just wanted to know the general gist of it, nothing specific."

"Annul? Whose marriage?" said Franz, surprised. "Was Ruth thinking of annulment?" He looked very puzzled.

"He didn't say, and as I said, it was the very general aspect of the thing," said Vargas. "Now, if we could go into this will." He squinted while he put on his eyeglasses and rifled some papers.

It was a very short will. Aside from bequests to charities, to several household help, 'spending money' to his parents and siblings, bequests which Vargas had already taken up with the other heirs, everything else he owned he left equally to Franz Steiner and Laura Steiner. He did not even acknowledge that she was now carrying somebody else's name. Or perhaps he realized that, if their plans succeeded, she would be a Steiner again.

Vargas peered at them from the top of his glasses and said, "I should like to point out that, should anyone question the will, they won't have any leg to stand on. This is a very valid will, by a young man who knew what he was doing, as I and the two witnesses could attest."

"Nobody is going to contest. I am not accepting this." Laura looked at Denis, silently asking for support and got it. He nodded and gave her a small smile. "How do I go about giving my part to somebody else?"

"He wanted you to have it," said Franz.

He thought we were going away. Oh, Bud, you know I can't take it now. "He'll understand. Do you want it?"

"Of course not," said Franz.

"Then I shall give it to *Tito* Ray. Since that's mostly Gomez money, to RJ, as well." She looked at Vargas. "We are leaving this week for California. Can you draw up the papers as soon as possible and send it to my house for me to sign?"

"That can be arranged," said Vargas.

"Please draw up the papers. I am giving up everything he left me in favor of his father, Ray Steiner, and his brother, Ray Steiner, Junior. *Tito* Ray will decide. You know the address."

"I'm sure we can manage that."

"Thank you then," said Laura. Goodbyes were said and they left.

"Can we go up to my office for a bit?" asked Franz. "I have a small matter to attend to. It won't take long." He looked at Denis. "Come visit our office."

* * *

Denis had never been to the offices of Steiner Corp. Outside, the Steiner Building was a modern building of glass and steel. There was nothing modern inside the offices of Steiner Corp.: large rooms with high ceilings, wood panels, ornate furniture, distinguished, smelling of old and moneyed.

Mae met them when they came out of Franz' office. She handed an envelope to Laura. "Mrs. Richards, I found this among Mr. Steiner's things. I was about to mail it to you."

"Thank you," said Laura. She looked around, wanting to be alone.

"You may use Mr. Steiner's office," offered Mae.

"Thank you." She hesitated. She did not want to go in there. Her heart broke the last time she was in that room. It had not mended yet. She looked up and met Denis's eyes. Very often lately she would catch him looking at her with a disturbing stillness and she had to look away. "You'll wait for Franz here? I won't take long," she said and left him stranded.

She went inside, closing the door behind her. The day had cleared; the sun had broken through the drizzle. Sunlight poured through the tall, drapeless windows, the haze making the room look ethereal, otherworldly. The radio was still sitting on the console, still tuned in to the classical music station and, in a most eerie and dreamy way, still playing Heifetz. Last time he was soothing Joe's savaged breast. Now, she could hear him coaxing, coaxing, a plaintive Rachmaninoff's *Vocalise* from his violin. She looked around. The room was so exactly the way she saw it last, she half expected Joe to come out through the bathroom door. She waited but of course he didn't.

She sat down and looked at the envelope and at her name in the middle. She broke the seal and opened the envelope. The letter was written in his neat, lean hand. There was his signature small j at the bottom of the page. He never used capital letters whenever he signed his letters to her and Franz, but just to her and Franz. "I never imagined loneliness such as this could be until you left me a lifetime ago yesterday. The thought that this is just the beginning of endless days and nights feeling this way just crushes me. But you had given me more happiness this week than I thought possible, had given me more happiness than anything or anyone, in a lifetime where happiness seems to mean just one thing, you, and for that I thank you. I love you, Laura Steiner, how much you could never know.

"You've always loved miss millay. Here's one again for you.
there is a word i dare not speak again,
a face i never again must call to mind;
i was not craven ever nor blenched at pain,
but pain to such degree and of such kind
as i must suffer if i think of you,
not in my senses will i undergo.

She sat there reading his letter, crying quietly. The door opened and she could hear Franz giving indisputable instructions with authority. Franz always presaged his entrances with leftover sentences flung over his shoulders. He swept into the room, with Denis trailing behind.

The first thing Denis saw when he entered the room was the giant picture on the wall of a young girl, unmistakably his wife, standing between Joe and Franz, three sets of light-colored eyes stark against sunburned faces, three sets of teeth displaying the Steiner overbite before their parents had them straightened, three stunning Steiner faces in open laughter, teasing the camera. Even at that age, then, she could already take your breath away.

"He left you a letter?" Franz asked and put out his hand to his sister for the letter. She ignored him and put the letter in her handbag.

"Let me read it," Franz demanded.

"It's not for you." She wiped her face with the back of her hand. Denis took out his handkerchief and handed it to her. She looked at his initials on one corner, the gray, small dsr. This, or a relative of this, was the offending culprit that started all this tragic mess in the first place. She gave it back, unused, and searched in her handbag for her own.

"Well?" pursued Franz.

"Well what?"

"Well," he said, with hands gesturing impatiently for emphasis, "what did he say?"

"He said you should take better care of your sister now that he's not around." She stood up and left the room.

* * *

"Can we visit Isa before we go home?" Laura asked Denis.

"I wish you would. It's been a long time."

"Where's Isa?" inquired Laura, when the door was opened to them by a maid in white uniform.

"She's out in the garden, Miss. If you will wait, I shall call her."

"It's all right, we'll find her ourselves."

Isa's garden. Just what you would expect Isa's garden would be, like her, sensuous and exotic, a luxuriant display of lush plants sprouting everywhere, flowers displaying all sorts of colors, and orchids clinging to every available space.

Laura had not seen her since that afternoon when heated words were exchanged between them.

Isa met them when they came out into the garden. Her twin daughters looked at Laura and Denis with saucer-like eyes, thickly lashed. Laura drew in her breath. "Oh, God, they're so beautiful," she said as she drew them to her.

"You really should give Manuel an MG," said Denis. "Work like this should be rewarded. Really."

"Yes, I guess we outdid ourselves there," said Isa in character. Then she looked at her sister and became serious. "Are you all right now?"

"I'm fine."

"I went to the hospital but you were asleep."

"I know. Denis told me. Thanks."

"The doctor said you could still have another baby."

"Of course," said Laura.

They exchanged small talk, mostly about the orchids, which Isa and Manuel had parlayed into a flourishing business. "I never expected you could be capable of this domestication," said Denis and tousled Isa's short hair.

They declined her invitation to coffee, saying they had *merienda*. Then it was time to go.

Denis gathered Isa in his embrace. "I missed you, you know," he said. He did, miss this irrepressible girl.

"We're leaving tomorrow," said Laura, "When are you going abroad again? Promise you'll come and visit us." She then kissed her sister and the twins goodbye.

* * *

They brought the tiny urn that contained their son back with them to California, nestled in a bed of silk scarves and embroidered handkerchiefs, inside a jewel box Cecilia gave Laura that played bars from the Nutcracker Suite March when it was opened, playing four bars over and over, maddeningly, and stopped only when it was snapped shut. Denis carried it on his lap, all the way home.

The days passed, as they would do, as she willed herself to close her eyes through restless nights, straighten an already straight house, chew and swallow food she could not taste. And steeled herself from hurting too much when she would look up and catch Denis watching her.

He was ever so patient with her, who was weepy, withdrawn, her guilt over Joe's death a cross too overwhelming for her to carry alone, and yet who could she tell? She knew that she had opened Joe's Pandora's Box and once his demons had been let out, even for just the briefest of time, he was powerless to put the lid back on again and laid exposed to Ruth's dark needs.

He asked Charles to lighten his schedule so he could be with her more often.

"Is there anything I can do?" asked Charles, concerned for him.

"It's all right, she'll be okay in time," Denis replied. "Thanks, Charles."

18

*H*e bounded up the stairs. He was early, very early. He was in top form today, so was the orchestra, led by Michael, who, though sometimes could be uneven, could not be faulted today, and they finished recording with the first take. He forsook lunch, wanting to rest up a bit before he and Laura flew to San Francisco, where he was singing Hamlet.

He saw his bag and Laura's, all ready, standing on the floor. He heard music coming from her study.

She had been packing and putting away the classical records Joe had given her. How could she listen to them again? He had introduced her to classical music, everything about it had something to do with him. How many quiet hours had they spent listening to these records, not saying much, just letting the music wash over them. She had replaced them with new tapes by different conductors and performers, searching for different sounds from their different music-making. She placed the records in a box, which she put on the floor of the closet in her study. Like Joe, they would stay silent to her forever.

From the open door Denis saw her sitting on the floor, with records strewn about her. She did not hear him over the din of Mahler's Second, with the powerful first movement of the Resurrection Symphony played by the entire orchestra, the loud notes from the brass drowning footsteps and all other concerns of everyday living, but, looking at her tear-stained face, surely not despair. He looked at the surplus of records around her, records that he knew Joe had given her. She took one record, put it to her breast and motionless, wept, wept the heartrending weeping of the hopelessly despairing. Then she saw his shoes and looked up at him, her face going the gamut from misery, to alarm, to guilt.

"What is it, Lauren?" But even before she answered, he knew.

Then all the strange pieces that he refused to look in the face came together to him: her insistence on a divorce for which he thought he was entirely to blame, her announcement that she was having an affair, her hysterical outburst in church and her wails of heartbreak in their bedroom that night that reverberated through that vast house, Joe's will that he made that terrible week which left her a fortune, Vargas' evasive answers when pressed about the annulment, that letter Joe left her that she would not let even Franz read, Joe's ways that mirrored his own and that left him with concerns he did not want to probe, like scattered fragments of a jigsaw puzzle, and then one central magnet pulling all the pieces together, piece by piece, until every segment was sucked into one whole, forming one central picture, Joe. The realization sickened him.

"There was something I missed, wasn't there?" She could not look at him and turned her face away. He pulled her up until she had to face him. He held her face and forced her to look at him. "There is more to this than just the loss of the baby, isn't there?" She lowered her eyes so she did not have to look at his, boring into hers like a knife. "Something did happen, what was it? You did have an affair with him, didn't you, didn't you? Answer me, Laura," he thundered, shaking her, "answer me."

"It was not an affair. It happened just that one time. We did not mean it to happen. Oh, please, believe me, it happened just that one time. We did not mean it to happen. I am so sorry, so sorry." She was weeping a storm.

"God, I can't believe this." He thrust her away from him and without his arms to support her, she lost her balance and, arms flailing, fell on the sofa. He straightened up, and looked at her with disgust in his eyes. "How could you, Laura?"

She bent over in the corner of the sofa, pulled her knees up to her chest, crying her heart out. "I'm so sorry, oh, God, really I am."

"You're sorry," he roared. "You're sorry. Oh, oh," he raised his clenched fist in the air. She covered her face with both her hands, as though to protect it from his blow. He saw the gesture and thought, did she think I'd strike her? With this rage seething inside him, was he capable, he who had never said an unkind word to her? One cuff with the back of his powerful hand and he could send her frail body careening across the room.

"I really am. I was so miserable and he just wanted to comfort me. Oh, I'm so sorry. Please believe me." She reached out her hand to him, needing him to comfort her, but he shook it

away with such force it thrust her body backwards. She recoiled
from his rejection. He might as well have struck her, a blow
would not have hurt her as much. As if he had burned her, she
put her hand to her chest. His rejection dried her tears, made her
shiver. He was ominously quiet but she could not look at him. "If
you want to divorce me, I'll understand. You could ask Charles to
prepare the papers, I shall not contest."

"Divorce! Divorce! There you go again. For a Catholic you
are so fond of hiding behind a divorce," his voice blared in the
room.

"I never meant to hurt you and for that, if for nothing else, I
am very, very sorry. You can believe that or not," she looked at
him sadly. "I shall stay here until Charles brings me the papers or
until I have put my things in order. I shall not get a cent from
you, you know that. I shall return all the things you gave me. I
shall be out of here by the time you come back."

"Out of here? Out of here? To where?" He knew he was
getting out of control.

"You needn't concern yourself with me. I'll manage."

"Oh, I'm sure you will," he painted every word with sarcasm.
"You were left alone for a week, one week, damn it, and you
managed very well indeed."

She looked at him. "I have no excuse for what I did. It
happened just that one time, when I was aching so much and he
just couldn't stand seeing me so miserable. But I am not even
passing that buck to you. I take full responsibility for what I did,
but we never meant it to happen and it did not happen again.
Most of all, I never meant to hurt you. I have always loved Joe
but with a love that was completely different from what I feel for
you. Everybody knew that, including you, and I never tried to
hide it. What I feel for you never changed or wavered. I am not
trying to justify anything or even ask for your forgiveness. In His
mercy, I hope the one who would be granting me that would do
so, knowing how much I have suffered and how high the price I
paid. But it was not an affair. There was nothing tawdry or sordid
about it and it never happened again. You could divorce me or
you could shoot me. Unfortunately, Joe is not going to give you
that pleasure. But you could do with me what you will. At the
moment, I really do not care anymore."

"Oh, you don't, don't you? Well, good for you. Unfortunately, I do. It's too bad for me but I do."

She looked at him, but could not stand the anger and the hurt in his eyes, and looked away.

"But I do," he wailed. "I do, I do, damn, damn, damn it," he roared and struck his fist into the wall, but it was solid and drew blood when it met his clenched fist. Laura looked up when she heard the thud and saw his bleeding hand.

"Oh, Denis, your hand." Forgetting herself, she went to him and tried to take his hand but he pulled it roughly away.

"Damn the hand and damn you, Laura. Get away from me."

He swept past her out of the room, grabbed his bag without losing step, leaving hers on the floor, forlorn and rejected. She was shivering and it was not even cold. Then she heard his car speed away.

* * *

She could not bring herself to pack her things. She started to put his papers in order in her study. There was so much to put in order, for which she was thankful. She was numb but was thankful for that, then she could put off feeling and thinking. Her body ached but sleep was not about to be kind to her. Dawn would come and find her red-eyed and very much awake. She rifled through her drawers and plied herself with pills left over from what the doctor gave her after she lost the baby, and welcomed a tomblike darkness that engulfed her.

She inquired about travel to Spain and Switzerland. She did not think she could face relatives and friends and decided on Madrid first, where she did not have to see both. She went to her bank to see how she could liquidate her own money when she needed it. Then she asked Charles, who had been taking care of part of her own money as well, to free her money anytime she wanted it. She did not say anything about the divorce, she left that for Denis to do. She wanted to take care of everything and be out of the house before he came back.

* * *

He should have looked deeper into this thing about Joe and Laura, Denis thought. Did she notice him because he reminded her of Joe? That afternoon at Stevens', when she looked up with recognition in her eyes, did she see the shade of Joe in him? And when she smiled that smile that ravished him, was it because she saw in him a Joe without encumbrances of family ties, and incestuous impediments, and the horror of tainted children? Looking back now, their similarities were just too many and too startling, how could he have not seen them? Why did he not take notice then? Maybe he did, but he borrowed from her the art of looking through things that were too distasteful to look at and unlike everything in his life that he faced head on and on which he meted instant resolution, the thing with Joe and his wife was something he just dreaded to look in the face, not sure of its name, afraid to give it one.

He remembered one vacation when Ray invited them to dinner at the Manila Hotel. He had engaged Cecilia in a discourse on the crass commercialization of the music industry, and was not particularly aware of the conversation of the others at their table. All he remembered was his wife, sounding stern and disapproving, saying in a very cold voice, "Excuse me, excuse me, that's my cousin you're talking to."

"Well, it's true, that decision was not the best for the company," returned Azucena, a cousin, who earlier had joined their table.

"That's business, Suzie," said Franz, trying to placate her, "you lose a little, and then you win a lot."

Denis heard his wife, who never cared for business and never ventured into the midst of a business discussion, rushing to Joe's defense. "That company had six ships when these two started to work there. Now it has ten. An impressive growth in just five years. Tell me if you know of better."

He never heard his wife talk about their family business. He knew there were ships but this was the first time he realized just how many there were.

"Give Francis and Ray credit for that," said Azucena.

"Papa and *Tito* Ray couldn't have done it alone, on their own. That company could not have grown as fast without these two there. And it would be nice once in a while if people remembered that Joe and Franz came to this job prepared to their eyeballs, which I think should make any relation proud. But if you're not happy with the way things are run, why don't you sell out?"

"Sell out?" Azucena sputtered. "Sell out? And who would buy us out?"

"We would, the three of us."

Azucena snickered. "The holy trinity who could do no wrong. Perfection personified."

"Now, Suzie," said Franz, always the pacifist, "don't mind my sister here. But she's right, you know, you couldn't put your money in a better company, if I may say so myself."

Then Joe, who had been silent in all these, said, "Say so yourself, Franz." And unexpectedly, he let out an earthy, whooping laugh that startled Denis, a staccato hahaha that came from deep inside him, a lusty laugh so eerily like his own that Denis felt chilled. In a moment, he remembered thinking, in a moment I'll know why I am so disturbed by this.

"You're drunk," said Azucena scornfully. She might as well have said "as always," the words hang heavily in the air, everyone knew she wanted to say them, "as always," but even she, termagant though she was, did not dare. There were limits to what one could say to Joe to his face.

"Yes, I guess I am," said Joe, and started laughing again.

"There's just no use talking to you," said Azucena, as she gathered her handbag. "Goodnight," she said, looking at Cecilia and Denis, and included the rest with a broad glance while pointedly ignoring the three. Then she tottered back to her table on three-inch high heels.

Joe looked at Laura and said, "Thank you but you don't have to fight my battles, you know. I can manage, if I cared, but I don't."

"Nobody criticizes," she paused, "nobody criticizes a Steiner in front of me."

"She's all talk, Lauren, she gripes about everything, don't give her a thought. But thanks, anyway," said Joe. "Don't think I don't appreciate it." He patted Laura's hand, distractedly dug into his pocket, and came up with his cigarette case. He took out a cigarette, leaned over to one side to put the case back in his pocket and lit the cigarette. He took a deep drag, exhaled and realized he was blowing a cloud of smoke in the air. "Oh, I'm sorry," he said and tried to fan the smoke away with his hand. He twisted his cigarette, still long and smoldering, absently on the ashtray. "I must say goodnight. Becky is waiting for me."

"Becky?" somebody echoed.

"Becky. Mom's most recent project."

"She's such a nice girl, *hijo*, and so good-looking, too. What else do you want?" said Maggie.

"What I want is to get her to the back seat of my car, that's what I want."

"Oh, Joe," his mother said reprovingly.

"But she wanted to impress me first, after being cued by you, I'm sure, Mommy dearest; she wanted to talk, about me, about my life, for crissakes. God," he exclaimed, "who wants to talk.

"Oh, Joe!" Maggie said again.

"Oh, Mommy," he said, shaking his head at her. "You are an amazing woman, Marguerite, I should be ashamed of myself if I don't reward such persistence. Now off I go to see what magic this Becky woman can do." He rose, kissed his mother on both cheeks. "You behave yourself now." He kissed Cecilia, then Hazel, and nodded a sweeping goodnight to the rest. Then, passing behind Laura's chair, he touched her cheek gently with his hand. "And to all a goodnight."

Thus he left them, a tall, handsome figure, commanding attention as he weaved his way through tables and out of the room.

"Now, what girl wouldn't want to get in the back seat with such as that?" Denis said.

Yes, Denis thought, he should have seen it.

Even his presents to her through the years were not the perfunctory gifts of one cousin to another, but spoke volumes--- of patient hunts and painstaking searches into who knew what antique shops and out-of-print bookstores. And, strange and different as she had always been (wasn't that a big part of why he stayed captivated all these years?), she treasured these presents more than any other, more expensive ones, she received, except perhaps his own. First editions of poetry, rare prints of favored books, special publications of poems. And that exquisite book of Edna St. Vincent Millay's poems, with pages of colored illustrations of exquisite women with blowing hair and flowing dresses; or that volume of Omar Khayam's *Rubaiyat*, covered in rich leather, edged in gold, which sent her misty-eyed and calling him long distance. "Hi, it's me. Did I wake you?" (Throaty laughter.) "I'm sorry. But I had to call you. Oh, Bud, the book is so bee-au-tiful, thank you ever so much. You knew I'd love it.

Where did you get it? You must have spent a lot of time looking for it." Pause, then "Yeah, sure."

Which made him wonder if she loved the things Joe gave her just because it came from him? Or if it was possible for him to give her anything that she would not love.

There were other instances, numerous instances that left him, well, if he must say it, feeling jealous. There, it's out. Yes, jealous, of that golden youth that included Joe and excluded him, of that space inside her that Joe inhabited, of her regard for Joe that not even husband, not even marriage, not even the years of separation, dimmed. Even though she maintained that what she felt for Joe was entirely different from what she felt for him, he did not care, he just did not want him there, he just did not want him anywhere near her.

19

$\mathcal{H}$e went through the motions of living, hardly eating, hardly sleeping, apathetically rehearsing.

"Want to talk about it?" asked Peter.

"No." He put both hands inside his pocket and gazed, unseeing, out the window. "I wish I did not love her so much. No," he said, shaking his head in frustration. "No, I can't even say that. I love loving her so much. It's something that gives me a lot of pleasure. I guess loving her without reservations comes with the territory. If you did not love her then she could be exasperating. You, for instance, you don't like her much."

"Of course I do, how can you say that? Marta adores her. She's just different, that's all, but then that's what makes her special." He paused and said carefully, "I, however, wish you could tone it down a bit. Sometimes it gets out of hand and explodes, even if it happens only once in a long while. Still, I don't like the way it does to you. It's all right, married people quarrel once in a while, you know, it's just that you don't do it."

"Now you won't like what I'm going to do. I'm going home."

"Denis, not again."

"I have to, Peter." he heaved a sigh. "I can't change, it's too late now, what can I say? I'll be back in time for rehearsals."

* * *

He let himself in and went up to their bedroom. Her boxes were the first thing he saw when he entered the den, half a dozen of them, taped, tagged in green, with Cecilia's name and address in large letters, there in the middle of the den, and almost floored him. Her suitcase was standing amidst packing tapes and paper, with her name on it and a hotel in Madrid.

He went downstairs and sought out Milly. "Where is she?"

"She's in the grocery. Mario is picking her up. He had to go to the hardware store."

"It's all right, I'll pick her up myself."

* * *

She was standing in front of a shelf of books. Even in the grocery store she had to look at books. He stood looking at her until she looked up and her eyes met his, eyes that for a long time now had a sadness in them that he was powerless to console. He came toward her and took hold of the shopping cart. "Do you need anything more?" he asked.

She shook her head, still looking at him.

He took out his billfold and paid for the groceries. She did not pick up much; just enough to half fill a grocery bag. He carried the bag with one hand and with the other opened the car door for her. He waited until she was seated, closed the door after her, deposited the groceries in the back seat, and drove away. He could feel her looking at him, and at a red light he turned and returned her look but her eyes did not waver. They reached the house without saying a word.

He put the groceries on the dining room table and followed her up the stairs.

"I'm sorry," she waved her hand at the boxes, "I did not expect you." She tried vainly to clean up the mess, picking up ropes and paper here that she dropped back there. "I thought I'd send them to Mom." She saw him looking at her suitcase, all marked and labeled.

"Madrid?" he asked.

"There's this group tour. It's touring Spain for three weeks. I leave Sunday."

"Three weeks? Here I must come back to you after a week. You could stay away for three weeks?"

"I'll manage," she said, caught herself and shrugged. "But then you know that."

He let that pass. "Must you go?"

"I have to get away for a while, think things over."

"You want to get away from me? Maybe I shouldn't have come back. You want to think? Think about what? Think about him? You don't have to go to Spain for that."

"God, Denis, is that why you came back, to torment me some more? He's dead, Denis, dead, dead, lying in that closed, dark place there, alone there, in the dark," she started to wail, "and I put him there. How can I not be devastated by that? Would you love me more if I were so insensitive, so callous that I don't think of that? He's dead, dead, dead, oh God." She slid down to the floor, put her head against her updrawn legs and wailed, "dead."

He looked at her and let out a forlorn sigh. He went to her, pulled her up to him and enfolded her in his arms. She was so small-boned, had always been a perfect fit. He buried his lips in her hair. It smelled of a new perfume, one he did not recognize. "Hush, it's all right now, I'm sorry, I'm sorry. Don't. Don't think about it anymore." He kissed her cheeks, wet with tears. "I'm just no good without you, what can I say. I guess you could do whatever you want with me, and I'd still be in love with you. There was a time when we could work anything out. Let's work this out." He smoothed her hair and pressed his lips to her forehead.

She stopped controlling herself and let go, heaving great sobs, wailing great wails, while he held her and let her until she had it all out.

"I'm sorry," she said, her lips against his chest. "So sorry, so sorry."

"It's all right now, it's all right now, let's put this behind us and start all over again." He kissed her eyes, tasted salt, lightly touched her lips with his. "All right? All right?" He stroked her hair, patted her back, held her close until she calmed down. "Would you like to pack some things and come with me?" She buried her face in his shirt, wiped her eyes and blew her nose on it.

She looked at the mess on the floor. "What am I going to do with this? And my ticket and reservation?"

"Milly will put these back while we're away. I shall take care of the rest when we come back."

* * *

They spent the following days in communion with each other. They passed moments in silence, and when she started to talk, he would take up the thread of her thoughts and find that their thoughts were in accord all the time, synchronized even in their silence. They clung to each other in stillness or they talked well into the night. And dawn would find them still in rapture.

They went out to watch the sun come up, he standing behind her, holding her, while the morning breeze ruffled her hair into his face. They walked the beach, deserted at the early hour, the golden glow of dawn reflected on their faces. Then they would go inside and she would nestle back into his arms and they would sleep thus until he had to go to rehearsals.

Then he would hurry back to her.

His first honeymoon was a hushed, tremulous union with a girl young in age and younger in knowledge. Now he was looking at her with new eyes, no longer the pristine innocent that she had been to him all these years, but a woman now with passions that another could awaken and claim, a new kind of sensuality that he bestowed on her.

That she and Joe would come together was inevitable, and he, especially, should have foreseen it. When she stood on the brink of a fall---without his protection, exposed to Joe's passion that had been kept well under wraps all these years, stripped bare in the face of her misery and his elation that he could come out in the open at last and claim her---when she stood on the brink of a fall and fell, somehow he could not fault them both entirely and knew that it had to happen. In a strange, ambivalent way, this strange unfamiliar emotion consumed him; the thought of her brief seduction fanned his passion into a conflagration that frightened him but at the same time he did not want to subdue.

She filled his every moment; most of all, they talked about Joe. Joe occupied their conversation, hovered over them, stayed with them even in their silence. He wanted to exorcise him from her thoughts, and the only way he knew how was to get him out in the open.

"I hate to burst your balloon but I think Joe was just chicken. He saw those cousins and just got scared. Because there are ways to get around that. You could choose not to have children, for heaven's sake."

"You don't understand. The only birth control allowed Catholics is the rhythm method, which is most, most unreliable. If the stakes were not so high, then it would not be so scary. You make a mistake, well, you have another child. But with me, with him and me, a mistake could be just disastrous.

"Franz tried that delayed-action contraceptive."

"Franz' intention was not not to have a baby, but just not to have one every ten months or so. If there's a mistake, so there's another baby, nothing catastrophic. Besides, Franz does not take his religion as seriously as Joe did. Franz would never miss a Sunday Mass, for instance, but he would not go so far out of his way to attend a weekday Mass either. With Joe, his religion was his life, or better to say, his God was his life. Those Jesuits formed him since he was just a small boy. I know, they did Franz, too, but Joe also surrounded himself with their writings, absorbed their ideas, absorbed what he read. Those books you saw him carrying around, those were mostly books on the ideas and teachings and philosophies of those Catholic saints. He was a Catholic through and through, if he was anything. At school, he would make time to go to chapel and just stay there, with his eyes closed, conversing with God, filling himself with His peace. He had a personal relationship with Him that was just awesome, a love and a faith and an obedience that was total. He was such a good person, with such an uncompromising sense of what's right and what's wrong. And that's why I knew he could never have gone through with the annulment. I may have been just nineteen, but he knew that I entered this marriage knowing full well what it entailed, and neither a philandering husband, nor even a love that just won't go away, was no justification at all to dissolve it, even if the Church would grant it, because then, annulment would just be another name for divorce."

* * *

"I cannot believe that that one indiscretion could have such heartbreaking consequences, could punish me so much," she said. "It took away Joe. It took away the baby. I had not wanted a lot of things in my life, my wants are so few, but it took away that one thing that I wanted so much. And saddest of all, for you, it ended your generation, at least with me."

"We could try again. I did not try hard enough that time. There must be someone there who could do something for us, so many couples have done it. Maybe we don't even need help. We did it on our own before, we can do it again."

She touched his face. He took her hand and put it gently to his lips. She smiled at him sadly. "It's not going to do any good. There's no help for me now. I'm afraid that was it for me, there is no more second chance."

"Don't say that. You don't know that, you can't be sure about something like that."

"I know, and I'm sure and I am so very sorry."

* * *

He promised himself he would put things behind them, start anew, mend what broke, prop up what weakened, better what was not very good, forget what could destroy them.

That shattering experience made them stronger so that when his resolves overwhelmed him and he found himself on the other end of the line, the one who needed comforting and a lot of open loving, too, but feared to let go lest he lost control again, she was there to ease and soothe and reassure.

He was brushing his teeth when she came out of her bath. He finished up and kissed her lightly. "I'm very tired. Good night."

He was in bed when she came into their room. She sat on the bed and watched him looking at her. "Talk to me," she said.

"I'm tired."

But she wouldn't take that. "Talk to me," she repeated.

He looked at her a long time. "I was thinking how I can't go through another harrowing time like that," he said, shaking his head slightly, "not again, Lauren. I will go crazy, or my heart will give out, or maybe I'll do a good job with a car crash and just end it all. But I can't go through that again."

"Have I given you any reason to think it could happen again?"

"I just want you to know."

He had silences that were getting longer. She would catch him looking at her in a strange way and she knew she had to calm his fears, too.

She took his face in her hands, with the furrows in some part she had not noticed before. When had he gotten older? She had been so wrapped up in her own sorrow she had not given much thought that he might be suffering, too. She uncreased with two fingers the knit on his forehead. "He was my hero and my best friend ever since I can remember. He taught me about things that matter, and by his example, about honesty and fairness, and about right and wrong. Most of the things that you love about me now, he had a hand in shaping. The Joes in one's life come but once, if one's lucky. His mom said that at the rate he was drinking he'd need another kidney soon, and I thought, I'll give him one of mine, I'll give him anything I have without thinking twice. He was the most righteous person I know, and that sad, sad time, if it were not that I was hurting so and he couldn't stand seeing me that way, if he had but given it a thought, that wouldn't have happened. I have been thinking about these things, and you know, I would give up everything, the good life, the trips abroad, all this money, if I could just buy back that week. Yes. I'd give up everything I have, save one, if I could just erase that terrible week and bring him back." She touched his face.

"I know you sometimes think that I fell in love with you because you reminded me of him. Not so. I had my head down the first time I heard you speak. I was sure I had never heard a voice so full of melody. Then I looked up and there you were, with the sun behind you, and I thought you looked like a shining god.

"I don't know how I can make you understand how I can feel this way towards Joe and still love you this much, but I do."

"Save one?"

"Save one. I would give up everything, except you. Just leave me you and I could survive anything." She touched his face gently. "You don't worry about anything anymore. You're safe with me, I'll make it so."

After that, he didn't.

20

For some time after the affair ended, Ruth's family tried to talk her into going abroad, maybe go back to school, finish what she left off. But the ironic thing was that now that she was free to go, she preferred not to. Joe had wanted her to go back to the children and now that he was gone, that was what she wanted to do.

Accompanied by her mother, she went to Georgie's house, the one that Georgie had built for her. Georgie was coming down the wide stairway when they entered the house. He stopped when he saw them, his hand in mid-air; all the disgust he felt for Ruth he did not even try to hide.

"Camilo," he hollered, coming down the stairs. When the boy came in, he said, "Didn't I tell you that that woman is never to be allowed in this house?"

"Please, Georgie, it was not his fault, we let ourselves in."

"And you may let yourselves out."

"Oh, Georgie, please, I just want to talk to you. Couldn't you bring yourself to just talk to me?" She went to him, but he flung his arm wide, caught her straight in the face and she fell on the floor.

"I know why you came. You are not sorry, you are afraid. Well, don't worry, even though I hope that you fry in hell, I don't want to add a murderer for a father to my children's misfortune of having the town's slut for a mother."

"Your children, your children! They're my children too."

"No, they're not. Not anymore. When you started bitching around, you forfeited your right to them."

"I know I did wrong, but you were at fault too. Joe asked you to stop thrusting me to him, as if I were a piece of chattel that you could just pass around. But you just couldn't tear yourself away from your cards. You were at fault, too."

"How dare you smear me with your dirt." The hatred in his eyes made her wince. "I had never fallen short in my duty as a husband. You had everything a wife could want, you never lacked for anything, anything. But you had to itch for him. When you were making a *puta*," he spat out the word contemptuously, "of yourself, it was just you, it had nothing to do with me. But you made me the laughingstock of the town, the cuckold who couldn't satisfy his wife. So go and look for another one who could and I'll blast him, too, to kingdom come. That's what you think, don't you, that's what everybody thinks, that I soiled my hands with Joe's blood for a bitch like you. You make me sick. Just mark this: you may grovel there to the end of your days for forgiveness but you will never find it here. Now get out of here and never ever let me catch you again anywhere near here or my children, unless you have a death wish."

* * *

For a while, Ruth's family mulled the idea of going to court to force Georgie to give Ruth visitation rights to the children, but, given the temper of the Hernandezes at the moment, their lawyers strongly advised against it.

Old folks in the countryside believed that tragedy came in threes. The affair with Joe, every one said, was the first misfortune, the second, Joe's tragedy. But who would count having an affair with Joe Steiner a misfortune? When the affair erupted in the open and into the gigantic scandal it was, nobody blamed Ruth for straying. George Hernandez, Junior might have been a very good catch, but Joe Steiner was, simply, Joe Steiner. Let the woman stand up who could have said no had he just made the move. That he never did put him way up there on top of the ladder, an unattainable prize any girl would have given an arm and a leg, or a soul, as Ruth did, to take. And so, although they did not sympathize, they understood. Karma, everyone said, a doomed, doomed fate.

While Ruth's family covered her with their protection against Georgie's wrath, the real enemy, the real threat to her safety, which was really she herself, reared its head. Engulfed by guilt for not feeling repentance or regret or remorse---for how could she regret Joe, ardent and passionate Joe---even now, after all the scandal and the tragedy, she still lusted for him, for his arms around her, his lips on hers, his body covering hers---Ruth sank deeper into depression.

What would cause a vital person to call it quits and take her life? A marriage shattered, a social stigma, a life in shambles, these would not do it. But this, on top of those, would: a loved lover, so sadly missed, now irrevocably gone, and the knowledge that she was responsible for his going, just as surely as though she had pulled the trigger herself.

She would have accepted the fury of Georgie's gun; oh, would that he would send her to join Joe wherever he was now, but she knew that was not to be. Georgie was her judge and her jury, but not her executioner, who, to add to her sentence of eternity in hell after this life, would make sure that she served an additional lingering term of hell on earth as well. He would see to that. Now, with Joe out of the way, the full force of Georgie's bitterness and vengeance would surely be spent on her. She knew that the next time she would see her children, they would be children no longer. She knew, too, that after a thorough brainwashing from Georgie, they would be lost to her forever. And so her family was caught unawares when the third misfortune struck.

She never left the house now, did not even leave her room. When her family again broached the subject of going abroad, she acceded. "All right," she told her sister, "make plans, we'll go on your next leave," which was in a month. "Meanwhile, please just leave me alone to sort things out with myself."

They respected her wishes, hoping that the projected trip, at least, would give her a reprieve from this overwhelming sorrow, not knowing just how much she was hurting now, mired as she was in despair, and they left her alone.

* * *

When her mother entered Ruth's room and saw her daughter dangling from the rafter, the red rope around her neck looking like a grotesque choker clasping her throat too tightly, she suffered a heart attack, which almost made it the fourth misfortune, or the third, if one canceled out the affair with Joe as the first. But that would not have been right. This enormous tragedy started out when Ruth, throwing not just caution to the wind but marriage, home, husband and children as well, gave in in wanton abandon to this lapse in her moral fiber. That was really the first misfortune. Coming full circle, Ruth ending her own life closed the set of tragedies.

There was no fourth. Ruth's mother rallied.

Her doctors were adamant that she did not attend the funeral and the Hernandezes, once again, were advised that their presence at the funeral would be most unwanted.

Before the tragedy could be grasped by the children, just babies, really, aged three, four and five, Georgie's mother packed them up, and with two of her daughters to render assistance, off to Disneyland they went, grateful to fantasy when reality was too heavy to bear.

BOOK 3
LAURA

1

*T*he recording of the soundtrack of Kiss Me Kate went smoothly and they finished earlier than Denis expected. He was glad he was getting home early. Charles was hosting a dinner party and he wanted to take a leisurely time getting ready for it.

Producers of his latest movie were coming over. He had barely finished filming Kiss Me Kate. Now they were trying to interest him in The Merry Widow. With interest in musical revivals on the rise, and with the tremendous success of his movie The Student Prince, he was deluged with offers to record Broadway musicals and operettas.

Laura was not in their bedroom. He heard music coming from her study and went inside. She was on the bed, her arms flung at her side, very much asleep. He looked around him. He had not been in this room in a long time. He heard himself singing September Song. He always had the impression that she did not care much for Kurt Weill's songs, especially the ones Weill did with Bertolt Brecht, which he found rather odd, since she loved all the other German operas and songs that he had recorded.

He looked around. There were stacks of his tapes near her player. There must have been a dozen of his pictures around, with a very big one on the wall in front of the divan, the one with a hint of a smile on his face, where one eye squinted smaller than the other, where that expensive watch she gave him rested on a hairy wrist. This was the cover of his latest recording. There was evidence of him everywhere. A photo album choking with his pictures was on her desk, and a manila folder crammed with clippings from newspapers and magazines. This was her study, it was his shrine.

He had taken to writing the notes that accompanied his classical records himself, delving into history, into the lives of Schubert and Brahms and Mahler, and the Schumanns. She was trying to help him, mostly in researching materials, and this occupied a good part of her time. Mahler's life had always fascinated her, his music stirred her. The first time she heard Denis sing the *Kindertotenlieder*, she sat through the applause, so moved was she by the music and his performance. That was her introduction to his Mahler and she had been an ardent follower since then.

Books on Mahler were strewn on the bed beside her. She obviously was working on them before she fell asleep. He looked at her, at the frown on her face. He pushed a stray lock from her forehead and expected her to stir, she was such a light sleeper, but she did not move. He heard movement outside the room and went out to find Milly.

"Has she been sleeping long?" he asked her.

"She has been having these pains for many weeks now. She takes these medicines that make her sleep."

"What pains? Where? Why don't I know about this?"

He went inside and sat on the bed watching her. He kissed her face, which looked drawn and very white. She stirred, opened her eyes and was about to get up when she saw him but his hand stayed her. "It's all right," he whispered.

"What time is it? Have I overslept? Are you hungry?"

"Hush. It's all right, I came home early. How are you feeling?"

"Just give me a few minutes, I'll get the sleep out of my eyes and I'll tell Milly to see to dinner." She was obviously disoriented.

He touched her face gently. "We're going to Charles' for dinner, remember?"

"Oh, I forgot. I'm so sorry." She still couldn't seem to open her eyes. "Denis, would you mind very much if I did not go?"

"If you don't feel like going, then we don't go."

She looked at him and knew he would stay home with her if she did. Charles had been planning this party for weeks. She knew she had to go with him. She sneezed, produced a handkerchief from her skirt pocket and blew her nose on it. "I'll just take a hot shower, I'm sure that will bring me around." She placed her hands on his shoulders and lifted herself up, but he put his arms around her waist and pulled her down to his lap.

He held her face between his hands. "You have been having pains? Why didn't I know of this?"

"Because it's nothing, really, and you're such a worry wart."

"Pains where?"

"Hey, it's nothing. Just upset stomach. Now you've really wakened me up."

"Since when have we been having pains that we don't tell each other about?"

She touched his face gently. "It's all right. If I don't think of it, it will just go away." She squirmed out of his arms and stood up.

He rose and held her by the shoulders. "It won't and you know it."

"It will," she said and turned to go to their bedroom.

"Will you be still, woman?" He pulled her to him. "Now, tell me, what is this all about?"

"It's nothing, really."

He heaved a sigh, shook his head. There was no getting to her. "Let me take you to Enzo tomorrow." Dr. Enzo, Jo's husband.

"He's a heart doctor," she sighed. "There's nothing wrong with my heart, except that you shake it sometimes."

"And I'll shake it some more if you don't call him up."

"Oh, all right. I shall call *Tita* Jo first. Then maybe Enzo can recommend a lady doctor."

"Good. Let me call Charlie. We don't have to go to this dinner and I don't have to attend that rehearsal tomorrow."

"Yes, we have and yes, you have. I'll bathe and get dressed and I'll go by myself tomorrow."

"I want to go with you."

"No."

"Ah, there she goes again," he sighed. "Promise me you'll go. Promise." She rose but he held her. "Promise."

She looked at him and knew there was no getting out. When Denis got himself into this state, she might as well save her energy. He could not be budged. "All right, all right. Guess I shall have to have lunch with *Tita* Jo or something. I haven't been in touch for quite some time and she'll think I only call when I need anything."

"Which you do. Why don't you call her more often, have lunch more often?"

"She has other things to do, and so have I." She smiled up at him and said, "Now, may I take my shower?"

He smoothed her hair and kissed her gently. "It's going to be all right."

"Of course. Very all right."

Sadly, it was not.

* * *

Laura awoke to a lot of pain. She did not move and studied the ceiling. This is not my room, she thought, disoriented, and I think I'm painfully wounded. She turned her head and saw Cecilia and Jo. Then she remembered---the visit to the doctor Enzo recommended, the panic she felt when the doctor and Enzo conferred, the frantic long distance calls to and from Manila, Cecilia's sudden advent while they prepared her for surgery, and through it all, Denis, his strong arms around her like a wall against harm, master of the situation as always, collected, dependable, her rock of reassurance, firmly sure that everything was going to be all right.

Cecilia and Jo rose from their vigil when they heard her movement. "How are you feeling, dear?" Jo asked, smoothing her hair.

She was in so much pain she did not have time to think of sparing them. "Not too good, I'm afraid."

She looked around the room and did not find what she was looking for. "Where's Denis?"

"He went to the doctor's office," replied Cecilia. She looked at her daughter's face, the skin almost translucent, biting her lips to ease the pain. "Let me call the nurse," she said and turned to go but Laura held her hand.

"I'm glad you're both here," said Laura, and gave them a faint smile.

Just then the doctor came in. "So how are we feeling?" she asked. Laura wondered why people say we when they only meant you. Well, she thought, I don't know about you, but as for me, "May I have something for the pain," she asked.

"We'll take care of that in a minute. I gave your husband a list of doctors who could give you chemotherapy. You could ask Dr. Enzo's opinion, of course." Cecilia was about to raise her hand to stop her, but the doctor was not looking at them, she was looking at Laura, unaware that she had not been told yet. "It will make you feel sick and if you don't want to continue, you just tell me. As I told your husband, my feeling is that, our concern should be to make you as comfortable as possible."

Denis, at the door, was galvanized into inaction and rendered mute. He wanted to shout, don't say anything, I shall tell her myself, in my own time, but no words came out.

Chemo? Laura thought, chemo? "Did you say chemo?"

All of a sudden she felt cold, her entire body was freezing, and she couldn't hold the trembling that came from within her.

Denis now released from stupor, rushed to her side. "Oh, darling, it's all right, it's all right, I'm here." The doctor gave her a shot and Denis held her until he knew she was asleep.

* * *

The next day after Laura's consultation with the doctor whom Enzo recommended, Enzo called Denis and asked him to lunch. "I hope this is a purely social lunch, Enzo," said Denis, dread touching his voice.

"You have always been one of my favorite people, even though you keep yourself so scarce," said Enzo. And he was one of Denis', but except when their wives arranged it, a social lunch was something they never shared. A chill gripped Denis' heart, and he knew, even before Enzo fed him, before shattering his world to pieces, before he voiced his suspicion and suggested surgery, even before then, Denis knew that with all the excellent genes that his wife inherited from her parents was that fatal one that already had done away with several family members. "We were given good genes." Maricris once said. "We reach our eighties still looking and feeling great." "Unless cancer gets us first," added Isa, always with the last word.

The ensuing surgery confirmed Enzo's fears and this time he told Denis in the hall, standing outside the operating room, too distraught to pause for convention, too heartsick to break for formalities.

"Is it bad?" Denis asked. Enzo nodded. "How bad?" Denis asked.

Enzo shook his head and sighed deeply. "It's very well in its advanced stage."

"How long?" Denis asked.

"In most cases, it takes three, four months, maybe less."

Lunch was the last thing both of them would ever want to share again. Denis insisted on telling his wife himself, but went around in dazed circles, helplessly wringing his hands, silently shouting his grief, angry and sick and heavy of heart, putting off the terrible task of telling her, until, he told himself, he had steeled himself and made himself strong enough for both of them, not wanting anybody else to do it for him and yet dreading to tell her himself. All the time, he refused to come to terms with what he knew was true: there wasn't time.

* * *

He removed himself from his wife, lying there on the hospital bed, drugged to oblivion, sleeping away the cruel hours. But for him there was no refuge anywhere. He held onto the headboard, hoisted himself up, but feeling too heavy to rise on his own, he sat back down and covered his face with his hands, let out an anguished cry, "Oh, God, God, God."

Cecilia could not help him. Her own grief was too heavy for her to bear, she was bearing Francis', too. To bear Denis' as well was just too much for her.

It was Jo who came to his rescue. "Denis, it's a very trying time for all of us."

After a while, regaining his composure, he let out a sigh that resonated with pain. "I'm afraid I'm not taking all this very well. I'm sorry. I'll go take a walk."

He came out of the building into the crisp March air. March, true to form, did not disappoint, and blew up a storm. The day was just as dark and gloomy as his state of mind. He walked briskly with his hands buried deep in his pockets, in a hurry to go nowhere. No matter where he went, he couldn't escape his thoughts, angry, frustrated, and grieving. How could You take this child who was on her knees in front of You everyday of her life. He always thought she was invincible, would stay on forever, live to a still-beautiful hundred, for why would the gods want to recall her so soon, whom they had created perfect. It had always been his gift, that he was an ace problem solver. Everybody could always depend on Denis to mete out a swift and wise resolution. But on this, his most heavy problem, he staggered in helplessness.

Then he thought of Laura, and he knew he must get hold of himself, and bear up for both of them. The blowing wind lashed his face and he was chilled to the bone. He had better hurry back. He wanted to be there when she awakened.

2

*A*fter a week, Denis brought his wife home. He canceled all his engagements and never left her side. And so it was to the end.

He nursed her himself, fed her, helped her bathe, dried her hair. He gave her a short haircut, now it was just curls all over her face, which made her look like a little girl. "Had I known you'd look so good in short hair, I'd have done this a long time ago."

He refused any help. "It's all right. I don't have anything to do, I'll take care of her myself." Cecilia, sensing that Denis did not want any interference in taking care of his wife, left them alone as much as possible, and spent most of her time with Jo.

He served her meals in bed when she was tired, they ate together in the terrace when she could make it, spending with her every moment of this last spring, fragrant with roses, bright with sunshine, drenched with heartache.

"Now let's see how long it takes before you tire of having me around twenty-four hours a day," he told her. His shoulders had taken on a permanent slope these days, as if his burden was physical, and too heavy to carry.

Then one day Denis informed Cecilia, "She wants to go back to New England."

"Do you think that's all right?"

"What harm could it do her? I'd like to show her as much of New England as she can take." Cecilia kept her peace.

Once again, Riverside Drive came to the rescue. They made the apartment their base, stayed there to rest when Laura was tired, and revisited the places he brought her to that first spring nine long years ago. The laurel blooms were not yet in profusion, it was too early, spring was late in New England this year. Still the countryside was radiant. The place that rented the canoes was still there. They took another cruise down the river and again he showed off, rowing with strong strokes as he led the canoe along the serene countryside. They ate in the place that overlooked a waterfall, again took the back roads and passed the church with white steeples, the quaint red brick houses, but the cows under the leafy trees were not there anymore. "They're on vacation," he told her, "but if you're good and don't leave, I promise you cows too many for counting, if you just hang in there for me."

They picnicked on a grassy knoll near a brook rushing to nowhere, and he read her the poems she loved. "Remember this? The first poem you read to me that first night, and I was falling in love with you." He read the first lines.

"When I too long have looked upon your face,
wherein for me a brightness unobscured,
save by the mists of brightness has its place,
and terrible beauty not to be endured."

He closed the book and looked at her. He did not need to read the rest.

"I turn away reluctant from your light,
And stand irresolute, a mind undone,
A silly, dazzled thing deprived of sight
From having looked too long upon the sun."

She smiled. "You memorized it."

"I have written it in my heart."

From masses of wildflowers, he made posies for her.

He apologized. "I don't have any jewelry to go with this, but would a kiss do? These are precious kisses. A lot of women would prefer them to jewelry." He started kissing her and wanted to know, "Can we make love here?"

"If you don't mind the ants, I'm sure they won't mind you."

"They won't come up the blanket," he said, looking at the white sheet they had spread out on the grass.

"Not yet, but they will. Don't you know that ants have a great curiosity about the human reproductive processes?"

He looked at her, all seriousness. "Now you're making that up," he accused her. He tried to pin her down to the sheet while she tried vainly to escape from him. She did not try hard enough and he was all over her. "Let's see how curious those little devils are."

"Denis Richards, you get off me, you dirty old man."

But these good days were few. Most times she was tired and they stayed in Riverside Drive. Soon, she was more exhausted, less valiant. "Let's get you a wheelchair, then I could wheel you around when you feel too tired."

"I don't need a wheelchair, it would make me feel sicker. Is sicker the right word?"

"I guess. Irving Berlin said so, when Annie got her gun."

Against her protests, he insisted on the wheelchair and got his way. He wheeled her in the park nearby, stopping under some trees and, with her eyes closed, she listened while he read to her.

How precious to him these moments of escape were. But time was running out and now an ever-present chill gripped his heart. He couldn't take his eyes away from her, searching for ways to make her more comfortable. She had a high threshold of pain and wanted to be alert for as long as she could and only when the pain became too unbearable would she allow the painkillers to give her a measure of relief.

She saw the sadness, now a constant on his face. "My one regret is that I cannot leave you that faith that has sustained me through this time of sadness, this faith that has given me peace. You've gone to church more times than most other Catholics. Now I am sorry I did not ask you to join me."

"Why didn't you?"

"Because you would if I asked you and I did not want that. I wanted you to join because you wanted to." She traced his face with fingers that felt cold as snow. "Now I am leaving you without any support to hold on to. I know you are going to miss me but try not to grieve too much."

"And how, do you suggest, do I do that?"

"This is one thing I am sure of. God will not give you a burden you cannot bear. That I believe. For as long as I can remember, a dozen or so people bent over backwards that I would spend my life in the utmost comfort. Now whence came this endurance to pain? What practice did I have that prepared me for this? None at all. That's why I believe God gives us just as much as we can handle."

* * *

During the night, she took a turn for the worse. He brought her to the hospital and called Cecilia. A priest came to hear her confession, give her Holy Communion, administer the Sacrament of Extreme Unction. Most Catholics believe that after the last rites were administered, the sick person very often rallied. But she never did.

* * *

Denis knew she was slipping away fast. Thus he sat, holding her hand, holding on to her, feeling his life slowly draining away with hers. He dared not look away lest she should open her eyes for one last look at him, or draw one last breath or bid him one last goodbye and he would not be aware of it, or that he would not be there to witness even the most minute detail of her final passing.

And then it was over. He knew she had drifted away, was gone, even though she had not moved, taking away with her his energy too, leaving him completely depleted, totally spent.

Tomorrow would have been the ninth anniversary of that day I first set eyes on you. Tomorrow? He looked out the window at the slowly-lightening sky. That tomorrow had become today. Time was a haze since he started taking care of her. It flew fast, or it crawled slowly and it did not matter to him. The days passed into nights but the restless nights did not bring surcease from this unbearable suffering, hers physical, his breaking his heart.

Again his eyes drifted to the window. Dawn slowly filled the room with light, but it did not find his heart.

Cecilia entered the room and when she saw him there, his desolation pervading the room, she knew Laura was gone. A sadness so piercing swept her, not only for this daughter, but for this man who had loved that daughter so. She knelt by the bed and held Laura's other hand. She had done her share of crying for her. Now she knelt there, with a strength she drew from that faith that had always been her support. They sat immobile, left to their own thoughts.

Finally, he stirred. "If it's all right with you, I'd like to take her home."

Cecilia and Francis listened without comment when they heard that Denis had bought this plot big enough for him and his wife, in a cemetery of his choosing. They would have wanted her in the family mausoleum where at least, until Denis would join her, she would not be alone. But they knew that would never be. Denis would not want the Steiner mausoleum to be his final resting place, and he would never let them take her to where he could not join her when his time came, watched by the departed Marquezes and Steiners though she might be for now.

"If that's what you want," Cecilia said. "Is there anything else, any other particular arrangement you want made?"

"I just want to take her home with me, that's all. The rest is up to you. I guess you shall have to tell the others. When is Francis coming?"

"He'll be in L.A. tomorrow. Do you want me to call Charles as well?"

He nodded slightly. "Thank you, Cecilia."

Cecilia left the room and he sat there holding his wife's hand. She looked like a little girl asleep, her short hair framing that face that not even death could touch. "It's our anniversary, dear. Like everything about you, a wonder, one last surprise. You went out of my life on the same day you entered it. Nine years ago today I came to New York, found you and how you changed my life. Now you must teach me how to live that life in the coming days without you."

3

rom the private plane that Denis chartered, the cortege went directly to the church where the rest of the family waited. The Mass was short, silent, strange. Denis did not want music played, or last words spoken. From the church, they brought her to this cemetery, chosen by him and approved by her, this green place of trees and grass and willows weeping with the wind. She said she liked it, this place with the sky over her head and roses at her feet and the willows for company. And so it was, instead of the Steiner mausoleum, where that one departed Steiner now rested. In death, as in life, Denis denied Joe that one thing he would have given up everything for, to spend the rest of his eternity with her.

* * *

It was a raw June afternoon when they buried her, just the kind of weather she would have found fitting and that would have pleased her, a weeping, wailing, whimpering afternoon, too blustery for June, with a turbulence that came suddenly and unannounced. A howling wind wildly whipped the willows, furiously thrashed the ladies' skirts against their legs, lashing their faces.

As suddenly as it came, the wind subsided, tired out from too much tumult, and swiftly stopped, its job done. Then the sun came out, at first peeking tentatively from a leftover cloud, then pouring down a blessing of yellow sunrays as the sad-eyed mourners dispersed.

* * *

He roamed the house, went through her things, handled her clothes and her jewels. He would wake up mornings and his eyes would search for her through the bathroom door, from where she would come out when she heard his waking-up noises---sneezing and sniffling and clearing his throat.

Her smile haunted him wherever he went. He passed her portrait above the sofa in the den, and caught her smiling at him. He removed the portrait, brought it to their bedroom and hung it in front of the bed so he could look at it first thing in the morning and last thing at night.

He went to her study. He played the record that was on the player and Ravel's *Pavanne* filled the room. *Pavanne to a Dead Princess*, the macabre piece was called. Even her records mourned her.

He went through her closets, smelling her dresses, fondling them as though by doing so he would feel her inside them. He caressed her underclothes. He always delighted in looking at her in them, silken and lacy and full of seduction. Once he commented why she always bought such exquisite underclothes, nobody would see them anyway. She was surprised at the question. "You would," she replied, "so would I." His favorite nightgown was hanging on a satin hanger where she left it, the silk one with the thin strap that he would just flick away from her shoulders and the silky column would slither down in a heap on the floor. This was what she wore the last night she spent in this house, still smelling of her soap and baby powder and a scent of her perfume. He brought the nightdress to bed with him, he could almost feel her body through the fabric, and he ached for her with an agony that was physical. But rest eluded him even in sleep.

He awoke one night to find moonlight streaming into the room, white and ghostly. He was roused from a fitful sleep by movement and he looked up at the curtains, partly drawn, stirring in the breeze. He had opened the window earlier and had forgotten to close it. He had flopped into bed and fallen asleep; he had not even changed into his pajamas. He was cold from the night breeze, his body trembly. He reached out his hand to her as he had done all those years when he awakened in the night. But she was not there. "Lauren," he called, disoriented, "Lauren," and then remembered. She would never be there again. "Oh Laura," he lamented, "help me get through this, I can't go through it alone," and his body shook with the cold and the heartache. But she was not there to comfort him.

* * *

That was how Peter and Marta found him, after days of sorrowing, unkempt, uncombed, his beard, like his hair, sprinkled with silver, his face peaked. He looked like he lost twenty pounds, pounds he could not afford to lose. Marta's heart just went out to him, loved friend for so long. She could not control herself and embraced him, crying. "You have not been taking care of yourself," she scolded him.

"We're having Marta's birthday party Saturday. We just thought we'd remind you," said Peter.

"Oh, yes," Denis said. And everybody would be there, playing their roles of comforting, consoling, whispering to him stories of other people who died just as fast, just as young, and those who were still here, years after they were not supposed to be. What did it matter to him if a multitude died the morning she did? What cared he if they found a miracle that raised up everyone of that multitude, if she was not one of them? What cared he if he never saw people again, if all plants wilted, if nothing remained but windswept barrenness, as long as she was here now, comforting him, consoling him, taking away the sadness, this sadness that permeated the house, stuck to walls, stopped all other thoughts, silenced all conversation. "Well, I'll try but I don't think I can make it," he said to Peter. "There is just so much to do during the day that I just drop into bed at the end of it and fall asleep just like that," he said, snapping two fingers.

"Yeah, you look like you do," said Peter, noting his bloodshot eyes. "Oh, Denis, you have to snap out of this. You cannot nurse grief so long. Work has always been good for you. Let's do that European tour. They sent out feelers again. Let's say yes, Denis," Peter entreated.

Denis knew he did not have to pretend with them, they had been friends since they were kids, he could not put on a brightness he did not feel. "It's just harder than I thought. Maybe in time I shall care about singing, care about something again. Meanwhile, just let me be. I do have a lot of things to take care of. She left a lot of things unfinished that I have to finish for her."

"I think the first thing you should do is sell this house."

Denis looked at Peter, appalled. "You cannot be serious. It would be like cutting off my arm or something."

"This is her house, this is her. She lived here more than you did, she has her imprint all over the place. Get out, Denis."

Marta was crying unabashedly now.

"Hey, hey, what's with the tears?" said Denis, putting his arms around her. "All right, I'll try to snap out of it."

"You'll come Saturday?"

"All right, I will."

4

ecilia called Denis when they arrived from Europe. She and her sisters decided they deserved a rest after all the misery they had been through and the four of them decided Europe was the best place to do it.

"How's Spain?" inquired Denis.

"Simply wonderful. We made a pledge. Next time we go, you must come with us."

"Yes, I will," Denis replied, and meant it. He remembered how, in Santo Niño, he wanted to see everything, listen to all the stories that had anything to do with how his wife spent her youth. They had planned to go to Spain, rent a car and drive to all the other Basque towns that Laura had been to. They planned to look up her other Basque relatives there. She showed him pictures of some of them, women with names like Maitechu and Arantze and Begonia, women as delightful as their namesake flowers with their glossy leaves and fat blossoms that flourished in their garden.

They also planned to visit Switzerland, where the first Francis' family came from, and visit the school where she went. "Let me see which side of your family gave you that face," he said. But although they went to several European cities where he performed, they never went to Spain and Switzerland. His program did not include countries wherein he was not singing. And so they made plans for a next time that never took shape and never came. How could he know that they would not be given the time? No amount of regret and recrimination could bring a minute back. How did those Rubaiyat lines go? *The Moving Finger writes: and having writ, Moves on: nor all thy piety nor wit, Shall lure it back to cancel half a line, Nor all thy tears wash out a word of it.* How true.

"We're going back home Sunday, after Franz' baby is baptized" Cecilia continued. "Franz is wondering if you would honor them by being the godfather."

"I've never been asked to be godfather to any child before. The honor is mine." He was pleased.

"Good," said Cecilia, "It's this Saturday, ten in the morning at the same church. By the way, they are naming the baby Laura."

"Laura Steiner," he said, and thoughts of spring came unbidden. Spring and Central Park and New England. And a girl more breathtaking than laurels in bloom.

* * *

As he did early evenings after they buried her, just an hour or so before sunset, he went to the cemetery and placed the single red rose that he brought, on the tombstone on her grave. A single red rose every day, that was what she wanted. It started as a joke, when he first read her James Joyce's *Now Have I Fed and Eaten Up the Rose*. "That's what I want when I go, a red rose every day." And then when she got really sick and they both knew that she was really going, she made him promise her that. "Red," she said, "Don't confuse me with any other color." He got angry then, why, he could not understand, except that he hated the poem. He excused himself and told her he was taking a shower. And with the steaming water raining full blast on him, drowning all other sound, he cried his heart out, the tears breaking out in torrents as though they could just stream on forever. It was the first time he faced the horror of her lying there. But then, of course, that was what he brought her when she was gone, a single red rose, every single evening, driving straight from his house, just an hour before the clouds turned dark against the orange sky. And the wind would shake the willows, telling him to get up and go, and he would drive straight home, to loneliness and desolation and emptiness beyond bearing.

He sat on the grave and told her of the new Laura Steiner. The first baby I'd be godfather to, isn't that something, after all these years? He told her what he did today, not much, but more than what he did the days before. Sorry, dearest, I must have been very dull company all these evenings. Nothing much I did to tell you about. Just the constant heartache, which I don't want to burden you with. Just sitting around, thinking of you, thinking of the years with you.

It was a good life, wasn't it, the best nine years a person could ever hope to have, only because you made it so. Thank you, and although I would have wanted you to linger longer, I never had any regrets, and I thank you. I don't even regret Joe because when we weathered that storm, it made our marriage stronger. See, I have kept my promise, I have not thought of Joe in a long time. You asked if I had forgiven you. I could forgive you anything. That is what love does; it can let you forgive anything. There is nothing you could ask of me that I would not give you.

He stayed until the sun hid behind the trees and a chill hovered over him. He wondered how long this ache, this anguish in his heart would stay, or if it would have tarried so long if he did not allow it to come in and remain, as he had done.

* * *

He bathed and shaved and managed to make himself look human again.

When he arrived in church, everyone was waiting in the courtyard, in full force, including his wife. His heart stopped. There she was, in the shade, leaning against the church wall. But the dress was wrong, the stance was wrong, the picture was wrong. Then he realized, the girl was wrong. It was Madeleine.

There were warm greetings truly meant and kisses straight from the heart, and embraces full of love, for this man who for nine years had shown them that that love was his because he earned it. He was happy being with them again, he missed being with them. Some of the happiest times of his life were spent with them, in Manila and Santo Niño and San Sebastian. Did they know how much he loved them? He would always belong to this family, even though she, who brought him to them, was no longer here. They, on their part, were happy to see him, although looking thinner and still with that sad-eyed gaze, looking better, looking well.

He handed Hazel a small package. He had started packing Laura's things and had chosen a gold and ruby bracelet with Laura's name engraved on it, one of his yearly dandelion-and-jewelry offerings to her. "For the baby," he said. "Now let me look at her."

There she was, a small, pink thing, looking at the world with Franz' gray eyes, a Steiner all the way. Had their baby survived, he would have been a Richards all the way, his hair, his face, his eyes, his everything. She had wanted it that way, didn't she? A boy who looked exactly like him. Sebastian Denis Richards. That was his full name. Given the Filipinos' penchant for nicknames, his wife's family would have wanted to call him Butch or Junior or even that ubiquitous, androgynous name given to a child in almost every Filipino household, Baby, heavens forbid. Well, his son would have insisted on Sebastian, a manly name, no lazy, funny, shortened nicknames for him. Too late. Oh God, for someone who was so unwanted by his father even when he was just an idea, he had been grieved and mourned and longed for so much. Later, when he realized that he did want a son, why didn't they strive for another one? He had been given to recriminations lately, thinking back to all the things he wanted to do with her, later. How was he to know that that later would not be given them? He remembered the time he and Laura read the other Laura's diary, full of recriminations, not so much for things they did but for things they didn't, who, like him, waited for the later that never came. He should have learned some lessons there.

He prodded the baby's fat hand with his finger, this new Laura Steiner, whereupon she opened her clinched fist, grasped his finger tightly, brought it to her tiny baby mouth and, quite simply, found his heart.

"May I hold her?" he asked. Hazel helped him. "Laura Steiner," he whispered. He looked at her in his searching way, and did not want to give her back. (They had placed the urn that contained their baby on Laura's breast, ensconced in the folds of her white gown, the day they buried her.)

"It's time to go inside," Hazel whispered into his thoughts.

"May you have a life full of light and laughter and love, as she had," he whispered, and handed her back.

And may you find as good a man as this one, must have passed through everyone's thoughts. Throughout the years, Laura's family had learned to love him, this person who was good through and through.

*   *   *

He declined Cecilia's offer of lunch. "I am putting my house in order. There's just too much to do. Another thing, I have asked Charles to prepare the papers to transfer to your name all the property she brought with her when she married me. That really should go back to you. The papers should be ready by the time you go home." He kissed Cecilia. "I must go."

Madeleine, who was leaning languorously against the wall, said, "I have to go, too. Can you take me to my hotel?" She did not let his hesitation bother her.

"We'll take you," Franz volunteered.

"Oh, it's all right, Franz. Denis will, won't you now?" She stood, resolute, in front of Denis. There was nothing else he could do.

"Of course," he said. He bade everyone a fond farewell and opened the door of his car to his ravishing passenger.

He was silent during the drive. She was one family member he did not know well, having met her only a couple of times. She lived in Spain and Italy through three marriages (and one live-in relationship that lasted longer than her longest marriage and which produced a son), the short-lived last from which she was in the process of extricating herself. Three marriages in a dozen years. No wonder Ray gave her credit for his head of gray hair, long before it turned completely silver when Joe died. Denis could feel her looking at him for most of the drive, obviously wanting to see how uncomfortable she could make him.

5

$\mathcal{I}$t was an afternoon such as this, he remembered, a time for story telling, when his wife told him about the Gomez side of the family.

"Although my Mom's family has a measure of wealth, wealth in Santo Niño's dictionary is much different from wealth in the Steiners' or especially the Gomez' book. Compared to them, my Mom was of good family but no money. I guess that was why my grandmother liked my Mom better than *Tita* Maggie, who came from too much wealth and too much spoiling. Now she was spoiling her children as well, my grandmother said. By the way, story has it that she was conceived in Paris, after her parents went to see Gounod's *Faust*. Don Jose was so impressed with the opera, he named his eldest daughter Marguerite.

"Anyway, *Tita* Maggie never liked me. She always complained that Joe spent too much time with us. Well, she's always complaining about one thing or another. About the only things that she does not complain about are her children. They could do no wrong. Especially Joe. But then, Joe could do no wrong in the family's eyes. He's the *niño bonito*, adored and doted on by his grandfather and aunts and cousins. I guess *Tita* Maggie was just jealous of the time Joe spent with us, that's why she was always critical of me. Not that I minded," she shrugged her shoulders. "She was a master of condescension, too. After we got married, she said, 'An actor, Lauren?' 'An actor and an opera singer, *Tita* Maggie," I replied, "and very handsome too, but then everybody says that.'" She laughed. "No, she never liked me." Denis had a list of what he loved about her, a generous list, bursting to the brim, and this must be one on top: if she was unimpressed by praise, she was unconcerned by criticism as well. She knew what was right, did what she had to do, and did not care what people thought after that.

"*Tita* Maggie's daughters are very good-looking. The oldest one, Madeleine, got married to a Spanish count or one of those guys. You met her at a party in the house. The first time she saw you she said, 'My, Lauren, where did you find that?' Obviously another Steiner who had not heard of you. You do remember her. She was the very sexy one, with that provocative way of tossing her hair and crossing her legs."

"Yes, I remember," he said drily. "When she shook my hand she gave it such a grip and would not let go for quite some time."

"Don't let it go to your head too much, dear. She's always been crazy and does crazy things and enjoys making people uncomfortable."

I'm sure she did, he thought. He remembered looking at his wife and Madeleine talking to each other and thinking that they had many physical similarities. It was evident they were related, the same full head of light hair, the same small-boned build, the same knockout legs. Madeleine wore her hair loose and long, her skirt tight and short, and very much aware how good her legs looked, kept on crossing and uncrossing them. Every once in a while he would look up and there she was, looking at him with narrowed eyes, intent and provocative. But he was not open to seducement in any form, especially not from family members. He cut short whatever else might brew inside Madeleine's head, turned away and looked for food and never cast another glance in her direction again. He had heard stories about her, and he was not playing. It was amazing how two people could look so much alike, he thought, and be so different. While one was flashy and flamboyant, the other was quiet and still. He was glad he had this one and not that other.

"Anyway," said Laura, "she lives in Spain now, divorced her count. She's going to marry A VERY RICH BANKER, caps courtesy of *Tita* Maggie. Those are the things that make a deep impression on her."

"Divorced? I thought you Catholics don't divorce."

"It's all right, dear, I'm Catholic, you're not. Just tell me anytime you want out, and I'll give you yours."

"You would?" he said, winding a strand of her hair around his finger.

"Why not? Catholics do un-Catholic things these days, if it's convenient. It's called cafeteria Catholicism, you know, pick and choose. If we find the Church's teachings inconvenient, then we challenge and criticize the priests, the cardinals, or even the pope himself, or we just stop going to church. Or worse, join another

congregation not related to the Catholic Church. So why not."
She removed his hand from her hair, bit one finger playfully.
"Anytime you want to be free, just say. Then you could go the
way Madeleine goes."

"Enough of the Gomezes," he had said. "The more I hear of
them, the more unpalatable they get, the shallow Maggie, the
capricious Madeleine." And Joe. Well, somehow he found him
the most unpalatable of all; too rich, too good-looking, too
brooding, too easy for women to fall for, too close to his wife for
comfort.

6

*T*hank goodness her hotel was not far and they were there in no time at all.

"Come up," Madeleine more commanded than invited.

"I don't think so," Denis declined. "I have things to do. But thanks."

"Oh, come on. Just for a few minutes. You've been with this family for nine years and I have not spoken nine words to you. Have the valet park your car. He looks like he could use the tip."

Up he went with her to her room, not just a room, but a suite of rooms, very large, which must cost her a pretty penny. "What do you want to drink?" she asked. She went to a cabinet full of bottles.

"Nothing, thanks."

"Oh, yeah, I heard you don't drink. No vices, actually. Well, it's time you took up a few."

"And which ones would you recommend?"

"The major ones, most definitely. Nothing like indulging in heedless recklessness to make you feel good. You're not Catholic, are you?"

He looked at her without answering, unsure of where she was leading the conversation.

"Pity you're not." Of course she knew the answer. Anyway, if she didn't know it, she would presume it. Her presumptions and opinionated convictions, copies of her mother's, were stuff of family legend, told on evenings when stories of family eccentricities held sway, after a good dinner, over a glass of wine, with tolerant laughter.

"All our lives," she went on, "we're taught that if it feels good, it's bad. But it's also human to sin, our God is a forgiving God. So we succumb willingly and ah, it feels good. Then the guilt comes in, as it always does. We Catholics are built for guilt, it's rooted in our fibers, cast in our system, since they poured that holy water on our baby heads and named us after those saints in heaven. Oh, we squirmed and kicked and hollered in protest but a lot of good it did us." She took out two glasses and a bottle from the cabinet. "But then, there our maker is, working his mysterious ways, his wonders to perform. We can unload to a good priest in the dark anonymity of a confessional," she sniggered and gave out a snort, as though she found the forbidden cookie, "and ah, all is forgiven. And we can do it again and again. Imagine that! Good Saturday and Sunday, happy Monday to Friday. Better than a shrink, believe me."

So she was one of the thorns on that good Father's side, Denis thought. "Especially if you go to a slightly deaf priest, then you're not scolded and given an entire rosary for penance," he said. Two Catholics, born to and raised in the same family, went to the same school, but whose concept of God and sin and forgiveness and right and wrong, was as different as white from black.

"Who told you that? Oh, she did, of course. Well, although she never patronized Father Santos' business, I'm sure she never got more than a couple of Hail Marys, for all the sins she must have committed."

She came towards him carrying the glasses and the bottle. She had lost some weight since he saw her last, looking more like his wife now, the short skirt showing off those long legs, the fitted blouse, the full breasts underneath. She handed him a glass and poured him his drink. "Here, a good vice to start with."

He took the glass from her with a murmured "Thanks" and settled himself into a chair.

She gulped down her drink as though she really was thirsty, picked up the bottle and refilled her glass. She sat down on the sofa with her fresh drink and patted the space next to her. "You'd be more comfortable here," she said.

"I'm all right here," he replied.

"Afraid of me?"

"Should I be?"

"No. I'm really very nice once you get to know me. I don't bite." She watched him watch her from the rim of her glass. "And I enjoy being stared at."

"I'm sorry. It's just that you look so like her, and..." He left the sentence hanging there.

"You still got it bad? Wine, women and song don't work for you? Oh, I forgot, you're not singing your songs yet. Well, well, no wine and no song. No wonder you're looking like a sick dog. Well, there's always," she paused, "women...." Her voice trailed as she looked at his inscrutable face. "The women don't work, too?" She looked at him, then her eyes narrowed. "Why, I'll be damned, Mr. Richards. Why, you don't say! No women, too? Oh, this is too much. Oh, don't tell me you have been a good boy all this time? I mean a good boy in your dictionary. A good boy in mine is something else. Well, well." She looked at him, her lips working up a mischievous smile. "You could have any woman in the world to help you forget, and you prefer to do it alone? Oh, for crissakes, why, you're even worse than I heard, and I heard bad."

He was about to ask how bad but thought better of it. He really did not want to know. He checked himself and let it pass.

But she did not care if this conversation was going one-sided. As though she divined what he preferred to keep to himself, she continued, "Like you were the soul of faithfulness. Like you were under her thumb." She ran her forefinger over the rim of her glass, drew circles, studied him with half-closed eyes. "Like Denis Richards does not play around."

Somewhere in their lives, they had expected that one day, Denis would be true to that breed, the superstar, in whose book the word faithful was not written, and would start to look around. But he had been true to the image that everyone had of Denis Richards, a vanishing breed, an anachronism, a one-woman man. "God, nine years! An awfully long time to be faithful to one woman."

He was very still, just looking at her.

"Oh, what a waste, what a waste," she gulped down the last of her drink. She poured more drink into her glass but got just a few drops. She shook the bottle and poured again but could not squeeze liquid from glass. She went over to the cabinet again and refilled her glass. "What was it with her, anyway. My brother loved her all his life, never recovered from her, did you know that? I bet they had an affair, you know?"

"How could that be," he said evenly, "we lived a world away and we were together every day of our lives."

"Except for that one week when she came home without you." She looked at him, expecting some reaction but got none. "That terrible, terrible time he died." She gulped down her drink again. Her eyes misted at the memory and took on a faraway look. "Something must have happened between them. I was home, you see. I saw him pluck a rose, jump over a hedge, fling his arms out wide in exhilaration. My dearest brother, remote, aloof, stranger to displays of emotion, looking so, so..." she searched for a word, "so sensually fulfilled. I knew she was there, I knew she came home without you, I knew she arrived in the morning and did not get to Forbes until very late that night. Oh, it broke my heart." She shook her glass and ice tinkled against the crystal. "Anyway, that's what I think." She looked into space, talked more to herself. She stood up, went to the cabinet, took the bottle out, poured herself another drink and plunked the bottle down on the coffee table and herself on the sofa.

"Ha! Little Miss Perfect, everybody's role model, Miss Goody Goody, committing adultery with my brother, and incest too. For that would be incest, wouldn't it? They looked the same, acted the same, why, he looked more like her brother than Franz or Nacho did." She laughed bitterly. "Incest. Conjures dark, shameful, forbidden deeds. But then there was nothing new about that. That was normal in *Tita* Ceil's family." She gloated, malice written all over her face. "You could never talk about incest in Joe's presence or he would swat you," she slapped the table with the flat of her hand, "like a fly with a fly swatter." She leaned forward and in a hushed, conspiratorial voice said, "You must have seen those strange children, those bitter fruits of those incestuous couplings, those.. "

"Stop it," Denis shot out from his chair. He plopped his glass on the table; his drink, untouched, splattered quivering crystalline drops on the wood.

He had been ominously quiet that the reaction surprised her and stopped short her diatribe. He loomed in front of her and for a minute really scared her with that horrible anger on his face. "Stop it," he said again, in that low voice that she thought very seductive, and found more so now. Strong, masculine, take-charge males had always excited her and she could not find one more male than this, this angry, oh-so-handsome giant towering in front of her. "I won't have you talking about my wife like this. How dare you malign her who cannot defend herself! And how dare you bandy around accusations like that." Or more weird, she thought, mourning his dead all this time.

The scared moment had passed and now she was more aroused than alarmed. But then, she was attracted to him the first time she saw him, stimulated by his largeness into fantasies of larger dimensions. She had always preferred baritones to tenors, with their darker roles more voluptuously menacing, the larger timber of their voice carrying more power, their propensity for mischief promising more excitement.

"Oh, shut up, Denis Richards. Dead all this time and you still talk of her in the present tense." She put her glass on the table. "Sit down." But he stood there determined, holding in his anger. "I'm sorry. Really I am. Sit down, please. Come on, please."

She refilled her glass, which was not empty yet. She had been doing this, filling her glass before it became empty that he wondered if there was a stick behind her that was propping her up. "It's just that I'm sick and tired of her. You would be, too, if you grew up with the idea of her hovering over you. Laura this, Laura that. You look so much alike, why can't you be like her. Always Laura, she could do no wrong.

"Everybody thought the world of her. Even RJ, that hard-to-please Gomez boy. And Joe. Ah, Joe. He worshipped her, compared her with every girl he went out with and found all of them wanting, because who could compare with Laura? And so he went alone and drank himself to death. That was the hardest thing to bear. She expropriated him, took him away from us. He belonged more to them than to us, sleeping over in their house on weekends, spending vacations with them, always with her and Franz. And then there's Papa. You should have seen how gentle he always was with her. I went to their bedroom looking for him, but he wasn't there. I thought I heard someone outside, on their verandah, you know, the one facing the garden. I went through that French door and there he was. He thought he was safe; Mom was out I don't know where. He was sobbing his heart out. We had just gotten word that Lauren died, you see.

"Ah, my father. I could see it in his eyes when I misbehaved, which was ooohh, sooo often! Why can't you be a little like her? Because I did not want to, that's why. She led such a boring life, how could she not have bored you? I can't understand how you lived with her so long, and so faithfully, too, I heard. Miss Iceberg, I can't imagine her making love to you, I can't even imagine her naked in front of you, *o mejor dicho*, I can't imagine you making love to her." She had a small, sensuous smile on her face, which left no doubt that she could indeed imagine it.

"'Xcuse me, 'xcuse me," she whispered. "My breeding goes thataway when I've had too much to drink." She took the glass to her lips, her tongue sought out a swimming cube of ice, caught it into her mouth, worked on it with sucking noises and pursed red lips, looking at him through slumbrous eyes. But she did not draw encouraging waters from him. Something in his disapproving stance brought up remembrances of things better forgotten, often not.

"Papa caught me in a compromising position with this boy when I was fourteen, and the disgust in his eyes was something I had to live with for a long time. Of course nobody could touch her until you came. How could anyone? *Tita* Ceil's army of chaperones was always around, led by Franz and Joe. And Joe, well, though I'm sure he wanted to, he was not the one to do it, either, not without the blessings of marriage, for crissakes! "

Everyone in this family said 'for crissakes.' He wondered who started it.

"You should have been in the house when we learned that she gave up that money Joe left her. Papa just sat there and cried, I mean, cried. Just when everyone thought there was nothing more she could do for an encore, she pulled that one out her sleeves. That would surely go down in the Steiner history books as the good deed of the century that just couldn't be matched."

She laughed. "All the boys were scared of her, cold, cold Miss Frigidaire, with her chauffeur-driven Mercedes, and that frigid look that could chill you to the bone."

Denis looked at her, this pathetic creature, filled with a festering resentment towards his wife who must have sailed through all this bitterness without even being aware of it. Not, he thought, that she would have cared if she was. How could I have thought that they looked alike? Like heaven and hell, that's how alike they were. His anger slowly dissipated, flowing out of him, deserting him.

"Did it never occur to you that maybe, if you had spent less effort trying to be different from her and more into being a better person, if not a better daughter and sister, then maybe your father and Joe would not have had reason to wish you were someone different?"

"Do you have any idea how it was, trying to compete with someone like that? You think it was easy, being compared to her, and always coming up short? It would not have been so bad if our families were not so close, then my so-called imperfections would not have been so glaring. But we were always doing things together. If *Tito* Francis wanted to go anywhere, Papa would want to go there, too. They had to be together all the time, picnics, parties, weekends. If Mom did not put her foot down and simply refused to go to Santo Niño, we would have spent our vacations there, too, heavens forbid. It was as if they were not working every day in the same office. But they were just inseparable, like Joe and Franz were. We were always thrown together so much that it was a wonder nobody thought that Joe might be drawn to Laura."

They were both quiet, and then she pointed a red-tipped finger at him. "And then," she said accusingly, "you had to come along. Little Miss Perfect bags big, big Mr. Perfect. Oh, really, it was just too much. How could my husbands compare?"

Wasn't all that drink getting to her, he wondered. She was rambling, true, but she was not slurring her words. "Oh, the first one was all right. But we were too young. And the second one, well, he was even more promiscuous than me, than I am, was, whatever. The next one, too. And Luigi, well, you've met Luigi."

Yes, he had. Too rich, too conservative, too old for her. "I thought he was a most decent fellow."

"Well," she said, bobbing her head from side to side, "girls' hearts don't really flutter over the most decent fellows."

"Who do they flutter over? No, no," he said, holding up a hand, "don't answer that" Familiarity, no matter how short, was slowly breeding contempt, and he did not want that. She was still family, after all, and he was all for family, distasteful though he found this one member. But what did it matter how repelled he was; he was not going to see her again, he would see to that. "Why did you marry him then?"

"Have you heard of the words 'banks' and 'millions' and such? He owned the banks, I wanted the millions in it."

"How could you? Your family has more than enough."

"Sure, like I just stayed home and hated shopping and partying and going out."

She wanted to marry me, thinking I was unemployed, he thought, that was how much she valued money. Or then, maybe, that was how much she valued me. Yes, me. She wanted me, struggling, impoverished, unemployed me. The thought warmed him, lifted up his dejected spirits and, at last, gave him peace.

"But it's all right now," she continued. "That most decent fellow made me a woman of very, very independent means. Yes, so independent that I don't have to care what anybody thinks of me. Now I can afford to do what I damned well please, pleasing nobody but myself, beholden to nobody but myself. Yup, the name of the game is pleasing Madeleine."

"Ah," he said, letting out a deep breath, "we are a pair, you and I. You're blaming her for what went wrong with your life. I'm blaming her for the pain I've been going through. But you know, it was not her, it was just you. You both started with the same gifts, wealth, family and that face. And I, I could sit in the dark for the next ten years feeling sorry for myself, blaming her for going away, blaming her God for taking her away. Or I could get down on my knees and give Him thanks for lending her to me for nine years, brief though they might seem to me, and then get on with my life. We could keep on screwing our lives, you see, and blaming her or we could get on and make the best of it. It's our choice, really, not Joe's, not your parents'."

I could have made a mess of my life, he thought, could have ended up with a screwed-up, angry woman like this, and shortened my life a dozen years. But *you* are still here, still taking care of me. Thank you, dear. And thank you for coming into my life, and what a life you made for me.

He walked to the door. "It's late, I have to go, so much to do. Then I'm going back to work." He surprised himself. He had not thought of working since his wife got sick. "Take care of yourself, Madeleine. You have so much going for you. Don't throw your life away. Don't prove everyone right. That face could carry any day, carry it well."

"There you go, comparing me to her. You're worse than all the others there."

"Yes, I am. She's my wife, remember?"

"There you go with your present tenses again," she said.

A female Joe, he thought, he had not seen anyone drink as much but could still talk as straight.

He laughed and started to go.

"Must you go?" She pulled herself up and walked him to the door. She looked at him with eyes that somehow, now, did not look anything at all like his wife's. "I'm so sad. You're so sad. The world is so sad. Stay a bit. I could help you, make you feel very much better, you know."

"You just did." She had. He kissed her check slightly. "Thank you."

She looked up at him, surprised at the kiss. "You're not afraid of me anymore?"

"No," he shook his head slightly and smiled, "you talked away the bogeyman." He looked at her face, so like his wife's, and yet... He could not believe anyone, much more he, could have thought they looked alike. His wife's face might have stopped him on his tracks, but it was much more than that that made him stay, and that was what this face in front of him lacked, and why those men went away. "Goodbye, Madeleine."

* * *

He called Cecilia when he reached the house. "Are you all still there?" he asked.

"Yes, we're still gabbing. How's Madeleine?"

"She was the worse for wear when I left her. I'm afraid she's going to finish that bottle. Anyway, I just miss you guys, that's why I'm calling and to give you the news. I was offered the title role in The Return of Ulysses in Berlin. I want you to be the first to know, I shall accept. There are a couple of others, too, but first this big European tour. So back to work I go. I guess I shall be in Europe for quite some time."

"Hey, that's great news. I'm so happy for you. Maybe we could catch you in Spain sometime. Is Spain in your itinerary?"

"No. But Spain is not for working in. Spain is for going to with you people. Let's plan this thing right. Then I shall go with you next time. One more thing. Are there some things of hers you and the girls would like to have? Some clothes and jewelry, perhaps? I'm putting her things in order. I shall set aside some I don't want to part with, the rest I wish, I'm hoping, you would take with you." He had not even thought of giving her stuff away until now. "Why don't you and the girls come tomorrow?"

"I shall ask them. May we call you later?"

"I wish you would," he said.

7

$\mathcal{O}$n the day of departure, Peter and Charles picked up Denis from Amalfi for the airport. Marta came along to drive the car back. Mario and Milly, happy that he was going back to work again, but saddened that he would be away so long, bade him an emotional goodbye.

"Take care of yourself," said Milly, her eyes misting, to this man whom they had served faithfully for nine years, a better man than whom she couldn't think of, except perhaps Francis. And Joe.

"You take good care of the house, and don't forget the flowers," Denis said.

"Well, I guess we're all set," said Peter to Denis when all the suitcases were finally stashed away in the back of the car.

"Yes," said Denis, "I guess we are." He looked up, and took one last look at their bedroom window. He thought he saw her there, smiling down at him. Maybe he did, for with all his might, he willed it so. The curtain fluttered, perhaps from a breeze, though there was none, perhaps from her touch. Perhaps she was there now watching him, and bidding him farewell, as well.

There he stood, looking up, very still.

As he bid her goodbye, he closed his eyes, to a sun-gold lake in Central Park and yellow dandelions, to laurels thick on a crisp June day, to a misty white beach bathed in magic moon glow, and moons peeking through palm trees, bright and full, on nights that moved him so. And through it all, to the ghost that had made a permanent home of his hazy world, a girl with a face and a smile that dazzled and consumed his senses the first time he saw her, in a sweet long ago.

"Goodbye, dear," he whispered and got in the car.

The end

WHEN SHADOWS FALL

A Novel

By

NILDA ABERÁSTURI

July 2015

www.ingramcontent.com/pod-product-compliance
Lightning Source LLC
Chambersburg PA
CBHW070838250626
47159CB00003B/839